"A brilliantly executed novel, perfectly paced, beautifully described and a true joy to read."
SFBook.com

"Adventures in a nightmare citadel – a story that hits the ground running and doesn't let up."
Liz Williams

"The elements which constitute this novel may be familiar – a vast, stratified community, a ragamuffin on the run, criminals and officials vying for supremacy – but Whates's assured prose, slick pacing and inventive imagination make for a gripping read. His first novel is the work of a born storyteller."
The Guardian

"Brilliantly inventive."
SFX

"It is his characters who live through the story and make the reader need to know just how it's all going to pan out, human characters who may seem familiar but then there's that one thing, that shifted alteration that changes the world and changes the reader too."
Michael Cobley

"All in all, it is an excellent book. The city is almost a character on its own."
Gnostalgia

IAN WHATES

City of Hope & Despair

The City of a Hundred Rows
Vol. II

**ANGRY
ROBOT**

ANGRY ROBOT

A member of the Osprey Group
Midland House, West Way
Botley, Oxford
OX2 0HP
UK

www.angryrobotbooks.com
Sideways

An Angry Robot paperback original 2011
1

A catalogue record for this book is available
from the British Library.

ISBN: 978 0 85766 087 9
EBook ISBN: 978 0 85766 089 3

Set in Meridien by THL Design.

Printed in the UK by CPI Mackays, Chatham, ME5 8TD.

For Natasha,
the best daughter anyone
could ask for.

ONE

The Four Spoke Inn failed to be all manner of things. It wasn't the cheapest place around, nor was it the warmest, the most welcoming, the largest, the busiest, not even the most convenient. Yet it was a little of all of these. The landlord, Seth Bryant, was well aware of this. He had long since come to terms with the hostelry's strengths and limitations, determining to make the most of the former while learning to live with the latter.

Seth knew his clientele and what to expect of them. Many were regulars, but, the inn being situated where it was, just as many weren't. This was one of the things he loved most about the place – it offered constant variety to spice up the underlying sense of stability, as comfortable as a well-worn chair, provided by familiar faces who could be counted on to appear more nights than not, picking up on conversations begun the previous evening or the one before that as if the world had stood still in between. There was little opportunity for boredom to set in, for life to grow stale, because new faces were ever imminent if not already arrived. Every time the door swung open and an unfamiliar figure strode through, the dynamics of the tap room would shift – sometimes by only a subtle degree, but by no means always.

This particular evening the bar was dominated by a group of bargemen who sat clustered around the long table by the window. They weren't yet deep in their cups but a few of them were well on their way, the volume of the conversation from that part of the room rising steadily as the ale continued to flow. Ol' Jake had taken to scowling in their direction at regular intervals from his accustomed perch on a stool at the right-hand corner of the bar.

"Don't know why you put up with them," he said to Seth as the latter drew him a pint of darkly sweet Dancastre ale.

"Yes you do," Matty said from beside him. "It's for the sake of their coin, eh, Seth?"

The landlord smiled. "What can I say, Mat? You've got me bang to rights. The old women'll be whispering in each other's ears and word will spread like wildfire through Crosston and all the villages beyond – the shock of it! Respected innkeeper caught accepting honest coin in return for ale!"

Matty laughed and slapped Jake on the back.

His friend's scowl only deepened. "All well and good, but do you have to accept it from *them*?"

"If you want the inn to still be here so you can keep coming in and moaning about every new face that wanders in then yes, Jake; I have to take coin from whoever's willing to part with it. Besides, they're not that bad."

"So you say," the old man muttered into his beer.

There were nine in total crammed around the long table – the crew of two barges, all male. Seth knew this lot; they'd stopped here before. Not all did. Some stayed close to their boats, sleeping on the great vessels as well as working them, irrespective of how prosperous a trip might have been, but not this lot. Their owner-captains were happy to let the crews enjoy an evening's relaxation from time to time when a trip had gone especially well.

As long as their tankards were frequently replenished and nobody riled them, there would be no trouble from this mob, while the inn's coffers would benefit considerably from their custom. Seth had ensured they were in good hands – he'd asked Molly to make a point of looking after them and she had plenty of experience with the like; knew how much cleavage to show as she leant across to collect the empties and how much of a wiggle to give her hips as she walked away again, while she wouldn't take offence at their coarse humour or ribald comments and coped admirably with wandering hands. Thank goodness Bethany wasn't on tonight. Younger, slimmer, less buxom, and by most estimates a good deal prettier than Molly, that one had a sharp tongue on her and a habit of not standing for any nonsense.

With no one waiting to be served at present, Seth left his station at the bar and wandered over to where the bargemen sat. "Everything all right, lads?" Contented murmurings rippled around the table. "Molly looking after you, is she?" At this the murmurings grew louder and more enthusiastic, with a few appreciative chuckles thrown in for good measure. "If you're hungry at all, we've a few of this morning's catch left – good plump sandfish, only a few, mind, which we serve basted in butter and lemon juice on a bed of fresh river samph – or there's some mutton stew, steeped in a rich ale gravy, and we've a fully mature Cabrian cheese if you'd prefer. That comes with home-baked bread and I might even find you some really spicy Deliian pickle if you've a fancy." He smacked his lips at this last. "Just let Molly know when you want to order anything."

They assured him that they would and, with a final smile, Seth sauntered back towards the bar. He stopped en-route to exchange a few pleasantries with Lal and Si, who occupied their usual table in front of the hearth and were deeply absorbed in a game of checkers. No need to have the fire lit at this season, thank goodness, but this would form a cosy focal point later in the year as winter began to bite. Seth just hoped that, when it did, this winter would be milder than the last, which had been especially bitter, with even the Thair threatening to freeze over – something Seth had yet to see in his lifetime – icy skirts forming on both banks, though they failed to spread out and meet by covering the truly deep waters in between. A little chill could be good for business, encouraging people to seek solace in front of a roaring hearth while warming their hands around a cup of mulled wine or cider, but when it was *that* cold they generally stayed at home and battened down the hatches.

With a rueful shake of his head, Seth banished memories of such lean times and headed back towards the bar, where Matty looked ready for a refill, only to be stopped by two merchants at another table, who had evidently been discussing the origins of the inn's peculiar name and were hoping for some enlightenment.

Seth smiled, trying to do so without any hint of indulgence; this was hardly the first time such a question had been asked of him.

"There's been much speculation over the years on that very subject," he told the two men – younglings both; the youngest sons of noble families most probably, who, seeing no opportunity for rapid advancement at home, set out flushed with dreams of making their fortunes by ferrying goods common in one area to places where they were not, little considering how many had already trod that path before them and how rare it was to find such undiscovered or unexploited commodities.

"Some would have it," he continued, "that a vintner travelling from far Kathay suffered an accident on the road and, unable to make proper repairs, had to continue with one of his precious wagon's wheels badly damaged and only partially mended, so that it boasted just four spokes rather than the original six. Yet that patched-up wheel carried him for many leagues, finally giving out here, where the great trade road meets the Thair. Taking this as an omen and judging it a likely spot, he set up shop where the wagon foundered and proceeded to sell his wines, doing very well in the process and establishing this inn as a result.

"Others claim the place was established by four strong-willed brothers who determined to go into business together but could agree on little else, arguing about every pernickety detail, until they found this spot. For the first time, all four agreed that this was where they should establish an inn, which they did, naming the place to reflect the four strands of their divergent personalities – all of which led away from each other in every instant but came together here and here alone."

"And do you favour either of these origin tales, sir?"

Seth smiled. "Truth to tell, no. Both have their appeal yet strike me as fanciful. I prefer the more pragmatic theory."

"Which is?"

"Well, you'll see that the inn is situated on the great trade route, that mighty road of commerce which stretches from distant Deliia in the east to the Atlean Sea in the west, bisecting the continent like the corded belt around some lanky cleric's waist. It also stands on the banks of the mighty Thair, the river that stretches from fabled Thaiburley, the City of Dreams, in the south to the distant northern mountains. I believe that these are your four spokes, gentlemen: the road stretching in two opposing directions on the one hand, the river doing likewise on the other. Four passages to distant lands, representing the greatest trade routes in the world, all four conspiring to meet here, at the hub."

One of the young merchants laughed. "Good fortune for you, then, landlord."

Seth nodded. "Good fortune indeed. Now, if you'll excuse me…?" He looked towards the bar, where Matty still waited.

"Yes, of course."

There was a deal of truth in what Seth had told the merchants, though by no means the whole truth. Few people alive knew or even suspected that, and Seth certainly had no intention of enlightening anyone. Best to let sleeping dogs lie, as far as he was concerned.

Having reached the bar without any further interruptions, he took Matty's battered pewter goblet, which the man insisted was reserved especially for him though Seth couldn't imagine why – it was as worn and sorry a piece of tat as you could imagine. Even when new the cup could hardly have been remarkable, yet Matty would drink from nothing else. Presumably for sentimental reasons, though Seth had to wonder whether any self-respecting sentiment would truly wish to be associated with such an uninspired piece of metalwork.

As he placed the brimming tankard down on the counter in front of Matty, the door swung open. Seth glanced up in time to witness the most beautiful man he had ever seen step inside. This was not a description he had ever expected to make about any man – beauty being something he considered to be sole property of the fairer sex – but it was the one word that sprang instantly to mind. The newcomer was tall, with golden blonde hair which seemed to have captured a stray sunbeam or two as a net might snare and hold an insect. He had piercing blue eyes and the sort of face which a truly gifted artist might aspire to produce one day, were he perhaps to render the image of a god. Despite being muffled beneath a heavy dark cloak, his physique looked to be well-toned and muscular.

All conversation ceased; even the bargemen went quiet and simply stared as this golden youth crossed to the bar, where Seth stood gaping.

"What can I get you, sir?" Seth asked, remembering his manners.

The eyes flashed with what? Amusement? "I have a fancy for some wine, please, landlord. White." His voice matched the appearance; clear, fully masculine, yet a little higher than some might expect and with a lilting, almost musical quality. "Do you by any chance have any Abissian white – a bottle of sundew, ideally?"

Seth swallowed on a suddenly dry throat. The stranger had just asked for one of the rarest wines in existence, a label prized by connoisseurs irrespective of vintage. The given year made a difference of degree alone, not to whether the bottle cost a fortune. Nobody would think to order such a highly prized drink at a mere roadside tavern.

Correction: one person would.

Seth was glad to note that conversation had started up again in the room around him. It gave proceedings a welcome sense of normality as he smiled at this newcomer, this individual who had just uttered words he had never expected to hear, and said, "If you'd care to step into the back room, sir, I'll see what I can find."

This earned him a few odd looks from Matty and Ol' Jake as he ushered the golden youth behind the bar, but there was no helping that.

Glancing over his shoulder as he led the unusual visitor through the dimly lit hallway that led to the back room, Seth couldn't help but note that the dimness seemed dispelled by the youth's passage, almost as if the lad glowed with light. Once they were away from prying eyes and inquisitive ears, Seth turned to the stranger. "You have something to show me, I believe."

"Indeed."

The youth dipped a hand inside his voluminous cloak and emerged holding something; a quite unremarkable length of wood, roughly as long as a man's forearm, perhaps a little more. It was slightly broader and squared at one end, more rounded at the other, but nothing special, you might think.

Seth stared at the crudely turned stick as if this were the holiest of all relics being presented to him. He licked his lips and said, a little hoarsely, "The fifth spoke."

"Just so," the golden boy said, and then smiled. He reached up to the clasp at his throat and, with a shrug of broad shoulders, sent his cloak drifting to the floor. The garment dropped languidly, as if in slow motion – a curtain drawn to one side at some major unveiling. Beneath, he was naked from the waist up, revealing the toned, bronzed torso of a young woman's dream, every muscle perfectly defined and not an ounce of fat in evidence.

And then he spread his wings.

White and pure, they filled the room and more, unable to fully extend yet still magnificent. The light was unmistakable now, shining forth from the visitor in a blaze of golden glory.

Seth found that he had fallen to his knees. "What do you want of me?" he asked in a voice full of reverence. And the other proceeded to tell him.

The room felt oddly smaller once the visitor had departed, as if the youth had taken something more than simply his presence with him. For long seconds the man who had been calling himself Seth Bryant for more years than he cared to remember stood as if frozen, his attention focused on a single simple word which burned deeply in his thoughts; two fateful syllables he hoped passionately would never need to be uttered while fearing that they inevitably would, or why else had he been told them? Drawing a deep breath, he picked up a glass from the side, polished it, and then poured out a generous measure of brandy from the accompanying decanter. His continued absence would no doubt set tongues wagging back in the tap room, but what if it did? He needed a few additional moments to compose himself before facing the customers again. No one could blame him for that, surely?

After all, it wasn't every day that a man came face to face with a demon.

TWO

From the Streets Below to the Market Row,
From taverns and stalls to the Shopping Halls,
From trinkets so cheap to exclusive boutique,
From the Cloth-Makers' Row and people who sew,
To haberdashers, tailors, and upward we go…

His name was M'gruth and he was on a mission. Yet these were unsettled times. Brief days ago gangs of subverted street-nicks had rampaged through the City Below, looting and killing, throwing themselves into pitched battles with the City Watch while strange spider-like mechanisms haunted the shadows. Nothing like it had been seen since the war. The Maker was dead, the Dog Master was dead, and the street-nicks were now a broken force; it would be years before they could hope to re-establish their grip on the under-City and its trade, if ever. In the aftermath, territories were shifting, unexpected alliances had been forged and new powers had begun to emerge and flex their muscles, keen to fill the vacuum left by the street-nicks' demise. Any journey undertaken at such a time promised to be a hazardous one, as the various pretenders scrambled to establish a position of prominence in the new order.

Most chilling of all, the Blade had once again returned to the streets of the City Below.

So M'gruth's movements were governed by two conflicting imperatives: haste and caution.

But M'gruth was a professional. He had lived with such pressures all his life. His progress was therefore swift, while every move was considered and every shadow scrutinised.

As a result, he was not the wisest choice of target for an ambush, as the three over-confident nicks were about to discover to their cost. Over-confident, because they must have known who he was; not by name, perhaps, but certainly by generic type. After all, it was written all over his body. Yet still they were lying in wait.

The terrain was broken; derelict buildings and shattered homes – the former pens and living quarters, guard stations, cook houses, weapons stores, practice yards – all part of the enclave that had sprung up around the Pits. Empty now, abandoned when that hellhole closed down; gone to wrack and ruin and left to the mercies of looters and scroungers, local folk who had undoubtedly dismantled the buildings piece by piece, wasting little time in taking what they needed for their own homes. Death by increment; no more than anywhere associated with the Pits deserved.

He ducked down behind a partially demolished wall, heading at a right angle to his original course. Crouching low and moving quickly, he circled and came up behind the first kid while the would-be ambushers must still have been wondering what had delayed him, where he'd gone to. The lad had a crude sling in one hand and a pile of half a dozen oval stones beside him. The weapon was made from braided rope, even to the pocket in which the shot would sit. M'gruth crept up unnoticed, tapped the kid on the shoulder and, as the wide-eyed boy turned quickly around, waggled an admonishing finger in the lad's face as he struck him hard across the forehead, using the pommel of his sword as a cudgel.

Transferring the blade to his left hand, M'gruth took up the sling from where the unconscious nick had dropped it and fitted one of the stones into the vacant pocket. Peering beyond the small heap of rubble the kid had chosen to hide behind, he saw the second nick, now standing straight, craning his neck to try and spot the man the group were intending to ambush.

M'gruth whipped the sling round and around, only a couple of times, before letting fly. Perhaps the nick heard the sling slicing through the air as it spun or even the missile hurtling towards him, certainly he looked around just in time to meet the stone head-on. Two down.

The third, closer than the second and doubtless alerted by the collapse of his mate, raised his head and stared at M'gruth, who smiled and lifted his arm, hand still clutching the sling.

"Are you mad? See these?" and he rotated the arm, displaying the continuous pattern of ochre tattoos that ran up the limb before disappearing beneath his shirt to re-emerge at his neck and run on to adorn the bald pate of his head. "I'm a Tattooed Man for Thaiss's sake! Did you really think the three of you could take me?"

"S-sorry." The nick was backing away, fear obvious in every contour of his body.

"I don't have time to deal with you properly now, so breck off!" This last the Tattooed Man yelled.

The boy needed no further encouragement, but immediately turned and ran, almost tripping over his own feet in his haste to escape. M'gruth smiled. The irony of being attacked here of all places hadn't escaped him. He'd enjoyed this little diversion, for all that it had caused him a momentary delay. The thought brought his focus firmly back to the mission, and he hurried on.

If he were ever asked to name one place in the world he would least like to return to, this would be it; but needs must. He was now in the very shadow of that detested theatre of blood known as the Pits.

A moment later and he was passing under the arena's walls, something he had vowed never to do again.

He heard them before he saw them. Sounds that came rolling down the tunnel like echoes from a past he had tried so hard to forget. Sounds that sent cold shivers tingling down his spine, causing him to falter, to stumble to a halt for a second with his eyes closed. For a moment he was back there, sword clasped tightly in his hand, guts screwed up in a knot of terror and heart pumping with both fear and anticipation, as he wondered whether this was to be the day he died. It was the sound of combat that had halted him; the harsh clash of steel meeting steel, the gritty shuffle of feet manoeuvring for better balance, the grunt of expelled air from extreme exertion as muscles powered an attack or strained to repulse one. M'gruth gathered himself and ran on, reassured that he was not yet too late and afraid that if he delayed any longer he might be.

He burst from the tunnel into a large amphitheatre, flanked by curving banks of seats to all sides – crude

wooden benches, many of which were now broken or
absent entirely, presumably scavenged for material and
fuel like the buildings outside since it wasn't that long
ago the place had closed down. Other than that, everything was much as he remembered it. The Pits, where
people paid to see men die, and where friend was forced
to slaughter friend simply to survive. M'gruth had always
imagined that, if viewed from above, the arena and its
seating would resemble some wide-opened mouth screaming obscenities to the heavens, those on the floor of the
Pit a snack about to be swallowed by that unholy maw.

On this occasion the snack in question consisted of two
women, girls really, though it was often hard to remember the fact, especially when you saw them like this, with
knives drawn and battle joined. Both were dressed in
black, even down to the leather boots, belts and accou-
trements. Occasional flashes of silver studwork the only
relief. The two girls wove an intricate dance of flowing
limbs and flashing steel in the centre of the arena, strikes
and counter strikes that challenged the eye to keep pace.
M'gruth was a Tattooed Man – the fiercest warriors in
the City Below, yet even he was dazzled by the speed of
attack and riposte before him.

One of the girls was marginally larger than the other
and perhaps a few years older, though the difference was
slight and seemed to have had little impact on the fight
as yet. Both were covered in a sheen of sweat and had
suffered minor cuts, where blades had kissed against flesh
and drawn blood, though presumably without causing
any real damage, since neither seemed in any way hampered. Another thing that was impossible to ignore was
how alike the pair looked.

M'gruth knew them both, respected and even perhaps feared them both, and at one time or other he had called each his friend.

The task that had been entrusted to him was a thankless one, though not impossible, or so he hoped. His job was to stop these two lethal girls from killing each other in a senseless fight. Each thought they couldn't carry on living while the other did; neither had yet stopped to consider how difficult it might be to live *without* their counterpart. Sisters. He was just glad he'd never had one.

"Stop it, both of you!" His call sounded small and impotent even to his own ears, a mere whimper which was instantly swallowed by the vastness of this place, so he tried again, louder this time. "I said *stop it!*"

"Breck off!" Kat, the slighter of the two snarled without sparing him a glance, too intent upon her opponent.

"What are you doing here, M'gruth?" the other asked, without pausing in the fight.

"For Thaiss's sake, listen to me will you? She's back. The Soul Thief is back."

The two girls froze. For long seconds neither moved, though their gazes remained unflinchingly fastened on each other.

"You sure about this?" the older, larger girl said at length.

"Positive. Now will you both stop this madness?"

Slowly, ever so slowly, weapons were lowered, though neither girl stood straight, neither gave ground, and their eyes never wavered.

The older girl, Chavver, was the first to stand up, gradually abandoning her fighter's crouch. As her sister warily followed suit, Chavver looked at the Tattooed Man for the first time, if a glare infused with such fury could ever be considered a mere look, and said, "If this is some sort of trick to stop us from killing each other, M'gruth, you're a dead man."

He didn't doubt it for a minute.

Tom was more nervous than he could remember ever being before; certainly more than he was prepared to admit to the prime master. Not terrified, as he'd been when cornered by the demon hound, convinced he was about to die, and it was true he'd felt a little scared when first setting out to reach the Upper Heights – that distant Row at the very crown of the city – but that had been nothing compared to this. Somehow, the Heights hadn't seemed entirely real; a fable of a faraway place which had no relevance to him. His aborted attempt to go there had been part adventure and part impossible dream. Deep down he'd never expected to actually reach the roof of the world and had always known he'd be back in the under-City by morning.

This, however, was different in every way.

For long seconds he simply stood there, breathing in great lungfuls of sweet air, so cool and fresh, feeling the unfamiliar spring of grass beneath his booted feet and letting the wind stroke his face as he glanced up at the vast, distant sky. *He was outside.* That reality would take some getting used to, for all that the prime master had brought him out here a couple of times beforehand to acclimatise. Those earlier visits did help, a little, but they were just brief tasters, akin to quickly popping your head out the door before scurrying back inside. This was the real thing.

He turned and looked back. Seen from here, the city was a truly awe-inspiring sight. There were no balconies or terraces at these lower levels, the austerity of the faintly yellow stonework broken only by the occasional window. Yet the eye refused to dwell here but was rather compelled to look higher, drawn that way by the thrust of sheer stone walls erupting from the ground and reaching ever upward towards the heavens, as if the city somehow pulled at everything in the vicinity: the ground, the landscape, the very air surrounding it, even the attention of those insignificant people standing at its feet.

Seeing Thaiburley like this, Tom could well understand why this was considered to be the City of Dreams. Snatches of the levels verse, that childhood guide to the city's complexities learnt at his mother's knee, played through his mind, as they had during his ill-fated climb to the Heights.

> From Residence Rows where Kite Guards patrol,
> And learned folk study the soul,
> Arkademics and masters with wisdom to share,
> The city's leaders, entrusted to care,
> To the topmost Row, the Upper Heights,
> Where stars and demons frequent the nights,
> The end of this verse, fair Thaiburley's crown,
> From which lofty peak you can only fall down!

He gave an involuntary shiver, as the verse brought back memories of his fleeting visit to the Residences and the first time he'd glanced over the city walls, the sudden disorientation and the sense of absolute dread that had engulfed him. Without the prime master's help he felt certain a similar horror would have overwhelmed him now in the face of all this open space. It still didn't feel natural, but at least he was managing to cope.

"Liberating out here, don't you think?" his mentor said from beside him.

"I suppose so," Tom replied. Liberating was not quite the word he would have used.

The prime master chuckled. "You'll soon get used to it."

The old man was probably right. What might take a little more getting used to was the nature of the companions chosen to accompany him.

He wished fervently that some of the old crew were going, the Blue Claw, even Barton with his boasting of improbable deeds and his cocky swagger. But the Claw were gone like so many of the traditional street-nick gangs, their members scattered or detained. Perhaps they would regroup in time and rebuild, but even if they did so it would be without him. Tom was coming to accept the bitter fact that he didn't have a place among the nicks anymore, that the streets were no longer his home.

Funny, being a street-nick was a grim and desperate existence at the best of times, yet here he was regretting the loss of that life. The thing he missed most was the companionship, that sense of being a part of something, of belonging. His time with the Blue Claw might have been hard, but they'd all suffered that hardship together and had been able to draw strength from one another. He'd forged true friendships with kids of around his own age, and that more than anything else was what his life had lacked in recent days – the comfort of such close-knit friendships. Since being taken under the prime master's wing he had seen so many wondrous things and learned so much, and he was certainly living far better than he'd ever expected in his wildest dreams.

Yet none of that stopped him from feeling lonely.

More even than the Claw, he missed Kat. He'd only known the renegade nick for a few days but they'd been through a lot together. With her flashy black clothes, sassy attitude, twin short swords and a wealth of experience far beyond her years, she was one of the proudest, fiercest and bravest people he'd ever known and he would willingly have trusted her with his life. If it had been just the two of them setting off on this journey he'd have felt a lot happier, but he hadn't seen her since she left him with the Blade and didn't even know whether she'd survived the final chaos of that fateful day. Instead of Kat, he'd been lumbered with a right pair of oddballs, neither of whom he knew.

That was the most unsettling aspect of this whole business. He was embarking on a venture that would take him far beyond the city, on a journey to places that lacked even the solidity of tables but were instead complete unknowns, a trip that seemed more likely to take months than days, and he was expected to do this in the company of two complete strangers.

The prime master had selected them personally, and he had learned to respect the elderly man and to trust him. But that venerable gentleman was not the one who was going to have to travel and live with this pair. Tom was.

As if on cue, the first of these two companions wandered over to join Tom and the prime master, or rather to tower over them. Kohn was a veritable giant, standing roughly twice as high as a full-grown man – taller even than one of the Blade. Tom still remembered the first time he'd met him, just a few days previously. "This is Kohn," the prime master had said almost casually, as if trying to convince Tom that here was someone he just knew was destined to become a firm friend. All Tom could do was gape. His surprise didn't end with Kohn's size, because this was not just *any* giant, but rather a bald one-eyed giant, whose Cyclopean eye was rheumy and opaque. The huge figure was clearly blind.

"Kohn is one of the Kayjele, a long-lived race who make their home in the northern mountains," the prime master went on to explain as the giant came to stand before them, almost as if at attention.

"I know you," Tom had murmured.

His mind instantly raced back to the walls, where he had been fleeing a murder scene, stumbling along a kinked corridor to emerge into a large chamber where a vast, heart-like contraption beat and pulsed. The daunting contrivance, which he had since learned to be one of many pumps used to circulate water around the city, had been tended by this same creature or its twin. On that occasion the baleful gaze of that great, milky eye had sent the young street-nick scuttling away in terror.

When seen in the full light of day with the whole world open before him, the giant seemed much less intimidating, though he was still far from Tom's ideal choice of travelling companion.

The former street-nick now knew that Kohn had just finished a term of indentured service to the city and was about to embark on a journey back to his homeland. Since this meant he would be travelling a course that paralleled Tom's own for much of the way, the prime master thought it only sensible that they should travel together.

Sensible, perhaps; but definitely not good for his nerves, for all that the old man assured him Kohn was reliable. Tom also wondered how the giant was going to manage the journey when he couldn't see. When he'd asked the prime master this, he was told: "Kohn *is* able to see, Tom, though I daresay the world appears very differently to him than to you or I. He sees with his mind. All his people are capable of this, but in his case the ability is far more acute, no doubt developing that way to compensate for his lack of normal vision. Don't worry, Kohn won't slow you down in the least. In fact, quite the contrary. His unusual perspective may even prove to be of benefit."

Tom would never admit to doubting the prime master, yet he felt far from convinced, notwithstanding cryptic references to "unusual perspectives". He was beginning to regret agreeing to this expedition in the first place; or rather he regretted allowing himself to be talked into it; he wasn't sure he had ever actually *agreed* as such.

The giant now stood with them outside the city walls, silent and unmoving, his face looking directly at Tom, presumably 'seeing' him despite the opaqueness of that single central eye. For his part, Tom went to speak, then hesitated, remembering that, in addition to being blind, the giant couldn't reply. "Kohn is mute, so won't necessarily be the liveliest of company," the prime master had explained. "But he can hear and understand you perfectly well and will make his meaning clear with gestures when necessary."

His other companion didn't promise to be much of an improvement on the giant either.

As if on cue, Dewar, the man in question, was coming towards them at that moment, walking up from the banks of the Thair. The great river flowed in majestic splendour a short distance downslope from them, vanishing into the brief canyon which developed into a broad cavern mouth: the entrance to the City Below.

Dewar was among the least remarkable people Tom had ever met. A little more meat on his bones than the average inhabitant of the City Below, so presumably he came from up-City somewhere, one of the more comfortable Rows, but otherwise he could have blended in just about anywhere. On the younger side of middle age, a tad on the shorter side of medium height with slightly receding brown hair, he had a rounded, homely face and a very ordinary physique. Yet the prime master had assured Tom that this man was more than capable of looking after himself. If so, his outward appearance certainly offered no clue. As far as Tom could see, the only features which seemed even remotely noteworthy were the man's eyes. Living on the streets, as Tom had for most of his life, you learned to judge people quickly and the eyes were often the most important indicator. Dewar's were intelligent; more than that, there was a coldness in their depths and an intensity in their stare which caused Tom to give an involuntary shiver and led him to reconsider his assessment. Perhaps after all there was a little more to this man than immediately seemed apparent.

As he watched Dewar approach, he couldn't help but wish that the prime master had thought to send at least one familiar face along on this venture. A selfish thought and one which probably showed his age, but he didn't care.

"The barge has arrived," Dewar said to the prime master with a typical lack of deference that irritated Tom.

If Tom could find one redeeming aspect to the whole venture, this was surely it – he was finally getting a chance to go on a boat. Tom had often watched the great barges unloading at the docks or riding the deep centre of the Thair as they came and went along the river, sitting low in the water due to their loads and then riding high once relieved of them. The young Tom had dreamed of some day going on one of those boats, and here was his chance. Their ill-assorted group were to travel the first part of the journey aboard one of the huge vessels, which was making an unscheduled stop at the little-used dock outside the city walls in order to pick them up. A measure arranged by the prime master to avoid attention, which suggested to Tom that all was not yet as secure in the City Below as some would like to claim.

The boy felt a jolt of excitement at hearing the barge was already there waiting for them, waiting for *him*, and it was all he could do not to run down the track to see it.

"Tom?"

He was checked by a woman's voice calling from the direction of the city, a voice which sounded oddly familiar. He turned to look back and saw two figures approaching. One he recognised as Thomas, recently installed on the Council of masters, the highest rung of Thaiburley's government. The other wore the green of a Thaistess, the representatives in the city of the goddess Thaiss, or so it was claimed. Tom had little faith in such things for all that his feelings towards the Thaistesses had softened following recent events. When he thought to look beyond the robes at the woman who wore them, Tom suddenly realised that he *did* know her.

"Mildra!" Here was the young Thaistess who had

tended him in the aftermath of his hard-fought battle against one of the Dog Master's creatures.

She laughed, reminding him how young she was to be wearing the green of a full priestess and how patient and kind she had been in the face of his surliness and suspicion. "Is that a smile, Tom? Don't tell me you're actually pleased to see *me*, a Thaistess." Her grin robbed the words of any sting.

He looked down, sheepishly. "Sorry about last time, and right now I'm happy to see *any* familiar face." He said the words quietly, so that the prime master and Dewar, who were conversing with Thomas close by, wouldn't hear.

"Oh dear."

She didn't say it in a way that suggested he was being unreasonable or childish, or in any sense selfish. So the feeling that he was must have been wholly of his own making.

The young Thaistess positioned herself deliberately so that her back was towards the small knot of other people, standing between Tom and them as if to emphasise that this conversation was private. "Sometimes, when there are things that need to be done, it's easy to lose sight of the cost for those involved, of how difficult the things we expect from a particular person might be."

He understood what she meant. "I know the prime master means well and that he has the whole of Thaiburley to worry about, but…"

"But you don't really want to go on this journey."

"No." This was the first time he had admitted as much to anybody, and the word emerged as a whisper.

Mildra took a deep breath and then said, "Let me talk to him. It doesn't matter how important he deems this to be, he can't ride roughshod over your feelings and your needs like this. Not after everything you've already done for the city. We haven't actually set out as yet so it isn't too late to call the whole trip off. Leave this to me." She went to move away, towards the prime master and the others.

"Do *you* think it is? Important, I mean," he said quickly, stopping her.

The girl hesitated, before saying, "I won't lie to you, Tom; yes, I rather suspect it is."

"Wait a minute," the rest of what Mildra had said penetrated his thoughts, "did you say *we*?" He suddenly noted the bag she was carrying, a rucksack as green as her robe so that it tended to blend in with her clothing.

"Yes," and her grin was as broad as the Thair, "I was intending to go with you. Didn't anyone mention that?"

"No… no they didn't."

"Well, since you were going in search of the goddess Thaiss, the very heart of everything we teach and believe in, it seemed only natural that a Thaistess should accompany you. And as the youngest and, perhaps – how can I put this? – most flexibly-minded of my sisterhood, I was chosen."

"Oh." Tom found himself smiling. He didn't really know Mildra well, but she had shown herself to be a warm and generous person and had helped him when he'd most needed help. At some instinctive level he both trusted and liked her, despite her being a Thaistess. All of a sudden, knowing that she was going to be there as well, the trip didn't seem nearly so daunting. And there was still the lure of going on a barge…

"Mildra," he blurted out, before he could change his mind, "please don't say anything. Forget my moaning. If this journey really is that important, and if you're willing to go all that way, then I guess I am too."

She stared at him for a silent second, before asking, "Are you sure about this?"

He looked her unblinkingly in the eye. "Yes."

"Right," said the prime master, coming over to join them, "are we all ready then?"

"Ready," Tom replied, and was surprised to discover that he meant it.

The prime master watched with troubled heart as the small party disappeared towards the Thair and the waiting barge. There was so much at stake here, and he had just gambled with four people's lives despite having no real idea of the dangers confronting them. He felt himself to be a man involved in a game of chance in which the other players could see his hand while he remained blind to theirs and didn't even fully grasp the rules.

Evidently, he wasn't the only one with reservations. "Are you sure this is wise?" Thomas asked from beside him.

He raised his eyebrows. "Ah, Thomas, now there's a question."

"I suppose you're going to tell me that wisdom is grossly overrated."

"No, far from it. Wisdom is deserving of the greatest respect and is something we're in the habit of dismissing far too readily. It's merely my capacity for wisdom that I would question. Is this wise? Sending an ill-matched quartet quietly off into the unknown, without fuss or fanfare, without military escort or any of the Blade to watch over them?" He shook his head. "I really don't know."

"Then why are you doing this?" The young master's

frustration, his desire to understand, was apparent in every syllable. The prime master could still remember when *he'd* been that eager, in those long ago days before the weight of responsibility had taught him the value of hesitancy.

"To protect him, Thomas, to remove him from harm's way." Both knew he was referring to the younger master's namesake, the former street-nick Tom.

Thomas shook his head, clearly exasperated. "With all due respect, that doesn't make any sense. By sending him outside the city aren't you doing exactly the opposite: placing the lad beyond our capacity to protect him?"

"Perhaps," the prime master acknowledged.

He hesitated, wondering how much he dared share with Thomas. When all was said and done this was his burden, yet it made sense for someone else to know of his suspicions. Well-established layers of bureaucracy ensured the day to day running of this vast metropolis, yet ultimately the responsibility for everything that went on in Thaiburley fell on the shoulders of just a dozen people – the Council of Masters. Inevitably, all twelve were forever short of time and overstretched; it seemed unfair to trouble any of his established colleagues with his concerns, but Thomas was still finding his way and was not yet inundated with the demands of government which would swamp his attention soon enough. If the prime master were going to talk to anyone, he could do a lot worse than trust this astute and keen young man.

"You're right, of course," he said, "this is something of a gamble; but, I fear, a necessary one. If you examine all that happened in the City Below of late and look beyond the subversion of the street-nick gangs, you'll see that much of what went on was aimed at Tom, designed to either capture or kill him."

"But surely that's been dealt with and those responsible either captured or killed."

"It would seem so, and yet..." This was the moment; did he dare risk saying more? He took a deep breath and continued. "I'm not convinced we caught or even identified everyone involved. My fear is that the real mastermind managed to elude us and is still at large in the city somewhere."

The younger man studied him. "That's an unpleasant enough notion, but there's more, isn't there? Otherwise why not keep the lad safe in the Heights and assign a squad of the Blade to guard him? Whatever the threat is, it seems confined to the City Below."

The prime master smiled. The assembly members had enjoyed a particularly good day when they nominated Thomas as candidate for the Council of Masters. There was no doubting the sharpness of the young man's mind. "Yes, there's more. Something is wrong, Thomas, fundamentally wrong. How else could a monster like Magnus arise and come within fingertips of reaching the rank of master?"

"And you think that the lad is capable of righting whatever's wrong, and that this expedition is the way to do so?"

"That's my hope, yes. Perhaps not solve everything, but at least show us where the real problem lies." The prime master shook his head. "So much was lost to us during the war. The city's data stores ravaged, much of the history and knowledge our ancestors took for granted gone forever... But there's *something* at the source of the Thair. The Thaistesses would have us believe that this is where their goddess lives. I'm not convinced that's literally true, but it might very well be symbolic of a deeper truth. Whatever is there is connected to the very core of all that Thaiburley is. Where better to seek answers? If this doesn't work, I'm not sure where else we can turn to, what more we can do.

"I don't believe an army could achieve this, nor the Blade in all their might, but between the four individuals in that little group there are some remarkable talents. I dare hope these might prove enough."

An awkward pause followed, while both men pondered their own thoughts. Then the prime master asked abruptly, "Do you believe in the goddess Thaiss, Thomas?"

Thomas blinked, clearly nonplussed, and he studied the older man, as if trying to decide whether or not the question was meant seriously.

"I only ask because if you do, even to a small extent, might I suggest you pray to her? Only I've a feeling that we and our four departing friends are likely to need all the help we can get during the days ahead."

Thomas went to answer but clearly thought better of it. Instead he simply turned to gaze at the broad ribbon of the Thair, its shifting waters sparkling in the sun, keeping his thoughts to himself.

THREE

The customer, Sander, took the small crystal phial gingerly, as if afraid it might sting him; though in truth it already had, financially at least. He had come to the apothaker in the past for the odd preparation, but none of them as significant as this. He really was a sorry excuse for a man, she reflected. Seemingly old beyond his years; spindly thin, tall and slightly stooped, with an unfortunately sombre expression which suggested he carried the weight of the world upon his shoulders rather than merely the administrative concerns of a middling import business. He smelt of camphor and his complexion didn't do him any favours, either. Sallow cheeks were marred by a number of unsightly indentations, akin to stud marks, the legacy of a childhood illness. Doubtless they were barely noticeable in the full glare of the sun globes, but here and now in the apothaker's home the fickle illumination from candle and lantern conspired to highlight the pock marks so that they took on the semblance of mini craters; it was impossible not to stare at them. The old woman had to consciously avert her gaze, forcing herself to focus only on his eyes.

The man turned the small bottle slowly between his thumb and the tip of his forefinger, as if to examine the contents by the lantern's glow.

"And you're sure this will work?"

The woman smiled thinly. She had expected something of the sort: a plea for reassurance. But she wasn't in the mood, so offered harsh reality instead. "As sure as I can be."

He looked up sharply, offence manifest in his scowl. "But you said..."

"Sur Sander, nothing in life is entirely certain, as you well know. You accept a shipment from a supplier who has been sending you such packages for years, a man you know to be reliable, but you open it up to discover that on this one occasion the contents have turned rotten. This can happen, yes?" The man nodded reluctantly. "In that phial is a potion mixed of proven ingredients and instilled with the correct essence, a formula I know has worked on countless previous occasions and so should work again, but nothing can be guaranteed. If the girl you intend this for already despises you, then there is no power in the world that will transform her feelings into love. The potion might soften her heart a little but the rest would be down to your own endeavours. If, on the other hand, she is merely indifferent to you or better still is already disposed to liking you, there is no reason why true affection shouldn't take root in her heart and blossom."

He looked worried now. "She does like me, I'm sure of it," he muttered, sounding anything but.

"Well, there you are then. If that's the case, you have nothing to be concerned about."

He flashed her a fragile smile, looking far from reassured. The old woman stood, anxious to bring an end to the meeting, and proceeded to usher him towards the door. Her face bore a confident expression which disappeared the instant he was gone. She returned to slump into her familiar chair at the small table that dominated one end of the room, suddenly feeling her age. It didn't matter whether she was in the City Above or the City Below, men remained the same: malleable, insecure, and more inclined to listen to their hormones than their brains.

In her youth, in far finer surroundings than this, her looks and well-proportioned figure had proved formidable advantages; weapons which few men could resist for long. And she so enjoyed their capitulation. Now, since the scandal that had brought about her dramatic downfall and banishment to the under-City – not to mention the fading of her looks with the passage of unkind years – she had to rely on her wits and on other talents, while being forced to live out whatever time remained to her down here in the stinking bowels of the city.

The curtain at her back moved and Kara entered, to walk past and sit in the chair facing her.

"He's gone then?"

"Yes."

"Wretched, pathetic man; he makes my flesh crawl. The way he looked at me that first time…" She gave a melodramatic shiver. "I hate the fact that we have to deal with the likes of him."

The old woman laughed briefly and bitterly. "I wouldn't worry. I doubt the young girl whose head he's so desperate to turn feels much different. Most likely the potion, for all the essence you poured into it, will only make her pity him at best."

Kara was still young, tact a skill she had yet to master, which was why the apothaker took great care over which clients she presented the girl to. When dealing with Sander, she tried to keep Kara well out of sight.

The old woman first encountered Kara sitting on a stool at a street corner, selling freshly baked cakes and pastries made by her mother. Not yet a teen, she was already strikingly pretty despite being filthy and near-emaciated. High cheek bones, sparkling eyes, and a tumble of auburn hair transcended the outer coating of grime, but that wasn't what caught the apothaker's attention. She sensed in this young waif an inner fire, a talent not unlike her own but fiercer and stronger, far stronger. It seemed a tragedy that such a girl was destined to end up running with a street gang and embroiled in petty crime, or, more likely, whoring, as happened to so many in the City Below where there were far more people than there would ever be decent jobs, or even half-decent ones.

Following some extended bartering with the girl's mother – an old shrew with a keen eye for a profit – the apothaker secured the girl's services as her apprentice. In effect, she bought her. Yet she never once begrudged doing so, considering every coin to have been well spent. The girl was a revelation, her raw talent beyond anything the apothaker had seen before.

Kara rarely mentioned her father and when she did it was generally to the effect that he was drunk much of the time. These comments were invariably expressed in such an uncomfortable manner that the old woman suspected the man had abused her in some way.

With great patience she began to tutor her young protégée, teaching her to harness her emerging talent. Kara
proved to be a willing pupil and took to the disciplines as
if born to them, so that she was soon able to draw out the
potential of distillations, powders and elixirs far more effectively than the woman herself could ever have done.

They had been together now for nearly two years, during which time the girl had entered her teens. Clearly
destined to be a great beauty, she was already drawing
attention from men who ought to have known better
and boys who had yet to learn to. With the onset of pu-
berty her abilities blossomed and their partnership went
from strength to strength; the old apothaker with her
knowledge of chemistry and scientific process, brought
with her from the City Above, the girl with her raw talent to manipulate and set potentials. The old woman's
flickering abilities helped to guide the younger's bur-
geoning skills.

In addition, Kara loved her stories, loved to hear all
she could of life in the City Above. If the old apothaker's
experiences had been predominantly mundane in the
living, they grew to be so much more than that in the
telling. To a young girl condemned to live out her life in
the slums of the City Below, these tales provided treas-
ured glimpses of a magic kingdom forever beyond her
reach, and she lapped up every syllable.

What could she tell the girl this eve? In truth, she'd
long since run out of stories about her own life, even the
heavily embellished ones, and had all but exhausted the
gossip she remembered from friends and acquaintances
of those days. She was having to rely increasingly on
pure invention and sensed that even Kara was starting

to doubt some of the more outlandish claims; she resolved to be less flamboyant this time around.

They prepared the evening meal and ate in comfortable silence for the most part – cold meat, day-old bread and watered ale all slipped down a treat. This standard fare was then supplemented with a pickled egg each from the jar that Sander had brought as a gift. These proved less successful.

"Thaiss, that's disgusting!" Kara said, screwing up her face at the sharpness.

"Yet they're considered a great delicacy up-City," the apothaker lied. She'd been able to taste nothing but vinegar when she bit into her own egg and could well understand why Sander was reduced to giving these revolting things away.

"Really?" The girl examined hers with obvious suspicion.

"Yes, really; an acquired taste, perhaps, but delicious when your palate is accustomed to them." The old woman nibbled daintily at the pallid ovoid. They couldn't afford not to eat everything that came their way, and she was hanged if she was going to be left with an entire jar of the wretched eggs to polish off by herself.

Kara copied her, gingerly biting off morsels of vinegar-infused white, but she still wrinkled her nose every time she chewed.

The meal was soon finished and dishes cleared away. As they settled in for the evening by the hearth, the apothaker said casually, "Did I ever tell you about my cousin Andresh?"

"No," the girl said, "I don't think so." Actually the old woman was quite sure so, since she'd never had a cousin Andresh.

"Well, a bit of a black sheep was Andresh – a distant cousin, I should stress, on my mother's side. Not often talked about, which is doubtless why I haven't mentioned him before. Anyway, he kept some very suspect company did cousin Andresh, so much so that on one particular occasion his exploits came to the attention of the Kite Guard..."

"What was that?" The girl looked up sharply.

"What was what?" the old woman replied, a little testily because she was just getting into her stride.

"I thought I heard something from out back."

The apothaker frowned. She hadn't heard a thing but was willing to concede that her ears weren't all they used to be and that the youngster's were by far the sharper.

She stood up, cocked her head but still couldn't hear anything. "What did it sound like?"

"Something breaking... or being broken."

The old woman grunted. Street-nicks most like. She knew the local gangs and paid her dues like everyone else, but so much had changed since the riots and the fighting that all bets were now off. She wouldn't put it past some opportunist or other to break in looking to steal her distillations in the hope of increasing their chances of thieving and dodging the razzers. Best way to deal with this was to teach them a lesson; if they got away with it once they'd only come back for more. Signalling Kara to stay where she was, the apothaker picked up an iron poker from the cold hearth and headed purposefully towards the curtain at the back of the room. Beyond lay the rest of their meagre home: a short hallway ending at the back door with two internal doors leading off; the first opening into the cramped room where both women slept and the second to a slightly larger space with its apparatus and jars of ingredients – their workroom. The latter was doubtless where the intruder was at that very moment, creeping around and trying to decide what was what.

Gripping her fire iron tightly, the old woman pulled aside the curtain, ready to storm down the hall and into the back room, already rueing the damage which she felt certain would result from the incident, only to be confronted by a swirling mass of darkness born of some deranged nightmare. The stench was the first thing that struck her; a smell of dank decay, of something rotting – the smell of death. And the darkness had a face; eyes which fastened on her and seemed to tug at her very being, as if drawing the soul out of her body and pulling it inexorably towards that mass of twisting shadow.

She shuffled a few involuntary steps back into the room as the thing advanced, shrinking away from its touch. The nightmare form moved swiftly and the apothaker pressed herself against the wall, cowering, wishing the wall would absorb her, let her pass through. The apparition brushed her in passing, seeming to have no substance, no physical pressure, yet its touch felt as cold as a tomb.

The apothaker was wrenched from her funk by a scream. Kara! With a conscious effort of will she forced her arm to lift, raising the fire poker which still somehow dangled from her limp right hand. Desperation lent her energy. She prised her body from the wall and stared at where Kara was sitting. The girl had disappeared, enveloped in roiling black mist, yet that nebulous swirling now took on a semblance of form and the apothaker fancied she could make out the hazy shape of a woman standing over Kara's chair, arms spread as if to embrace chair and girl alike. If so, the figure was draped in a large black cloak, unlike any garment she had ever seen before. It billowed and flowed and floated, never still, as if constantly disturbed by breezes and gusts that simply weren't there.

The apothaker had no idea what was being done to her protégée, but she doubted any good could ever come out of this walking nightmare.

"Leave her!" she roared, surprised at the strength of her own voice.

The thing looked at her; definitely a woman's face, though distorted beyond anything that could still be called human. As the eyes turned to her, she again felt that awful sense of something pulling at her inner being. And then the creature flowed towards her.

The apothaker caught a brief glimpse of a withered, limp form where Kara had sat, and then gagged as the awful smell grew stronger and the darkness was in her face, twin pits of hell staring into her eyes.

"Too old, too spent," a voice akin to the crackle of dried paper said. "Your talent's weak and fickle; not worth the effort of taking. The girl, though... she was delicious." The last syllable emerged as a protracted, sibilant hiss, and was accompanied by a stomach-churning waft of fetid breath and the sense of something stroking her chin.

The apothaker recoiled and gagged, suddenly terrified beyond all reasoning.

Without warning the dreadful presence withdrew, floating across the room and past Kara's chair, where a desiccated husk now sat, and onwards towards the door. The apothaker was able to breathe again, to think. She stumbled forwards, legs shaky, the poker dropping from numb fingers as she stared at the body in the chair. Moments ago this had been a beautiful, vibrant teenager, bursting with life and energy – a young girl poised on the threshold of realising her potential and only just beginning to learn how to enjoy life. In seconds all of that had been snatched away, snuffed out in the blink of an eye, to leave behind a wasted, white-haired cadaver, a vessel drained of everything that had made Kara so beautiful and alive.

"You brecking monster," she screamed at the thing's back, "you've killed her!" The old woman couldn't bring herself to touch the ashen husk that now occupied the chair, for all that she wanted to reach out and hold her precious Kara, to cradle her in her arms. At first she had hoped, somehow, that the girl might yet live, that she was merely damaged and could be nursed back to health, but it was immediately obvious that all hint of life had gone.

What now? How could she possibly survive without the girl's talent and the preparations it infused? The tears came unbidden; for Kara and for herself.

The living nightmare barely paused. It gathered before the front door, which abruptly exploded outward, and the thing flowed through, to vanish into the thinner darkness of the night.

Irrationally, the old woman followed, stopping in the vacant doorway to shout in the nightmare's wake, "Come back! You might as well take me as well! What am I supposed to do without her? You've already killed me, so come back and finish the job!"

But the killer had gone.

The old woman suddenly realised that she wasn't alone out here, as a face turned towards her, doubtless startled by her shouts. The apothaker nearly screamed anew in shock, but stopped herself, fascinated by this new apparition. Wide eyes stared out of a face covered in a pattern of intricate runes and markings. She suddenly realised what this had to be. *A Tattooed Man!* She saw others now, slipping through the pools of light and shadow cast by the street lamps. They were questing, hunting. Instinct told her that they were after her monster. She dashed back into the house, opened a cupboard and snatched up a particular phial before returning to the shattered door. She looked out expecting to see the Tattooed Man or someone similar but they'd moved on and instead she was confronted by a wiry black-clad girl, short sword clutched in either hand.

The apothaker gasped anew. "You're one of them, aren't you? *The Death Queens.*" The legendary warrior sisters said to rule the Tattooed Men.

"Get back inside, mother. This isn't a night to be outdoors."

So young. "It's been here," she blurted, desperate that the girl should understand, "that thing. It killed my Kara." The tears flowed again, as the image of the desiccated body in the room at her back flashed through her mind's eye. She wasn't ashamed of her grief and held her head high.

"I'm sorry... for your loss." The girl was obviously uneasy, wanted to be away. "You're not alone, but when we catch it, we'll claim revenge for you and everyone else, I promise."

"Here, take this." The old woman thrust the precious phial towards this girl. She looked to be no more than a few years older than Kara, yet there was a fire all her own glowing within this feral girl's breast. The apothaker sensed that this mere slip of a thing, this Death Queen, might actually stand a chance of killing the creature. There was a talent in her, nothing like Kara's, but something bright and strong all the same.

The girl stared at her as though she were mad.

"I'm an apothaker, and a good one," she explained, pride refusing to be dismissed so readily.

"Yeah, I'm sure, but just go back indoors..."

"No, you listen to me! I might not be able to hold a sword and could never hunt that thing down, but I can do this much. In here is the most potent elixir of luck I've ever distilled. Genuine talent went into this; not mine you understand, *Kara's*; and she was special, *really* special. Why else do you think that creature came here?"

The girl hesitated for an instant, then nodded and, after transferring one of the swords so that both were held in her left hand, snatched the phial.

"Drink this and you'll catch that thing, and beat it, and kill it."

"Thank you. Now, please..."

"I know, I know, I'm going back inside." Yet still the woman lingered. "One thing, before I do, though..."

"What?" The word was snapped, the girl's patience clearly at an end.

The apothaker had suddenly realised she didn't even have a label to attach to her hate, didn't know what to call the creature that had just stolen her life away. "This monster, does it have a name?"

The girl smiled grimly. "Yeah, it has a name all right, one straight out of a children's tale, maybe even a story you threatened your Kara with on nights when she was being stubborn and wilful and wouldn't go to bed. It's called the Soul Thief."

Being back among the Tattooed Men felt odd. In fact, if Kat were to be entirely honest, it felt odd being alive at all. She had returned to the Pits expecting to die.

The two of them, these sister-strangers, had walked back from the Pits in silence, M'gruth between them. Each refusing to acknowledge the other. Then Kat had found herself back in a world she thought she'd abandoned forever – that of the close-knit tribe known as the Tattooed Men.

She could never have actually killed Charveve – or Chavver as she preferred to be called – while she had no doubt that her sister would happily have slain her. Therein lay the vital difference. Kat was prepared to fight with every scrap of strength and will at her command to avoid being killed herself, but that was never going to be enough; not when her sister was prepared to go that crucial step further.

Kat was under no illusions. She knew their fight to the death wasn't over but had merely been put to one side while the pair of them concentrated on hunting down the Soul Thief. Afterwards, they'd finish it; one way or another.

All of which gave the present circumstances a surreal edge, even though everything was so familiar in many ways, like stepping back in time. Around her people moved with unhurried efficiency. The sounds of provisions being shifted and weapons readied – the rap of wooden crates on solid floor, the hiss of blade edge on whetstone, the gentle slap of feet and creak of leather harness – the Tattooed Men were preparing for war. Here was

Shayna fussing over her wounds, there was Charveve balling out M'gruth. The old crowd, together again; except for Rayul, her closest friend among all of them.

Rayul would never again be part of such gatherings. Because Kat had killed him. No one else here knew that as yet. Now *there* was a conversation she wasn't looking forward to.

Her wounds were mere scratches but Shayna brushed aside all such protests. "Even scratches can become infected."

Kat knew better than to argue, so surrendered to the healer's ministrations, relaxing as the older woman placed gentle hands around the edge of each wound. Warmth emanated from those hands, coursing through her body and producing a sense of tremendous wellbeing. She had to fight the urge to close her eyes and simply drift off to sleep, struggling to stay focused so that she could watch as each cut and minor wound closed and rapidly disappeared, leaving no more than a faint scar. Kat had seen this done many times before, but the sight never ceased to amaze her.

"That's some talent," she said, more drowsily than intended.

Shayna shrugged. "It's nothing really. All I do is speed up the body's natural healing processes."

"And you call that nothing? Seems pretty special to me."

"We're the Tattooed Men, Katerina. There's no one else like us in the whole of the city, most likely the world, so we're all special, even you. Especially you."

Kat grinned, willing to overlook the use of her full name – Shayna was one of the few she'd let get away with such things. "Tell that to my sister sometime, will you?"

"I've tried, believe me, I've tried." So saying, the healer stood up and moved away, leaving Kat to rouse herself to full wakefulness once more.

Chavver was in her element, snapping out orders and organising the Tattooed Men with well-practiced ease. Kat wondered whether her sister's injuries had benefited from Shayna's healing hands as hers had and, if so, why the older girl wasn't acting as woozy as she herself felt. Probably another manifestation of her famed iron will. After all, a queen couldn't be seen to show weakness in front of her subjects.

Well, anything she could do, Kat could match. So thinking, she pushed her body upright and swung her feet off the bench, planting them firmly on the floor, before forcing herself to stand. After a moment to make sure she wasn't going to wilt back onto the bench again, she strode purposefully towards her sister. Chavver turned at her approach and favoured her with a withering "Oh, so you're still here are you?" look.

"What about me?" Kat demanded. "And don't even think of trying to leave me out of this, Chav."

For an instant Kat's gaze locked with her sister's and she saw the hatred that still burned in the depths of eyes so like her own, then the older girl's focus shifted, sliding past her, and she called out, "M'gruth – Rel and Kat are with you," not even deigning to acknowledge her younger sibling.

Kat glanced around towards M'gruth, who stared back at her wide-eyed, clearly not relishing the prospect of giving orders to someone who had once led the Tattooed Men, but Kat smiled to reassure him. She couldn't care less about status. All that mattered was that she was involved, that she would have a chance to hunt down the abomination that had murdered her mother.

Besides, did Chavver really reckon that M'gruth had the balls to order *her* about? She suppressed a smile as she turned away and went to make her own preparations, determining to grab a bite to eat at the same time – nothing too heavy with the night that lay ahead, but she was going to need energy and plenty of it.

Night time and the tattooed Men were out in force. Kat had almost forgotten how good it felt to run with them; the sense of casual power, the feeling that nothing could harm her. In the year or more since she'd left them Kat had become a solitary skulker, flitting through the under-City like a ghost, moving across the territories of several established street-nick gangs, often unseen, always unchallenged. This had enabled her to believe that she was apart and somehow superior to the nicks and other petty denizens of the streets as she watched their furtive comings and goings without being involved.

Running with the Tattooed Men was akin to that in many ways but more so. Arrayed to either side of her, strung out in a long line so that they were in eyeshot courtesy of the under-City's flickering lanterns – if at times just barely so – were men of similar competence to herself. They ranged across territories with impunity. No need to skulk now; only a fool would consider standing in their way. The Tattooed Men were hunting. Like some far-flung human net they trawled the streets of the City Below.

Kat was positioned towards the right-hand tip of their line while Chavver would be holding the centre. Kat looked to her left, seeing M'gruth emerge from an alleyway,

then to the right, spotting a shadowy figure at the ex-
tremity of a lamp's glow – Rel. They didn't pause, didn't
acknowledge one another but moved on, again separated
by intervening buildings until the next branching street
or alley. In this fashion they advanced across a broad
swath of the under-City.

Something swept into sight, dipping down to head
height and then away again, causing Kat to tense, but it
was only a bat. In theory, she didn't need to worry about
the brecking things this time out. Before the hunt began
each of them had smeared some of Shayna's protective
ointment to face and arms and other exposed areas of
flesh. The unguent repelled the blood suckers to the point
where none would come near them, or so the theory
went. Shayna was tight-lipped about what actually went
into her salve, proclaiming, "That's my pension, for when
this is all over."

She was probably right. Many of the under-City's inhabitants were paranoid about the bats and would
doubtless pay handsomely for protection that actually
worked. For her own part, Kat remained sceptical. After
all, she'd survived down here for well over a year without the healer's salve and hadn't been attacked by the
bats once, though there were always tales of street-nicks
who'd been less fortunate.

At least the ointment didn't stink, in fact what little
smell it carried could almost be described as pleasant,
which had come as a surprise the first time Shayna produced it. In Kat's experience, most lotions and potions
that did you any good were guaranteed to smell and taste
foul. She commented as much to the healer, who
explained, "Bats don't hunt by scent, they use sound."

"So what does this cream of yours do, then?" Kat wanted to know. "Shriek at them?"

Shayna's response had been a simple knowing smile.

Kat reckoned that either bats noses were more sensitive than Shayna was letting on, or the ointment did nothing more than bolster the wearer's confidence. Whatever her reservations, she didn't refuse the salve when it was passed around. Better to be safe than sorry.

This time as she emerged from between two buildings and glanced across at M'gruth, it was to see him beckon her over. She felt a jolt of excitement and instantly turned and repeated the gesture to Rel, before sprinting across to join M'gruth. Someone along their line had caught sight or hint of their quarry and the hunt was about to begin for real. Kat was itching to move and could barely contain herself as they waited the brief seconds needed for Rel to join them. As soon as he did so they were off, funnelling in towards the centre of the line, as other groups would be. This was where the groupings designated by Chavver came to the fore. Now that the line had broken, they slipped smoothly into their allocated team of three – a pattern which Kat knew was being repeated up and down the line. Discipline came naturally to men raised to combat, men who had learned the hard way that teamwork could make the difference between life and death. This was exactly the sort of instinctive efficiency that gave the Tattooed Men their edge.

Kat slotted in as if she'd never been away.

As the line contracted inward they came to a figure who simply stood and pointed the way. Kat was so intent on the hunt she didn't even note who it was. Their team followed the finger, seeing the backs of another team a little way ahead, four in this one.

Kat felt a heady mix of excitement, anger and elation welling up inside. Once before, not long after the Pits had been closed down, they'd hunted the Soul Thief and had failed to catch her. Kat was determined the bitch wouldn't escape her again.

They ran through deserted streets, the under-City's inhabitants staying safely cosseted in their homes after globes out, as tradition down here dictated. They ran in virtual silence; there were no shouts, no outward sounds to indicate that their quarry had been sighted, just the gentle pad of feet on compact ground.

Kat had forged a little ahead of Rel and M'gruth, unable to entirely curb her enthusiasm. The Soul Thief was close, she could sense it.

In front of her, the group of four had stopped, hesitating by a shattered door, but only briefly. They were away again before she reached them. Pallid light seeped from the gaping doorway. Something had happened here. The murderous bitch had been at work. Instinctively, Kat drew her twin blades. A face appeared in the doorway, making her jump. An old woman.

The face looked as startled as she felt. "You're one of them, aren't you? *The Death Queens.*"

Kat hadn't been called that in a long while. The title, which she'd once worn with such arrogance and pride, now sat uncomfortably. If she were a queen at all, then it was a deposed one. Something else struck her. Kat had heard the occasional old dear with delusions of grandeur affect an up-City accent before, but this one sounded genuine. Rather than the hesitant precision of the self-conscious imitator, she fancied she heard here the easy delivery of a natural speaker.

Despite this curiosity Kat was itching to be gone, sensing that the Soul Thief was slipping further away with every passing second, but the woman refused to go back indoors and despite herself the girl felt sympathetic, fully understanding her loss. After all, she'd suffered in much the same way herself – a while ago perhaps, but the memory and pain were rarely more than a thought away. The woman thrust something at her, a small bottle, claiming it to be a potion for good luck or something. She would have scoffed at such things a few days ago, but that was before she'd cowered with Tom while a demon hound slobbered over them and the boy's ability had effectively hidden them in plain sight. The great beast never even knew they were there. So now she hesitated, sensing that the old woman believed her own words, and when she started muttering about talent and a child who was 'special', Kat began to believe a little as well. So she took the proffered phial, tucking it away in her clothing, which seemed to satisfy this self-proclaimed apothaker enough that she finally vanished back inside.

Kat felt released, as if the woman's presence had somehow held her trapped and only once she'd withdrawn was the girl free to pick up the hunt once more. Rel and M'gruth had caught up with her, so the three of them ran together again.

"You shouldn't dash ahead like that," the latter said, managing to sound both angry and offended.

"You should try to keep up," was her retort.

The night's stillness was shattered by a strange, piercing wail, sounding as if it were only a short way ahead.

Kat broke into a sprint. She knew what the inhuman cry had to mean: the Tattooed Men had caught up with the Soul Thief, the monster that had sucked the life from her mother and turned her and Charveve into orphans; the creature responsible for their ending up in the Pits. She wanted to be there, wanted to be part of that bitch's death more than she'd ever craved anything in her life. So Kat ignored M'gruth's calls imploring her to slow down and instead ran for all she was worth.

FOUR

Dewar had to give the prime master credit. Here was quite possibly the most formidable man the assassin had ever encountered. He thought he'd found the best that Thaiburley had to offer in his former employer, Magnus – powerful, suave, cunning and ruthless. Yet in comparison to the prime master, Magnus was as naïve as a newborn hatchling and all his scheming and manoeuvrings amounted to nought. True, the senior arkademic had projected a sense of destiny and purpose, sufficient at least to persuade an ambitious man to throw in his lot with him, but the prime master was destiny personified. Furthermore, he understood human nature and the workings of the mind, knowing exactly how to bind Dewar to his cause – which buttons to press to ensure the assassin's loyalty. Not an astonishing feat, perhaps, but more than Magnus had ever achieved. Initially, Dewar worked for the senior arkademic because it had suited him to do so. Later, the burden of shared guilt over the various acts Dewar perpetrated on his employer's behalf bound the pair of them together, each dependent on the other's discretion. Such relationships were fragile at best, destined to collapse as soon as either party lost faith in the other. The prime master was not about to rely on such uncertain half-measures to secure his loyalty.

When the old man interviewed him following his failed attempt to flee the city – meant as a temporary measure, a way of lying low and allowing things to settle before his return – the assassin knew at once that his future was on the line. Faced with the prospect of permanent banishment from the city, Dewar had listened carefully to all that the prime master had to say, noting the exact phrasing and inflections and seeing in them a glimmer of hope.

Only then, once he was confident that he understood precisely what his options were, did he make his pitch, choosing each and every word with infinite care. "I understand why you feel reluctant to allow me to remain inside the city, but might there perhaps some way in which I could serve you initially *outside* the walls, and so prove my loyalty?"

The prime master regarded him thoughtfully, the ghost of a smile played at the corners of his mouth, leaving Dewar in no doubt that this was exactly what the man had been waiting to hear. "Now there's an interesting suggestion."

First Thaiburley's senior official dangled the carrot. "In many ways you're an enigma, Dewar. You clearly value your citizenship but have flouted our laws from the very first moment you arrived here. Now you propose to redeem yourself by performing some service *outside* the city. A strange proposition by any estimation.

"Yet it just so happens that there is a small task which, if accomplished, *might* persuade me to overlook your past conduct and rescind your banishment."

Dewar bowed his head respectfully. "I'll do anything, prime master."

Then came the inevitable stick, which the prime master brandished with equal deftness. "I would require a small amount of your blood, of course."

Dewar froze. "My blood? Why?"

"Oh, nothing to worry about." The old man smiled and waved a dismissive hand. "Just a pinprick on a finger, that's all. You'll barely feel a thing."

Dewar licked his top lip, a nervous habit he thought abandoned decades ago. "And why exactly would you need this blood of mine?"

"A mere precaution, which I'm sure will prove redundant. You see, the service I mentioned involves you safeguarding the life of a certain individual as they undertake a potentially perilous journey. In the unlikely event that you should have a change of heart while fulfilling your task and abscond, or, worse still, should anything happen to the person you're supposed to be guarding, well, with a drop of your blood there isn't a corner of the world you can hide in where I won't be able to reach you."

Dewar stared at the prime master. The man's smile remained as warm and guileless as ever.

The assassin had seen some of the things arkademics could do and didn't doubt that masters were capable of a great deal more. He sensed that here before him was a good, a decent man, but he didn't make the mistake of assuming that this was an indication of weakness. Here was the person who was ultimately responsible for the whole of the city and everyone in it, who must be well used to making tough choices when such were required.

After all, he hadn't hesitated in deploying the Blade to the under-City, where their very name was a dire curse.

The assassin was not about to dismiss the threat couched in the old man's soft-spoken tone as an idle one.

The prime master was speaking again. "I apologise now for taking such unnecessary precautions, but you do understand why I have to take them, don't you?"

Dewar's own smile was thin and humourless as he nodded in agreement. "Of course."

"Excellent! Oh, by the way, the person you'll be looking out for is someone I believe you're already aware of, a former street-nick by the name of Tom."

Dewar struggled to keep his face passive, feeling simultaneously shocked and amused, and undecided about which reaction was the stronger. He had just been charged with safeguarding the life of the very lad he'd originally been sent into the City Below to kill.

As if that particular irony were not enough for any man to have to deal with, the prime master had another surprise up his sleeve, casually revealed to Dewar as he was leaving the man's presence, having donated a few drops of blood.

The prime master suddenly said, in the manner of a man who had almost forgotten to ask, "Incidentally, is there anyone among your network of informants in the under-City you would like me to keep an eye on in your absence? Anybody who you feel might otherwise be vulnerable?"

Dewar paused and looked back at this deceptively frail man, this cunning manipulator and consummate politician. The question left the assassin in no doubt that somehow the old man knew all about the retribution he had dealt the bargeman Hal on Marta's behalf. Dewar had left the slimy brecker bleeding his life away in an alley close to the runs; one more unsolved murder for the local razzers to puzzle over – just another night in the City Below – but he didn't doubt that someone of the prime master's abilities could identify him as the perpetrator should he be interested enough to investigate. Evidently, he had.

The assassin found himself strangely reluctant to answer. He had a choice here and it wasn't one he relished. Before making it, he was going to have to do something he'd been trying to avoid: analyse what he truly felt for Marta, if indeed he felt anything at all. She was, after all, a whore; a particularly pretty, young, and spirited one, granted, but still a whore.

He licked his upper lip again, much to his own annoyance, and said, as nonchalantly as he could manage, "Thank you, prime master, but not really, no." Then he added, as if he too were susceptible to afterthoughts, "Though, having said that, there *is* one girl, now that you mention it; a tavern wench by the name of Marta – she means nothing to me personally, you understand, but she's had a particularly rough time of it lately, and she did provide the information that led me to the Blue Claw, which in turn set events in motion. I do feel she probably deserves a certain consideration."

"Marta," the prime master repeated thoughtfully, as if memorising the name. "Very well. And she operates where?"

"Around the market area, at the fringes of the runs," Dewar replied, seeing no harm in playing the prime master's game but wondering what advantage he was handing the old man even as he did so. "As I say, no real matter, but since you asked..."

"No, quite understood. From what you say, the city owes this girl a considerable debt. I'll make sure she's safe in your absence."

"Thank you." Dewar felt completely off-balance, his thoughts rattled and fragmented, as if he had just been outclassed in a mental fist fight and was still reeling from a series of well-placed blows. This was a feeling completely alien to him, a man who took pride in his self-control. He forced his thoughts into order, and, as his mind began to regain some semblance of equilibrium, was suddenly appalled by his own words. He had just made himself vulnerable in a way he would never have believed. Did Marta *really* matter that much to him?

Apparently, yes.

Tom was finding sleep frustratingly elusive, perhaps unsettled by the gentle yet unfamiliar motion of the boat. Dewar seemed to suffer no such problems and, to judge by the regular rhythm of his breathing, had dropped off almost at once. But then Dewar had been busy almost from the first moment they came aboard, making himself useful to the crew by helping with this and that, while Tom had simply spent the day watching the river go by and waving at people on the banks. He would have helped, if asked, but had a feeling he would only have been in the way.

For him, this first day away from Thaiburley had been a wonderful, exciting, almost magical experience. He'd especially enjoyed it when they'd passed other barges going in the opposite direction, particularly the first time one of the great vessels came surging towards them, looking from a distance as if it were going to meet their own boat head on. Only as the other craft drew nearer did the illusion evaporate, as it became clear the two boats would slip past each other with a good deal of water between them. The barges were invariably heavily laden, carrying loads either to or from Thaiburley, and so were restricted to the deeper channels towards the centre of the river; hence the illusion of imminent collision. Crew members would sometimes pause to acknowledge their counterparts with curt greetings and the odd good-humoured insult.

Much of the comment coming their way had to do with Kohn. The giant sat at the prow of the boat, the only area of deck large enough to accommodate him.

His sightless eye stared towards the riverbank and Tom wondered what he 'saw' and whether the experience was as enjoyable for the Kayjele as it was proving to be for him. Somehow, he felt it was, and he sensed in the giant a kindred spirit at a level he could never have put into words.

The most convenient place to position himself, where he wouldn't be in the crew's way, was close to Kohn, and the pair of them had spent long hours sitting beside one another, neither making a sound while they soaked up the experience and 'watched' the world go by. He found the great solid presence beside him oddly comforting, and began to regret some of the less than charitable thoughts he'd harboured concerning the giant earlier. After they had sat there for most of that first day, their silent communion growing, Kohn reached into his jerkin and pulled something out. It was a pendant, a great orange-brown stone, faceted and shaped like a teardrop, which hung around the giant's neck via a simple leather thong. Kohn leaned forward, holding the stone towards Tom without taking it off. The boy sensed that this was a display of trust, that Kohn was sharing a confidence. He reached out hesitantly and took the stone in his hand. It was surprisingly warm to the touch, almost as if generating its own heat, but Tom guessed this was because the pendant was habitually pressed against Kohn's body.

"It's beautiful," he said, because he couldn't think what else to say but also because it was, in a bold, brazen way. His response seemed to satisfy Kohn, who smiled, took the pendant back and slipped it inside his jerkin once more.

Tom wouldn't have swapped that river ride for the world, whatever the rest of the journey might bring. His fascination with the barges originally stemmed from a sense that they had just arrived from some exotic faraway place or were about to set off to visit one. He'd always been a little in awe of the hard, dour men who crewed the vessels and envied them their freedom and independence, though perhaps that particular assumption deserved some rethinking, certainly to judge by the amount of work he watched the crew get through that day.

The barges were essentially gigantic floating containers, with a point at the front and an engine at the back. No space was wasted. Every inch not taken up with cargo storage was a fraction less potential profit, so all such areas were minimised. Steering was situated on a small part-covered platform built above the cramped cabin in which the family lived. And it *was* a family, this crew. Man, wife and two sons. Not all were, as Tom well knew. Many were all male, with the crew hired, but not this lot.

As you stepped from the deck down the five steps that led into the cabin, there was a small, black stove to the left, where all the cooking was done. Beyond that was an area that didn't look big enough for four people to sit and eat in comfortably, let alone sleep, yet they did, and somehow there were now going to be seven sleeping there. Boards had been moved, sacking and bedding produced – even a curtain, which was pulled across to separate crew from guests; not men from women as Tom first assumed, which meant that Mildra was forced to sleep in the same small area as him and Dewar.

Tom didn't have a problem with the arrangements – he'd slept in worse conditions than this – but he wasn't sure the Thaistess had, though she made no complaint.

Kohn would have to make do with spending the night on deck where he'd spent the day; he certainly wouldn't fit down here.

After a prolonged and fruitless period of tossing and turning, Tom finally accepted the inevitable, rose from the section of floor which served as a bed, and felt his way to the stairs. He went as quietly as he could and managed to successfully avoid bumping into Dewar beside him, so reasoned there was a fair chance he hadn't disturbed the others.

On emerging from the hatch, he was stopped in his tracks by sight of the sky. The breath caught in his throat and for long seconds all he could do, this lowly street-nick raised in the confines of the City Below, was stare at the myriad pinprick lights that punctured the darkness, while basking in the pure wonder of it all.

"Beautiful, isn't it?" a voice asked from behind him.

The sound made him jump – he'd been so absorbed that he hadn't even heard Mildra climb from the hatchway after him.

"Sorry," the girl said, though her mischievous grin suggested she was anything but. "I didn't mean to startle you."

"That's all right, I was just…" he gestured wordlessly at the heavens and shook his head.

"I know what you mean," the Thaistess said wistfully. "A wonderful sight; it's been years since I've seen the stars."

Tom never had, not even on the night he'd climbed the city's walls, when these flecks of light must have been obscured by clouds. Either that or he'd been too busy, too frightened and too excited to notice them.

"On a night like this, with a clear sky and without the ambient light from the city to mask them, they're quite, quite magical, aren't they?"

Perhaps that was it; perhaps there'd been too much light all around for him to notice these pinpricks of silver brilliance above him when he'd gone up the walls.

For long moments the pair of them stood there, simply gazing upward, though Tom was aware of Mildra's presence at his shoulder, a distinctly feminine presence, for all that she was a Thaistess.

"Well," she said after a while, "first day's ended. How are you coping?"

"Not bad. Being on the barge helps. Something I've always wanted to do."

"Good." Then, after a further pause, the girl said softly, "You miss Kat, don't you?"

Not for the first time, Tom wondered whether Thaistesses could read minds. "A little," he admitted.

"I saw her fight once, you know."

Tom grinned, the words brought back memories of his own. "Yeah, she's really something isn't she?"

"I mean," the Thaistess continued, a little hesitantly, "I saw her fight *in the Pits*."

"What? Tom was shocked. The Pits were anathema, a dark, shameful episode in the recent history of the City Below which most tried to forget. Even the street-nicks tended to avoid mention of the place. He'd never before heard anyone admit to actually having gone there.

"I wasn't always a Thaistess, Tom," Mildra went on, clearly uncomfortable at his reaction but also a little amused. "Before thoughts of joining the priesthood ever entered my head I was... well, it doesn't really matter, but I used to know this boy – young man I suppose – though most of the time he acted more like a kid than you do. Anyway, he used to enjoy going to the Pits, so I went with him. He loved it, watching the fights and all the blood. He'd gamble on the outcome of bouts, on who was going to survive and who would die first, and he'd flash his money around. Liked to think he was the big man but it was nothing more than brash bluster and posturing. That's what got him killed in the end – acting tough in front of the wrong people." She drew a deep breath. "So, yes, I went to the Pits more than once."

Tom was fascinated despite himself. "What was that like?"

"In general, do you mean? Or seeing Kat?"

"Both, but tell me about Kat first."

"Well..." The Thaistess drew a deep breath. "It was incredible; *she* was incredible. I've never seen anyone move so fast. She was only a child, a wiry slip of a thing, dressed in black much as she wears now – I've no idea whether that was her choice or whether they made her wear black and she's never lost the habit. Three of them came into the arena together – Kat and two men, both of whom were a lot bigger than her and a several years older, and yet she was calling the shots. They followed her without question. At first I thought this was some bizarre joke, an extra handicap imposed by the people who ran the place, but no, the men followed her because she offered the best chance of survival.

"The three of them walked to the centre of the ring, where the two men – both bearing tattoos to show they were veterans of the Pits – flanked the girl like towering bodyguards. There came this horrible, inhuman squealing, as if a pig was being strangled, then the gates at the far side of the arena lifted and an enormous borquill came charging out, bearing straight down on the three in the middle."

As she mentioned the borquill, Mildra glanced towards Tom inquiringly. He shook his head, never having heard of the beast.

"The borquill looks a bit like a wild boar but it's bigger," the Thaistess explained. "Plus there's a ruff of stiff, hollow hairs protecting its most vulnerable parts – the neck and throat. These quills can be raised when the animal's threatened and the reason they're hollow is to allow the borquill to pump venom through them, which it stores in two throat sacs. The venom isn't strong enough to actually kill a man, but it doesn't have to be. If you get pricked by one of those quills, you'll become drowsy and disorientated within minutes, and that's as much of an advantage as any animal needs when it has tusks as sharp as the borquill's.

"I don't know what I expected, the three in the middle to fight for themselves I suppose, or perhaps for the two men to step forward and shield the girl, but I certainly didn't expect what actually happened. It was the girl who came forward, snarling and shrieking insults at the animal, while the two men faded into the background.

"The borquill tore straight towards Kat, covering the distance in a flash. There looked to be no way this insignificant little girl could avoid being gored and ripped apart on those vicious tusks. Then, at the last minute, she simply skipped to one side. The move was so delayed and so deftly executed that the animal had no chance to adjust but simply charged past her, squealing in frustration.

"Kat was instantly goading again, waving her arms and yelling at the beast, which hadn't stopped running but turned in a great arc of scampering feet and churned-up dust to come charging straight back at her for a second time. Again she danced aside, delaying the move even longer, or so it seemed.

"By now the crowd were oohing and ahhing. The two men were still in the arena, but they might as well not have been. All I or anyone else there had eyes for was that huge, angry animal and this seeming waif of a girl who defied it.

"This went on for several minutes, with Kat nimbly dodging charge after deadly charge by the narrowest of margins. And she laughed! She was actually enjoying herself. We were cheering now, the crowd, even me. Every time the borquill shot past her a great roar went up.

"At last the beast slowed and then came to a halt, staring at its tormentor, tail twitching from side to side while steam rose from the brute's bristly hide and its great sides pumped in and out as the it panted for breath. While Kat kept its attention, perhaps not as energetically as before, but still moving and making enough noise to distract the beast, one of the men, all but forgotten until then, darted in from behind and slashed at the back of the borquill's legs. The poor animal let out its loudest squeal yet, one of the most heart-wrenching sounds I've ever heard. It tried to spin around but the injured rear leg gave way, causing it to stumble, and Kat was there, darting in to hamstring the other back leg.

"With the borquill crippled the contest was all but over. The three of them circled the injured beast, which was trying desperately to keep its feet and face them, before moving in to finish things off quickly; the famed quills were never even allowed to be a factor."

Mildra paused and fidgeted slightly, as if the memories had somehow overwhelmed her ability to speak of them. Tom was enthralled and said nothing, willing her to continue. Finally, she drew a ragged breath and did so. "The sounds coming out of the animal in those last few minutes were awful. I've never heard anything so plaintive, so pathetic. Even now, thinking of them chills me through and through."

Tom gave an involuntary shiver, and then wondered, "Did you actually *enjoy* watching things like that?"

Mildra smiled at him. "It's just as well the prime master has shown you a new life, Tom; you're far too sensitive to be a street-nick."

Tom scowled.

"I didn't mean that as an insult," the woman said quickly.

"I know, but you're not the first person to say something like that." And what really stung was the private suspicion that the accusation might be true.

"To answer your question, when you hear people talk about the things that went on in the Pits they sound terrible and inhuman, which they were, but at the time, when you were actually there, it was very easy to get swept along by the excitement, by the raw spectacle of unrestrained combat and people fighting for their lives. The place was usually packed, and with everyone around you caught up in this wave of anticipation, the startling thrill of people and animals fighting for their lives, the horror to think that this warrior you've quite taken to might not survive the coming bout... I suppose there was a sort of mass blood-lust, but it was incredibly real and exciting and dirty and breathtaking – an intoxicating, potent feeling that grabbed you by the heart and the throat and wouldn't let go. It was impossible not to succumb. When people gasped as their favourite was wounded or narrowly escaped death, that was a genuine reaction not some theatrical flourish. The whole thing was so intense, so... *real*.

"Intellectually I might be disgusted with myself, but the truth is that at the time, yes, some primordial part of me did enjoy the Pits, however much it shames me to admit that now."

They sat in silence after Mildra finished speaking, Tom having no idea what to say in response. He didn't know how old the Thaistess actually was, and didn't want to think how young she must have been then. His age? A little older? Not much, certainly. He shivered, feeling suddenly chilled. He must have been so absorbed by the Thaistess's story that he hadn't noticed the steadily falling temperature.

"Cold?" Mildra asked, reaching out to clasp his hand.

Warmth flowed from her touch, making his arm tingle on its way to spreading rapidly through his body.

"I was, a little," he admitted.

"Once the sun goes down it can turn chilly surprisingly quickly." She stood and held a hand towards him. "Shall we go back down?"

Tom nodded, letting her help him up. Mildra's grip was firm and he was intensely aware of how smooth her skin felt and how delicate her fingers. He let go quickly, because part of him didn't want to let go at all.

After one more glance upward at the stars, he followed Mildra back to their quarters. He wondered afterwards whether the Thaistess had imparted more than just warmth when she clasped his hand, because this time he fell asleep almost immediately his head hit the pillowed sacking.

Dewar felt a great ambivalence towards his current situation. He had originally come to Thaiburley to lose himself within the vast multi-layered metropolis, to hide from a past which he knew would catch up with him at some point anywhere outside the city's walls. Yet here he was venturing half the length of a continent, exposed once more. All in order to be allowed to hide again. Life certainly didn't get any simpler with the passage of time; leastways his didn't.

He felt no such ambivalence towards those who were travelling with him. One a scruffy street-nick risen above his station, the second a Kayjele – a subhuman race whose intelligence barely rose above that of pack animals – while the third was a Thaistess. As far as the assassin was concerned, Thaistesses came in just two flavours: those gullible enough to swallow wholesale a creed of ludicrous myth and ritualistic ox shit, and those cunning and manipulative enough to perpetuate the same for their own advantage.

He had no intention of getting to know his companions at any level, all three of them were worthy of nothing other than contempt. This was a job, and not a particularly pleasant one at that. The sooner it was done with the better.

Dewar had crewed briefly on a cargo ship not dissimilar to the barges in the past – part of an assignment undertaken long before he ever came to Thaiburley. So he stepped aboard with a sense of confidence, noting in passing where the fenders – hand-woven balls of rope – hung from the barge's side and prevented the boat from knocking against the jetty and damaging itself. And he almost smiled at the slight sway of deck beneath his feet. Was that a twinge of nostalgia he was feeling? Ridiculous, yet being here stirred memories of a life now past and a home he could never see again.

Dewar guessed that this crew must have been pushed for time and struggled to make the rendezvous to pick up their passengers, because they hadn't even covered the cargo yet. Large wooden crates stacked one upon another rose from the sunken hold to form an apparently solid block which stretched along almost the entire length of the boat. A narrow strip of deck, wide enough for a man to walk around but little more, bordered this mass of crating to either side. And that, in essence, was the barge in its entirety.

Famously, these vessels were flat-bottomed, to minimise their draft and maximise their capacity, but even so they sat deep in the water when fully laden like this, which meant that the river bank must fall away steeply here to allow the barge to come in so close. Just as well; Dewar would not have fancied the prospect of trying to cross in anything as small as a rowboat or lighter with Kohn sitting beside him. The giant's mass would surely have been enough to overbalance them.

The captain, who introduced himself as Abe, was a short, solid-looking man with a face as craggy as the scenery that surrounded them. He didn't waste any time but got underway as soon as the party was aboard and Kohn had been ushered to the prow, where there was space for the giant to sit in a semblance of comfort.

Four passengers, and four crew as well by the look of it. Abe's wife – a matronly, grey-haired woman with a perpetual scowl that looked fit to curdle milk – steered the barge from a small platform towards the boat's aft, while the two sons, neither of whom seemed long out of their teens, scurried around to secure the cargo. No hired crew here, all family.

"Can I help at all?" Dewar offered.

Abe stared at him. "I don't know, can you?"

"I've worked cargo before."

"Pitch in, then. 'Nother pair o' hands is always welcome."

Dewar would far rather keep busy than not. He joined the three men in getting the cargo clothed up. This consisted of lifting two vast, heavy sheets, infused with tar as protection against any rain, over the mass of crates, one from either end. They fetched the aft sheet first. Dewar took one side, Abe the other, while the two lads clambered on top of the crates. Even with four this proved back-breaking work and Dewar could only wonder how they would have managed with just the three of them. Eventually, both sheets were in place, which just left the ties – strong ropes pulled tight against the cargo and cloths to keep both firmly in place – two dozen in all, ranging along the length of the hold. Again they worked as a team, with Dewar now on top of the crates, passing rope and holding it taut; Abe preferring to trust his son to tie the actual knots rather than a stranger.

With less effort involved, Dewar spared more attention to his surroundings. The river ran through a deep canyon. Sheer cliffs rising on either side. The course ran remarkably straight and he had to wonder whether it was entirely natural. Of course, diverting such a major river would be a remarkable feat for anybody, but would it be an impossible one for those who had built a city of nearly a hundred tiers into the very heart of a mountain?

By the time they'd finished the final tie and Abe had expressed terse satisfaction, the barge had emerged from the gorge and was moving through more open countryside.

They passed fishing boats and then a village. Children ran along the bank, their shrill laughter carrying across the water like the distant whisperings of playful spirits. Dewar hardly noticed. He sat slumped against one side of the cargo, aching in muscles he'd forgotten he had. It was a long time since he'd attempted any form of labour as physical as this. Perhaps volunteering to help hadn't been such a good idea, particularly bearing in mind the journey ahead, but, on the other hand, he always said that the best way to strengthen any tool – the body included – was to temper it. The fire in his joints would doubtless do him good in the long run, or so he tried to tell himself.

Abe came over to join him. A sense of mutual respect approaching camaraderie had begun to develop in the

wake of the task so recently shared, and Dewar felt he'd
been accepted by the bargemen in a way that the rest of
the party hadn't.

"You ever made fenders?" Abe asked.

"Can't say that I have."

"'S not hard. I'll show you." He handed Dewar a
length of rope. "Just follow me."

The assassin watched the first assured movement of
stubby fingers and rope, and then copied. He'd always
been good with his hands and prided himself on being a
quick learner. In short time he'd picked up the knack and
began to see how this was all coming together. Realising
as much, Abe picked up his own pace and completed a
plump oval of interwoven rope – a wasp nest made of
string – long before Dewar had finished his novice effort.
Once the assassin felt his own was close enough to the
bargeman's, he held it up for the other's approval.

Abe took the would-be fender and hefted in his hand,
as if weighing it. "Not bad," he said. "A bit slow, perhaps,
but all in all not bad at all."

High praise indeed.

Confident that his charge could come to no harm here
in the middle of the Thair, Dewar took the opportunity to
ignore his companions as best he could. That didn't prevent him from noting that the Thaistess, Mildra, was
surprisingly young for a priestess and might even have
been considered attractive in a haughty, well-scrubbed sort
of way, were she ever to wear anything other than the
ubiquitous green robes of her calling. She seemed to spend
a lot of time in conversation with Tom, doubtless trying to
convert him to her spurious faith. Dewar promptly made
a unilateral decision that his duties extended to physical

wellbeing alone and didn't include such things as intellectual poisoning. If the kid really was that gullible, let the pair of them get on with it.

He was awake when the two of them sneaked out of the cabin on the first night, and briefly entertained the notion that there might be something more than friendship between them, but dismissed the thought. One was only a kid for goodness sake, while the other was a priestess, and, as far as Dewar was aware, the Thaissians hadn't yet sunk so low as to use sex to ensnare their victims.

The second day on the barge was a more relaxed one, which was just as well, because Dewar's muscles were telling him in no uncertain terms just how much they resented the previous day's misuse. As the sun slipped down below the tree line, the barge arrived at Crosston, which was as far as the boat went. Here the cargo would be unloaded and a new one sought for the return trip to Thaiburley.

Dewar bid Abe and his family a fond farewell and led the party towards a nearby inn on Abe's recommendation, a place where the bargeman assured him they'd find good food, decent ale and a soft bed for the night. Intriguingly, the tavern was called the Four Spoke Inn.

FIVE

Kat paused, considering the hurried scrawl before her with bemusement but no real concern. Everybody knew that things were changing in the streets; this was merely further evidence of that fact. It was the second time she had seen this particular motif daubed onto the wall of a building, which pretty much confirmed that here was the badge of some gang or other staking a claim to the area. This used to be Thunderheads territory. Not any more, it would seem.

Daubed in white, the sign was a simple one, which showed either a lack of imagination or a degree of intelligence in recognising that not everyone rendering it was likely to be an artist. It consisted of an oval, a circle stretched horizontally, with what were obviously intended to be a pair of fangs dangling from the upper 'lip': a mouth in the process of either screaming or biting.

This second example was a lot more competently executed than the first, and where that one had looked almost comical, this had an air of the sinister about it and made a far more effective warning. Particularly as the door beside it had been kicked in, as if for emphasis. "We Mean Business!" the shattered wood and gaping hole seemed to declare.

Kat moved on. The previous night had proved frustrating. They had come so close to their quarry that she could almost taste success – or the leading trio of hunters had, even managing to get off a single shot with a crossbow, and the quarrel seemed to hit home; hence the inhuman scream that had spurred Kat on. Yet by the time she and the main force of Tattooed Men had arrived on the scene the Soul Thief had vanished, and they'd found no further trace of the monster that night. It was like trying to hunt down a shadow, or a fragment of mist in a fog.

Hence Kat's early morning outing, even though she was dog-tired. If they were ever going to catch the Soul Thief they needed to try something different, they needed an edge. And Kat had a plan. Not a particularly noble one, but if everything worked as she hoped, the only victim would be her mother's murderer; and Kat could live with that.

She only hoped that the new order represented by this graffiti-scrawl didn't mean there had been wholesale changes in this area of the streets. The last thing she needed was for Annie to have moved on. Kat had already made one visit that morning which she'd been putting off and called in a favour in the process. She'd hate to have gone to all that trouble for nothing.

In the event, her concerns proved groundless. Annie sat on her accustomed step, engrossed in a game of flip with a street-nick, a kid Kat felt sure she vaguely recognised as having run with the Blood Herons. There was a reassuring sense of the familiar to the scene, as Annie took a flat, rounded stone in her leathery hand and, with a flick of her wrist, sent the stone spiralling into the air – this could just as easily have been happening weeks ago, before the City Below went to hell in a handcart. After spinning through several rotations, the stone thudded to the ground between Annie and where the nick squatted. It landed beside another similar stone, both displaying a white cross emblazoned on their upper face. A pair, which entitled Annie to flip over a nearby stone, one that currently showed a single white stripe. The flip converted that stone from the boy's to Annie's, revealing the cross it bore on the reverse side. Annie now had five in a row. Game over.

"Huh," the old woman cackled gleefully. "That's three to me!"

"Yeah," the boy said, with a tone of sullen resignation that made Kat grin, "I know, I'll get started on cleaning out the kitchen."

"Good boy; and do it properly, mind!"

Kat waited until the lad had disappeared inside before bending to pick up one of Annie's winning row of five. She held the smooth stone in her hand. As she'd suspected, it was weighted, deliberately imbalanced so that it was bound to land with the cross exposed more often than not. The difference was only slight, but it was there.

Kat shook her head. "Hasn't he caught on yet?"

Annie shrugged. "He's new. He will eventually, but till then, might as well make the most of 'im."

The first time Kat encountered Annie, she hadn't even been certain there was a person beneath what seemed to be nothing more than a heap of rags piled haphazardly on the step, until the old woman moved. Only then did a human form become discernible among the sacking and the cloth and the filth. In streets where poverty was the norm there was nothing unusual about a person wearing threadbare and tattered clothing, but Annie seemed to live in the rags which others threw out when they found newer, better and cleaner rags. Even her lank grey hair was a matted and unkempt mess – a pile of dust and fluff that sat atop the apparent mound of discarded cloth. Yet this was Annie, and no one expected her to be any different.

"Now, what can I do for you, my little Death Queen?"

Kat shifted uncomfortably. This was the second time in a space of hours that someone had used that all-but-forgotten title.

Annie was many things; a smelly, filthy old woman, a beneficial mentor to the waifs and strays who couldn't find a place even within the street-nick gangs, a collector and dispenser for the various waves of gossip that coursed regularly through the streets and, most importantly for Kat's purposes, a fixer, a broker, a deal-maker.

If you wanted something and couldn't get it through any of the usual sources, if you'd exhausted every other possible avenue, you came to Annie. She wasn't cheap, but if what you were after was out there, Annie would find it. Kat had discovered long ago that Annie had a weakness for pretty things, for baubles and trinkets, and that there was one sort the old woman coveted above all else.

The sun globes had only just been warming up as Kat hurried down the oddly featureless street, passing quickly between twin rows of houses without any windows. She never had figured out why the flatheads' buildings were built this way – after all, the flatheads themselves seemed to revel in basking in the sun globes' warmth, so you'd think they'd want to open their homes up to it rather than shut it out – but there you are.

Returning to the Jeradine quarter was something Kat had been putting off, and she wasn't entirely certain why; perhaps it was merely a reluctance to return to the patterns her life had fallen into during the recent past. She hadn't been here since the day Ty-gen bribed her into seeing the street-nick Tom safely back to his home turf; and what an eventful trip *that* had proved to be. Technically, she'd completed that task successfully by her reckoning, but she had never come back to collect her commission. Then again, she'd had no need of it until now.

Not many of the Jeradine were around at this early hour, and those few of the tall, bipedal reptilians that she did encounter ignored her, as usual.

Despite the buildings looking much alike, she had no trouble finding the one she was looking for. A Jeradine's face is pretty much unreadable to a human, but Kat thought she detected a hint of surprise in Ty-gen's eyes as he opened the door to her knock.

"Hello, Ty-gen," she said, a little awkwardly, "remember me?"

The flathead pointed at his throat, and Kat realised he wasn't wearing his voice simulator, so couldn't reply. He stepped back inside and gestured for the girl to follow, leaving her in the front room as he disappeared into the back. Funny, but she'd never seen him before without the 'translator' – his name for the little crystal mechanism – and had assumed he always wore it. Seconds later the Jeradine reappeared, with the familiar black band around his throat, fronted by the faceted grey khybul construct. Before all this started Kat had earned a pretty good living selling the delicate and beautiful khybul sculptures that Ty-gen produced to contacts she'd made up-City, yet she felt little empathy with that part of her past, so recently abandoned, which now felt as if it had taken place in somebody else's life entirely.

"Kat, seeing you once more brings me great pleasure and relief."

The flat, emotionless voice produced by the translator and the Jeradine's awkwardly formal sentence structures still made her smile, whatever her misgivings about coming back here.

"Yeah, it's good to see you too, Ty-gen."

"Have you returned in order to resume our previous trading relationship?"

"No, no, at least not just yet," Kat added quickly, not wanting to close the door too firmly on any possibility when life could be so unpredictable. She took a deep breath, feeling a bit ashamed that she had sought out the Jeradine again only now when she wanted something. "I got that boy, Tom, all the way across town to the edge of Blue Claw territory like you asked." Which was pretty much true in as far as it went.

"Ah, and now you have come to collect your reward."

"Yes, no... well, sort of."

"I have kept the sculpture safe for you here."

With a sweep of his arm, the Jeradine pulled back a curtain in the wall behind him, to reveal a particularly large and intricate khybul sculpture; a magnificent city of impossibly tall, sweeping walls topped by tiny, needle-point towers, the whole lit artfully from within the alcove that held it. Thaiburley, the city of dreams, in miniature. This remained perhaps the most beautiful single thing Kat had ever seen, yet she shook her head.

"No, I don't want that."

"Oh?"

"Don't get me wrong." The last thing she wanted to do was offend the Jeradine. "It's incredible, wonderful, the best thing you've ever done; but I was thinking about this as I took Tom across the under-City. What would I do with something like that? You know how I live. If I attempted to keep this it would only get stolen or, worse still, damaged or even broken completely."

"What do you wish as reward in its stead, then?"

"I thought perhaps I could take a few smaller pieces – you know, less valuable ones, easier to keep – three, say."

"I see."

"And... well, perhaps you could let me have one now?"

"I've got something for you, Annie." Kat produced the sparkling crystal statuette which Ty-gen had handed over without hesitation or comment. It was the image of an eagle or some other bird of prey, wings spread, feet clasping a rock which also formed the figure's stand. The rays of the sun globes twinkled from the bird's outstretched wings as Kat turned it slowly.

She watched as the old woman's eyes lit up with excitement and avarice; a look which was quickly replaced by a narrow-eyed calculating stare. "And what would Annie have to find for you to get her hands on this lovely bauble?"

The encounter two nights ago with the aged apothaker had brought Annie to mind. Kat still had the phial the

woman had thrust upon her tucked away in a pocket.
She didn't know whether this 'luck potion' would work
or not, but there had to be *something* they could do to affect the Soul Thief, and she finally had a good idea what
that might be.

"Demon dust," she said simply.

"Demon dust?" Annie repeated the word slowly and
nodded wisely. "Why, you plannin' on invadin' the
Upper Heights?"

"No, nothing like that. I saw some used once, that's
all; it took out a demon hound in the blink of an eye."
At odd moments in the past few days Kat had found herself thinking of Tom and wondering what had become
of him. She'd heard rumour of a boy with extraordinary
power who had saved the whole of the under-City. She
knew at once this could only be Tom. No point in
dwelling on him though; by now he'd doubtless been
whisked away up-City to live a life of pampered luxury.
Out of her world for good, and, besides, she had more
pressing concerns.

Annie had evidently been mulling over her words.
"Heard there were plenty o' reasons for folk to stay off
the streets last night; the Tattooed Men among 'em."

"We weren't the only ones out hunting, Annie," Kat
said quietly.

"Heard that, too. So, you and yer sister patched things
up then?"

"I wouldn't exactly say that."

Annie nodded and pursed her lips. She then skewered
Kat with an intense gaze that seemed to strip away all
her carefully built defences and pierce right through to
the marrow. "Only one thing I can think of that'd see the

Death Queens runnin' side by side again. Yer lookin' to bring down the Soul Thief, aren't yer?"

Kat said nothing; she simply returned the old woman's stare with an intensity all her own.

Annie thought for a second and then said, "I've heard of demon dust, yes, but I've never come across the stuff meself, nor even anyone who's actually seen it before, let alone who knows how to make it." Kat's heart sank. "For all that, I might know of someone who can help yer.

"Leave this with me. I'll ask around. You come back before globes out tonight, and we'll see what's what."

"Thanks, Annie." Not demon dust perhaps, but the hope of something at least. "Here, take this." She held out the khybul sculpture.

"You sure? I ain't done nuthin' yet."

"I trust you, Annie."

The old woman gave a curt nod. They both knew she wouldn't dare cross Kat, especially now that she was back with the Tattooed Men.

Kat walked away, leaving Annie to resume her customary perch on the step. She felt oddly buoyed by the encounter, as if there were now some genuine reason to hope.

Perhaps that explained her complete lack of alertness when she turned a corner and walked straight into the three men. They *were* men, not boys, but in every other respect they looked like street-nicks on patrol.

"Well, what have we got here?" the lead lout asked, before answering his own question. "A pretty little girl all done up in black."

The three were dressed alike. Not leather as much of her own gear tended to be, but they wore uniform black and white. Gang for sure, but which gang?

"Aren't you a little old to be playing at street-nicks?"

"The street-nicks time has passed, darlin'. The big boys are in charge now."

"And you would be...?"

"The Fang." She remembered the open-mouth motif noted earlier. "And you're on our turf," the man added.

Was that really the way of it? Were grown men taking over where the teenagers and kids had left off? Surely the Watch wouldn't stand for that sort of escalation. Hardly her problem, of course.

"Not for long," she assured them. Kat stepped out to go around the trio, but as she did so the lead man, the one doing all the talking, moved across to block her path.

"What's yer hurry, sweetheart? I'm sure we could find plenty to talk about, you an' me."

Kat stepped back, a little wearily. The last thing she wanted right now was a fight, but since when had her preferences counted for anything in the balance of things? Where were all the razzers when you needed one? Doubtless keeping their heads down until any hint of violence was past, in the time-honoured tradition of the under-City's law enforcers. Kat's hands came to rest casually on twin sword hilts.

"I'd let the lady through if I were you, gents," said a voice from behind her. M'gruth; she'd know his rasping tones anywhere.

The lead Fang looked beyond her, and she could see the surprise in his eyes. "And what if we decide not to?" The words sounded confident enough, but his two companions were already looking nervous.

"Well, then I guess we'd have to settle matters the old-fashioned way, and you wouldn't want that, I promise you."

"Three against one; those odds don't sound too bad to me."

"Really, and how do your two friends feel about that?"

One of the other two Fangs had reached forward to tug urgently at the leader's arm, muttering, "Come on, leave it. He's a Tattooed Man for Thaiss's sake."

Perhaps realising the support he might have hoped for wasn't there, the man's gaze switched to Kat. He shrugged. "Hardly worth the effort really, she's only a kid." He looked back to M'gruth. "We'll let it pass this time."

"Good decision," M'gruth assured him. He and Kat walked past the men and away, the lead Fang's surly gaze on them the whole while.

Kat was fuming, but waited until they were out of earshot before rounding on the Tattooed Man. "What the breck do you think you're playing at, M'gruth? No need for you to get involved – I could have handled them."

"I don't doubt that for a moment," he assured her. "It wasn't you I was worried about."

A sudden suspicion crossed the girl's mind, causing her to stop in her tracks. "Were you following me?"

"No, I was just out stretching my legs and trying to keep out of Chavver's way. She's in a foul mood this morning."

Kat snorted; since when was her sister ever in any *other* sort of mood? She still wasn't convinced by M'gruth's claim of innocence but couldn't prove anything, so she was forced to let it go for now. The pair resumed walking.

Annie wasn't on her usual step when Kat returned – presumably even she had to stretch her legs and answer the call of nature occasionally – but a quick word with the unruly-haired girl who came to greet Kat when she called soon brought the old woman shuffling out from the dilapidated building the step fronted.

"That time already, is it?" Annie said, squinting at the pair of lamplighters with their hand-pulled cart and long tapers who were busily working their way along the street discharging their duties.

"Yes, Annie, it'll be globes out before you know."

"And you an' yer bald-headed tribe will be off a huntin', I suppose."

"Most likely," Kat replied with more impatience than she'd intended. In truth, after last nights' fruitless pursuit she was fast coming to the conclusion that their current hunting methods were never going to work, but she wasn't in the mood to discuss the subject. "Did you have any luck?"

Annie grunted, not replying immediately but rather lowering her aged frame onto her step before fidgeting to get comfortable. After all the years the old woman had sat there, Kat wouldn't have been surprised if the step bore a shallow bum-shaped depression, and fleetingly regretted not checking before Annie appeared.

"Well," the old woman said once she'd settled, "depends on what you mean by luck. Didn't find no demon dust but I'd already told you I wouldn't. Got you this, though."

She held out a scruffy bag. Inside was what looked at first to be a coiled serpent with glistening thorny jewels decorating its skin. Kat frowned and looked more closely. "A whip?"

"Yeah, but not just any whip. It's from up-City; apothaker skills have gone into that. See those gems? Real sharp and they're supposed to be capable o' holding onto anything, even a demon, which is why I got interested. If it's good enough for a demon, should be good enough for this Soul Thief. Can't say for sure it'll work, 'cos I ain't 'ad a chance to try it, but I trust the source."

"Really?" Kat knew the disappointment showed in her voice. She didn't want to offend Annie, who was a more than useful contact, but she'd hoped for something better than a gaudy piece of trinket-encrusted foolery.

"You don't 'ave to take it."

"No, that's all right... Thank you, Annie." Kat took a closer look. In its own way the whip was beautiful. A coil of lacquered brown leather, intricately woven to produce a diamond criss-crossing pattern on the surface; perhaps she'd been overhasty in her dismissal; some fine workmanship had gone into this and no mistake. Whether or not the jewelled thorns could really trap a demon was another matter.

Even so, when she said, "Thank you," again, she did so with considerably more conviction.

"Also," Annie said, "there's this man, says he can help. Name of Brent. Not local, fresh off the barge, but 'e's askin' questions 'bout the Soul Thief same as you, and says he knows how to kill it."

All of which sounded unlikely. "If this Brent is from out of town, how has he even *heard* about the Soul Thief? Most folk in the City Below reckon she's nothing more than an old wives' tale, so how come an outsider knows anything about her?"

"I don't breckin' know." Annie waved an irritated hand, as if to ward off such stupidity. "Ask him, not me. Do you want me to set up a meet or what?"

Of course Kat did, though every scrap of common sense in her body told her that something wasn't right here.

Kat had a lot of things on her mind as she left Annie. She'd pinned a great deal of hope on the old woman and now felt frustrated, as if opportunity were somehow slipping from her grasp. This stranger, Brent, was a new factor, one she neither understood nor trusted. Yet she had to follow up on any possible lead, just in case. At least there was still that night's hunt to look forward to. Even if it proved as fruitless as she feared, running around the streets was still a great way of letting off steam.

"Well, well, if it ain't the little girl in black."

Kat froze, recognising the voice and cursing her own lack of alertness for the second time that day. Too little sleep, too much on her mind. This time, if they were spoiling for trouble, she was in just the mood to oblige them. She turned around slowly, to see a group of five men fronted by the Fang who had taken such delight in goading her that morning. He had a knife in his right hand and ran the flat of the blade casually back and forth across his left palm as he spoke. One of the others hefted a crude club. The intention to intimidate was as blatant as it was amusing.

"Wonderful. Playtime for the Fang Gang. That's all I need."

The man appeared not to have heard. "No Tattooed Man 'ere to protect you this time, my little darlin'." His smile was lecherous, triumphant and sly all at once; pure evil in a single leer. He went to step towards her.

Kat laughed. There was nothing theatrical or exaggerated in the sound, it was just a laugh. The Fang looked a little uncertain and his grin faltered; this clearly wasn't the reaction he'd anticipated.

"Is that what you think?" Kat demanded, incredulous.

"You brecking idiot! M'gruth wasn't protecting me, he was restraining me!"

It wasn't so much a red mist that descended upon her then as a thrill, a singing of the blood, a sense of elation that here finally was a chance to let loose the beast inside her; that element which had enabled her to survive the Pits and emerge as one of its greatest and most feared champions. She welcomed the primordial presence as the old friend it was, opening herself to the bloodlust and allowing it free access to her mind, her heart, her soul. Kat snarled: a chilling, animal sound. She drew her two short swords in a single smooth motion and danced forward, swift as a striking serpent. An expression of almost comic startlement now graced the first man's face – her cocky would-be tormentor. He struck out with his own knife but Kat's move had caught him off-guard and he hadn't troubled to set his feet properly; the result was a poorly timed blow made in panic by a man who'd thought he was in charge of the situation and hadn't yet caught up with dawning reality. Kat swayed and ducked, while never interrupting her forward momentum. The man's arm and blade flashed past and above her shoulder. She plunged her own sword forward, feeling sudden resistance as the blade bit home. At no point did she even consider leniency.

The man screamed, others were yelling and cursing; Kat paid them no heed. She lashed out with the other sword, feeling it rake across a man's side to her left even as she ripped the right-hand blade from the leading Fang's torso, conscious of the splatter of warm blood on her arm. She didn't push the second blade deeper, wary in case it became entangled in the ribcage. Someone tried to grapple her right arm from behind. She brought her elbow back sharply, feeling it crunch into the attacker's face, mashing his nose. The arm came free again.

A fist swung towards her. She didn't have time to register whether or not it held a blade, she simply ducked, swivelled and kicked out, the heel of her foot slamming into the man's knee. It hit at an angle and she heard an audible crack as the leg buckled and the joint or bone gave way. Another scream. Another one down.

Suddenly she was free of attackers and had some breathing space. She turned, adopting the fighter's crouch which came as naturally to her as breathing. Mollified by this brief taste of freedom, the beast began to relent, to slip away into the recesses of her subconscious once more.

The five Fangs no longer looked quite so menacing. Two were on the ground. One lay in a foetal position, curled up as if to protect his belly, dead or dying; the other writhed and clutched his knee, groaning in marked contrast to the other's silence. Of the three standing, one pressed a hand to his nose, blood flowing freely from beneath to cover mouth, chin and throat. A second was brave enough to still hold a sword, though the wound to his side wept redness and was plainly visible through the rent in his black shirt. The final Fang, the one she hadn't come to grips with in those few brief seconds of explosive mayhem, just looked stunned.

She felt the anger cool; not disappear, but no longer irresistible. "I didn't start this," she reminded them, "but I will finish it if you want me to; shouldn't take long. One or two of you might even live to talk about it. Or we can stop fighting here and now and all walk away." *Those who still can*, she thought but didn't add.

The Fangs exchanged glances and seemed to reach a silent consensus. The one with the injured side slowly lowered his sword, knives were dropped and there was an obvious slump in all of them as they relaxed a little; the droop of resignation, of defeat. Kat stood straight and dipped her own blades. She didn't sheath them – wouldn't until they were cleaned, but she no longer menaced the gang members with them.

"If you Fangs want to stake out some turf around here, that's fine by me," she told them, "but there are a few things you need to learn if you want to keep hold of it." There might be a new order in the Under-City, but she intended to see that a few things stayed the same. "The first is that you leave the Tattooed Men alone. Let them pass where and when they want without interference – you don't trouble them, they won't trouble you. The second is that you don't ever, *ever* mess with their Death Queens.

"You got that?"

She watched their eyes widen as her meaning sunk in. They'd seen her with a Tattooed Man for Thaiss's sake and yet it still hadn't occurred to the stupid breckers who she was. They'd just taken her for a cocky girl with a sword. That was the problem with reputations – everyone expected her to be older and bigger. At least they would recognise her next time, she felt certain of that much.

Two of the Fangs nodded, acknowledging her words. None of them seemed keen to meet her gaze.

SIX

Tom had never seen anywhere quite like the Four Spoke Inn. He'd been to a few taverns in the City Below and could see the resemblance, but he was also acutely aware of the differences. This was like some younger and more vibrant cousin to the under-City's dingy drinking dens. It was bigger, brighter, airier, and somehow more welcoming than any tavern he'd experienced before. Even the seats and tables looked more comfortable, as if the furnishings had room to breathe here, which sounded ridiculous but it was how the place struck him.

The only uncomfortable aspect was fleetingly provided by the man standing station at the bar, who stared at their party in apparent horror as they entered, for all the world as if he'd just seen a ghost; or three in this instance, Kohn having remained outside. The man recovered quickly enough, however, and introduced himself as Seth Bryant, the inn's landlord. He soon had the three of them seated with flagons of ale – liberally watered in Tom's case – and bowls of hearty stew standing on the table before them.

Seth even took the presence of Kohn in his stride. "We've had the odd Kayjele stay over before," he explained, "on their way to and from the northern mountains and Thaiburley. He'll have to sleep in the barn, though – the inn doesn't have rooms big enough for folk his size."

Tom found himself quickly warming to this Seth, who had a ready smile and was proving a jovial and attentive host. Dewar seemed considerably less enamoured, as if he too had noted the landlord's initial reaction and wasn't about to dismiss the expression so readily.

The tap room began to fill up as the evening progressed. Mildra vanished at some point. Tom initially assumed she had retired to her room, but learned from Seth that instead she had gone outside to see Kohn. Feeling a little guilty that he hadn't done so himself, Tom followed.

Unused to drinking, he found himself less than fully steady on his feet, despite the watered-down ale.

Night had fallen while they were in the bar; a few stars speckled the sky and a half moon graced the world with subtle radiance. Muffled light also spilled from the inn's windows, so he had little trouble making his way around the back of the Four Spoke Inn to where the stables were situated.

He found the pair of them sitting on bales of hay just inside the stable door. Either Mildra had taken a candle-lamp with her or Seth had provided Kohn with one; the tall white column of wax shielded in a bubble of glass now sat off to one side, presumably placed there to prevent its flickering flame from interfering with their view of the stars.

The Thaistess looked relaxed and greeted Tom cheerfully. Even Kohn smiled and made an inarticulate noise.

"Kohn's pleased to see you," Mildra supplied.

"You can understand him?"

"Yes. Not the vocal expressions, well, no more than you can – they don't contain words as such, only emotional indicators. Kohn and his people speak with each other directly mind to mind."

"And you can hear this?"

"After a fashion. You probably could to, with enough practice and a little training."

Tom stared at the amiable giant and concentrated, willing some form of meaning or understanding to come through, but nothing did.

Mildra laughed. "I didn't mean you'd be able to do it straight away."

Tom gave up, and asked instead, "Is that how they can understand us? Do they hear our thoughts rather than the actual words?"

Mildra looked at him with evident surprise. "Yes. The Kayjele don't have a structured language as such, they've never had need of one. When you say something you also think it, and the Kayjele can skim the meaning from the surface of your mind."

Tom had the feeling that he'd just impressed the Thaistess, and didn't want to spoil that by showing any alarm at the thought of what else Kohn might have skimmed from his mind – the horror he'd felt on first meeting the giant and the dismay at having him as a travelling companion, for example. So he tried to keep his features impassive and simply nodded.

When they left Kohn and headed back to the inn, Tom thought that perhaps he did sense something from the giant – an impression of contentment – though that could just have been wishful thinking. As they walked, Mildra slipped her arm inside Tom's. It was a casual gesture, at least it seemed so as far as she was concerned. For his part, Tom became instantly conscious of the gentle pressure of her arm resting on his and of where it pressed against his side. He also had no idea how best to hold his own arm to accommodate hers. The last thing he wanted was for the young woman beside him to break this intimate contact and pull away, so he did his best to keep in the same position he'd held originally. Trying to do this caused his arm to stiffen and freeze in place, transforming it from a mobile and flexible limb into an ungainly lump which had little to do with him but just happened to jut out awkwardly from his shoulder blade.

The brief walk around to the inn's door was therefore a mixed experience for Tom. He was thrilled at Mildra's touch but at the same time frustrated by his own sense of clumsiness. Thankfully, the Thaistess seemed completely oblivious to his discomfort, chatting enthusiastically about the two days spent aboard the barge and how much she'd enjoyed the experience.

They'd evidently saved themselves many days' journey by travelling on the river. The road between Crosston and Thaiburley was far from direct due to the mountainous terrain around the city. Tom only hoped they could make the next stage of the trip in similar fashion and, by the sound of it, so did Mildra.

Tom's good mood was punctured as soon as they stepped back inside the inn. Dewar was waiting for them. He said quietly, "We'd best all get an early night. I want to start out first thing in the morning."

"Why the rush," Tom asked, a little petulantly.

"Because our landlord is not to be trusted. Don't be fooled by the ready smile and false joviality; he's not all he seems and the sooner we're away from here the better."

Mildra raised her eyebrows in obvious surprise. "Presumably you can't be that worried, or why are we still at the inn at all?" she asked.

"Because unless I miss my guess our arrival has caught him by surprise. Besides, I don't believe he'll try anything while we're under his roof – that would draw too much attention – so moving elsewhere might actually make us *more* vulnerable. But we should be off as early as possible in the morning, ahead of whatever surprises he might be cooking up."

Mildra was clearly sceptical, and Tom instinctively wanted to take her side, but then he remembered that look on Seth's face as they'd arrived, which seemed so at odds with the rest of the man's behaviour. Grudgingly, Tom had to admit that perhaps Dewar had a point. So he kept his mouth shut and headed for bed.

Seth was stunned when the three ill-matched strangers walked into his inn. He knew immediately who they were – how often did you find a Thaistess wandering the roads? Their mention of a Kayjele travelling with them only confirmed things. This was the party the demon had warned him to watch for and charged him to stop, to kill. So how the breck had they reached Crosston? What had become of the men he'd sent to ambush them on the road? A force recruited in secret – no point in blowing his carefully constructed cover at this point – at no small cost to him in terms of time, effort and coin.

Had those men failed him? Had they been too lazy or cowardly to actually launch an attack? It seemed unlikely; he had yet to pay them anything more than a trifling retainer. What then?

He soon learned the truth, after slipping into the familiar persona of cheerful landlord and making an appropriate fuss of these new guests. They had arrived by boat. *By boat?* Impossible; the Kayjele always walked to and from Thaiburley, hating the river and mistrusting boats – everybody knew that. He'd depended on that very fact when setting up the ambush. Apparently, everybody was wrong. Either that or these were exceptional circumstances, or perhaps an exceptional Kayjele.

Whatever the truth, his scheme had failed – not something he cared to report to the demon – which meant he needed to come up with a plan B, and quickly. Poison was always an option, but he'd prefer not to kill guests staying under his own roof, valuing this identity and this life too highly to throw it all away needlessly.

The newcomers themselves seemed nothing out of the ordinary, though there was something vaguely familiar about the man, an uncomfortable stirring of memory that suggested Seth should recall a long forgotten mention of just such a person, though he couldn't for the life of him think what.

The hired thugs he'd dispatched to intercept the group would be waiting for their intended prey some distance out of town – necessary to create the illusion that the ambush was the work of brigands, to disassociate any connection with Crosston or with him. If he sent a messenger recalling them now and the men rode through the night, they could be back here by late morning of the next day.

He settled on Wil – young enough to still be excited at the suggestion of intrigue and adventure, naïve enough to be trustworthy and, most importantly of all, the lad had access to a horse.

Wil lapped up Seth's claim that the newcomers were not all they seemed, that they were in fact fugitives fleeing from Thaiburley after having committed heinous crimes. As landlord, Seth had been alerted to keep an eye out for just such a party – said to include a Kayjele and a beautiful trickster posing as a Thaistess; could you believe such nerve? When Seth went on to explain that there was a group of Thaiburley officers not a day's ride away, Wil insisted on riding immediately to fetch them. How could the landlord refuse such an offer? Wil finished his drink and left, his sense of righteous purpose apparent in every stride. Seth smiled; oh what he'd give to be that young again, if not that impressionable.

This night held all the promise of being as frustrating as the last. Kat crouched over the withered husk of a man who less than an hour ago had been alive. She was searching for some clue, which in her heart of hearts she knew wasn't there to find. M'gruth was trying to get some sense from the traumatised wife, who stood with her back pressed firmly to the wall as if to make certain no nightmare could creep up behind her, and whose body shook as violently as her voice. Somewhere nearby a baby screamed, its cries going unheeded. The wife's wide-eyed stare never left her husband's corpse.

One step behind again, as they'd been the previous night and as they were always going to be.

With nothing more to be done, Kat and M'gruth left, passing through the open doorway, avoiding the splintered shards of wood which were all that remained of the barrier that was supposed to have shut out any darkness from the outside world. Rel waited anxiously for them in the street beyond.

"Looks as if we're in for another night of withered corpses and the wailing of the bereaved," M'gruth muttered.

"You mean another night of chasing shadows," Kat replied.

The two shared a glance, and she knew then that the older man shared her reservations about current tactics, and she suppressed a small triumphant smile.

"Hey, you three!" The shout came from a little way down the street and carried with it the arrogance of assumed authority, a tone which never failed to rile her.

She stared in astonishment. "I don't frissing believe it." There, clearly visible in the glow of the street lamps, stood a man wearing the dull brown uniform of the City Watch. "A razzer, patrolling after globes out?"

"What are you up to?" the officer asked, striding towards them.

"Trust me, you don't want to know," M'gruth replied.

"That's for me to decide. Now stay where you are, all of you."

"Keep out of this, razzer, it's none of your brecking business."

Something wasn't right here. The Watch rarely ventured into the streets after globes out and *never* did so solo; where was the man's partner? Kat heard a hissing sound from somewhere above her head. It reminded her of a suppressed sneeze, and she glanced up to catch a fleeting glimpse of a dark shape flying quickly past and another expanding one plummeting towards her.

"Net!" she yelled, diving to one side even as the word screamed from her mouth. She was conscious of Rel and M'gruth also throwing themselves in opposite directions, though presumably the older man was a little slower or had simply been in the wrong place. The net caught Kat's trailing foot but she pulled her heel free without any difficulty; twin swords drawn as she sprang to her feet, to see Rel staring wide-eyed at a floundering M'gruth, who'd been caught beneath the weighted net. The older man, still on his feet, stopped struggling and said to the younger, "Well, what are you gawping at? Cut me free."

"Leave that net alone!" the razzer commanded. He'd nearly reached them.

Ignoring him, Rel grabbed a handful of netting and started to hack at it with his sword. He didn't get far. A large form swooped down – a man – thumping into Rel feet first and sending him sprawling before disappearing upward once more, though not before Kat caught a glimpse of uniform and outstretched cape. A *Kite Guard!* What the breck was a Kite Guard doing in the City Below? They were cloud scrapers, the razzers of the elite, to be found only in the rarefied environs of the city's upper Rows, not slumming it with the grubbers down here.

The razzer without a cape had arrived now, brandishing his puncheon as if he wanted to hit somebody with it. Kat leapt over the winded Rel to face him.

She'd never taken a blade to a razzer before and didn't particularly want to start now, though she had a feeling there wasn't going to be much choice. They might be synonymous with incompetence and corruption, but the

Watch still represented authority, and matters tended to run far more smoothly down here if you kept "authority" out of things.

Predictably, the razzer acted as all razzers will and fired his puncheon at her without further warning. Kat was ready, dodging to her right and flicking out the sword in her left hand to deflect the club as it sprang towards her. Before the puncheon could retract into its sheath again, she danced forward to bring the flat of her other blade smartly down onto the razzer's hand, causing him to drop the weapon with a surprised yelp. Then she was behind him, sword edge pressed to his throat.

"Don't move," she hissed. Probably unnecessary, but she'd hate the embarrassment of the man slitting his own throat by fidgeting or trying something heroic.

"Kite Guard, we don't want any trouble, but nor are we going to stand around quietly while you catch us in your net and pummel us with your puncheon." She strained to see upwards and thought she caught the suggestion of something moving past just beyond the reach of the street lamps, but couldn't be sure. "So come down here and let's talk things through."

Rel was back on his feet and, between them, he and M'gruth had managed to get the older man free of the webbing.

"A Kite Guard, down here?" M'Gruth asked quietly. "Are you sure?"

Nets dropping from the sky and a flying man kicking people over, what else did he think it could be? "I'm sure."

"Release the guardsman first," a voice said from above them.

He was on one of the roofs on the opposite side of the street. Rel and M'Gruth both looked at her, but she shook her head; subtly, slightly. No point in antagonising him by attacking. Strange how the command structure of their little trio had undergone an unspoken adjustment.

"Happy to let him go, if you agree to come down here and join us. It's not just because of the crick in my neck, I hate talking to someone I can't see – makes me nervous."

"Let the officer go first," he repeated.

"Done, if you agree to come down once I have."

There was a pause. "Very well."

She withdrew the sword and stepped back. The razzer spun around to glare at her, then crouched to retrieve his puncheon. There was a sigh of displaced air or perhaps of rustling cloth, and a blue uniformed figure landed beside the guard.

Kat stared. A little. Well, she'd never seen a Kite Guard before. Certainly a step up from the razzers she was used to if this one was anything to go by. He was almost handsome in a clean-cut, well scrubbed sort of way. "What are you doing here?" she asked.

"I was about to ask you the same thing," he said. "Some strange bodies have turned up, desiccated and withered, and there's been rumour of a dark creature haunting the nights, so we came to investigate."

The Guard paying attention to petty murders? Would wonders never cease? "They're more than just rumours, but that's not what I meant. What are *you*, a Kite Guard, doing all the way down here in the City Below?"

He pursed his lips. "Long story, but you might as well get used to it. You'll be seeing a lot more of us here before long."

"Really? Have the disturbances finally persuaded someone up-City to pay attention to what goes on around here?"

"Something like that. Now, you still haven't explained who you are or what your business is…?"

"You're Tattooed Men, aren't you?" the razzer in the dun-coloured uniform said. If Kat had been staring at the Kite Guard, this one was gawping at M'gruth and Rel.

"Yes, laddie, we are," M'gruth replied.

"I've heard of you but never…" His attention darted between M'gruth and Kat. "Then you must be…"

"A Death Queen, yes," she said, growing a little tired of such exclamations.

"*Death Queen?*" The Kite Guard looked alarmed.

"Hey, I didn't choose the name, others did. I just have to put up with it, all right?"

"Fine," he said with a hint of a smile. "Sorry." He looked towards the Watch officer, and she wondered what the two of them would make of all this later. "You still haven't explained your presence here, standing outside a shattered door," he said, presumably in an attempt to reassert some authority.

"We're hunting the same thing you are. Inside you'll find a traumatised woman and what used to be her husband. We're aiming to track down and kill the monster responsible, the Soul Thief."

The Watch officer sniggered. "The Soul Thief?"

"Yes, and despite what you think you know she's no laughing matter." In the face of her glare, the sniggering stopped.

The Kite Guard looked thoughtful. "If what you say is true, perhaps we should join forces and work together."

Kat stared in astonishment. Had a razzer really just said that? The world was changing, no question about it. Still, if she were ever going to work with a razzer, she could do a lot worse than team up with this one. "Maybe," she said. "But first you'd better check on what I said, hadn't you?" she nodded towards the open doorway. "And we'd better get back on patrol."

He looked as if he wanted to argue and insist they waited there, which could prove a little awkward, as Kat had no intention of doing anything of the sort, but in the end he simply nodded. "All right then. See you around."

"Yeah, you just might."

As the three of them hurried away, M'gruth said to her, "Chavver will be looking for a good explanation as to why we broke the patrol line, but being rousted by a Kite Guard ought to cover it."

"Reckon so," Kat agreed. "Interesting times, hey, M'gruth? Interesting times."

"Yeah. Aren't we the lucky ones?"

SEVEN

At Dewar's urging they were up and about early, snatching a hurried breakfast at the inn. Seth was so charming and helpful that Tom found himself regretting his suspicions of the previous evening, which he concluded were just the result of tiredness fuelled by Dewar's assertions. It all seemed so foolish after a night's untroubled sleep and Tom felt embarrassed at giving such paranoia any credence whatsoever.

Their host was evidently untroubled by their early start and obvious haste, making sure they were well fed on hot oaty porridge with deep-golden honey on the side and great chunks of grainy, still-warm bread which smelt and tasted wonderful. Suitably fortified, they said their goodbyes and set about seeking passage upriver.

Tom had been looking forward to visiting the wharves, yet it proved a vaguely unsettling experience. He'd lived much of his life in the shadow of somewhere similar – the City Below's counterpart. The Blue Claw's territory ran from market square to docks, and pilfering goods from the warehouses around the latter had been regular practice. So he expected to feel wholly at ease here. In reality, Crosston's wharves proved a mix of the familiar and the strange, just as the Four Spoke Inn had been.

Even at this hour, the docks were busy. The hustle and bustle, the noise and underlying sense of organised activity that teetered on the verge of tipping over into complete chaos at any moment, were all things he recognised. As he watched, a huge crate was being lifted from a river barge similar to the one they'd arrived on; hoisted high in a web of ropes controlled by a crane – a broad-based contraption of metal and wood that looked far too frail for the job but presumably wasn't, the whole controlled by a man in a raised cabin, his face creased in a frown of concentration as he wrestled with a series of long levers. Behind stood a team of four broad-shouldered oxen, which were harnessed to the mechanism and, in a manner Tom couldn't quite fathom, appeared to be providing much of the actual lifting power for the crane. A second man stood by the animals, directing them via clutched reins, a switch, and shouted commands. The system struck Tom as crude when compared to the great cogs and chains of Thaiburley's fully mechanised hoists.

Once lifted from the boat, crates were then loaded onto a series of horse-drawn carriages, one per cart, which stood in line awaiting their turn. And here was another major difference. Horses were virtually unknown in the City Below – Tom had never even seen one before – all such draught work being conducted by oxen. He found the great carthorses with their huge feathered feet shifting restlessly, tails twitching and breath snorting, oddly intimidating.

"What's the matter, boy?" Dewar asked.

Tom shook his head. "I don't know; this is all just so different."

"What, missing the stench of rotten fish, sewage and stale smoke, are we?"

There was that, too, Tom had to admit.

The big barges didn't tend to venture any further than Crosston, though Tom was never entirely clear whether this was because the going became too shallow for their laden holds further upriver or it was for purely economic reasons, with this being where the Thair met the great trade road. Whatever the truth, their group was forced to seek passage on smaller cargo vessels; something which was proving frustratingly difficult, much to Dewar's obvious annoyance.

"What's the matter with these brecking yokels?" he muttered at one point. "Aren't they interested in earning some honest coin?"

Tom tried to hide his sense of satisfaction at seeing the man so agitated, sharing a smirk with Mildra when Dewar's back was turned.

Once or twice, Tom had the feeling that they might have found passage were it not for Kohn's presence, but each time a captain hesitated as if in consideration, their gaze would flick to the Kayjele, lips would purse and then would come the familiar shake of the head.

In the space of an hour they'd walked the length of the docks asking at every opportunity, but had failed to secure the berths they were after, and even Dewar was forced to admit that the river was closed to them for now.

Nor did the man have any more success when it came to buying horses – a prospect which Tom was none too

keen on in any case. For all that their self-appointed
leader claimed he was primarily interested in beasts of
burden to carry the group's provisions, Tom still was still
far from disappointed when the dock master, whom
they'd consulted on the subject, shook his head in a
manner they were getting increasingly used to.

"But there must be a horse trader somewhere in a
town of this size," Dewar insisted.

"Used to be," the bewhiskered local confirmed, knocking out his briar pipe against the stanchion of an idle
crane. "Beaman and Sons." He then set about refilling
the pipe from a small cloth bag, evidently paying their
party only minimal attention. Dewar looked fit to explode. "Shut up shop some three years gone," the man
continued, apparently oblivious to any impatience. "Not
enough demand, you see. Most folk who come to
Crosston are just passing through, and they tend to bring
their own horses with them."

"So what do the locals do when they want a horse?
Buy them from passing merchants?"

The dock master shrugged. "Some might. Most'll find
what they're looking for at the horse market."

Dewar stared at the man with the sort of look that Tom
hoped would never be directed towards him. "You have
a horse market." The words emerged as cold as ice.

"Once a month, every month."

"And the next one is…?"

"Oh, not for a good few days yet."

"Of course it isn't," Dewar muttered.

Was it Tom's imagination, or had the dock master
taken particular pleasure in saying that last? Certainly
there was the shadow of a grin on the man's face as they

moved away, led by a tight-lipped Dewar. The grin
quickly vanished amidst plumes of smoke as he sucked
hard on the rekindled pipe.

While the rest of them were at the docks, Mildra had
gone to the market, intent on bolstering their already
considerable supply of provisions. She met them at the
edge of the wharves, having enjoyed considerably more
success than they had.

Kohn, who thankfully had little by way of personal
luggage, was going to have to carry much of their bag-
gage in lieu of a packhorse. He seemed happy enough to
do so, an impression which Mildra confirmed.

So they set off, quickly leaving behind the environs of
the docks with its warehouses and dingy dwellings as
they followed the river north, passing along the way
rows of tall, fine houses, many with neat lawns before
them; riverside homes that put anything Tom had ever
seen in the City Below to shame.

As they walked, Tom began to realise the wisdom of
Dewar's search for a horse. He'd spent most of his life on
his feet, and had grown up dodging razzers and running
from disgruntled marks, but that was very different from
spending a whole day walking. Especially when this was
likely to be the first of a whole load of days filled with
the same. If he found this a daunting thought, what
about Mildra? How much exercise had she done during
all those years tucked away inside Thaissian temples?

They soon reached the outskirts of Crosston and the
blanket of human habitations started to fall away. They
now had the river on one side and fields opening up on
the other. He felt fine so far but wondered how long it
would be before muscles complained at unfamiliar use

and feet developed blisters. Mildra had shed her priestess's robe – currently bundled within the luggage carried by Kohn – in the face of what was already proving to be a warm day. In its stead she wore a simple tunic, dyed pale green; presumably as a token concession to her faith. This was the first time Tom had ever seen her without the heavy garment synonymous with her office and he was surprised at how much of a difference it made. She really did look like a girl now, and he found himself wondering how old she actually was. Mildra glanced up at that point and caught him watching her, smiling happily as she did so. Her youth wasn't the only thing made more apparent by the robe's absence; he also couldn't help but note how pretty she was, and it came as bit of a shock to see how feminine a figure had been hidden away beneath those concealing robes.

For all that Seth had implied the Kayjele were not that uncommon in these parts, enough people had stopped to stare at them that Tom was relieved when they left the town behind and entered the countryside. By the time they took a break for lunch, even the skirt of fields that surrounded Crosston had fallen behind and they were walking through a wooded land of silver-barked trees and more greenery in the form of shrubs and brackens than Tom had ever seen before. He was nearly as glad to be away from the fields as he was the houses; the landscape had been far too exposed for his liking. At least here among the trees there was a comforting sense of enclosure, of protection against all that openness.

Yet the woods too had their sinister aspect. Noise accompanied the party as they walked. It wasn't just the occasional birdsong; there was a constant rustling murmur from the higher reaches, as if the trees themselves were whispering about these intruders.

"It's just the wind blowing through the leaves," Mildra assured him.

In his mind he believed her, but a deeper, more instinctive part of him refused to be convinced. Though, by the end of the day, he'd grown more accustomed to the sound and could almost understand why the Thaistess insisted it was soothing.

Tom's fears regarding his own fitness became reality as the day wore on, and his legs felt heavy and ached by the time Dewar called a halt. Even his trek across the City Below with Kat hadn't involved this much uninterrupted walking, but he determined not to say anything, refusing to display any such weakness in front of Dewar, or Mildra for that matter; though it was obvious that the Thaistess was finding the going at least as tough as he was.

When they did eventually stop, in a clearing a little removed from the road they'd been following, the girl sank to the ground, managing to instil a degree of elegance to the manoeuvre which Tom didn't even bother trying to emulate as he slumped down close to her.

She looked across at Tom and grinned, admitting, "I never thought it was going to be this tough."

The fact that Tom *had* didn't make his limbs ache any less. "Can you imagine what tomorrow's going to be like – walking on legs that are already stiff and sore?"

She frowned. "True. Take your trousers off."

"*What?*"

Her smile this time showed genuine amusement. "Tom, I've already seen you naked."

Had she? He thought back to when they'd first met. He'd been taken to her temple with that mechanical creature fastened to his back. It was possible. He'd been pretty much out of it at the time and didn't particularly enjoy reliving the memory now. "I was unconscious then."

She looked at him, suddenly professional and sincere. "Trust me. This is what I do."

All he could think was how beautiful she looked.

After an awkward moment he sighed and unbuckled his trousers, pushing them to his ankles and then pulling his shirt down, adjusting his position so he could sit on his shirt and use it to cover himself as much as possible.

Mildra, clearly amused at his coyness, placed both hands on his left knee. Instantly a sense of warmth flowed from her touch, loosening cramped muscles and banishing aches. Tom closed his eyes and it was all he could do not to moan with the sheer pleasure of relief. After a few seconds the hands were gone, transferring their attention to his other knee before he could even feel disappointed at their absence.

He tried to concentrate on the warmth and the healing, doing his best not to react to the fact that a beautiful woman had her hands clasped around his naked legs. Yet it was hard, and when those hands moved up to hold his thighs, it became even more so. He jerked away, pulling his legs together and up to his chest for protection, embarrassed by his reaction and feeling the blood rush to his cheeks.

"Tom, it's all right," Mildra said gently. "I'm just healing your muscles, relieving the aches."

"I know," he said. "I'm fine."

He wanted desperately to turn around, to move away from Mildra until the stirrings in his groin subsided, but

knew that if he did so, the effect her ministrations had produced in him would be obvious to all, so he stayed where
he was, simply wishing that she would leave him alone.

Dewar and Kohn gathered kindling and set a fire, without troubling either Tom or Mildra for help. Tom was
almost tempted to believe that their dour leader realised
how tired the pair were, though if so he made no comment to that effect. Assuming that was the case it came
as something of a surprise to Tom, who would never
have suspected Dewar capable of such kindness or tact.

The short period between stopping and sleeping, during which they ate a meal of bread and salted meat from
their provisions, proved an awkward one for Tom. He
found it difficult to talk to or even look at Mildra, and
was grateful when Dewar suggested they should get
some sleep ready for another early start.

Part of him still wondered what he was doing here,
how he, a simple street-nick, had become caught up in
all this. His thoughts turned wistfully to his time with the
Blue Claw. Deep down he still hankered for the days
when his most daunting challenge had been winning the
affections of Jezmina, the sweetest, most innocent member of the Claw, whose briefest glance could surely melt
any man's heart. It was largely to impress her that he'd
accepted the challenge of climbing to the roof of Thaiburley, which, in many ways, had set all this in motion.

With a pang of guilt, Tom realised that he'd hardly
spared Jezmina a thought in recent days and still had no
idea what had become of her. There was a time, not so
long ago, when he'd have found it difficult to think of
anything else. He had attempted to ask about her in the

days following the chaos, but these had been no more than half-hearted queries which he then failed to follow up. On reflection, perhaps it was better that he didn't; with all that was happening in his life of late Jezmina was probably better off without him, though part of him still wanted to impress her, to see adoration in those deep, dark eyes once she realised how important he'd become – on personal terms with the prime master no less.

Just before Tom sank into the deep sleep of exhaustion, he determined to find Jezmina on his return to the city, once this daunting trip was out of the way; if only to make sure she was all right for his own peace of mind. Yet, even as the thought formed and was then brushed aside by sleep's soothing caress, part of his mind acknowledged that this resolve would probably not even be remembered come morning, and his very final thoughts before oblivion claimed him were not of Jezmina at all, nor even of Kat. They were of Mildra.

From the Medics' Row where lives are saved
To the streets of the Bankers where fortunes are made…

The prime master surveyed his image in the mirror with critical eye. He didn't dwell on the face, disliking the way time's passage had resculpted features he remembered as being more vigorous and youthful than cruel reflection insisted they now were. It was the overall impression that interested him. Gone were the ceremonial robes and the insignia of office; gone was any indication of either opulence or authority. Instead he wore simple, plain clothing, which made him seem somehow smaller and even frailer than usual. The figure who looked back was surely not a person worth paying attention to – which was exactly the effect he was seeking.

There were parts of the metropolis, the City Below for example, where a simple shedding of his expected uniform would all but guarantee anonymity. The same wasn't true of the Medics Row, where he was headed tonight, but it would certainly help.

Nobody could know of this imminent visit. Nobody. Not even the council guards, who at that very moment stood vigil outside his home and were charged with accompanying him everywhere, were to know that he was even gone. He could draw upon his talent to achieve that, selectively blinding them so that they wouldn't notice his coming or going, but such an exercise of power might be noted by anyone with reason to watch him and, besides, he shied from interfering with the minds of others unless strictly necessary. Thankfully in this instance there was a simpler, cleaner alternative.

He moved into his study; the back wall dominated by a pair of matching floor-to-ceiling book cases, their shelves full of varied tomes, most of which he hadn't glanced at in decades. He approached the leftmost stand and removed from its third shelf a particularly weighty volume, the spine of which declared it to be *Hibelicus's Guide to Intestinal Disorders, Volume Two (third revision)*. He then pushed the two books beside it to the left and replaced the *Hibelicus* on the shelf, pressing it firmly into its new position.

The whole bookcase proceeded to move slowly forward, before sliding smoothly across to overlap its twin on the right. Behind stood an area of wall, blank apart from a single wooden door. When opened, the doorway revealed a spiral stairway leading downward. Melodramatic, perhaps, this secret passage, but it worked. Clearly whoever designed this residence had been an individual of considerable foresight.

The way was dark, while the air both felt and smelt dank, reminding the prime master of how rarely he utilised this escape route. He wondered briefly what might have brought his numerous predecessors this way, whether their motives would have been altruistic or self-serving, perhaps even sinister. Given the number of individuals involved, doubtless the stairs had carried in their time people whose intentions fell into all three categories.

He didn't bother with a light but concentrated on feeling his way with his thoughts, a very minor use of talent which ought to go unnoticed, particularly in these elevated Rows where practitioners proliferated. The fact that he even considered someone might be watching him was an indication of how paranoid he was beginning to feel. Overwork, stress; he knew the likely causes, but that didn't remove the feeling. Somewhere in the city lurked an unknown enemy, he was certain of it, and until the threat was identified, he wasn't about to take any chances.

All of which meant that progress was slow, as he concentrated on not misstepping, and this was proving a great deal more tiring than anticipated. Dependence on instantaneous travel had made him lazy it would seem. Unfortunately, such time-saving jumps were possible only to specific points within the metropolis, such as the Thaissian temples he used when visiting the City Below, and none were located conveniently enough to be of any help on this occasion. So he was reduced to relying on man's most primitive form of travel: his own feet.

Finally the passageway ended, having brought him down through the Heights and the Residences and the Bankers Row, to the Row of the Medics; though that title was perhaps a little misleading these days. He'd often thought that it should be renamed the Row of Research, since expertise in just about every conceivable scientific field had long since been concentrated here, not simply medicine.

However, once you started messing around with the traditional names of the Rows, it would necessitate rewriting the levels verse, which so many children still learnt by rote, and he was hanged if he was going to open up that particular can of worms.

The corridors were all but deserted at this hour, so he slipped unnoticed from the passageway's concealed exit and hurried to the designated address, along a route he was coming to know well. The only person likely to discover him was a patrolling Kite Guard, and he'd deal with that contingency if and when it arose.

He arrived without incident and let himself in without knocking, the door opening to his touch. A stunted corridor lay before him, with five doors leading off, two to either side and one directly in front. The format and indeed the uniform functionality of the doors themselves cried 'workplace' rather than 'home'. He strode immediately to the furthest door and pushed it open, stepping into what was clearly a laboratory.

Clean surfaces, white or smoothed wood, surrounded him, while mysterious glass cabinets and domes festooned walls and worktops, many of them containing objects of even more dubious purpose. Off to one side a small metal burner produced a constant blue-tinged flame. For an irreverent moment, the prime master wondered whether the burner served any practical purpose but was instead there merely to declare to a casual visitor that this was a place of serious research, in case they were in any doubt.

The room had a single occupant; white coat turning her form almost androgynous, while her auburn hair was tied back in a simple band. She was titrating something yellow into a glass beaker, her back to him as he entered.

"Come on in, PM," she said, without pausing or looking round.

He refrained from pointing out that he already had.

"Be with you in a minute."

He shuffled closer, though not so close as to be a distraction, and tried to peer around her to see the beaker and fluid more clearly.

"Does that have anything to do with why you called me?"

"No, this is just routine," she replied. "But I thought that, since I was here anyway, I might as well finish this off while waiting for you."

Apparently satisfied, she turned off the flow from the fragile-seeming burette, carefully pushed the metal stand holding the slender glass wand back against the wall and sealed the beaker with a stopper. Only then did she turn around to smile at him, the crows-feet at the corner of her eyes merely emphasising the bright warmth of the expression.

"Thaiss, you look awful," she said, the smile transforming into a concerned frown.

"Thank you; and there was me about to comment on how lovely you look."

"Go right ahead. Don't let my candidness stop you."

And she was lovely. The flashes of grey in her hair and the laughter lines around her eyes did nothing to diminish that; rather they were indications that the prettiness of the young woman he could still picture so clearly had matured into a deeper, more profound beauty.

Her frown was still there, though. "You're working too hard as usual, aren't you? You've got to ease up."

"I would love to; in fact, I determined only today to have an early night of uninterrupted sleep and recuperation, but then..."

She held up an apologetic hand. "I know, I know... I'm sorry."

"Jeanette," he said softly, "when have I ever complained if you're the one summoning me, whatever the hour?"

For a moment their eyes locked, memories of what they'd almost shared passing between them in a glance. Then she looked away.

"Right," he said, trying not to sound in any way awkward or embarrassed, "so what's the latest?"

Her expression darkened. "Not good news, I'm afraid."

He'd guessed as much, or she wouldn't have troubled him at such an hour. Before Jeanette could continue, however, there was a discreet knock at the door. She looked startled, clearly not expecting anyone.

"Sorry," the prime master said quickly, "I forgot to mention, I gave one of my colleagues the address and told him to meet me here." He then raised his voice and called out, "Come through, Thomas."

The door opened and the young master stepped in.

"Thomas, I'd like you meet Jeanette, one of my dearest friends, Jeanette, this is…"

"…our newest master. Delighted to meet you, Thomas." Her smile took in first the younger man and then the older. The prime master could well imagine just how delighted she would be. Jeanette was always going on at him to share the burden of office and to not take on so much responsibility himself, so this development would please her no end.

"Jeanette, would you mind bringing Thomas up to speed before sharing your latest news?"

"Certainly." She then slipped into a toned-down version of the lecture mode which the prime master had seen her adopt so often when addressing a roomful of attentive students or arkademics in training. "It began in the Artists' Row," she explained. "Several people succumbing to a mysterious malady which local healers seemed unable to treat. As more fell victim, we were called in to try and identify the cause and provide an antidote. Meanwhile, the number of victims began to rise alarmingly and we were forced to impose a quarantine to prevent this from becoming an epidemic."

Thomas looked shocked. "I haven't heard anything at all about this."

"Good," the prime master said. "We've attempted to keep a lid on it but you never know how successful you've been, especially given the way word of mouth travels around here."

"Why keep quiet about it at all?" Thomas asked.

"Because of the nature of the disease." The Prime Minister looked towards Jeanette, who gave a shallow nod and picked up the story again.

"What we're dealing with here is not simply a fever; it's worse than that, much worse. The disease physically attacks people, transforming them, killing them in the process."

"Attacks them how?"

The woman looked at the prime master, who nodded. She moved to the back of room, where a large shuttered window dominated the far wall. At a touch of her hand, the shutters started to lift. The prime master took a deep breath; he knew what was to come.

A single table occupied the centre of the small room. On it lay a body, which, despite being the shape and size of a human, could never actually have been human, surely. So the brain insisted. The supine figure appeared to have been crudely chiselled from some form of rock or perhaps bone. Where there should have been skin and hair, there was instead a seamless film of an off-white substance that looked to have been dug from the ground rather than being anything that once breathed. Nor was this coating smooth and skin-like; instead it was lumpy and covered with bumps, like some interrupted statue which the sculptor had yet to return to and complete.

"Gods," Thomas murmured. "Was that ever human?"

"Oh yes," Jeanette assured him. "A few days ago this was a living, breathing man."

"It's hideous." Thomas seemed to be searching for a more dramatic description without being able to find it.

The prime master knew exactly how the other felt. He'd seen this several times before and still found it disturbing in the extreme; words, any words, were inadequate.

"For reasons that should be obvious, we call this disease bone flu." Jeanette continued. "The hands are the first to go, and then the arms. Sufferers complain of a tingling sensation, then an itching to the skin. This is swiftly followed by a loss of feeling to the affected limb which is accompanied by a process we've dubbed calcification. Calcium starts to permeate the skin, apparently drawn from the bones. Soon the skin is transformed into the brittle and inflexible sheath you see before you. The depositing of the calcium isn't entirely regular, hence the gnarly bumps and protrusions you see here. From the transformed limb the infection spreads, rapidly. As the process progresses across the body, it starts to attack the vital organs as well. Once that happens the end isn't far away, though sufferers would doubtless wish it to be even nearer. Left to face the consequences unaided, they die in excruciating agony."

Thomas was staring at the body on the other side of the glass and shaking his head, as if to deny such a thing could happen. "I never imagined…" His voice trailed off.

"Now do you see why we're keeping this quiet until we've found a way to combat this abomination?" The prime master said quietly.

Thomas nodded, and then surprised his older colleague by saying, "I wouldn't have thought there was enough calcium in the entire body to do this."

Not for the first time, the prime master found himself impressed by this latest colleague's perception. Even in the face of such horror, the man's brain continued to function with remarkable clarity. "There isn't, and that provides our disease with a final wicked twist. As far as we can tell, bone flu attacks only those with a smattering of talent, and it's somehow able to draw on that talent, using it to manufacture additional calcium within the body in order to complete the transformation process. Bone flu turns a person's own talent against them."

"What?"

"This is something new Thomas, a threat the like of which the city has never faced before, if our damaged records are to be believed. We don't know where this bone flu originated, nor how. All we do know is that it's here, it's spreading, and to date the disease has proved 100% fatal. Everyone who contracts bone flu has died."

"And I'm afraid I have some more bad news to add," Jeanette said.

"Go on," the prime master said, bracing himself.

"There's been a new outbreak, in the Residences. Bone flu has started attacking the arkedemics."

He nodded, absorbing this. It was the sort of development they'd been dreading. Not unexpected news, but still a bitter blow.

"Has this new outbreak been contained?"

"For now, but I don't hold out any great hopes that we'll be able to do so in the long run." Jeanette sounded as weary and frustrated as he felt. "How can we hope to contain it when we don't even know for sure how the infection's spread, for Thaiss' sake?"

"But you will work it out," he assured her, "you will."

He had to believe that. More importantly, she had to believe it.

As the two masters slipped out into the gloom of Thaiburley's night-time corridors once more, Thomas turned to him and said, "You have to tell the rest of the council."

The prime master nodded. "I know."

Now that the infection had spread, there was little choice. "But can you not see the implications here, Thomas?"

The other looked at him expectantly.

"A multitude of people have settled in Thaiburley over the centuries, Thomas. The blood of the founders, those who built the city, still flows through the veins of many, but so diluted as to be all but insignificant. Only in a very few does it flow pure enough for the core to recognise that individual as founder stock and so allow them access to its potential, manifesting the various forms of talent. Yet talent is what enables this city to function. We masters and arkademics use talent every day to fulfil our duties; without it, Thaiburley would very swiftly devolve into anarchy.

"And yet we're about to tell the most frequent manipulators of the city's core, the most important dozen people in all of Thaiburley, that the very talent that makes them special might leave them vulnerable to a horrifying death. Could you blame them if they stopped exercising their abilities? And what would happen if all the things those individuals do for the city were no longer done?"

"It would be the end," Thomas whispered. "Of Thaiburley... of everything."

"Indeed." This was a bleak assessment, but hardly one the prime master could fault. "Now you understand the nature of my dilemma."

EIGHT

The attackers didn't use bows, though whether that was because they were intent on taking their quarry alive or merely a reflection of the darkness and the likelihood of shooting their own men, Dewar couldn't be certain.

As he listened to their stealthy approach he cursed, fluently and silently. There were more of them than he would have expected – ten at least – in addition to which this was not really his kind of a fight. He was a skulker rather than a head-on brawler and preferred conflict to arrive at a time and place of his choosing, not to have it thrust upon him like this. Still, he'd little choice but to play the hand that was dealt him. The assassin had moved to one side of the clearing, back pressed against a tree, braced and ready.

He was just grateful that they'd been granted some warning of the attack; Kohn had somehow sensed the enemy's approach, though it wasn't the giant that shook him awake but the Thaistess, whom Kohn had evidently woken first. Even so, they didn't have much time, but at least they weren't destined to die in their sleep and could meet their attackers with weapons drawn. Mind you, judging by the way Tom was holding his sword, Dewar doubted whether the lad had ever handled one before. He looked more like a knife fighter whose blade had out-grown him. Discounting the Thaistess, who appeared to be unarmed, there were only three of them as it was, so he just hoped the former street-nick proved to be more accomplished than he looked

No further time to worry about that – the first attackers were already advancing into the clearing. Dewar raised his kairuken, took careful aim and fired. The weapon, a deceptively simple spring operated catapult with a hand-grip and trigger, was designed to be quickly reloaded, giving it the edge over a crossbow in Dewar's opinion. Even as one razor-edged metallic disc flew towards a shadowy assailant, a second was being slipped into place. He fired again, catching another attacker a split second after the first target hit the ground.

That was to be his last opportunity to get a shot away though, as two grim-faced men turned and hurried to-wards him. He was forced to abandon the kairuken and draw his sword.

Dewar was a good swordsman when he needed to be, verging on expert. But he avoided such intimate ex-changes whenever possible, especially in forests, where twisting your foot on an exposed tree route or tripping over other woodland detritus offered such golden oppor-tunities for cruel chance to kick a man in the balls.

He pushed himself away from the tree, ever conscious of his footing, angling the move so that one of the at-tackers was slightly behind and so hampered by the other. Peripherally he was aware of a great roar that could only be Kohn, and of men's curses and movement to his right, but he shut that out, narrowing his focus onto these two men before him.

There didn't seem to be any plan here – no attempt to make the most of the fact that there were two of them to his one. They simply came on. Their mistake.

He danced back to avoid a crude cut from the first attacker, using the foot that had gone backward to spring forward again immediately, so that he was upon the man even as the blade sailed past, thrusting with his own sword. His lunge only scored what amounted to a deep scratch, as the fellow twisted in the wake of his strike; either a very clumsy move or a quite brilliant one, since it saved his life. Dewar wasn't taking any chances, kneeing this first opponent – who doubled up with a dramatic *whoomf* of expelled breath – and slamming the pommel of his sword into the side of the man's head. That way, the blade was still facing in the right direction to parry a blow from the second attacker. Hampered by his colleague, this was never going to be more than a hopeful thrust, but the man quickly moved around to engage the assassin properly. Dewar had planned to finish the first man off before facing the second, but he wasn't given the chance.

What was more, this opponent actually seemed to know what he was doing, taking the assassin's measure with a well rehearsed combination of strikes, the first high and the second low, while keeping his own guard high enough to leave no obvious openings. Dewar feinted and then jabbed in earnest, once twice, was parried each time and then had to jump back smartly to avoid the other's riposte. They were closely matched, and he had neither the time for this nor the desire to see which of them would eventually better the other. Then he remembered the tree roots.

Stepping back hurriedly in the face of another attack, Dewar seemed to trip and fall backwards, twisting around desperately as he did so. Seizing the opportunity, his opponent closed in, and the assassin barely blocked an otherwise lethal strike. Yet even as the two blades met Dewar's other hand was in motion, swinging up to sink into the man's groin the dagger he had surreptitiously drawn under cover of the apparent fall and roll. The brigand let out a scream of pain and surprise as Dewar twisted the knife, feeling the warmth of fresh blood coat his hand.

He was on his feet again in an instant, ignoring the stricken swordsman for the moment as he faced the first attacker again, now recovered but still not in the same class as his colleague. Dewar easily blocked a wildly aimed blow before driving the edge of his own blade through the man's collar bone and on.

The other swordsman was desperately trying to staunch the flow of blood from his groin and didn't seem to offer much of a threat, but there was no point in taking any chances. Dewar ran him through and then turned his attention back to see what else was going on around him.

The first thing he saw was Kohn. The Kayjele fought like a man possessed. As far as Dewar knew, the giant was usually as bereft of weapons as the Thaistess, but the tree bough he'd picked up instead of a blade made the point pretty much irrelevant.

If you were going to pick a fight with a Kayjele there was one thing you really had to be aware of. Not necessarily

that they were big and so had a long reach, though that
was certainly worth bearing in mind, nor the fact they had
only one eye and so perhaps suffered from a lack of depth
perception. No, what you most had to bear in mind was
that they were strong. Really strong, not just because of
their size; even when proportions were taken into account
a Kayjele packed far more punch than your average man,
which was why they made such ideal tenders for the
pumping stations dotted around Thaiburley's multiple levels, where from time to time heavy equipment had to be
moved and regulated. The Kayjele could perform unaided
tasks that would otherwise have required the help of an
ox or two. Dewar supposed this disproportionate strength
had developed in response to the harshness of their
mountain home.

So, if you choose to place the trunk of a small tree in
the grasp of hands powered by that sort of muscle, the
result is always likely to be impressive. A fact which several of the attackers were now discovering to their cost.
The giant was holding off a semi-circle of four armed
men, roaring and snarling defiance while brandishing his
length of tree as if it were a twig.

The men feinted and darted, making a fine show of
looking for an opening while doubtless hoping one of the
others would be the first to chance their arm. The crumpled forms of a couple of their colleagues lying around
Kohn's feet offered a clue as to why the quartet seemed
a tad reluctant to push forward. As the assassin watched,
one of the fallen pair moved, slowly, trying to drag himself away. The other one didn't.

No sign of the Thaistess or the boy. Dewar assumed
they must have made their escape into the trees. Probably

wise; they would only have been in the way judging by what he'd seen earlier of the boy's sword knowledge.

The assassin thought about going back for his kairuken, which should still be close to the tree where he'd dropped it, but decided to make do with what was to hand, or rather foot. Of course he could have employed the sword which hadn't been sheathed as yet, but he was curious. The man was so focussed on the Kayjele and that intimidating bough that he seemed oblivious to Dewar's approach until the assassin's boot landed squarely in the brigand's back, sending him stumbling forward.

What followed lived up to Dewar's expectations in every way. Kohn's hefty club came whistling around in a two handed swing, catching the brigand while he was still trying to recover his balance. The bough struck the unfortunate man's head with a sound like the clap of thunder, lifting him from his feet and sending him flying through the air to land in a heap some distance away. Dewar doubted he'd be moving again in a hurry.

The brigand furthest away then gathered his courage while the other two gawped and, seizing the half opportunity offered by his colleague's demise, chose to move in. However, in mid-stride he seemed to think better of the notion as Kohn's club came whistling back towards him, and tried to retreat without following through on the attack. He wasn't quite quick enough. Tree trunk smashed into hand and, with a yelp, the man dropped his sword.

Dewar had to concentrate after that, as he crossed swords with the man who'd been closest to the fellow Kohn had just attempted to swat into the forest's canopy. Unlike the first two the assassin had fought, who if anything had seemed overconfident, this one didn't seem to have his heart in the contest. Younger than those others, his stance was wholly defensive and he gave ground from the first. Then Kohn roared, a sound chilling enough to give any man pause, let alone a lad already looking for a way out of a scrap. The youth flung his sword at the assassin, and then turned around and ran, hot on the heels of the other surviving attackers.

Dewar sheathed his sword and deftly drew a throwing knife, confident that he couldn't miss at this distance. Yet, as he took aim, a vast shape hove into view; Kohn, chasing after the brigands himself and doubtless ensuring they wouldn't stop running for a while, but robbing the assassin of a clear shot in the process.

"Kohn!" Cursing, Dewar slipped the knife back into its sheath and set off in pursuit. This wasn't some random attack, he felt certain, which raised such interesting questions as who had sent them and why. Questions which the assassin was determined to hear answered.

Only once he was well into the trees and knee deep in bracken did he remember how awkward blundering around in a forest at night could be. Woodcraft was a skill Dewar hadn't needed to call upon in years, and he was quickly discovering that, like all mistresses, she demanded a certain level of dedication. Dare to ignore her and she'd desert you. Despite his best efforts, it sounded to his own ears as if he was moving through the undergrowth with all the elegance and precision of a heavily pregnant goat.

Fortunately, those he followed were making no concessions to stealth at all, so compared to them he seemed an insubstantial spirit on silent feet.

The assassin caught up with the fleeing men as they were scrambling onto their horses, cursing and squabbling the whole while, each with their own opinion as to why the supposed ambush had turned into such a shambles – all of which doubtless laid responsibility firmly at someone else's feet. There were the expected ten or eleven horses, though only three carried riders, still hastily settling into their saddles. Only three? Had they really taken care of so many, or had others simply fled in the wrong direction?

Dewar didn't stop to wonder, but drew the throwing knife from his belt as he ran towards the mounted men, and flung it without missing a stride. His aim was satisfyingly accurate and he watched the knife bury itself between the shoulder blades of his target. The man cried out and slumped forward over his mount's neck, but he didn't lose his seat.

Somebody yelled, "Ride!"

Horses whinnied and reared and pulled at their tethers. Either the fleeing men had released all the steeds, not just the ones they needed, or the mounts hadn't been properly secured in the first place, because suddenly horses were running everywhere and Dewar found himself surrounded by barrelling bodies and threatened by flailing legs and hooves. He did his best to shield his face, smelling warm horse flesh and instinctively closing his ears against the snorts and angry whickering, the sounds of snapping branches and crushed foliage that surrounded him, as he tried to follow the fleeing riders. He saw that one of them had grabbed the reins of their wounded fellow's mount, and the three were quickly away, out of Dewar's reach.

The assassin cursed, as annoyed at losing a good throwing knife as he was about the trio's escape.

The loose horses had bolted, but two remained, either not freed when the others had been or more effectively tethered. They were skittish and alarmed, but he set about soothing them with quietly spoken words. He approached with exaggerated care, using a constant flow of gently voiced imprecations to woo them.

He would love to lead the pair of them back to the others, but knew how difficult that was going to be with two nervous horses, so settled for doing this one at a time, deciding to begin with the one that seemed most amenable – a brindle mare. After making sure the other was firmly tied, he led the mare back the way he'd come.

She wasn't entirely happy about the idea and he was instantly glad he hadn't tried to bring both together. She shied and snorted, but fell short of actually digging her hooves in and refusing.

Dewar used gentle but firm strength to cajole the horse forward, walking beside her head and talking to her all the while. "Come on you mangy excuse for a horse," he said in his sweetest, softest voice. "The glue pot's waiting to welcome these tired old bones of yours if you don't come this brecking way," he cooed. "It's a long while since I've feasted on horse meat. Roasted over an open fire, on a spit. Lovely." And so on until he and his newly acquired mount entered the clearing.

The boy and the Thaistess were huddled together on the ground. At first he thought they were merely hugging each other for reassurance, but then her realised it was more than that.

The boy looked up, distraught. "It's Mildra," he said, "she's hurt."

Dewar could see that much. The clue had come from the wound in her side and the blood that soaked her top around it. Plus the fact that she had evidently lost consciousness.

Kohn was gesturing frantically, trying to attract the assassin's attention. He looked over to discover that the Kayjele had grasped a partially charred stick from the fire, and, holding it by the burned end, had started to carve an image in the ground. First he drew a crude circle, then he marked a cross within it. Dewar stared at the image, determined to understand what the giant was trying to tell him. Kohn pointed repeatedly at the drawing and then forcefully back in the direction they'd come. As he pointed, he grunted repeatedly, clearly agitated.

A cross within a circle... or perhaps a wheel with only four spokes!

The assassin nodded to show he understood. "Thank you."

He still held the horse's tether, and now prepared to mount the beast for the first time. Almost as an afterthought, he turned to Tom. "Mind the girl. I'll be back before sunrise."

The lad looked up in puzzlement and obvious consternation, but that wasn't Dewar's problem. He climbed onto the horse without another word – never mind that he hadn't ridden in years and this steed and he were complete strangers; they could get acquainted on the road. Before any such concerns could be conveyed to the horse, he set off, riding hard in the direction of Crosston. Babysitting the boy and his friends could go to hell for the moment. That bastard of an innkeeper had some explaining to do.

• • • •

Seth Bryant was cursing himself for being a fool. Years of living the contented life of an innkeeper had turned him soft. As time passed he'd started to think like an innkeeper, to *be* an innkeeper, steadily growing into the persona adopted only as camouflage. The man who first arrived at the Four Spoke Inn would never have worried about protecting an assumed identity and would have done what was necessary without qualm or hesitation. The boy and his companions would have been, should have been, dead before morning. Instead he had made them breakfast with a smile and watched them walk away, knowing they wouldn't find passage upriver and happy to rely on the hired help to hunt them down and do his dirty work. As Seth hurried through night-time streets towards a pre-arranged meeting, something in the pit of his stomach told him that this had been a calamitous mistake.

Nor did he see any reason to revise that opinion when he entered the disused warehouse by the waterside – a place brimming with the stink of dampness and riddled with draughts courtesy of the rotted and broken timbers that comprised its walls. Only three figures waited for him. They sat slumped on assorted crates and bore the look of defeated men. One was lying rather than sitting, his body spread over two broken crates and his cheek pressed to one of them. The man was clearly injured, most likely close to death.

"Well?" Seth demanded, without preamble or ceremony.

"They fought like mad men," the nearest mercenary offered, not bothering to get up.

Seth glared at him. What had the fools expected, that their quarry would roll over and accept a knife to the throat without protest? "But did you kill them?" he asked, already anticipating the answer.

"Course we did," the other still-sound mercenary asserted, springing to his feet, suddenly all cock and swagger. "Got the woman and the boy for certain, and stuck the giant so full o' holes that he must be a goner."

"So only the man escaped?"

"That's right." The man was strutting now, as if to assert who was boss here. "He 'ad some fancy weapon with 'im that fired these razor-sharp discs. Took out Ed and Bart 'fore we even knew he was there."

A kairuken? Somewhere at the back of Seth's mind old memories stirred, and his unease about the man called Dewar grew, but time to consider such things with greater care later. "So the boy is definitely dead."

"Yeah, no question."

He was lying. Seth could see it in the man's eyes as well as in the way his friend looked on anxiously, gaze flickering between them, willing the innkeeper to accept the falsehood and terrified that he might not.

The cocky one had come to stare into Seth's face, as if daring him to challenge the assertion.

"And what proof have you brought me of this triumph?" the man who called himself Seth Bryant asked, in a voice none of the Four Spoke Inn's patrons would have recognised.

"Didn't have time for no proof, did we? Not with that brecker sending his discs whizzing round our ears. Why d'you think there's only the three of us here? But the lad's maggot food for sure; you can count on that."

"I see."

"So… if you'll just pay us what was promised, we'll be on our way."

The man who had once been Seth smiled. Split three ways or perhaps even just the two, payment promised to a dozen would go an awful long way. "My agreement was with your captain." He gazed pointedly at the injured man.

"Yeah, well, the cap'n's in no state to talk right now, so I'm standin' in for 'im."

"What happened to him?"

"Knife in the back from the brecker with the disc weapon as we was leavin'," the mercenary said, looking back towards his injured colleague who continued to pay them no heed and had yet to even open his eyes.

As the man glanced away, Seth moved. He hadn't let every skill go to seed, and even after all these years he'd kept up his knife work. The blade was out of its sheath and in his hand in an instant, moving through a smooth arc to bury itself to the hilt in the mercenary's side before the man had a chance to register what was happening. A good strike, sliding between ribs and ripping open the heart.

Seth allowed the knife to drop to the ground still embedded in the corpse, drawing instead his sword as he stepped over the body and advanced purposefully on the remaining mercenary, who had come to his feet and was fumbling to draw his own blade. Was this really the calibre of man he'd been relying on to accomplish a task he himself had been charged with? At least the lad had his sword out now, but it was hardly a contest. Seth strode forward with a momentum that would not be denied. The terror in his opponent's eyes only spurred him on.

He feinted to strike high, drawing the lad's blade up in a clumsy attempt at defence, but instead switched with

a deft turn of wrist and elbow and struck low, easily pen-
etrating the other's ineffectual guard. Easier than taking
money from the gullible Wil in a hand of cards. The blade
sank into the lad's abdomen. As his thrust ended, Seth
yanked the weapon sideways and out. The young mercenary's mouth and eyes gaped wide as realisation of his
own death penetrated. Seth swatted the limply-held
sword away and, with one scything stroke, decapitated
its wielder, relishing the brief resistance of bone and
sinew as the blade swept through. A bit melodramatic,
perhaps, but a great means of venting frustration and a
fitting way to welcome back the person he used to be,
the person he had always been, somewhere deep inside.

He casually retrieved his own knife from the first body
and then crossed to examine the mercenary captain,
who hadn't moved or reacted throughout the exchange
– presumably either unconscious or already dead.

Seth checked the man's pulse; there wasn't one.

The blade that had killed him was still embedded in
the man's back. Presumably his fellows had either been
wary of removing it in case they caused further damage
or simply couldn't be bothered. Not a problem anymore
either way. Seth pulled the knife free and considered it
for a moment. Good weapon – well made and perfectly
balanced. He wiped it clean on the dead captain's tunic
and tucked it into his belt.

In the language of a distant nation, Ulbrax meant
"shining strength", with a strong undertone of implied
masculinity. It was also a proper name; one cast aside
several years ago by the man who subsequently answered to Seth Bryant. Perhaps cast aside was putting it
too strongly; rather, that identity had been submerged,

folded up and sunk into the furthest recesses of memory against future need. To accomplish this submersion, a process of determined self-delusion had been applied, a means of persuading himself not to remember certain thought patterns, habits, mannerisms and abilities. However, in recent days the barriers had eroded and Seth had found himself thinking less and less like a Crosston innkeeper and ever more like Ulbrax the subversive, Ulbrax the spy. Ulbrax the killer.

Events in the warehouse had accelerated this reversion, which was now all but complete. The man who strode back towards the Four Spoke Inn was a very different proposition from the one who had entered the deserted warehouse a few moments before. There was little of Seth Bryant remaining, and Ulbrax felt nothing but contempt for the person he had become in recent years and particularly for decisions made in recent days. Now was the time to rectify those mistakes before the situation became irretrievable.

The hour was late; the inn's last customers had made their merry way home long before he'd set out for the clandestine meeting, while those few staying over ought to be fast asleep. He let himself in via the side door, familiarity guiding his feet in the darkness.

The restoration of his true persona proved timely. Seth Bryant would have stepped into his own room without the faintest suspicion that anything might be amiss, but Ulbrax possessed skills Seth had never even dreamed of. A little rusty, perhaps, but they were still there, as he discovered immediately he crossed the threshold of the room's door. Whoever the intruder might be they were good. There was no sign of a forced entry, nothing overt to arouse suspicion, and there was no sound to give the man away, not even the gentle rise and fall of breathing. Yet Ulbrax could sense him, smell him, *feel* him – this unlooked for, unwanted visitor.

The space was too cramped for a sword. Ulbrax slid a hand towards his knife.

"If your hand moves any nearer that blade, you're a dead man," a voice said calmly from the dark.

"Who… who's there?" he asked in a fair imitation of fear, hiding behind the tattered remnants of Seth.

His question was ignored. "Unbuckle your sword belt and drop it to the floor."

Ulbrax moved to obey. He couldn't see the intruder but was confident he'd pinpointed him by his voice – a voice he recognised instantly as Dewar's. That being the case, the verbal threat was most likely backed-up by a kairuken, assuming the mercenary's account could be believed.

Even allowing for the intruder's eyes being better adapted to the darkness than his own, vision couldn't be that certain. Had Dewar really seen his hand straying towards the knife or was that just an educated guess? Whatever the truth, Ulbrax knew that he had to act now if he was going to do anything at all.

He bent his knees, crouching slightly as if to allow the sword belt to drop to the floor, but instead converted the crouch into the springboard for a leap which he hoped would take the other by surprise. Not intended as an attack, the leap carried him further into the room, where intervening furniture combined with the darkness ought to make accuracy impossible. Rather than dropping the sword belt he dragged it with him, feeling along its length for the knife he knew to be there even before he'd landed.

His shoulder hit something – a solid thump of pain that travelled down his arm but which he ignored – and sent it crashing over; the table by the sound and feel. His landing was hampered by the impact but he still managed to complete the intended roll, coming to his feet in a squat and casting the now freed knife at the patch of darkness from which Dewar's voice had emanated. If the kairuken had been fired during this it must have gone well wide of the mark, because Ulbrax wasn't aware of any razor-edged discs coming his way.

Predictably, the thrown knife clattered against the wall and then the floor. He'd have been amazed if Dewar hadn't moved, but it was worth a shot. His eyes were starting to adapt to the dark a little, though nowhere near as quickly as he needed them to. Enough, however, for him to make out where the window was. Even as the thrown knife thudded to the ground he was moving, throwing himself at the window, face down and arms raised to shield his head. He felt the impact of glass and then the give of it shattering, followed by the sharp sting of shards scraping his body as he hurtled through. More stung his back as he landed and rolled. Something whizzed by, striking his upper arm just below the shoulder; a glancing blow, but enough to shred clothing and slice into skin as it passed. The kairuken! He was on his feet immediately and running, before his opponent could reload, dodging around the corner of the inn to put something solid between him and the weapon. He didn't look to see if he was being followed, assuming that he would be and knowing that the best chance of survival depended on his acting as if all the spawn of hell itself were at his heels. He knew these streets intimately whereas Dewar didn't, knew where to dodge and turn and climb. Pursuit wouldn't be impossible, but he intended to make damned sure it was difficult.

As he ran, something fell into place in his mind, doubtless nudged there by the threat of the kairuken, and he recalled exactly where he'd heard of a man answering Dewar's description wielding such a weapon before. The shock of revelation struck like a physical blow, causing him to stumble to a halt, hands clasping the rough wood of the nearest building for support as he gasped for breath.

How could he have failed to see it?

The words "King Slayer" hissed from his lips. With realisation came a new perspective –this whole situation took on a darker and sharper significance. It had just become personal.

NINE

Tom had done most of his growing up with a knife in his belt. Necessity had insisted that he gain some mastery over the weapon, but during the two days spent crossing the City Below in Kat's company, he'd grown increasingly frustrated at how limited a knife was when compared to the twin short swords the renegade nick wielded with such skill and ferocity.

Before setting out on this expedition into the unknown, he'd asked the prime master for a short sword just like Kat's, so he wouldn't have to feel inadequate if and when any fighting were needed. Now, as he stood at the back of the clearing and waited to meet whoever was trying to creep up on them, that opportunity had arrived and it dawned on him, belatedly, that he had no idea how to actually fight with a sword.

He'd wanted Mildra to run, to hide in the forest somewhere, but she'd refused. "No time," had been her response, "and how do we know there aren't more of them circling behind us?" Which wasn't the cheeriest of thoughts.

She now stood behind him and it really was too late for her to go anywhere else as armed men started to emerge from among the trees – grim-faced brigands whom Tom would have given a wide berth had he met them on Thaiburley's streets, let alone out here in the woods at night.

One of them suddenly convulsed and went down, victim to a flash of silver fired from Dewar's strange weapon. Two of the intruders changed direction and headed towards the sniper, even as a second of their number fell.

That still left far too many coming towards Tom. A couple were closing in, and it was obvious from their confident grins that they didn't rate a short sword in the hands of an inexperienced boy much of a deterrent. Increasingly, nor did Tom. He started to shuffle to one side and backwards, conscious of the Thaistess at his back, but the intruders simply spread out to widen their approach. Short of turning tail and actually running, there was nowhere else for him to go, and he couldn't flee for fear of leaving Mildra exposed. His heart was racing and his breathing turned ragged and fast. His gaze darted this way and that, but he couldn't think what to do. In the streets he would have run and dodged and hidden, but not here. The cold realisation that he was about to die seeped through him, and that Mildra would be left defenceless. Fear robbed him of all strength, clenching muscles and paralysing his arms; the blade in his hand was suddenly too heavy to lift. He watched in dread fascination as the nearest attacker raised his sword to strike.

The night was abruptly split by a blood-curdling roar, and what looked to be the trunk of a fair sized tree came whistling through the air to smash into the man poised to run Tom through. Kohn! The blow caught the attacker in the chest, lifting him off his feet to land in a crumpled heap several feet away.

Tom's paralysis broke and he rushed to take advantage of the distraction, darting forward to stab at an opponent still too surprised by the Kayjele's impressive intervention to do much more than gawp. Fear and shame at his own weakness lent strength to his arm, and the sword sank deep before the brigand even realised what was happening. By the time the man sank to his knees – a look of complete shock on his face – Tom had pulled the blade free again and stepped back to stand by Mildra.

Now that the paralysis had gone, Tom felt energised and was eager to convince anyone interested that he hadn't been scared at all. But there were still too many. Even as Tom stepped back he was aware of others pushing forward. A sword flashed towards him and he instinctively swaycd out of the way and raised his own weapon, deflecting the blow so that it slid past. The clash of steel on steel reverberated through his arm. It was jarring enough to make him wonder how people managed to do this again and again in battle, and, more importantly, whether he was going to be able to.

Yet as this concern flashed through his thoughts, it withered in the face of blossoming horror as he heard an, "Oh," of surprise and pain and realised that by deflecting the sword thrust, he had merely diverted it behind him – to where Mildra stood.

He swivelled around, to see the Thaistess crumple to the ground, her hands clasping her left side. The brigand responsible was already turning back to face Tom, and he felt a gathering rage to think that he had allowed this piece of scum to hurt Mildra. His throat let rip a snarl of inchoate fury as he drove his sword at that ugly face, only to have the blow parried with contemptuous ease.

Before either could strike again, Kohn was there, swinging his improvised club with crushing force to swat the man away. Something or somebody barrelled into Tom's back, knocking him off his feet. He nearly fell on top of Mildra, who was lying motionless on the ground, and he lost hold of his sword in the attempt not to. He ended up with his knees one side of the Thaistess and hands the other, supporting his body which hung suspended above her.

Tom pushed himself into a sitting position and tried to rouse Mildra, with no effect. He was conscious of Kohn standing before them, and several brigands beyond, but most of his attention was reserved for the young Thaistess. His questing fingers found a pulse; she was still alive. Instinct took over, and as he sat there, cradling Mildra in his arms, he began the recite the personal litany which had served him so well throughout childhood: *you can't see us, you can't see us, we're invisible, there's nobody here, nobody here at all,* over and over.

It brought back memories of when he'd hidden himself and Kat from the pursuing demon hounds, which had been the first time he'd ever attempted to hide anyone with his ability other than himself. The thought brought home just how much had happened to him of late. That had only been a dozen or so days ago, yet it seemed to belong in another life entirely. Sudden fear almost made him falter. The prime master had told him that he drew on Thaiburley's mysterious core when doing this. They were now a long way from the city; would his ability still work? How could it possibly over such a distance?

He refused to dwell on that, forcing the doubts aside and concentrating on his mantra with grim determination. This would work; it had to work, for both his sake and Mildra's.

He closed his eyes, letting the sounds of continuing struggle wash over the protective bubble of his looped words, as he fell into the familiar rhythm of repetition, determined to keep the two of them safe.

At length he realised that the sounds of fighting had ceased and opened his eyes, allowing the words to stumble to a halt. Kohn was staring at him, expression unreadable, and Tom had a feeling that the Kayjele had been able to see him all along, raising fresh concerns about whether or not his ability had worked. The bodies of attackers lay scattered around the clearing, and there was no sign of Dewar, though noises coming from somewhere beyond Kohn suggested that there might be some sort of pursuit underway.

Mildra remained unconscious and he felt the warm stickiness of blood on his hand where he'd cradled her. He stared at the serene features of the Thaistess with growing horror, willing her to open her eyes.

"Mildra?" No response.

For the first time he began to consider the unthinkable, that she might not wake up at all. There had to be something he could do. He'd been a complete waste of space during the fighting and desperately wanted to make up for that, quite apart from his determination not to lose someone he cared about.

Dewar reappeared, leading a horse and looking anything but happy. Tom felt a huge surge of relief. He wouldn't have to do anything now; there was somebody else to make the decisions, someone who hopefully would have a clearer idea of how to help the injured girl.

Yet no sooner had the man returned than he mounted the horse and left them, telling Tom in parting to, "Mind the girl."

Mind the girl? How was he supposed to do that? Mildra was the healer, not him, and she was the one now in need of healing. He stared at the Thaistess's inert form, at the wound, at the blood that was staining her top. Panic threatened to well up, to overwhelm and incapacitate him, but he fought it down, refusing to let fear be the master here. Think, he chided. What would he have done if they were back in Thaiburley? Larl reeds. How close were they to the river? Not far, surely.

He turned to Kohn. "Could you get the fire going again, put some water on to boil?"

Tom thought the giant understood, hoped he did, but didn't wait to find out. He hurried in the direction the river ought to be, and almost immediately heard it; not a great roar, but a gentle lilt of sound which might almost have been a sigh. He followed that soft noise and was soon at the side of the Thair. Visibility was better here, at the edge of the trees' sheltering canopy, where moon and starlight were free to tint the world. He followed the river's course for a while, scouring her bank, working his way in and out among trees whose roots dipped thirstily into the water and the clumps of thick-stemmed sedge and reed in between.

Within minutes he stumbled on what he'd been looking for: a clump of larl reeds, their rigid stems pointing pole-stiff towards the sky. Conscious of the passing minutes, he drew his knife and quickly harvested half a dozen, cutting them as close to the marshy ground they favoured as he could reach, then hurried back to the camp, holding his trophies inverted, so that the pointed tips trailed on the ground and none of the milky sap from their severed bases would be wasted.

He re-entered the clearing to discover that not only had Kohn set a pan of water on the rejuvenated fire as he'd asked but the Kayjele had also uncovered some bandages and a jar of salve from among the supplies.

"Thank you, Kohn."

Despite his anxiety over Mildra, Tom was feeling a good deal better about things. He might not have covered himself in glory during the fight, but at least he was now doing something useful. He just hoped it would prove to be enough.

He made a wad from a bandage and dipped it into the water and used it to clean Mildra's wound, then hurriedly cut a couple of the reeds into strips and loaded these into the pan, which was just starting to simmer. Next he squeezed the precious, sticky sap from one of the reeds, allowing it to fall in stringy droplets directly onto the wound. He'd seen enough knife injuries treated among the Blue Claw to know roughly what to do; the rest he was improvising. A smear of salve and then, using the tip of his knife, he manoeuvred the softened wad of fibrous larl out of the boiling water and placed it as gently as he could onto the wound, covering this with the broad section of a further reed, before wrapping the whole in a bandage. The result looked lumpy and ungainly; nothing like any of the work he'd seen performed on injuries before, but he felt certain he'd got the basics right.

Mildra hadn't stirred or uttered a sound throughout, but she was still breathing, which was infinitely better than the alternative. Kohn helped him lift her fragile form nearer the fire, where he then covered her with a blanket, after which there was nothing to do but wait; for morning, for Mildra to wake, and for Dewar to return.

Given a choice, Tom knew which of the three he could most easily have lived without; though the horse would have been useful, if only to get Mildra to a healer or medic.

Tom couldn't even think about trying to sleep again, so he sat watching Mildra, the looming presence of Kohn on the Thaistess's far side. Tom would have sworn that he barely took his eyes off of her swaddled form, yet found himself lulled into a semi-dreamlike state by the burning embers of the fire and taken completely by surprise when a remarkably calm and collected voice said, "Larl reeds, good thinking."

Startled, he jerked his head around to see the Thaistess roll over, if a little gingerly, and begin to push herself up into a sitting position.

"Mildra! Are you..."

"I'm fine." And she certainly looked and sounded it, though Tom was struggling to reconcile this very awake, very aware person with the limp and bloodied girl he had been tending such a short time ago.

Kohn made a noise which he took to be an expression of happiness.

"Thank you, Kohn," Mildra said. "And to you, Tom," she added, smiling at him. Then her expression changed, as her fingers explored his handiwork. "By the Goddess; how many reeds did you pack into this thing?"

"A few," he admitted uncomfortably. "You had us worried." *Us* seemed far easier and safer to admit to than saying that *he'd* been worried sick.

"Sorry, but the wound was a serious one and it's not easy to heal yourself. I had to turn my abilities inward, start rebuilding from the inside out, and the pain was... excruciating." She shuddered, and Tom felt a pang of guilt, remembering his own part in deflecting towards her the thrust that had done the damage, however inadvertently. "I had to sink into a healing trance in order to focus." She continued to fiddle with the bandage. "Would you help me get this off?"

Tom hesitated, abruptly embarrassed at touching the young woman's naked flesh now that she was awake, when he'd been perfectly at ease doing so when she was hurt and unconscious. He eventually made a token effort at helping but was relieved when she proved able to do most of the work herself. As she uncovered the actual wound, Tom could only stare. He'd seen healers at work before but rarely on anything as serious as Mildra's injury looked to have been, and the gaping, bloody hole that he'd seen mere hours before had now disappeared, a subtle ridge of scar the only thing to mark its position.

"My first war wound." She smiled again. "What happened after I went under?"

"Kohn and Dewar fought off the attackers," he replied. "I... hid us." It sounded pathetic even to his own ears, though evidently not to Mildra's.

"Thank you," she said again, reaching out to briefly squeeze his hand. "You saved my life as well as your own."

"But how did I do it? I thought my abilities drew on Thaiburley's core, so how do they work so far away from the city?"

Mildra smiled. "It's the river, Tom. Ultimately, the city's core is a gift from the goddess, and the Thair links Thaiburley to its mother as if the river were an unsevered umbilical cord. I can sense her presence in the waters constantly, and so long as we remain close to the Thair our abilities – my healing, your hiding – will continue to work as if we were still inside the city's walls."

Tom instinctively wanted to scoff at the idea of goddesses in rivers, but then stopped, for once doubting his own scepticism. After all, whether Mildra's claim had any basis in reality or not, their abilities did seem to work out here, and he could offer no better explanation as to why.

The Tattooed Men were running out of time. Two nights of hunting and they still weren't anywhere near snagging the Soul Thief. If the bitch stayed true to form she'd haunt the under-City for a period of around six to eight nights, feeding on those who took her fancy – which everyone was now willing to admit meant those with talent – before disappearing back into the Stain for another year or two. Out of their reach. Not even Kat would be crazy enough to continue pursuit into the Stain, that poisoned, polluted wasteland at the very back of the vast cavern housing the City Below; a place people tended to avoid even talking about, let alone visiting.

The Soul Thief had already been at work for three nights that they knew of, which meant they had perhaps three or four more before she vanished again. Their night-time trawls across the under-City weren't working, that much was obvious, and Kat was increasingly convinced they were never going to. Besides, she had a better plan. The only difficult part was going to be persuading Chavver. Not that the Tattooed Men's leader was inflexible or unwilling to listen to advice, no, not as a rule. It was only when the advice in question came from her sister that Kat could foresee a problem.

So, she'd have to make sure her idea reached Chavver's ears by a less direct route. After a few moments careful consideration, she chose Rel. Although a few years older than Kat, he was among the youngest of the Tattooed Men and had always been eager to make a good impression. The fact that he and she were teamed together made her chatting to him seem all the more natural.

"The problem is," she said as if in the mood to put the world to rights, "that when we *do* find the Soul Thief we're too spread out. The few who actually encounter her are never going to be enough to stop her, and by the time we can concentrate our strength, she's gone."

"Yeah," he agreed.

"There are two parts to this operation: finding the target and neutralising it. One's no good without the other. We've got the first part sorted out but are failing dismally with the second. What we need to do is stop chasing around after the Soul Thief and make her come to us, at a time and place of our choosing, where we're ready and waiting for her."

"Sure, but how?"

"Easy." She sat back and grinned, enjoying the hungry look that had crept into Rel's eyes.

"Well?" he asked on cue.

She leant forward again, and said quietly, as if sharing

some profound secret, "We know the Soul Thief feeds on those with talent, right? The healers, seers, illusionists, sages and all the other meddlers and pedlars who aren't out-and-out con artists but can actually do at least some of what they claim. So, all we have to do is round up everyone we can find with a scrap of genuine talent and put them together in one place, then sharpen our swords, load up the crossbows and get ready to nail the bitch when she turns up." Kat held her hands out. "Job done; the Thief'll never be able to resist!"

Rel was nodding vigorously, eyes shining as if he'd seen the light. "Yeah," he said. "You know, that might just work."

"Course it will, and it beats running around chasing our tails like we have been."

Kat wandered off feeling more than a little pleased with herself. All she had to do now was wait, though not for long as it turned out. Within the hour Chavver summoned everyone to a meeting, where the new tactic was revealed.

"Time we stopped chasing the Soul Thief and let her come to us," Chavver declared. Kat couldn't have put it better herself.

They were tasked with identifying and "recruiting" – willingly if possible, unwillingly if not – as many people as they could find who displayed even a scrap of talent.

Kat silently approved of the location her sister had chosen to set the trap. Iron Grove Square sat at the heart of a derelict district and was a place the Tattooed Men had often used as a training area. It was surrounded by abandoned buildings with enough vantage points to hide all of them while providing clear line of site of anything and anyone in the square itself.

Despite this being her idea, Kat was the first to acknowledge that the plan had its drawbacks, particularly for the unfortunates they were going to be using as bait. Given proper opportunity, the Tattooed Men could field enough fire power to stop a small army, and it would all be deployed here. Whether or not that would be enough to stop the Soul Thief was another matter; nobody had ever had the chance to find out.

If they couldn't stop her, they would just have provided the monster with the biggest feast she'd ever dreamed of. Even if they did bring her down, there was every chance that people would be caught in the crossfire, however unintentionally. Either way, Kat was glad that she wasn't going to be standing in that square when the shooting started.

In fact, if she dwelt on the fact that the people they were about to put on the front line were healers and apothakers and seers – folk who performed vital functions in the under-City – her conscience was likely to give her a severe beating; so she didn't. Instead she concentrated on the prospect of finally getting a real crack at the monster that had made her an orphan. That way, her conscience was reduced to resentful mutterings in the farthest corners of her thoughts.

She slipped away from the gathering, uncertain whether the Men would go hunting that night or not, but, if they did, she wouldn't be with them. Kat had an appointment to keep.

She would have chosen somewhere different for this meeting, anywhere different, had there been an option. Not that she couldn't understand the reasoning, far from it. For a stranger, unfamiliar with the City Below, the chophouses were a safe and sensible bet – good quality food at reasonable prices.

Kat wasn't a stranger, however, and the chophouses with their fussy ways and invariably waged clientele were so far removed from her usual haunts that they might as well have existed on a different Row entirely. Give her the smoky atmosphere of a dingy tavern and its suspect sandwiches washed down with sour ale any day.

Coalman's Chophouse was built into one of the arches supporting the grand conveyor – the elevated moving roadway that carried timber and other imports all the way from the docks to the Whittleson saw mill and factories – and it was reckoned to be one of the best. In fairness, Kat supposed a newcomer to the City Below would have trouble finding any of the places she preferred in any case.

Taking a deep breath, she pushed the door open and stepped inside. The place was bustling, proof positive that things in the under-City weren't all that bad despite recent events, since plenty of people could clearly still afford the clean cutlery and pretensions of Coalman's Chophouse. Despite her cynicism, Kat had to admit that the smells were mouth-wateringly good. On the tables around her she saw plates piled high with golden-crusted pies from which rich-gravied filling oozed, thick cutlets of griddled meat and juicy chops, plump brown sausages, hens' eggs and duck eggs with bubbled whites and bright yellow yolks, chunky slices of pink bacon and even thicker off-white slabs of tripe, all accompanied by mounds of boiled potatoes and roasted potatoes and peas and wilted greenery, from the sum of which rose wafts of steam and incredibly inviting aromas.

She did her best not to stare but it was a losing battle. Kat had never seen so much saliva-inducing food in one place before and the effect was overwhelming. She had to swallow, feeling suddenly hungry beyond all reason. Her view was abruptly blocked by a blue and white striped apron which proved to be worn by a tall man sporting a heavy moustache and even heavier scowl. "Can I help you?"

Kat had a tendency to stand out in most company, but here it was ridiculous. She'd never heard anything specific about the chophouses being male only preserves, but there certainly weren't any other women present just now, let alone of her age, or dressed in leathers, or carrying twin swords. Coalman's had abruptly gone very quiet, and Kat was acutely aware that every eye seemed to be looking in her direction.

"That's all right," a voice said very clearly and casually, "the young lady's with me."

The speaker was at a table behind the waiter. A tall man, slender and smartly dressed, with slicked-back hair and a rounded face dominated by dark eyebrows that perched above eyes which were perhaps a little too close together. Kat couldn't resist a small smile; at least she was no longer the centre of attention, as everyone had turned their gazes on him, including the waiter, who stood aside and, with a slight sniff, gestured Kat towards the stranger's table.

"Kat, I presume." he said as she slipped into the chair opposite. She nodded, but couldn't stop staring at the sumptuous looking meat pie and potatoes that sat before the man. He could only just have broken the crust, because curls of stream were still rising from the meat and gravy within.

"As you doubtless gathered, I'm Brent. Hungry?"

She nodded again, unable to tear her gaze away from the food. Too brecking right she was. The man beckoned the same waiter over, and soon Kat was confronted with a great golden-crusted pie all of her own.

She wasn't especially used to cutlery but knew the principles, and settled for eating with a silver-metal spoon, using its rounded bowl to break open the pie's crust and then pausing to savour the first release of delicious meat-rich aroma before tucking in. To her considerable delight, the food proved even tastier than it looked and at least as good as it smelled. She had wolfed down nearly half the pie before remembering why she was here and glancing up to see her benefactor studying her. Instantly she bristled; there was something sardonic and superior in the man's expression which irritated the hell out of Kat and made her palm itch for the feel of a sword hilt. Very deliberately, while still chewing a final mouthful of crisp pastry and tender meat, she sat back and pushed the plate away.

"Had enough?"

"For now." She would have loved to keep going but had suddenly lost her appetite. Besides, she was close to being outfaced, having already stuffed more food down her throat than she could ever recall eating at one meal before.

Kat forced her attention back to the man responsible for providing the feast and still didn't like what she saw, despite his generosity. "So, you're interested in the Soul Thief." She kept her voice low, reckoning a chat about the bogeyman from a kiddies' bedtime tale would only put her even lower in the estimations of the snooty so-and-sos around her, if that were possible.

"Indeed."

A tight-lipped brecker, and no mistake. Well, two could play at that game. She folded her arms and waited for him to say something. The amused twinkle in his eyes grew and a smile seemed to hover on his lips. This was all a game to him, Kat realised, and she was nothing more than a counter, there for his entertainment. Stuff that! She was no one's toy.

"Thanks for the meal," she said, preparing to stand up, "but if that's all you've got to say, I'm off."

"Your choice, of course, but if you really want to stop the Soul Thief, I'd wait and hear what I have to say if I were you."

He had her there, and knew it. She glared at him, sat back and did as he suggested: waited.

"Better." The word was spoken with such smug confidence that she despised him all the more.

Despite having stopped eating some time ago, Brent now paused to pick up his fork and break off a corner of pie crust from the thin crescent of pastry which was all that remained on his plate, speared it delicately on the tines without crumbling, and lifted it to his mouth. Done for effect rather than any lingering hunger, she felt certain. She glanced around, determined not to give him the satisfaction of having her watching the whole performance. At a table behind Brent sat another lone diner, an elderly man with a kindly face, who caught her eye and winked at Kat before smiling broadly. So warm was the smile and so conspiratorial the wink, that Kat nearly reacted with a grin of her own. However, her attention switched back to her dining companion, who had now finished chewing and dabbed delicately at the corner of his mouth with a napkin. The smile he then showed her was as different to the elderly man's as chalk is to cheese. This time Kat did respond, twisting the corners of her mouth upward in an expression without any hint of humour behind it; she could do patience when called for.

"Now, what do you actually know about the Soul Thief?" he asked.

"Enough."

"I doubt that very much. You see, the best way to defeat any enemy is to know them, and so learn their weaknesses."

"And what could you, an outsider possibly know about the Soul Thief that I don't?"

"You'd be surprised." That smile again; the one that made her want to reach across the table and slap him around the face until it disappeared. "I know what the Soul Thief is, why she feeds, how to prevent her from feeding and so weaken her to the point where she can be killed."

"Really? And how exactly do you know all this?"

"From my employer." A dramatic pause, but if he was expecting Kat to show any impatience, she disappointed him. "The creature you hunt is ancient, a left-over from another age, an abomination that should have returned to the dust long ago. I've been sent here to ensure that this small oversight is corrected."

Sent? This just got better and better. "And who sent you?"

"Ah, now there's a question; the answer to which you don't need to know and I'm not even certain of myself. But does that matter? We both want the same thing. With or without your help I will hunt down and kill the

Soul Thief, but I could do so a lot quicker with it, whereas without my help, you'll never succeed."

The waiter reappeared, reaching to collect both their plates. Kat's hand shot out, grabbing the rim of hers. No way she was about to let that much quality food get away from her. Brent raised his eyebrows and addressed the waiter. "Could the lady perhaps be provided with a box or bag in which to take away the rest of her meal for later?"

The man's brief nod was so stiff with disdain that Kat bristled, as he replied, "Certainly, sir. I'll see what I can arrange."

He could stuff his disapproval where the globes don't shine. Polite conduct wouldn't feed her tomorrow, whereas the rest of that pie would.

Once the waiter had left, Kat returned to glowering at Brent. She didn't trust him, and trusted even less the fact that he worked for some unseen employer whose real agenda might be anything. But, on the other hand, if he really could help bring down the Soul Thief... for that prize she'd take any risk.

"So," he asked, "do we work together, or not?"

She held his gaze for a moment and then nodded. "All right, we work together; but if at any stage you screw up or even think of double-crossing me and mine, you'll wish you'd never been born."

He smiled again and held his hands out, palms upward as if to demonstrate he was harmless. "Understood. In fact, I wouldn't want it any other way."

They left the chophouse together, Brent donning a brown coat with an elaborate upturned collar which might have been the height of fashion somewhere in the world but looked comically out of place here in the streets of the under-City. Kat watched him saunter off and was almost tempted to follow, when a voice spoke from behind her.

"Careful of that one, young lady."

She turned around, to see the elderly man who'd smiled at her during the meal from over Brent's shoulder. He was standing in the restaurant's doorway, evidently in the process of leaving.

"What do you mean?"

"None of my business, I know, but he smells of the East to me. Never trust a man who smells of the East." He smiled; the same warm and open expression she'd seen earlier. "Well, good night to you." He then strolled off in the opposite direction.

When Kat turned back again to look at Brent, he'd already disappeared from sight.

TEN

Tom came awake slowly, shedding layers of sleep like a snake casting off old skin. Not bad for someone who'd been convinced they wouldn't manage another wink for the rest of the night. True to his word, Dewar had returned before the sun rose. His mood seemed even blacker than before he'd ridden off and he refused to discuss where he'd been or what had happened. All of which irritated Tom no end. Who did he think he was?

"A couple of hours rest, then we'll break camp," their reticent "leader" declared. "We need to put as much distance between us and Crosston as soon as possible."

Crosston: was that where he'd disappeared too? Despite being curious and feeling frustrated at Dewar's insistence on treating him like the child the dour man doubtless thought him to be, Tom basically felt a huge sense of relief. He'd been afraid that Dewar might want them to move on immediately, particularly given the night's events. Had the man done so, Tom would have refused, not for his own sake but for Mildra's. The

Thaistess was clearly exhausted by the effort of having to heal herself and had nodded off to sleep long before Dewar reappeared. Quite what the outcome of such a refusal might have been he had no idea, and was glad he wouldn't have to find out.

Morning found Mildra still looking tired while insisting she felt fine. Not that Tom was fooled; nor presumably was Dewar, because he insisted she sat on the horse when they set out. Mildra protested initially, though without any great conviction. Apparently there should have been two of the beasts, but the second had seized the opportunity to escape while Dewar was off on his mysterious night-time ride.

One was quite enough for Tom, though as the morning progressed he overcame his vague mistrust of horses sufficiently to walk beside the Thaistess and even to spell Dewar in leading her mount from time to time.

"So, you can ride now?" he teased at one point.

"I wish," she replied. "Sit on a horse, yes; ride it, no. If Beauty went any faster than her current walk, I'd be on my backside in the grass in no time." She patted the horse affectionately.

"Beauty?"

"Well, I had to call her something. And she is, isn't she?"

Tom frowned at the horse, then back at Mildra. "You don't really want me to answer that, do you?"

Mildra laughed. "Men!"

Tom couldn't help but smile. It felt good to be called that. Especially by her.

He was finding walking easier this second day, less taxing on the muscles, though whether that was due to them growing more accustomed to the exercise or the lingering after-effects of Mildra's laying-on of hands the previous evening, he couldn't be sure.

The day's biggest surprise, at least from Tom's perspective, came when they stopped for lunch.

"Not you," Dewar said, singling out Tom, who only had eyes for the bread and dried meat he was in the process of unpacking at the time.

"What?"

"Come over here, and bring your sword. Let's at least make sure you know how to hold the brecking thing so you look less as if you just stumbled across it in a bin and more as if the weapon actually belongs to you."

So began Tom's first ever lesson in swordsmanship.

All too soon Dewar signalled an end to proceedings, sheathing his sword and saying, "Remember, practice!"

The session hadn't lasted long and barely scratched the surface of a few rudimentary skills, but Tom came away with a little more confidence; enough to justify missing out on the precious chance to rest, even if it did mean bolting some food down hurriedly as they were about to set off again.

Dewar's instruction to practice sounded like good advice to Tom, which he would have loved to have followed, if only he weren't so busy traipsing across the countryside at the time.

The Thair was a close companion for much of that day, and they saw stilt-legged herons high-stepping their way daintily through the river's shallows, snake-necked cormorants diving her depths to emerge with fish wriggling in their outstretched beaks, and V-shaped formations of ever-scolding geese flying above her waters, while boats frequently rode her central currents in both directions.

When leaving Crosston they'd chosen a less-travelled road in order to stay close to the Thair – Dewar in the ever-dwindling hope of finding a vessel willing to take them upriver, Mildra for her own reasons as Tom was now coming to realise. He hated to think what would have happened if the previous night's attack had occurred any distance from the river and the Thaistess had been unable to draw on her healing abilities. They encountered few other travellers. "Most who come this way do so in a boat," as Dewar muttered a little wistfully when watching yet another vessel at the river's heart steadily outpace them.

They passed several isolated dwellings hugging the river's bank, each with a boat or two moored nearby or sometimes out on the water, fishing, and they walked through two small villages that afternoon, with Tom hopeful that they might dally for a while in the second and perhaps end the day's walking early. He quite fancied the idea of a warm bed and of falling asleep with a roof over his head, but everyone else seemed happy to continue, which meant another night under the stars trying to get comfortable on the unyielding ground. At least they did stop long enough to pick up some fresh fish in the village, introducing a bit of variety to their evening meal.

While Mildra set the fire Dewar gutted the fish, before taking Tom to one side for a further quick but intense training session. Tom came away with aching arms and sweat dampening his clothes, but exhilarated and pleased with how the session had gone. He was more than ready for the fish, which proved delicious to the last flaky white-fleshed mouthful.

He fell asleep rehearsing sword moves in his head.

• • • •

The door had been repaired, after a fashion. Though Kat hoped this was only a temporary replacement and not the best the apothaker could afford. She rapped smartly on the faceless sheet of cheap plywood that now blocked the entrance; two knocks, which sounded dull and hollow, while the whole door vibrated beneath her fist.

It occurred to her belatedly that the apothaker might have moved away – gone to stay with friends or relatives after the traumas of the other night, but then she heard the shuffle of movement from within.

"I'm not open," a tired voice called out. "Try Sur Eames in Woodhouse Lane."

"It's me, Kat," she said, suddenly self-conscious and glancing around to ensure no passerby could overhear what she said next, "the Death Queen from the other night."

There came a rattle of chains and a scraping, as if a chair or some such had been pressed against the door's other side and needed to be removed.

The door opened a fraction, and a vertical strip of face appeared in the gap, complete with eye. "Kat, is it?" The face withdrew to a further rattle of chains and the door opened more fully. "You'd better come in, I suppose."

Kat followed her inside, having to manoeuvre around a solid wooden chair; presumably the one that had been used to block the door. The place smelt, and not of anything pleasant. She wondered if the old woman had moved from this room at all since the other evening, even to wash or pee.

"I presume you have something to tell me, about the monster that killed my Kara?" the apothaker said as she shuffled to a high-backed armchair and flopped down into it. The way she asked made it sound as if Kat dropping by to bring her an update was the most natural thing in the world.

On a small table in front of the armchair rested a drawing done in charcoal on a sheet of textured paper. It was a portrait of a girl, or young woman, smiling, a twinkle of mischief in her eyes and her face framed by a cascade of dark hair. Skilfully executed, the image seemed imbued with a sense of life, though it was only a sketch. Kat could sense the love and care that had gone into its crafting and guessed this must be Kara. "She was beautiful," she said softly.

"Yes, yes she was," the apothaker said, reaching forward to fiddle with the picture as if embarrassed to have her efforts on display and perhaps intending to move the sheet out of sight; but in the end she left it there. "I used to paint..." she explained. "In another life, when there was more time, and more beauty in the world." She shivered, and then straightened in the chair. "Now, what news?"

"Well," Kat said, a little guardedly. "I think we've found a way to trap the Soul Thief and finish her off once and for all, but we're gonna need your help."

"My help?" The woman cackled. "Never did learn how to use a knife, young lady, and if it's potions you're after, I've already given you the best I have. What help could I possibly be?"

"Not just you; we need everyone with talent, as many as we can possibly find."

The old woman's eyes narrowed. "And what would you want all these folk for?"

Kat took a deep breath, knowing that what she said next would either win or lose the apothaker's support. "As bait."

"Ah, I see." The old woman sat silent for a few seconds. "And you're sure that when the monster takes this bait, you can stop it?"

Kat smiled. "The Tattooed Men have weapons at our disposal you've never dreamed of; the sort of thing we don't get a chance to use too often. We'll stop her, don't worry." She spoke with such assurance and sincerity, she almost convinced herself.

"Very well, I'll help. Of course I will, if it means revenge... And I can help, perhaps more than you realise. I sense talent, you see, feel it within a person. I know if they're the genuine article or a pompous sham. It's how I found Kara. Would that be of any use to you?"

Kat stared at her host. She'd come here hoping the old woman could point her in the direction of other practitioners in the area, people who might have a smattering of genuine talent, but if the apothaker truly could tell those who did from those who merely claimed to, that was a boon beyond anything Kat had ever dreamed of finding.

"Maybe," she said, her usual guarded nature asserting itself. "You'll come with me, then?"

The old woman looked up and smiled – an expression that held no mirth or warmth but rather reminded Kat of a naked skull's grin. "What, the chance to catch the brecker that killed my Kara? Of course I will. Wouldn't miss it for anything."

"We could start with this Eames in Woodhouse Lane you mentioned..."

The apothaker shook her head. "I wouldn't bother – the man's a complete fraud. You don't think I'd send my customers to anyone who might actually take them away from me, do you?" She rose from her seat and pulled a sequinned shawl from a wall hook; a garment that looked as if it might have cost a pretty penny once upon a time. After wrapping the shawl with meticulous care around her shoulders and securing it with a pin, she ushered Kat towards the door. "Don't worry, girl, stick with me and I'll show you where the real talent lies."

Moonlight graced the land with fey shadows and an ephemeral beauty which Ulbrax was not even remotely in the mood to enjoy. By daybreak this would again be just one more barren and unremarkable hillside looking down on the great trade road as it made its way to Crosston.

"What are we doing here, Seth?"

Wil was getting on his nerves, and Ulbrax was finding the Seth persona increasingly difficult to maintain.

"I told you, seeking help. Trust me, Wil, everything will become clear shortly."

Better if he had undertaken this trip alone, but that was never really an option.

He'd brought with him the length of wood – the fifth spoke given to Seth by the demon – and followed the accompanying directions precisely. This was the right place, he felt certain, now all Ulbrax had to do was find the right rock.

Had *he* been involved from the start, Ulbrax would have come out here like a shot, making sure he knew exactly where the rock was so that he could go straight to it if and when it were needed. Forward planning: never hurt, often helped. Being a mere innkeeper, Seth had never even considered doing anything that intelligent, which left Ulbrax to blunder around in the dark looking for a particular lump of stone among many, with a whining yokel for company.

Wil had been the obvious choice. Anyone would have served, the lad was just unlucky; but there seemed little point in involving someone new when Wil had already been so helpful in recalling the mercenaries. Besides, there was no guarantee anyone else would prove this gullible.

"Bring that lantern over here, would you, Wil?"

The lad duly obliged; anything for his friend Seth, whom he clearly trusted implicitly. From the demon's description, the rock ought to be one of this clump before him... ah yes. Difficult to be certain in the fickle illumination of the lantern, but there looked to be a small hole in the face of one of them, a pit that was about the right size. He scraped ineffectually at the moss that partially concealed the indentation, then took the fifth spoke and brought it to the stone. If this truly was a fit, it was going to be a tight one. He wriggled the spoke around, increasingly confident that this was the right match, but unable to find the proper angle to push the stick home.

"Keep the light steady!" he snapped. Not that Wil was doing anything but; he just needed to vent a little steam at somebody.

Given the passage of years, it was hardly surprising if dust and dirt and moss had conspired to obscure and partially close the small hole. Setting the spoke to one side for the moment, Ulbrax took out his knife and used its tip to scrape away moss and gouge into the hollow, flicking out detritus as he went. He then tried the spoke again and this time, with only a minimum of coaxing, the stick grated home.

He rubbed his hands together and smiled at Wil, who looked vaguely uncomfortable and distinctly puzzled.

"Right," Ulbrax said, "Now comes the moment of truth!"

The key word which the demon had shared with him was no invocation in some long-dead mystical language, no tongue-twisting phrase laden with innate power, nothing that could be represented only by cryptic runes which dripped with eldritch energy. It was a simple, unimposing word.

"Arise!" Ulbrax declared, attempting to invest in those two mundane syllables all the drama that the occasion demanded.

He then stood back and waited, fascinated to discover what actually happened next.

Nor was he disappointed. The cluster of stones surrounding the spoke began to glow. Ulbrax ignored the sharp intake of breath from the lad beside him and concentrated on the steady transformation. The outline of individual rocks began to blur, as if the rocks themselves were somehow melting and flowing into each other. As the process continued, the affected area slowly took on a recognisable shape: that of a large person lying down, half wrapped around the keystone in what looked to be a foetal curl. Once this form solidified, the figure stirred, raising itself into a sitting position and then standing in one flowing, graceful movement.

Still the figure glowed, so brightly that Ulbrax would not have been surprised to see the grasses around the form char and wither or perhaps catch alight, but they seemed unaffected, so presumably the energy coming off the creature didn't involve a great deal of heat. Certainly

Ulbrax couldn't feel any against his face. In fact, if anything, the figure seemed to emanate cold.

"What... what is that thing?" stammered a voice from beside him.

"Our ally, Wil. Nothing to be afraid of."

In actual fact Ulbrax knew exactly what this was, but the knowledge would only panic the lad. Before them stood a Rust Warrior. The very last of its kind.

Time's healing qualities ensured that the Great War was barely thought about these days; the decade-long conflict which had seen Thaiburley tested and totter was the dread of generations past and had little relevance to the folk of today, for all that its scars could still be found here and there dotted around the landscape. Ulbrax had a natural curiosity about all things relating to death and destruction so had made a point of studying the war. He knew the conflict's effect had been profound. Thaiburley had all but withdrawn from the world as a result, becoming insular and far less concerned with what went on outside the city's walls. Before the war, her ambassadors were to be found throughout the continent and beyond, their influence on politics indelible. During the conflict itself her armies bestrode the land, pitching into titanic battle after battle against an enemy that very nearly matched her, but which, in the end, had been completely crushed and wholly eradicated. Thaiburley displayed a lack of mercy that left some observers stunned. In the aftermath of that ferocious and debilitating struggle, it was perhaps only to be expected that the city withdraw behind her formidable walls to lick her wounds and recuperate. But she had never truly ventured out again.

Both sides in that war had possessed terrible weapons and deployed fearsome troops: Thaiburley's Blade being pitted against the enemy's Rust Warriors – lethal and callous, engines of destruction said to be even less human than the Blade. Though formidable and greatly feared, the Rust Warriors had been outmatched and by war's end they had been utterly destroyed, stamped out to the very last.

Well, last but one it would seem.

Wil had taken a few steps back and raised a hand to shield his eyes, while even Ulbrax was forced to squint as he attempted to study the apparition. Nothing was clearly discernible beyond the shining nimbus, though he fancied something manlike lurked within.

Then the figure raised a gleaming hand, pointing towards Wil.

"Seth…?"

"Relax, Wil, our new ally is just making sure it knows you, so you'll be recognised as a friend in future."

As improvised lies went, that one sounded almost plausible.

Radiance shot from the outthrust hand, enveloping the cowering lad. Wil's mouth contorted, as if he were screaming, though no sound penetrated the engulfing cocoon of light. Then it wasn't just his mouth but rather his whole body which started to twist and shift: this was Wil viewed via a cunning fairground mirror. The next instant he seemed to come apart; not in a violent anarchic explosion, but rather in something close to slow motion, as if sliced into the thinnest sections which floated off in wafer-like slivers, hundreds, perhaps thousands of them. Almost as soon as they appeared, these shavings withered and darkened, many already crumpling and disintegrating as they drifted towards the ground. The light around the space where Wil had been standing died, but in the glow still emanating from the boy's nemesis, Ulbrax could see that these drifting flecks had acquired a dark, reddy-brown colouration, as if newly flaked from ancient iron.

"Ah, so that's why they call them Rust Warriors," he murmured.

The glow around the warrior started to fade, and Ulbrax was left facing a very human-looking figure, perhaps a head taller than him – tall for a man but not outlandishly so, certainly not enough to be called giant. He recognised the face, too. It was undeniably Wil's, though no one who knew the deceased lad could have mistaken this as the same person. The body was too large, too muscular, too imposing. Wil in a few years time had he performed physical labour every day during the interim, eaten well, and gained a bit of height along the way.

Such inconsistencies were irrelevant, however, since nobody who'd known the real Wil was likely to meet this impersonator and make comparisons. Ulbrax had no intention of returning to Crosston or the Four Spoke Inn; he was leaving Seth behind for good. His sole focus was on catching up with the King Slayer and the boy, and now that the Rust Warrior had replenished its energies courtesy of Wil's body, they could set about doing so.

The warrior's chameleon aspect didn't harm, either. It was going to be far easier travelling with a strapping lad at his side than it would have been with a faceless, glowing figure for company.

He addressed his new companion for the first time. "My name is Ulbrax. You will respond only to my voice, and will answer to the name Wil."

The tall figure nodded acknowledgment. Did Rust Warriors speak? He had no idea, but wasn't frankly bothered either way.

"Good. Come."

Ulbrax took one final look at the cosy glow of street lamps and unshuttered windows that marked Crosston, wondering briefly whether any there had noticed the great flaring of light on a nearby hillside. He could imagine the subject being remarked upon by some of the regulars at the Four Spoke Inn, with a shared frown and the odd stroke of stubbled chins, before they turned their attention to more pressing concerns such as the protracted dry spell in distant Angshé and the affect this was having on the price of soft fruit. A few days ago he'd have been there in the thick of it, discussing these weighty matters with the best of them, but life moves on. Ulbrax turned and strode away, the looming presence of the last Rust Warrior close on his heels.

ELEVEN

For the best part of three days after the body boys carted his mum's corpse away, he managed to keep hold of the home. On the third he lost it to a family – two boys older than him plus their mother and father.

Tom had never known his own father.

There were plenty of empty buildings scattered around the under-City but they were mostly falling down, dangerous, and in need of heavy investment in sweat and toil to make them habitable, which was why they were empty. His home was sound, so he knew it was only a matter of time before someone took it from him. Not that he went without a fight, but all that did was earn him a bruised ribcage and a smack around the face. They were too big, too strong, and too many. The knowledge that one of their boy's would have a peach of a black eye in the morning provided only minor consolation.

He was seven or eight years old – Mum never had been too good at keeping count.

He survived the first couple of days by scavenging scraps from the swill bins behind taverns, though little was thrown out in the City Below and pickings were meagre. At night he found an empty building and crawled into a dark corner of the only room which still had a bit of roofing in place, covering himself with a large sheet of rotting cardboard – a deconstructed, flattened-out box. He lay awake for hours, fearing that the bats or some other more formidable haunter of the dark would creep up on him while he slept and kill him without his ever knowing.

They didn't, so the following day he was still alive to contest with an obstinate spill dragon for a knob-end of stale bread and a bone which still had a few scraps of fatty, roasted meat clinging to it. The flecks of meat he devoured hungrily, and the bread wasn't too bad once it had been softened with a sprinkling of water.

Yet something, either the meat or stray saliva from the vindictive spill dragon, proved less digestible.

Within hours of the paltry meal he was struck by crippling stomach cramps. Remembering his mum's advice, he headed for the nearest temple of Thaiss, making it as far as the threshold before collapsing completely. The temple leant him a cot while they nursed him back to health, and he recovered quickly. With the benefit of hindsight, he realised the Thaistess was almost certainly a healer, but that possibility escaped him at the time. The boy was overcome with gratitude, not to mention a desperate need to belong somewhere. He determined to stay and serve at the temple, but they cast him out as soon as he was fit enough, the Thaistess explaining that the temple was not the right place for him. She was probably right and almost certainly meant well, though he failed to appreciate as much at the time. Her acolyte, on the other hand, was a spiteful cow who made his brief stay as uncomfortable as possible. He left the temple resenting their rejection and harbouring a bitter hatred of priestesses and religion which was to colour his attitude thereafter.

Returning to the life of a solo forager proved far from easy, and he was soon sliding towards starvation, ill heath and an early death, when he encountered a pair of cocksure nicks who seemed a great deal better off than he was. They proved to be members of a gang called the Blue Claw, and it turned out he was operating on what they assured him was their turf. After a tense moment which threatened to erupt into violence but somehow avoided doing so, with food again the cause of contention, he ended up going with them and was soon recruited into the gang; a move which almost certainly saved his life.

Tom blinked into wakefulness, sitting up and staring around, momentarily thrown by the absence of walls and the sense of space. "Wh... where am I?"

The face of a Thaistess loomed above him, smiling. "You're with friends Tom, and you're fine, though you were tossing and turning a bit in your sleep. Troubled dreams?"

He relaxed and sank back onto his sleeping mat as everything came flooding back. "In a sense. I was just remembering why I've always mistrusted Thaistesses."

"Oh." Mildra looked disconcerted, as if not entirely sure how to respond. "And do you, still?"

He grinned. "Not as much."

"Good."

He wasn't given much chance to lie around. The morning began with another training session at Dewar's insistence and to Tom's delight. He really looked forward to these lessons and had to concede that maybe Dewar wasn't all that bad after all.

Even so, as this third lesson started, he felt obliged to ask their self-appointed leader, "Not that I'm ungrateful or anything – I really appreciate this – but I can't help wondering why you're doing it."

Dewar stared at him in way that seemed to say "don't think for one moment it's because I like you", though what he actually said was, "Four days from Thaiburley, two days out of Crosston, and we're all still alive. I'd like to keep it that way if I can. Simple as that. Now, raise your blade and stiffen up that elbow! Your arm's flapping around like a piece of soggy cardboard."

Ulbrax sat on his horse and considered the ill-assorted trio before him. At his side, the Rust Warrior – whom no horse would carry – remained unmoving and unconcerned.

At least Ulbrax could appreciate the irony of the situation. He had gone to a lot of trouble to hire men much like this to kill the King Slayer and his party, who had doubtless passed through this area unhindered not long before, while here he was with three desperate men blocking his path to the front and three more behind. Men who required no hiring whatsoever.

"Where were you when I needed you?" he muttered.

"What wasat?"

"Oh, nothing," he assured the speaker – a particularly ugly specimen who looked capable of scaring most victims into submission with a single glower. So far, Ugly had been the only one to speak. Maybe his two companions couldn't – words being such troublesome things to formulate, after all.

Ugly grunted. Beside him stood a stick-thin shifty-eyed fellow who seemed incapable of standing still, forever twitching like a weasel on hot coals; that worthy sniggered.

"Now, we don't wanna hurt no one," Ugly assured him unconvincingly. "But me friend 'ere has a gammy leg and finds walking tough." He indicated the twitching weasel. "So if you just wanna get offa that horse o' yours and leave it with us, we'll let you be on yer way. Oh, and to show what considerate souls we are, we'll even take some o' the heavier stuff from yer: ye know, weapons, coin, any jewellery, that sort o' thing; just so's ye don't tire yerselves out with all the walking."

Weasel cackled at this, while the shoulders belonging to the big bear of a man on Ugly's other side – the thug holding the axe – shook in obvious appreciation.

Ulbrax held the reins casually in one hand and felt almost as unconcerned as he was attempting to appear. He leant forward a little and smiled. "I don't think so." He then turned to the figure beside him. "Wil, be a good lad and clear the road, would you?"

The Rust Warrior stepped up instantly. The big bear was closest and the first to react. He gave a snarl and raised his axe high, ready to cleave this impertinent man in two. He never got the chance. Wil's fist drove into the bear's stomach, travelling so far forward that it looked as if the warrior was somehow reaching inside the man to squeeze his intestines. The bear doubled up, eyes bulging and axe forgotten. Wil's left had then shot out, gripping the man's neck and twisting to produce an audible snap. That same hand caught the falling axe and, all in the one motion, swept it around to crush Ugly's skull, improving the man's looks no end as a good part of his face came away in a shower of blood and brains.

Ulbrax was having a struggle to control his horse, which was clearly spooked by the unfolding situation, so he missed the stroke that took Weasel's hand off at the wrist, alerted only by the man's agonised scream and the amount of blood pumping from the severed limb. He controlled the mount sufficiently to move it to one side of the trail where it wouldn't block the path of the ongoing mayhem, and looked back in time to see the Rust Warrior lift the injured man and fling him at the onrushing trio of brigands. Weasel hit sideways, catching one of the three with his legs, causing that one to stumble and pause and step to the side, while striking another full on, bringing him down in a tangle of limbs and blood and cursing.

The third charged on alone.

Ulbrax was delighted at this unlooked for opportunity to watch his Rust Warrior at work, and had to admit to being impressed by what he'd seen so far.

The brigand came straight in, either brave or stupid, face snarling beneath an unkempt beard, roaring defiance, and sword raised high with intent. Wil's axe met the man's blade with such force and speed that Ulbrax saw it only as a blur, while the resultant clash was loud enough to make him wince. He felt certain that one or both weapons must shatter beneath a blow like that, but in fact the brigand's sword simply went cartwheeling into the trees, steel evidently more resilient than the man's grip, however determined.

The Rust Warrior didn't pause, bringing the axe around in a sweeping arc which took his opponent in the side, crushing ribs and tearing through muscle and organs as the blade exited through the chest, dragging gore and blood in its wake. So much so that Ulbrax hastily urged his mount back a few steps for fear that some of the muck might reach him.

The man who'd been delayed by Weasel's flailing legs now faced the prospect of going one-on-one with the Rust Warrior. He clearly considered the odds carefully and didn't like what they totalled, because he took a few hesitant steps backward before turning around and running, dropping his sword in the process.

The warrior hefted up the heavy battle axe as if it were a feather-light trinket and flung it at the hastily retreating brigand's back. The axe flew like a bolt from a bow: true, straight and fast, smashing into the man before he had gone more than a dozen paces. Ulbrax couldn't have said which part of the weapon actually made contact first and didn't bother trying to work it out. The axe struck with enough force to shatter the runner, sending him tumbling to the ground with blood gouting from his mouth while limbs and body twisted at impossible angles.

The Rust Warrior strode over to where the final would-be robber was disentangling himself from the still-moaning form of Weasel. The warrior swatted away the man's hastily reclaimed sword, grabbed him by the throat and lifted him up, so that he dangled from one outthrust fist, toes almost scraping the ground.

As on the hillside the previous evening, the warrior started to glow; a radiance which spread along his arm to envelope the other man, whose body started to distort until it came apart in myriad dried-blood slivers. The glow faded and all that remained was a snowfall of rusty motes, while Wil's face was gone, to be replaced by an altogether more worldly-wise and menacing visage.

Ulbrax sighed, thinking that he'd probably stick with the name Wil, otherwise this could soon get very confusing. He'd been eager to put the Rust Warrior through its paces and had wondered how long before the thing would need to feed again and replenish its energies. Now both concerns were dealt with. All in all, a very rewarding encounter. Besides, he'd grown increasingly tired of having to look at Wil's fresh-faced innocence.

Almost as if acting on a whim or in response to some casual afterthought, the warrior trod down heavily on the back of the Weasel's neck, crushing vertebrae as he pressed him into the dirt. Following a convulsion, a strangled squawk and the single twitch of an eye, all sound and movement at ground level ceased.

Tom was amazed at how quickly his body had adjusted to the rigours of regular walking. Since that first day he'd found the going a lot easier and the aches and pains had grown progressively less, though how much of that was due to Mildra's ministrations he couldn't say. The Thaistess seemed to have recovered fully, and now spent more time on her feet than she did in the saddle, though she admitted to being glad that Beauty was there. He had a feeling she would have sat on the horse more often but chose to walk in order to keep him company; a kindness he was grateful for since, lessons aside, Dewar clearly considered Tom unworthy of anything as comradely as conversation.

On the outskirts of the first sizable town they'd encountered since Crosston, they stopped to chat with a family headed in the opposite direction, or at least Dewar did. Tom had already noted that their leader could be polite to the point of charming when he wanted something – information in this instance. It was only when you got to know the man better that the joy of his true personality shone through.

The father did all the talking. He had been striding beside a pair of oxen which pulled the family's covered wagon, and greeted them cheerily. His wife sat on the wagon itself and held the reins, while constantly trying to shoo their inquisitive daughter back inside as the girl kept scrambling forward to peek at the strangers. The wife's glare made it abundantly clear that she didn't trust them in the least, though Tom didn't feel singled out. He had a feeling this was her standard approach to all outsiders, and he wondered if she'd been like this even before the arrival of her daughter. Evidently her mistrust hadn't yet rubbed off on the girl in question, who could be no more than five or six and seemed determined to ignore the instructions of her over-protective mother, treating them all to a cheeky grin before being forced back out of sight again.

Tom had caught most of the exchange, but once the family moved on Dewar filled them in on what he'd learned in any case. "The town's called Sull, and we're going to have to take a ferry to cross a tributary river which feeds into the Thair here."

All of which sounded simple enough, but the reality of Sull itself proved to be anything but. Once they'd worked their way through a confusion of narrow streets and more people and barrows and carts and animals than they could possibly have anticipated, the party arrived at the ferry port, to be confronted by a broad and powerful river of mud-brown water, and a flat-decked boat. The water was flowing with daunting speed and the old boat – all that would be standing between them and the rushing torrent – looked frail and inadequate in comparison. Boarding had already begun, and they joined the short queue of people and occasional horses that were still waiting their turn. Beauty took some persuading, but eventually Dewar was able to lead her onboard. Tom's vote was with the horse, and had he been on his own he would undoubtedly have found an excuse not to step onto the deck; but with Dewar, Kohn and Mildra there beside him that was never going to be an option. The few seats were quickly taken, though the ferry was far from crowded, leaving the four of them to cluster around Beauty near the aft of the deck. Kohn drew a few stares and whispered comments but not many, suggesting that he wasn't the first Kayjele to pass this way.

Tom was momentarily distracted by Dewar's ongoing efforts to keep Beauty quiet. The man lavished more affection on that animal than Tom could imagine him ever sparing for a fellow human. As the ferry got under way, the former nick found himself staring at the water dashing beneath them, mesmerised by its power and insistent urgency, as it battered and frothed at the ferry's side. Reaching the far bank could not come quickly enough as far as he was concerned. Yet, so absorbed was he by the swirling patterns of water against the boat's hull that the abrupt jolt of their arrival took him completely by surprise, for all that it was an enormous relief.

They shuffled forward with the other passengers and Tom soon felt the luxury of solid land beneath his feet once more. Ahead of them stood a smattering of dwellings, but nothing to compare with the bustling town on the south side of the crossing. The houses clustered around the foot of a disconcertingly steep hill, and were soon left behind as the party climbed up to a point where they were able to look back at Sull, the ferry – which looked even frailer at this distance – and the merging of the two rivers. It was impossible not to be impressed by the power and sheer volume of water involved as the two powerful torrents clashed and eventually melded. The tributary they had just crossed was sufficiently large and impressive in its own right that Tom felt a moment of doubt and, as they left it behind and moved on, he felt compelled to ask, "How do we know we're following the right river?"

"Simple," Mildra told him with reassuring confidence. "I can sense the goddess in this one."

Had anyone else said that, Tom would have laughed; but this was Mildra, so he didn't.

Ulbrax felt sure his quarry would be sticking close to the Thair – the priestess would insist on that – which meant this was the only road they could take. And, unless they'd acquired horses somewhere along the way, they couldn't be too far ahead; but he really did need to know how far.

The covered wagon which now approached, pulled by a pair of plodding oxen, offered an opportunity to find out, as well as a means of testing a few other things. He stopped and waited for the wagon to draw closer. Beside him, Wil did the same. "Good day to you, Sir," he said, wearing his most disarming smile.

"Morning." The fellow holding the reins of the cart seemed friendly enough, but the sour-faced woman sitting beside him – presumably the poor brecker's wife – glared back with open suspicion.

"A lovely day to be travelling," Ulbrax said, casually patting the nearest of the two oxen, which had been pulled to a halt and now stood patiently swishing its tail. The Rust Warrior, for whom the wife had reserved particularly daggered glares, wisely stood some distance back from the animals. "Could you tell me, how far are we from Sull?" Ulbrax asked. Although he'd never visited the town he had lived in the area long enough to know the general lay of the land.

"Oh, no more'n a couple of hours ride, a bit more if yer walking," the man said, glancing at Wil.

"Excellent news!" Ulbrax's smile broadened. He then continued, with studied casualness. "We're hurrying to catch up with some friends and wondered if they might have passed you on the road. A party of four. You can't miss them – one's a Kayjele, then there's a man, a young woman and a lad."

"Friends, you say?"

Was that a hint of suspicion in the man's voice? Would they be forced to resort to threat and violence after all? No matter if so, but it seemed only fair to give politeness one more chance. "Yes, we were running late and missed a rendezvous, so are now desperately trying to catch them; you know how it is." Time to employ the smile again.

The man nodded, as if he'd done the same sort of thing himself before now. "Happens we did see a group like that just as we were leaving Sull, so you're a few hours behind, maybe more, maybe less, depending on the timing of the ferry."

There! Politeness did have its uses after all. "Much obliged. We'll bid you good journey and will be on our way, then. After all, we've a ferry to catch!"

"Hope you do, and that you catch up with your friends," the man said.

"Oh, we will, never fear," Ulbrax assured him as the man twitched the reins and yelled the team of oxen into lumbering motion.

Ulbrax was delighted with the exchange. This was the first time since being woken that the Rust Warrior had encountered people without killing someone. Welcome reassurance ahead of their venturing into a busy town such as Sull. He glanced across at his silent companion, who had no difficulty keeping pace with the horse's long stride. Now, unless Rust Warriors had some previously unsuspected inhibition against crossing open water, they couldn't fail, but one hurdle at a time.

TWELVE

Kat was surprised to discover how many people were willing to help. The Soul Thief's killing spree appeared to have stirred things up on the streets in a big way. Folk who lived near the wall and by the docks might still dismiss her as nothing more than a child's story, but those who dwelt nearer the Stain were fast accepting the Soul Thief as reality, particularly those who fell within the monster's likely prey group. The talented – all the minor practitioners who quietly went about their business and kept the creaking wheels of society in the under-City turning – were living in fear of their lives. Death was no stranger to anyone living in the City Below. Every street, every community, was accustomed to its cold, musty presence, pitching up when least expected like some long lost relative at a family gathering, never welcome but impossible to turn away. Yet what the Soul Thief was delivering went beyond mere death. There was something unclean and horrifying about the way she consumed the life force of her victims, an unnatural demise that was far worse than seeing a loved one carried away by illness or age or the simple rigours of life. The Soul Thief claimed as her own the essence of a person, the very part which was said to travel back along the Thair to reunite with the goddess Thaiss. For anyone with even a hint of faith, this was a fate too terrible to countenance.

So when Kat and the aged apothaker arrived at their doorstep and offered folk the opportunity to come out from behind the barricades and actually do something, many were only too willing. Not all, of course. Some simply shook their heads and set about building the barricades higher. Kat could hardly blame them for that. Nor did she intend to force people into helping as Charveve had demanded. She wasn't about to have that on her conscience if anything went wrong. Besides, with the apothaker's help she was recruiting plenty enough to the cause. In truth, she was a little surprised to discover just how many of these talents there were within a comparatively small area of the streets. It only emphasised how integral they were to the community.

One thing seemed increasingly obvious. This latest visit by the Soul Thief was exceptional. There had never been such a concentration of attacks before. The Soul Thief had been conducting these sporadic raids on the under-City's denizens for generations, but Kat had never heard of her killing in these numbers – so many that people couldn't help but notice and even the razzers felt obliged to investigate.

Kat had no idea why this particular visit should be so different, but she had every intention of making it even more so.

During the hours they spent together, systematically going from street to street, door to door, Kat developed a

growing respect for her companion, despite the residual
waft of foul odour that still clung to her following the self-
neglect of her grieving. There was a core of courage and
strength in the woman that belied her obvious frailties,
and, while Kat realised that her sense of loss included a
large chunk of self-interest, it was clearly more than that.
The apothaker had obviously cared deeply for her lost apprentice. There was also an indefinable air of dignity, of
class about the woman which prompted Kat to say, as
they headed home, satisfied with what they'd achieved,
"You're not originally from down here, are you?"

The woman paused and smiled. "No, not originally;
but I've been here for so long now that my life before
doesn't really matter anymore."

"Even so, when this is all over, maybe you could tell
me about it."

A faraway look came into the apothaker's eyes then,
as if she were remembering something precious, and her
features took on a tenderness and softness which rolled
away the years and hinted at lost beauty. "Yes," she said
at length, focussing on Kat once more, "I'd like that."

Kat had managed to snatch several hours' sleep the
previous night, for a change, which meant that once
she'd seen the apothaker safely home she still had plenty
of time and energy to burn up before globes out.

In theory, they were close enough to the Stain that the
Soul Thief could return there at the end of each night
and venture forth again each evening, but Kat didn't
think so. The nursery tale had it that the monster slunk
away into the derelict shadows of the streets to wait out
the day before returning to terrorise folk the following
night. The story had been pretty much spot on in every

other respect, and Kat's gut instinct told her it had this part right as well. Why waste precious hunting time going to and from the Stain at either end of the night when the killer could simply curl up in a disused building ready to stalk the streets again as soon as darkness fell?

If Kat could only find the creature's lair, she might be able to take it unawares during daylight and kill the monster while it slept. That sounded straightforward enough, like all good plans – apart from one minor detail: there were nearly as many derelict buildings in the under-City as there were fish in the Thair.

Fortunately, Kat knew exactly where the Soul Thief had killed over the past few nights, so concentrated her search accordingly. That still left a lot of streets and buildings to cover, but at least the task then seemed manageable. It would have been easier still had she recruited the Tattooed Men, or at least Rel and M'gruth, but they were still very much Charveve's tribe, and she wasn't entirely sure how far to trust them. Besides, in recent times she'd grown used to operating solo.

Where possible Kat took to the roofs, which she'd come to regard as her own personal highway during the years spent alone. The majority of buildings in the City Below were single storey and packed tightly together, which made the going easy. Many were also poorly built, and that added an element of hazard which kept Kat on her toes. One misplaced step and she could go tumbling down, taking the roof with her and maybe even landing in the lap of a startled resident within. It hadn't happened yet, but the risk was always there.

On this particular occasion, she used the roofways to get around but concentrated her search on the taller buildings. She reasoned that, were the Soul Thief hiding out at ground level, she might easily be discovered by scavengers – either human or reptilian. Disinherited street-nicks, opportunists, spill dragons, they all frequented the deserted slums. No, a taller building where access to upper storeys was made more difficult by crumbling stairways and collapsed infrastructure seemed the more likely. The number of such places that had gone to rack and ruin was limited, which narrowed things down still further.

The search took her from the solid brick delivery chute and corkscrew stairway leading to the City Above, once disputed by the Blood Herons and the Thunderheads, right up to the shadow of the grand conveyor, which was active at this hour – the chugging squeal of cogs and wheels as they conspired to push along the conveyor's endless rolling surface formed a discordant backdrop to her work.

During the course of the afternoon Kat found one recently dead body, a human skull, a pair of sleeping or drunk vagrants, somebody's stash of assorted valuables (most of which were undoubtedly stolen), a box of half-used candles and a battered brass lamp beside a pallet of filthy bed linen, two rusted knives, one decapitated clockwork toy soldier, a child's doll with a missing eye, and the shattered frame of a crossbow. In addition, she disturbed a rare night crow – the great black birds said to prey on the under-City's bat population – and stumbled on a naked thirty-something woman spreading her legs for a much younger man; either a lovers' tryst or a whore plying her trade. And, in a derelict tower attached to a long-disused building, she came across a heart beetle nest, which she gave a wide berth while inspecting the room from the far side due to her loathing of the flesh-eating bugs. Their glistening black carapaces and nipping mandibles made them the stuff of nightmare; hers, at least. Heart beetles were essentially scavengers, but they were notoriously unfussy creatures who would quite happily take a nip from living flesh given the chance.

In short, she found just about everything she might have expected to find in such surroundings, apart from any sign of the Soul Thief. Not a bitter blow in truth. She'd known from the outset that the chances of finding anything were slim, but that didn't stop her being disappointed.

Having covered every likely bolt-hole in the area defined by the Soul Thief's attacks she was forced to accept defeat, and was on her way back to the Tattooed Men when she saw something, or rather someone.

The view was good enough that she recognised him instantly, causing her to pause and lie down, clinging to the edge of the roof in order to get a better look. Tall, slender, the slicked-back hair: Brent. Nor was he alone. With him were two men, one she didn't recognise – an individual even more slender than Brent, and stoop-shouldered, as if his head was too heavy for the shoulder to fully support. The other she did know: one of the Fang, the man whose ribs she'd raked with her sword the previous day. What in the world could Brent want with a member of a street gang? There was something furtive about the way the trio hurried along, huddled close and talking in subdued tones, the stoop-shouldered man casting the odd anxious glance over his shoulder, as if keen not to be seen in such company.

The three of them were crossing an open square a little
ahead of Kat and she couldn't make out what they were
saying, just a murmur of voices. She didn't trust this
Brent, not in the slightest, and was having second
thoughts about their hasty alliance. Bringing down the
Soul Thief was too important a task to risk by involving
unknown elements. Despite the free meal and despite
her agreeing otherwise, she resolved not to tell Brent
about the trap being planned.

The man and his two friends were about to walk out
of sight. She almost went after them, but in truth she
was a little weary and a little despondent after the day's
fruitless search – not to any great degree, but enough
that she decided to take the path of least effort and let
them go. Whatever they were scheming she didn't care,
as long as it kept Brent occupied and out of her way.

This was a decision she would come to sorely regret;
one which would haunt her in the days that followed
and cause her to ask that most pointless and inwardly
corrosive of questions: What if...?

Tom felt that he was making real progress with Kohn.
He hadn't yet reached the point where he could understand the Kayjele as clearly as Mildra seemed to, but he
was beginning to get an ever clearer impression of the
emotions and general direction of whatever Kohn attempted to convey. Tom's desire to pursue this was
driven in no small part by his own insatiable curiosity,
his determination to learn as much about his abilities as
he could, but also by a persisting sense of shame at his
original reaction to the giant, whom he had since learnt
to both like and respect.

Whatever the motivation, he felt sure it was this developing' sensitivity that enabled him to detect the Kayjele's alarm at the same time as Mildra.

The land had risen sharply after they left Sull's ferry behind, the track following a serpentine course as it zigged and zagged its way against the gradient. They moved through a landscape of loose stone, low bracken, and small silver-barked trees whose spindly branches were adorned by feathery leaves. The way remained steep despite the path's meanderings, and the gravelly nature of the ground underfoot made the going less certain than it might have been. In the end they reached the top without mishap, and looked down to see the Thair some distance below. Sull and the tributary river were hidden from view by the trees, but the land ahead fell away gently – a sweep of hillside that brought their course more or less level with the river once more. This hill seemed to be almost an isolated ripple in the terrain; a bit of the land pulled back and ruffled up to make way for the tributary river.

They had begun the descent and were perhaps a third of the way down the gradual slope when Kohn became alarmed.

"Something's upsetting Kohn," Tom blurted out.

"He can sense danger," Mildra added. "A threat coming up from behind us."

They were still among the trees and although the track no longer followed the switchback pattern of their ascent, nor was it entirely straight, so they had only a limited view of their back trail. Tom noticed that Dewar already had the kairuken out and loaded, and he drew his sword a little self-consciously. This would be his first opportunity to put the lessons into practice and all of a sudden, with the sword held tightly in his hand and the prospect of using it in anger looming, they seemed far too few and far too incomplete.

Was that a horse approaching, the muffled, rhythmic thud of hooves? Sounded like it. He flexed his fingers while still clasping the sword, loosening and tightening his grip nervously, and took a step forward to stand between Mildra and whatever was approaching.

Then they came into view; two of them. One mounted, one on foot. The horse was hardly at an all-out gallop, but nor was it walking. Incredibly, the figure on foot kept pace. Tom had never seen human legs move so fast or arms pump so purposefully.

"Careful," Dewar said quietly, "the one on foot is a lot more than he seems."

Really? Tom would never have guessed.

The rider was hunched over his mount's neck, face partially obscured, yet there seemed something familiar about him. Then he sat straight and proceeded to rein the horse in. With a start, Tom recognised him: Seth Bryant!

Then he noticed the differences. Demeanour, expression, the whole set of body and face were at odds with the jovial landlord he remembered from the Four Spoke Inn. It was as if somebody else were wearing Seth's body. And when he spoke even the voice had changed, the words emerging with a clipped, nasal quality which reminded Tom a little of Dewar.

"Hello again, King Slayer." Seth looked directly at their leader. "I couldn't possibly let you leave without saying goodbye properly."

"So, you *are* one of the Twelve," Dewar said, as if this confirmed a suspicion.

"That I am, or rather was. Can't tell you what a pleasure it is to finally meet the man who betrayed us and destroyed my life."

"I didn't. It wasn't like that. The assassination was sanctioned."

"Do you honestly expect me to believe that?"

"No, not really," Dewar replied wearily, "but it doesn't alter the fact."

Seth nodded. "Agreed. And the fact is that you're about to die!"

At the final shouted word, the mounted man threw his right arm out in an arc. Tom instinctively jumped back, though the half dozen glistening slivers flew towards Dewar, not him. The assassin was already moving, leaping aside to land with rounded shoulder which enabled him to roll and spring to his feet immediately. Six needle-pointed darts thudded into the ground, none of them finding their mark. Seth urged his horse forward, driving it straight towards Dewar, who had managed to keep hold of his kairuken and was attempting to bring the weapon to bear. The assassin fired but the shot was a snatched one, the disc missing its intended target and slicing into the horse's neck in passing. The wound clearly startled the horse, which shied and turned its head sharply away from Dewar, almost unseating its rider in the process.

The large man who'd arrived with Seth started forward. Whoever it was, he was making a beeline for Tom, who raised his sword and adjusted his feet as Dewar had taught him. Nervous he might be, but his determination to defend Mildra steadied his hand and he drew strength from the recent lessons, casting doubts aside.

As on the night they were attacked in the clearing, Kohn stepped in, swinging a massive fist at the attacker. Tom watched the giant's blow connect, smashing into the man's head. A surge of relief coursed through him, only to turn to dismay an instant later as he saw how little effect Kohn's strike had. Tom had seen those hands pick up a small tree trunk and wield it as readily as a bat in some ball game, yet when struck in anger by such a fist the attacker barely flinched. His response, on the other hand, was far more decisive. Somehow, Tom had come to think of Kohn as invincible, an illusion that was shattered as he watched the Kayjele crumple beneath a dismissive swipe from the advancing figure.

Suddenly, Tom's own doubts came flooding back. If this unnerving figure was powerful enough to floor Kohn so easily, what chance did he stand? No point in using his ability to hide, the attacker knew exactly where he was. He glanced quickly around, hoping for salvation from somewhere, but Dewar was fully occupied with Seth, who continued to throw taunts at the assassin, though Tom couldn't spare the attention to catch exactly what was said.

The sinister attacker loomed large, almost upon him. Tom took a deep breath, prepared to make a thrust with his sword, and silently prayed for a miracle. It arrived in the form of Kohn. Somehow the Kayjele regained his feet and threw himself at the advancing figure. The giant's body slammed into the far smaller man, his muscular arms engulfing him. The attacker staggered under the impact but, against all reason, still didn't go down. The Kayjele grimaced and growled, his arms bulging with the effort to crush his opponent. Not a sound came

from the man held in that bear-like clinch, whose features remained unmoving while his eyes stared
relentlessly at Tom, sending a chill coursing down the
boy's spine. What *was* this thing?

As Tom watched, the giant's hold was broken, his
arm's forced apart by this stone-faced enemy. Finally the
thing's gaze deserted Tom to focus on Kohn, and its
whole body started to glow.

A golden radiance shone forth from the slighter figure,
slowly spreading along Kohn's arms from where the
thing gripped him until it enveloped the struggling Kayjele. Tom could no longer look at the attacker, the light
was too bright, but by squinting he could still make out
the form of Kohn, his face contorted in agony. Then that
form seemed to distort, stretching and bending as no living thing should.

At which point it silently disintegrated.

"No!" Tom realised he'd screamed the denial, as he
watched his friend die.

"Dear goddess," Mildra murmured from behind him.
"A Rust Warrior."

Had Tom not been terrified already, that would have
done it. The Rust Warriors were as feared and loathed as
the Blade. They were also supposed to have been wiped
out long ago. Yet here one was, standing before him as
big and bold as life itself.

Yes, Tom was afraid, but fear was just one of the emotions stirring within him. Anger and grief were there as
well. The glow around where Kohn had stood dissipated.
All that remained of the gentle giant was a flurry of rust-
brown flakes settling slowly to the ground like leaves
stirred by an autumn breeze. As he watched this, Tom's

fear was supplanted, withering away before the on-
slaught of those other feelings. The glow around the Rust
Warrior also faded and his form became clear again. Tom
heard Mildra gasp, realising at the same instant that the
monster's face had changed. As if to mock them, the Rust
Warrior had adopted the appearance of its latest victim.
It looked like Kohn.

Tom felt horrified, appalled. His stomach heaved and
he had to fight back the urge to heave up his last meal.
But beyond the revulsion, as he looked upon this abomination now wearing the face of their murdered friend,
he felt outraged.

Something within him snapped.

When Tom had felt his mind invaded by one of the
Dog Master's creatures during his trek across the under-
City he'd fought back, drawing on abilities he never
knew were there. When one of the hybrid creatures had
latched onto Kat, preparing to invade her mind and warp
her will, he'd used those same abilities to lash out and
destroy a whole swarm of them, and, later, with support
from the prime master and Jeradine crystal technology,
he had cleansed the entire under-City of those scuttling
mechanisms and their parasitic charges. On each occasions he'd paid with crippling headaches and exhaustion,
but this time he actively sought that coil of brooding
power within him, and there was no reluctance or internal conflict as he reached deep inside to draw it forth and
hurl it at the Rust Warrior with all his passion and will.

The result was spectacular.

This walking malevolent effigy of their murdered
friend stopped in its tracks and began to tremble violently. Eyes bulged in the closest thing to an expression

Tom had yet seen on whatever face the thing wore. The trembling ended as abruptly as it had begun, and then, without further warning, the Rust Warrior exploded.

Tom felt a great blast of heat and light wash over him. He was dazzled by the brightness and found himself blown backwards by the force, knocking into Mildra. They both went down.

As he sat up, desperately blinking stars from his eyes in an effort to see what had happened, he was amazed to discover no real injuries. He'd seen a boiler explode once and so knew about shrapnel, and had himself been hit by a shard when the sun globe came down, but there didn't seem to have been any this time; nor any real flames for that matter, despite the heat.

Tom climbed shakily to his feet, pausing to help Mildra up once he'd done so. From across the road Dewar stared back at him with obvious dismay. "I don't know what the breck you hit that Rust Warrior with, kid, nor where you've been hiding it, but good job – very good job. Don't suppose you got Bryant at the same time, did you?"

There was no sign of Seth or his horse. Tom shook his head. "No."

Dewar grunted. "Thought that would be too much to hope for; which means he'll be back, I suppose."

Tom didn't comment. He was staring at where the Rust Warrior had stood scant seconds before. A small black smear on the ground was all that marked the monster's passing. His second thought was *no headache!* He felt slightly disorientated, a little light-headed, but that was all.

Mildra also seemed to be examining the ground. She stooped and picked something up. Tom recognised it immediately as the dull orange-red gemstone Kohn had worn around his neck, the one the giant had shown him on the barge – their first step towards friendship. The strip of leather that supported it was gone, but the stone seemed undamaged.

"Kohn's heart stone," Mildra murmured. "Somehow it's survived whatever the Rust Warrior did to him."

"Heart stone?"

"Yes," she said, her gaze still fastened to the pendant. "Every Kayjele is given one at birth. They believe the stone forms a home for their essence, their spirit, everything that makes them who they are."

Tom found himself staring at the stone as intently as the Thaistess. It was now all they had to remember the gentle giant by. "What will you do with it?" Images of Kohn striding beside him on the road or sitting with him during their days on the barge chased each other through his mind.

"I'm not sure." She frowned thoughtfully. "I suppose I should try to get it back to his family, if I can. That's what he would have wanted." There was a quiver in her voice as she said this last, and Tom realised the Thaistess was close to tears.

"I... I wish I'd done something sooner," he said.

She put her arm around his shoulders. "Don't blame yourself, Tom!" This was spoken urgently, insistently. "You acted as soon as you could, and you saved us all from that awful thing."

All except for Kohn, he thought but didn't say. His gaze returned to Dewar, and he remembered then that Seth Bryant had seemed to recognise him. What was the name the former innkeeper called out? "King Slayer", that was it. What did that mean? What had Dewar done to earn such a name and the hatred which Seth so clearly displayed?

Ever the pragmatist, Dewar would miss Kohn principally for the Kayjele's strength and willingness to carry things. Their horse, which Mildra had named Beauty, must have bolted during the encounter, taking most of their provisions with her. Fortunately, Kohn had still been carrying some and the giant had possessed enough good sense to put his bundle down before attacking the Rust Warrior, which meant they each still had a change of clothes at least. The assassin always kept coins and any valuables about his person, a habit he had been grateful of more than once in his life.

While his two surviving companions seemed incapacitated by grief over their fallen comrade, he set about dividing their remaining possessions into three bundles. Might be an idea to trust the two of them with a little money as well, he decided, just in case they became separated at some point.

Despite his outward calm, Dewar was more shaken by this latest incident than he cared to admit. In many ways Indryl, fabled capital of the Misted Isles, seemed a lifetime ago, yet some details remained as fresh in his mind as if they were but recent yesterdays. He'd always known the surviving member of the Twelve were out there somewhere, keeping their heads down while building new lives for themselves under assumed identities, and he'd always known they would never forget.

Of course, he had no means of knowing how one of them came to be running the Four Spoke Inn in Crosston, but given their shared former profession, he could make a shrewd guess.

Assassination had been an accepted mechanism of government in the Misted Isles for centuries – part of the political order. Killings were carried out by the Twelve and overseen by the First. It had been an elegant, effective system, with each assassin working independently, rarely if ever meeting or even knowing who his fellows might be. They weren't public faces, weren't known to anyone apart from the First. The Twelve were self-policing, and would hunt down relentlessly any outsider who committed a murder and tried to pass it off as their work, or, indeed, one of their own who made a hit that had not been officially sanctioned. The system worked well, until Dewar was assigned the unthinkable. He had been tasked with killing the king.

In all his years of service he had never hesitated, never questioned a sanction no matter how prominent the target might have been nor, conversely, how apparently insignificant. But he paused to query this one. Regicide seemed a little extreme, even for the Twelve. However, the sanction was immediately confirmed, which meant that saying no and staying alive became mutually exclusive options.

They called him King Slayer; the irony obvious and fully intended. Because, for the first time in an otherwise exemplary career, he failed. It could have happened at any time: blind luck turning against him. The king leant forward at the wrong moment; the poisoned dart that would have killed him in seconds missing by a fraction and sailing past to bring an abrupt end to the life of a royal aide. There was no opportunity for a second attempt. Bodyguards surrounded his highness in an instant and Dewar made good his escape, avoiding capture by the skin of his teeth.

It took him years to make sense of what came after. The First disowned him, acknowledging that the attempt had been made by one of the Twelve but denying that the hit was officially sanctioned. In a fit of rage, the King declared all the Twelve outlaw, to be hunted down and tried for treason. Only the First was exempt. The rest of the order were forced to flee for their lives, and it was common knowledge that not all made it. Two were captured and very publicly hung, drawn and quartered, while at least three more were said to have been killed while trying to escape.

A political mechanism which had been in place for centuries was torn apart at a stroke, and he had been the unwitting instrument of its destruction. Had that been the plan all along? Was this a deliberate move to strengthen the royal hand by removing the Twelve, long seen as a counterbalance to imperial autocracy? But that made no sense. He'd come within a hairsbreadth of actually killing the king. No, this smacked more of desperation, of pragmatism by the First, who sacrificed the Twelve to save his own skin, and of opportunism by the king, who seized upon the incident as an ideal excuse to destroy the Twelve's power base once and for all.

Dewar didn't doubt that he'd been the pawn in some dark political machinations, but felt increasingly certain that unfolding events had skewed the outcome into a completely new form. The king and the First had become allies by circumstance, not by design, and Dewar drew some small satisfaction from knowing how uneasy an alliance that must be. Did either of them sleep well at night?

None of which altered the fact that he was the scapegoat, a figure of hate and the prime target for both a powerful national state and its agents, and also the surviving members of an exiled assassin caste. King Slayer they dubbed him; partly in cruel jest and partly because making the attempt made him just as guilty as succeeding would have done.

The only place he could ever imagine being safe again was within the walls of Thaiburley; the towering, dense hub of the human world.

Dewar was neither proud nor ashamed of his past. Regrets were pointless, nostalgia a luxury he'd never allowed himself. His past was simply there, a tapestry of events forever unfurling behind him as he progressed through life. People might occasionally see a part of that constantly evolving picture but the whole was his and his alone. Everybody had one, even someone as young as Tom or as sheltered as a Thaistess, but their histories were of no more interest to him than his was any business of theirs. So he said nothing to expand on comments already overheard and made no effort to satisfy the curiosity evident in the glances coming his way, particularly from Tom. Let them wonder. His past was his own.

THIRTEEN

The prime master's sense of foreboding grew more pronounced with each passing day – an irritation that wouldn't be soothed, an itch that refused to go away.

The incidents of bone flu had grown more frequent until it had become impossible to keep a lid on the situation. There were new cases reported among the arkademics each day, outbreaks occurring in rapid succession, and he had felt compelled to share what little he knew about the disease with the other members of the council. The prime master was impressed and more than a little proud of how calmly his colleagues took the news. These really were a fine lot of people, and their most extreme reaction was to censure him for not having shared the burden earlier. In truth, it made him a little ashamed at ever having doubted their character.

While he was now completely open with his fellows on the Council of Masters, he chose to be a little less candid when it came to the assembly, whom he had addressed on the subject of bone flu that very morning. There were considerably more in Thaiburley's second tier of government than the mere dozen of the Council, and while the prime master knew for a fact that the assembly boasted many dedicated and highly competent men and women, inevitably in such a comparatively large set of people characteristics such as integrity and courage varied. A vessel was only ever as strong as its weakest point, and he couldn't risk word of the darker implications of bone flu leaking out and causing panic across the city.

So he stood in front of the assembled members and smiled, projecting confidence and implying a far greater level of control over the situation than actually existed.

He explained that this was a new disease, told them that the causes and vector were as yet uncertain but that the medics were giving the problem their undivided attention and that a cure would soon be found. He stood there and blithely described the symptoms, advising anyone who experienced a persistent tingling in the arm, followed by a sense of coldness in the limb should seek the advice of a medic, just to play safe.

He didn't state that such tingling might have nothing to do with resting on the limb for too long but could instead be an indication of restricted blood flow for far more sinister reasons, a sign that changes were occurring. He didn't need to. They'd heard the stories. He wasn't there to deny the reports, but merely to make them seem more mundane and less frightening,

It was one of the most polished and accomplished performances of his life. As he spoke he could feel the tension in the assembly hall dissipate and watched as people visibly relaxed. He left the room surrounded by smiles and applause, whereas he had entered amidst furrowed brows and frowns.

It wouldn't last, this optimistic mood. All he had done was buy some time, but that was as much as he could do for now and time was what they needed most; apart, perhaps, from a miracle or two.

As the prime master walked back through the airy corridors of the Residences, flanked by half a dozen council guards in their ceremonial white and purple capes, his thoughts turned to Tom and his companions. Had it been a mistake to send the boy beyond the city? Could his formidable talents have been turned against the bone flu if he were still here? Perhaps; yet the gut feeling persisted that Tom's mission was vital to the long term future of the city, and experience had taught the prime master to trust such feelings.

He and his colleagues would have to find their own way of dealing with the disease.

The past couple of days had seen the prime master unburden himself to varying degrees, to both the Council and the assembly, but there was one thing he had yet to discuss with anybody, something he wouldn't disclose until absolutely the last minute: namely the tingling in his own arm, which had started that very morning.

The truth was that the prime master was scared; more scared than he had ever been in his long and eventful life. In the past he had triumphed in seemingly impossible situations, more than once when the odds were stacked precariously against him, but each time he'd been in with a fighting chance, whereas this was an enemy he had no idea how to fight.

The inn looked to have seen better days; in fact, the whole town did. There was a sense of tired resignation in the air, as if whatever reasons people may once have had to settle here were now long gone. The visitor scowled, wondering whether anything worthwhile could truly be found in such a place.

After a moment's hesitation the man pushed the door open and stepped inside. Ulbrax knew a bit about taverns, enough to know immediately that he didn't much like this one. It was the sort where everything stops when someone new enters; or at least it did when he came in – music, conversation, even the motes of dust in the air seemed to pause in their aimless flight to take stock of this stranger.

He was reminded of the moment the demon first stepped into the taproom at the Four Spoke Inn, but couldn't believe he cut anywhere near as impressive a figure.

He strode up to the bar, wearing his most engaging smile – an expression salvaged from the Seth days. After ordering a drink and ensuring that at least some of the conversation his entrance so effectively curtailed had sprung back to life, he said to the barman, "I'm looking for a man called Morca."

The barman stared at him but said nothing.

"Do you know him?"

Sill no response. If the suggestion to come here had originated from any other source, he might have thought this was a joke at his expense, but demons weren't noted for their sense of humour. He perched on a stool and supped his ale, conscious of still being the centre of more attention than he cared to be. He decided to wait only as long as it took to finish his drink. If this stony silence and complete lack of response to his query continued until then, he'd leave and seek help in more welcoming surroundings.

With perhaps two good quaffs remaining, a shadow fell over him. He looked up to find the sour-faced barman standing in front of him once more. "Follow me." So the man could speak.

Ulbrax slipped from his stool and did as instructed, heading down a narrow corridor that led off the taproom. The barman opened the door at the far end to reveal a darkened room and beckoned him to enter. "Wait in here."

Half expecting what might follow, Ulbrax stepped inside, to be suddenly grabbed from behind and held, feeling the cold kiss of steel at his throat and an iron-hard physique pressed against his back. "Don't move!" a voice hissed in his ear. He smelt garlic and something sweet on the man's breath while the stubble of whiskers rubbed against his ear tip. "If you so much as twitch a muscle, you're dead. Understood?"

"Understood," Ulbrax replied, determining to do as instructed even though his right arm was trapped a little awkwardly behind him.

"You were asking after a man named Morca."

"Yes."

"Who are you?"

"I'm the man who's currently holding a knife pointed at your balls," he replied, and did risk moving then, just enough to twitch the tip of the weapon in question against his captor's genitals.

"Hah!" The blade at his throat vanished and he found himself pushed forward, staggering several paces into the room before he could regain his balance and swivel around, just as a lamp blazed into life. Standing before him was a great bear of a man, arms crossed and the knife that had so recently been pressed against Ulbrax's jugular held casually in one hand. The man's face was stretched into a broad grin, though that was far from the most noticeable feature, because his face was also creased by a more permanent mark, a livid scar which began above his left eyebrow and continued down the cheek to disappear beneath thick brown stubble which almost constituted a beard. The scar was clearly the legacy of a slashing wound from a sword or perhaps a knife. By the look of it, he'd been lucky not to lose an eye.

"You've got nerve, I'll grant you that much," the man said, sounding more amused than angry.

Ulbrax had no intention of relaxing just because the stranger had a winning smile; he had little doubt that before him stood a dangerous man. "Morca, I take it," he said.

"Perhaps, but you still haven't told me your name."

Some cultures believed that herein rested a form of power, that knowing a person's true name gave you access to their soul. A load of hogwash as far as he was concerned, so he had little hesitation in saying, "Ulbrax."

The man nodded, as if this was the response he'd expected. "And I'm told you sometimes use a different name."

"Seth, Seth Bryant" though admitting as much felt odd now, even after so short a time.

"Good enough." The bear uncrossed his arms, half-spun the knife hilt in his hand and slammed it into a sheath at his belt. "I'm Morca. Understand there's folk need killing. If so, I'm your man."

Ulbrax slipped his own blade away but remained alert. "That's what I heard."

"From a mutual golden-haired friend, no doubt. And did this winged fellow happen to say anything else?"

"Only that you could mobilise a party of suitably vicious bastards in short order."

Morca nodded. "True enough. And who is it we'll be looking to kill?"

"A small party: man, woman and boy."

"A family, you mean."

"No, unrelated."

The big man shrugged. "Same difference. And do they all want killing?"

Ulbrax wondered whether this Morca simply enjoyed slipping the word "kill" into every other sentence or whether he had perhaps accepted a wager to do so. "The boy and the man. Do with the woman what you will – she's not unpleasing on the eye – but the man's mine. I claim the privilege of ending his worthless life and will take apart anyone who denies me that pleasure, one bone at a time."

"We'll bear that in mind. Now, where will we find these three unfortunates?"

"By my reckoning, they should have reached the edge of the Jeeraiy about now."

Morca gave a brief bark of laughter. "The Jeeraiy? Are you mad? Have you any idea how big that brecking place is?"

"Some, yes."

"And it's not just the size. The Jeeraiy is a mess of waterways and land spits and bogs and floating plant rafts, of shallow lakes and quagmires... Finding anyone in an area that vast would be tricky enough even if everything happened to stay where it is, but it doesn't! The geography constantly shifts with changing water levels and the movement of floating islands. There are no maps, because maps are pointless. You could send an army in there and still not stumble across who you're looking for!"

Ulbrax kinked an eyebrow. "I don't recall any mention of this being easy."

"I don't need easy, but by the same token I could do without impossible!"

"They're following the Thair going into the Jeeraiy and they'll be trying to do the same on the way out. I imagine if you travel along a straight line between where the river enters and leaves, you'll find them readily enough."

Morca shook his head, as if in exasperation. "You don't get it, do you? There are no straight lines, not in the Jeeraiy. It would take blind luck for us to find them, and there are more ways to die in that place than you could possibly imagine. I'm not about to waste my time by sending men blundering around in there with the odds stacked so heavily against us."

Ulbrax reached calmly to his belt and produced a knife, not in any threatening way but holding it out as if it were a gift. "Perhaps this might help."

"What is it?"

"A throwing knife. It belongs to the man, Dewar. Do you know of any decent diviners around here?"

Morca considered the knife. "You're sure it's his?"

"Positive."

The big man smiled. "Well, why didn't you say so before? We might just be in business. Even with this and a diviner's guidance, I'll have to hire more men – people who are used to the Jeeraiy."

Ulbrax shrugged. "Then do so."

Morca held out his hand. "The knife?"

"Of course." Ulbrax handed the knife across with a surprising sense of reluctance: this was the weapon he'd intended to kill the King Slayer with, but no mind – any blade would do.

"Wait for me back in the bar," the other man said, heading towards the door. "This shouldn't take too long."

"I'll be there," Ulbrax assured him. "And, Morca... don't fail me."

He paused on the threshold and looked back. "Oh, I won't." He grinned. "Your three friends are already dead. They just don't know it yet."

"This can only be the Jeeraiy," Dewar murmured, almost to himself.

"You've been here before?" Tom asked.

"No, but I've heard of it. The soil in the Jeeraiy is said to be the most fertile and productive in the whole continent."

"I can well believe that," Tom said, "at least to judge by the size of the grass they grow around here." Before them stretched a vista of tall, yellowish grasses that grew taller than even Dewar's head. Tom glanced at their leader. Of the three of them, he was the only one who had not been born in Thaiburley, the only one with any previous experience of the outside world. Not for the first time, Tom wondered about the man's past: who he had been, where he was from, and why he had chosen to settle in the City of Dreams.

They moved forward, following a path that had been forced through the grasses, where a swathe of great stalks were flattened and broken, leaving a way broad enough for them to tread comfortably in single file.

"Keep your ears open," Dewar cautioned as he led the

way. "This path is freshly made, and whatever's responsible can't be too far away."

Tom felt a sudden jolt of alarm. He'd assumed this was
a man-made track they were walking; it hadn't occurred
to him that an animal might have created it. He tried to
picture the undoubtedly huge and powerful beast that
must have been responsible for trampling such a wide
course through these tough grasses, and decided that on
reflection he'd rather not.

Tom was startled once as they walked through this forest of grass when they disturbed a long-legged bird which
took to the air voicing strident alarm, and he was troubled more frequently by buzzing, nibbling insects, but
nothing larger emerged to threaten them.

The grasses ended abruptly. One moment Tom was
plodding forward between towering stalks, the next they
had fallen away. It was as if the final veil of grasses were
a curtain, swept aside dramatically to reveal a stage. And
what a stage. The three of them stood for silent seconds
and simply stared at the panorama that had opened before them. A vast plain of water stretched away on every
side, interspersed with lumps and mounds and tufts of
land and grasses. Scythe-winged birds sailed lazily over
the water, mouths gaping as they presumably fed on the
abundant insects, and waterfowl bedecked the surface
like multi-coloured jewels. It was now late in the day, and
the sun sat bloated and orange a little above the water-
line, casting the scene in oddly subdued pastel light,
lending everything a magical, surreal edge. Even the birds
seemed to fly in slow motion.

This landscape was undeniably beautiful, but Tom was
puzzled. "What happened to the river?" he wanted to know.

"This *is* the river, Tom," Mildra said.

"These marshlands, this vast plateau of grassy swamps with its lagoons and islands and headlands, is what results when the great torrents that form the Thair pour out from the mountains and hit flatter land," Dewar explained. "The waters slow and spread out to become what we see here."

"And we're supposed to cross this how, exactly?" Tom wondered.

"We get help," Dewar said, nodding towards a cluster of crude wooden buildings that huddled on an apparently solid piece of land to their left. The buildings looked to be built on short stilts. "Don't be fooled into underestimating these people based on their homes," Dewar warned. "Wood will be far easier to come by in the Jeeraiy than stone. What you're seeing here is the product of expediency, not necessarily simplicity."

A great snorting noise drew Tom's attention back to the water, and he saw a large mud-grey head emerge, nostrils flaring and eyes staring at him. The face reminded Tom a little of a horse's, but stretched sideways so that it was broader and flatter. He wondered whether this was the animal responsible for the path they'd followed – it certainly looked to be large enough.

Somebody hailed them as they approached the village; a dark-skinned fisherman, standing upright in his boat and gathering in his nets. Seconds later a gaggle of half a dozen children came bursting from among the buildings to greet them. They didn't come to beg or pester, just to say hello. Mildra was enchanted, crouching down to gather in her arms the first girl to reach them, and even Dewar's frown seemed a little less sour than usual.

"Careful with that one," a matronly woman said as she came towards them in the children's wake. "She bites."

"No, I don't!" the girl in Mildra's arms asserted, and promptly stuck her tongue out.

"I'm Gayla," the woman continued, "headwoman of the village. Please be welcome to our homes and our hearths." Her face bore such an open, innocent expression that Tom couldn't help but grin in response to the smile the woman presented; a smile which broadened as her gaze fell on Mildra. "The goddess has touched you, child. You are truly blessed."

"I suspect I'm not the only one," Mildra said in return. "Thank you for your welcome. We won't trouble you for long but would be grateful of roofs over our heads for this one night."

"Of course. And food?"

"That would also be very much appreciated."

Dewar had appointed himself leader of their little group from the very first, and Tom was intrigued to see how he'd react to Mildra taking the initiative here, but if he resented the Thaistess's initiative he managed not to show it.

Gayla's promise of food proved to be an understatement. The villagers welcomed them with open arms and insisted on preparing a feast in their honour. Two plump fish, each as long as a man's arm, were slit open, rubbed with oil and stuffed with herbs before being wrapped in broad leaves then baked by burying them beneath hot coals; smaller fish were scored, seasoned and griddled; a large pot of a piquant soup – made from shellfish and vegetables that Tom could never have attempted to identify – was cooked over a fire pit, a small deer was spitted and slowly roasted, while balls of elastic dough were deftly kneaded and slapped onto hot plates above the fire pit to produce wonderfully fluffy flatbreads. Everything was accompanied by a salad of watercress and aromatic, flat-leaved herbs.

Tom bit into a piece of the bread, which seemed infused with a rich smokiness from the fire and was delicious, especially once he'd folded it around a chunk of freshly-carved venison.

The whole village had turned out, evidently determined to treat the party's arrival as cause for celebration. The more Tom saw of these happy, welcoming folk, the more convinced he became that they needed little excuse to stop whatever they were doing and hold a party.

As if to confirm this, Gayla said to him at one point as they sat in a contented circle around the glowing embers of a fire, "The goddess has been good to us. We have wonderful weather, our homes sit beside waters that teem with fish and attract deer and animals to drink. Every year the waters swell and cover our land, depositing fresh, rich soil which they have brought to us from the mountains so that when they withdraw again our crops grow good and strong in the sun." She shrugged. "Life is to be celebrated, and the arrival of pilgrims such as you three grants us yet another reason to do so."

The gentle light from the fire brought out in the headwoman's features a grace and softness that had only been hinted at in the full glare of day. Tom had no idea how old she was, but from things she had said and the weight of knowledge her words often carried, he guessed her to be on the far side of middle age, yet you would never have known as much to look at her. Flawless skin, unmarked by wrinkle or blemish, and she seemed to glow with an inner beauty that went far deeper than mere physical appearance. His gaze slid from Gayla to Mildra, who sat on the headwoman's other side, and the breath caught in his throat. She looked stunning. Her freshly washed hair was pulled back within a headscarf similar to Gayla's, revealing more of her face, which seemed to shine in the gold-red light of the fire, matching Gayla and more.

Tom looked away quickly, not wanting her to catch him staring, only to find Gayla watching him with a knowing twinkle in her eyes and a smile tugging at the corners of her mouth.

He was grateful then of the fire's subdued light; hopefully no one could see him blush.

FOURTEEN

Dewar was finding it hard to accept that a community like this could still exist anywhere in the world. Reconciling the complete openness, naivety, and plain niceness of Gayla and her folk with everything else he'd encountered during his life to date was proving something of a challenge. These people seemed too good to be true and he couldn't escape the thought that by rights they should have been conquered and ground into the dust centuries ago, their joy and optimism clawed down and suffocated in the drudgery and misery that the rest of the human race routinely had to contend with. Yet here they were, laughing, fishing, growing crops, basking in the sun, and laughing again, just for good measure. Mighty armies had swept across the continent, conquering, raping and pillaging, thousands upon thousands had perished in wars and plague, and all the while these gentle folk had gone about their lives untouched, oblivious to events that shook the very foundations of civilisation. Incredible. Maybe there was a goddess after all.

Perhaps he shouldn't have been so surprised; after all, the Jeeraiy seemed to exist outside of the normal rules. Dewar had always prided himself on being pragmatic, on dealing with reality as the world presented it rather than as he might have wished it to be. Yet this place had found a way of reaching under his skin. Everything here moved to its own rhythm and pace, as if time itself paused in the Jeeraiy to take a breather before deciding to move on, as slow and loose as the people who dwelt here. Dewar could feel the easing of tension, as the drive and urgency seeped from his body, the inclination to relax settling in as ready replacement. Which was precisely why they had to leave here as soon as possible. This place was dangerous, in a seductively innocent way. If they were to hang around much longer the prospect of staying, just for another day or two, might become too tempting to resist.

The others weren't up yet, but he decided to wait a little longer before rousing them. The sun had barely risen and it seemed harsh to wake them this early after the previous night's merriment, which had lingered long into the hours of darkness. Besides, he was rather enjoying the absence of their company and intended to make the most of it.

The assassin sat with his back against the hull of a fishing boat, doing nothing for once, simply soaking up what was happening around him: the essence of the Jeeraiy. Despite the early hour, some of the village's fishermen were already out. He watched as one bronze-skinned youth – naked above the waist – stood tall in his boat, balancing with apparent ease as he threw out his right arm in a wide arc and cast his net. It broke the surface in multiple tiny splashes, like a brief outburst of rain. Nearby, sickle-winged birds, their snow-white plumage catching the sun to glisten like new fallen snow, dive-bombed the water, bobbing back to the surface moments later, some with wriggling fish clutched in their bills, others with only a disdainful ruffle of their feathers as if to say that they hadn't really been going after a fish in any case. Movement caught his eye, and he looked across to see a large grey-green mottled spill dragon, or something closely related, emerge from a bank of tall reeds to his left and slide into the water, barely making a ripple.

Gayla walked over to sit beside him. Normally, he might have bristled at such assumed companionship, but here it didn't seem to matter.

"You're up early," he commented.

"Could say the same to you," she replied.

"I didn't really drink that much last night."

"Yes, I noticed you were holding back, not totally involving yourself in things. My excuse is that I'm used to it." And she smiled.

"Experience has taught me the value of a clear head, even when you least expect to need one; especially when you don't."

She nodded. "Sensible, very sensible. It also gives me the perfect opportunity to raise something with you. For the sake of everyone, I think you and your friends should be on your way sooner rather than later."

He stared at her in, surprise. This seemed totally at odds with the warm and welcoming character she'd displayed previously.

"Under normal circumstances you'd be welcome here as long as you please, but there's trouble coming," the woman continued. "Don't know what or when exactly, but it's close."

Dewar snorted. "Is this some message from your goddess? Sounds a bit vague if so, don't you think?"

"You may mock, but consider this: if I'm right, then you avoid potential danger by leaving, and if I'm wrong, you're on your way again, which is what you've been itching to do since you first arrived."

He smiled. "You might have a point there."

"You know I do."

"My impatience is not a reflection on your hospitality…"

"Oh, I realise that. But you have a job to do, and then of course there's always the fear that if you stayed too long you might actually get to like it here." She said the last with a twinkle in her eye.

The old woman was perceptive, no question. She was also right about the wisdom in not taking risks. With a word of farewell he stood up, intending to wake Tom and Mildra.

Gayla hadn't moved, but remained gazing out at the water, watching the fishermen. "Oh, they're already up," she told him without looking round. "I sent word before coming to see you."

Even as she spoke, Tom appeared, emerging from the hut the three of them had shared for the night. He paused in the doorway for a second, perhaps to savour the morning and the Jeeraiy, then waved to Dewar and came towards him. Normally, this was the point where the assassin would insist on another sword lesson, but frankly he was growing bored of them, and at least the boy now knew enough to put up some sort of defence. It wouldn't do any harm to give his sword arm a rest for one day, particularly if time was as pressing as the headwoman suggested.

"Breakfast should be ready by now," Gayla said, grunting with the effort of standing up. She was looking towards the embers of the large fire pit, where a woman squatted, stirring the contents of a big black saucepan.

"We can eat on the move," Dewar told her.

She raised her eyebrows, as if the very thought of sending guests on their way without feeding them was unthinkable, never mind the danger, but she nodded and said, "As you wish." Gayla then cupped a hand to her mouth and shouted across the water to the fishermen, who acknowledged and, as one, started to haul in their nets.

"What's going on?" a bleary-eyed Tom asked as he joined them.

"We're leaving," Dewar supplied.

"What?"

"Already?" Mildra asked, coming up behind Tom. She looked a lot more awake than the boy.

"Yes." He wasn't in the mood to explain himself.

Looking around, Dewar noted that it wasn't just the Thaistess and the boy but the whole village that seemed to be stirring. He didn't know whether word of their imminent departure had spread, or getting up this early was simply part of the normal routine around here.

"Gayla's advice," he added charitably, perhaps influenced by the bright chatter and sunny smiles that now surrounded him. "She senses trouble coming."

Villagers were approaching the woman by the fire pit, not in a crowd or a queue, but simply drifting over in ones and twos to accept a generous bowl of what looked to be soup thickened with rice. The squatting woman shared a few words or a joke with each, as she steadily ladled the broth into waiting bowls. No fuss, no apparent system, but there was always somebody there collecting breakfast, and before long almost everyone seemed to have a bowl of steaming soup in hand. Dewar couldn't recall ever witnessing a more impressive and understated demonstration of community in harmony.

The fishermen were starting to arrive – those who had been closest – and were pulling their boats ashore. No grumbles or complaints about being called back when they'd only just gone out, no fuss at all. They simply landed whatever fish had already been caught and got on with things.

Gayla waved to one of the fishermen before turning back to the three travellers. "Ullel here will take you in his boat, clear across the Jeeraiy if necessary."

"That's very kind, thank you," Mildra said, smiling at the fisherman, who smiled back. He looked to be older than any of them, including Dewar, but as fit and healthy as all his people were.

"He knows the Jeeraiy better than anyone," Gayla continued, "her moods and rhythms flow through his veins. Ullel will see you safe."

Villagers were beginning to come over now to say their goodbyes; people they had only met the previous day but who were already considered friends following the previous night's revelries. There were hugs for Mildra and Tom – the boy looking embarrassed as a young woman embraced him and even more uncomfortable when the man beside her did the same – though none for Dewar, which suited him just fine.

More welcome were the leaf-wrapped food parcels and sealed drinking flasks which several insisted on pressing into their hands.

It seemed the whole village had turned out to see them off. Mildra and Tom boarded the indicated boat, one of the largest in the small fleet, and took their seats. Dewar was about to do the same when an eerie noise floated across the watery plain. A horn, sounding like the forlorn baying of some bereft beast.

The villagers froze, and in an instant everything changed. Where there had been smiles there were now looks of concern, while relaxed idleness was supplanted by bustle and movement. Not panic, Dewar doubted these people were ever capable of that, but there was definite purpose in the way the crowd of well-wishers dispersed.

He looked at Gayla. "Raiders," the headwoman said. "You must go, quickly."

The fishermen were already working with quiet efficiency, tossing aside for the moment fish and nets not already dealt with and preparing their boats to take people. The first of whom – scampering children who came racing up to them, all gangly limbs and laughter – were already arriving. They thought this a game, Dewar realised grimly, already picturing how the laughter might turn to tears and screams as these same children were trampled beneath hooves or cut down by blades and arrows if they failed to reach safety.

All around him boats were being pushed back into the water. He watched mothers emerge from huts, babes clutched in their arms, elders at their side, all hurrying towards the sanctuary of the fishing fleet. Others – those men not manning boats – were loping towards the western edge of the village bearing weapons. He saw long knives, spears and bows.

"Please, leave!" Gayla demanded.

She was right. His job was to safeguard the boy and the Thaistess. Only by doing that could he guarantee his own future in Thaiburley. And there was no point in seeking out trouble, especially when at least one of the Twelve was on his trail. No question, the sooner he left the better. So why was he hesitating? Was that really his voice saying to Mildra, "You two go on, I'll follow later in another boat"? It must have been, since he emphasised the point with a gesture to Ullel. The man nodded and pushed his boat away from shore, standing tall at its bow and propelling the vessel by means of a long pole, as Dewar had seen others do before.

"This isn't your fight," Gayla said, still beside him.

"I know. I'm just... curious."

She shook her head, then called out to Ullel, who was lifting himself into his boat, "Take them to the Mud Skipper." The man nodded.

"What's the Mud Skipper?" Dewar wanted to know.

"You'll see when you join them."

Gayla then led him away from the water's edge and the tall reeds which were blocking their view of whatever lay beyond the cluster of stilt-based huts. In a land which was wetter than some baths he'd had, Dewar would have expected raiders to come in boats, but apparently not, at least to judge by the preparations being made.

Then he saw them; a party of horsemen riding hard in their direction. Villagers were shouting, gesturing, getting agitated at last. Men took position on the steps and in the doorways of the outermost huts, bows at the ready with arrows cocked.

"This is the only direction an attack could come from, unless they resort to boats," Gayla explained, her voice calm as if she were pointing out local attractions to a sightseer. "Water to our right, the high grasses to our left – impossible for a body of men to move through quickly or silently – and behind us more grasses with open water beyond. So they have to come this way."

"And how does that help you?"

"It means we can prepare. Watch."

The raiders had almost reached the outskirts of the village. The first of them charged across the narrow stretch of shallow water that lay across their path like a broad puddle. The raiders rode powerful mounts, short for a horse but tall for a pony, and all were a uniform ginger brown, with slightly darker manes.

"Könichs," Gayla murmured, as if reading his thoughts. "The fen ponies. There are still a few wild herds to be found in the depths of the Jeeraiy, though most have been domesticated now. Magnificent, aren't they?"

Dewar had to agree. Despite the riders on their backs there was something wild and untamed about these compact, powerful horses, with their blazing eyes and streaming manes, but the assassin was more concerned with the villagers' response, or lack of one. The raiders were almost upon them and he was finding Gayla's unfailingly casual manner increasingly difficult to understand.

Without warning, chaos erupted from the silt and sand beneath the lead horses' hooves. At first it wasn't clear what was happening; horses were whinnying their distress as they stumbled or were brought crashing down, sending riders skidding through the shallows, men's shouts of shock and anger only adding to the confusion.

As the edges began to lift clear of the water, Dewar realised what he was watching. A net. A vast expanse of

thick-stranded mesh that had been buried beneath the
water and under the sand below; a trap biding its time,
waiting until it was needed. He couldn't help but smile;
such a simple and elegantly appropriate defence. He was-
n't sure how the net was secured or triggered, the ends
being concealed within tall rushes to one side and even
taller grasses on the other, but there was no doubting its
strength or effectiveness. The charge had been halted,
the leading seven or eight raiders – perhaps a third of
their total number – were now tangled in the mesh and
floundering, while the rest of them were blocked from
the village by their enmeshed comrades.

Now the villagers let fly with bow and spear. Had there
been a division of archers firing in unison, they could
have wreaked havoc among the trapped men and those
stalled behind, but as it was there were a mere handful
of huntsmen, shooting independently. Several of the villagers ran closer in order to cast their spears, which
plunged into the hide of horse and man alike. Shrieks of
agony and shock joined those of anger and frustration in
a chorus all too familiar to the assassin. Battle proper had
been joined. The water was a churning mass of struggling
limbs as those trapped tried to find purchase, and a red
froth of blood began to spread across it as arrow and
spear took their toll.

The far end of the net seemed to wilt and give as a
rider appeared – one of those from behind, having either
cut or jumped the supporting cords. He snarled orders
to two of his fellows who followed more slowly behind,
goading them on, waving a heavy spear or lance above
his head. His horse was larger than the others and of a
darker brown, while the man himself looked to be big

by any standards. His face was marred by a long vertical scar slashed from top to bottom, giving him a demeanour as fierce as his snarl. The leader of the raid, Dewar felt certain.

Scarface levelled his lance and charged at those villagers still retreating after casting their spears. He bore down on one runner in an instant, somebody Dewar remembered from the previous night's feast – Myel or Mayel? – skewering him through the back, the lance punching out through the man's stomach. For an instant, as the lance tip struck, Mayel instinctively drew his body forward as if to escape, in the process pushing his shoulders and head back, arms raised in a parody of surrender, face lifting to the sky. Fleetingly, Dewar could see the smiling face from last night – happy, laughing, without a care in the world – superimposed on the grimace of agony as the villager died.

Without conscious thought, the assassin drew his kairuken and levelled the weapon at Scarface. However, other raiders were now catching up as the killer paused to free his lance, and Dewar was denied a clear shot. Rather than delay, he fired, taking out the nearest rider.

The attackers had bows of their own, and arrows trailing fire and smoke thudded into the nearest huts, catching swiftly in the dry timber.

He went to reload, only to find Gayla's restraining hand on his arm. "No! You have to go, now."

"But what about you?"

"We'll survive," she replied, interpreting his query as collective rather than personal. "Some of us will die while others live, as the goddess decrees, but the village will go on. Those who survive will rebuild. This is not the first time we've been attacked." So, perhaps these people were more fatalistic and worldly-wise than he had supposed.

Still Dewar hovered, torn by indecision, which surprised him no end. The sensible, logical course was obvious, and it wasn't like him to play at being a hero, or even to be tempted to, but something about these people had touched him at a fundamental level. He wanted to walk away from here knowing that this community went on, that it had a future, as if simply by doing so it made the world a better, more palatable place. The woman chivvied him with growing frustration. "Without you to protect them, what will happen to those two? They are mere babes in the world, vulnerable to every mishap. They need you. Now go!"

He knew she was right, so, with an effort of will, put aside his reluctance and set off towards the waiting boat, where the same young fisherman he had sat and watched casting his nets earlier that morning stood ready to spirit him to safety.

Was it the sound of thundering hooves that alerted him or did somebody shout a warning? Hard to tell in the heat of the moment. Either way, he turned to find the point of a lance hurtling towards him. He threw himself to one side and twisted. Too late to avoid the lance completely. Searing pain in his left arm as the tip punched through. He stared for a split second, not quite believing this was his arm the shaft had punctured, entering at the front with the point emerged behind. Yet even as that horror flashed across his thoughts he was falling, and knew instinctively that he had to keep the lance falling with him if he didn't want it to rip his arm open. He gripped the shaft as firmly as he could with both hands. The left still worked despite the wound, thank the gods, so presumably he'd been lucky and there was no major damage. Even so, his efforts sent the searing pain a few notches higher. The lance tip came free, his arm seeming to slide off it as he fell, without taking half the limb with it. He tried to hold and twist the weapon, but it was difficult, his grip slick with blood, and the shaft wrenched from his hands.

He landed heavily and lay there for a second waiting for his startled wits to regroup, seeing flying hooves and falling men from a somewhat novel perspective. He must have fallen more heavily than he realised, or perhaps the angle was misleading, because it seemed to him for the split second he lay there that the ground at the village's heart had turned to quicksand. Panicked horses and falling raiders appeared to be sinking and disappearing, swallowed by the ground itself. Then one particular man fell alarmingly close, without showing any signs of going any further. The assassin realised his efforts with the lance had not been in vain after all. He'd evidently done enough to unseat the rider, causing him to fall from the saddle, lance abandoned as the man raised both arms to soften his landing.

Dewar was on him in an instant; all thought of pain and blooded arm swept aside in a rush of adrenalin and necessity. He drew a knife as he clambered to his feet and drove the blade into the raider's side as he threw himself on top of him, striking once, twice. The man screamed, a roar of pain and anger, and punched Dewar in the face, clubbing him away.

The assassin rolled off, nose and cheek throbbing and hot, the salty taste of blood on his lips as it flowed freely

now from nose and arm alike. His opponent rose un-
steadily to his feet, hand feeling the two gashes in his side
and coming away glistening with blood. Dewar registered
for the first time that the man facing him was Scarface,
the presumed leader of the raid. They were even now,
both on foot and both wounded, though Dewar wasn't
groggy from taking a tumble off a horse, so perhaps not
so even after all. Scarface started to reach for his sword,
but the assassin had no intention of letting him draw it,
charging the man and barrelling into him. The impact
jolted his wound into fresh complaint. He ignored it and
brought the knife in quickly, but Scarface blocked the
blow with his arm, latching onto Dewar's wrist in the resulting tangle and squeezing, trying to force him to drop
the knife. Keen to protect his injured left arm, Dewar
headbutted the bigger man, his forehead smashing
against lip and chin. The grip on his wrist loosened and
he was able to wrench it free, stabbing immediately, driving the blade into Scarface's throat and upward.

The raiders' leader vented a choked gargle and then
collapsed as Dewar drew his knife free, the sticky
warmth of blood now coating both of his arms. He knew
he had to get something on his left one to staunch the
wound or risk bleeding to death, but time to worry about
that once he was clear of the battle. There was no sign
of Gayla, and he just hoped she'd reached safety. It was
definitely past time for him to get out of here in any case.

The boy still waited in the boat, standing up, beckon-
ing and yelling at him to hurry. Dewar ran, but even as
he drew closer, a figure rose out of the water behind the
boy and struck him down. To the assassin's adrenalin fuelled senses the whole thing happened in slow motion.

The figure emerging as if from nowhere, the blow, the lad falling forward out of the boat, water streaming from the unexpected assailant's form and more sheeting upwards as the boy landed face-down in the shallows. An arc of ruby red droplets seemed to hang in the air behind his collapsing form.

Dewar found a familiar figure confronting him. "Hello, King Slayer," said Ulbrax, the naked triumph in his voice bringing a snarl of rage to the assassin's lips. "Time to pay for your sins."

Dewar couldn't understand the proclivity this man seemed to have for talking before and during a fight. Who was he trying to impress – himself? As soon as the assassin had seen someone emerging from behind the boat he reached for a throwing knife. He drew and flung the weapon in one movement, an underarm throw which was nonetheless strong and accurate. Of course Ulbrax dodged it, but he was still knee deep in water, which hampered him, and Dewar had already sent a second blade flying in the wake of the first.

Dismissing his own injuries, Dewar followed up the daggers by charging. The second knife seemed to catch Ulbrax by surprise, and, though he again threw himself out of its path, the blade snagged his arm in passing. Nothing more than a flesh wound but it was something, and the need to evade left him unbalanced as the assassin slammed into him. They went down into the water, with Dewar on top, his face above the surface. He tried to hold Ulbrax's head down, while fending off the hand holding the blade with his own left hand, but that was weakened due to the wound and it soon became clear he wouldn't be able to do both for long. Beneath him,

Ulbrax thrashed and kicked and twisted, his free hand stretching towards Dewar's face and trying to claw at his eyes. The assassin leant away, doing his best to stay out of reach, and felt fingernails rake his cheek and neck.

In leaning away he shifted his centre of balance slightly, enough that Ulbrax was able to throw him off with a particularly violent buck of hips and twist of body. He landed almost out of the water but on his injured arm, which triggered fresh spears of agony. Yet even as he was being thrown off, Dewar brought his knee up, feeling it connect with the other man's inner thigh and then slide up to grind into his groin. Ulbrax came out the water spluttering and screaming, and, somewhere in the struggle and the roll, appeared to have lost hold of his sword.

The assassin pushed the other man away with his good arm and scrambled to his feet, but immediately felt hands fasten around his throat.

"Not so smug now, hey, King Slayer?"

Did the man never shut up? No wonder he'd made such a good inn keeper. Instinctively Dewar pulled both his arms together, forced them between the other's and then threw them apart, before Ulbrax could crush his windpipe. He put every scrap of strength into the move, ignoring the pain and the weakness in the left. The grip around his throat disappeared before it could bring any real pressure to bear.

They never quite left the water, and the fight degenerated into a blur of grapples, kicks, punches, attempted trips, throws and headbutts. The two of them were well matched, but Dewar knew he'd lost. The wound continually drained his strength and he was tiring far more quickly than his opponent. They both sensed it, and

Ulbrax redoubled his efforts, landing a solid punch to the side of Dewar's face which all but finished the assassin, leaving him clinging to the edge of consciousness.

His legs went, and he only remained upright because Ulbrax held him there with hands gripping his shirt front. Dewar's arms were two lead weights dangling by his side, his body a mass of bruise and hurt, and he didn't seem able to breathe fast enough to feed his lungs the air they craved, while every ragged breath brought a fresh parcel of pain. He knew he'd given a good account of himself and the other man couldn't be much better off than he was, but that brought small consolation. Not even the sneer on the victor's face, as he brought it close to Dewar's, was enough to rouse him. He was finished.

"So, King Slayer, this is it: treachery's final reward."

Talking, talking, always brecking talking; was the man *trying* to goad a response out of him?

Oddly, now that they'd both stopped struggling, Dewar had more time and opportunity to hurt his opponent than at any point during the actual fight. His left eye was starting to puff up and wouldn't fully open, and he felt more than half dead already, but knew that he'd soon be the rest of the way there if he couldn't muster the strength for one last effort.

So he did, though it was nothing glorious or noble. As Ulbrax's gloating face hovered close before him, he spat; but this was not simply a coarse act of defiance. He very deliberately spat into the other man's eyes.

Ulbrax instinctively flinched and jerked his head away.

Dewar seized on this sliver of a chance. With his opponent distracted, he forced spent muscles to move his right arm. The whole thing seemed ludicrously slow and he felt certain that Ulbrax would react at any second and stop him, but somehow he managed to pull a knife from his belt and plunge it into the other man's side. It wasn't the most clinical or powerful knife stroke of his life, and he could only hope it would prove enough, because he didn't have strength to try this again.

Ulbrax froze. He stared at Dewar in shock, and voiced a peculiar sound somewhere between a croak and a groan. His grip slackened and then slid off completely, as he collapsed into the water.

Dewar's feet and legs were being asked to earn their keep again. He stood where he was, swaying, and knew his limbs couldn't support him for much longer. That final effort had taken all he had. He started to turn, realising that if he fell over here there was a good chance he'd drown, but the effort proved one ambition too far. The world spun and his leaden legs refused to respond. Instead, they buckled. Suddenly the Jeeraiy came rushing up to meet him as he toppled forwards, racing towards the waiting water and into oblivion.

FIFTEEN

Tom felt sick at having to run away. He just knew that Dewar was going to get involved in the fighting, despite saying that he'd follow on after them. What had all those sword lessons and practice sessions been for if Tom was expected to flee at the first sign of trouble? In his heart he realised that he probably wouldn't have been much help but that didn't stop him feeling frustrated, angry, and more than a little ashamed.

Beside him, Mildra clutched his arm, gripping tightly enough that her fingers dug painfully into his skin. He wondered about saying something but didn't – glad of the contact and not wanting to disturb her thoughts or do anything that might cause her to shift and let go of his arm.

"It's for the best. We have to leave." She said this aloud, though he suspected the words were more for her own benefit than his. He glanced across to discover tears trickling down her cheeks.

"Look forward," Ullel advised, "never back. That way lies only regret and sorrow."

Tom was surprised to hear such philosophical advice from a fisherman, but then he'd been constantly surprised by these people ever since arriving in their village. Nor could he argue with what Ullel said. He turned to face the front of the boat, glad to do so as this meant he didn't have to meet the fisherman's eyes. He felt certain that he'd find only accusation there. The back of his neck tingled, as if the hairs were standing on end; he imagined he could feel Ullel's gaze boring into him and so shifted his shoulders, hunching forward slightly. Tom was acutely aware that this man had abandoned his home, his friends and family, all for his sake and Mildra's. He just hoped they were worth it.

"Where was it Gayla told you to take us?" Mildra said, the tears still audible in her voice. It was the question Tom would have asked, had he summoned up the courage to address the fisherman directly.

"To the Mud Skipper," Ullel replied. "Old Leon will see you across the Jeeraiy far quicker than I ever could."

As answers went, this was hardly the most informative Tom had ever heard, but Mildra failed to pursue the matter and he was still wary of speaking to the fisherman.

"And then…" Ullel continued, a little wistfully.

"You can return to make sure your family are all right?" Mildra finished for him.

"Yes."

Mildra lapsed into silence after this exchange, keeping Tom company – he'd been there well ahead of her. The village was already lost to sight behind a spit of land and for long moments the only sounds were the mournful keening of wading birds and the rhythmic splash of the pole entering and leaving the water, as Ullel took them ever deeper into the Jeeraiy. The scalding alarm call of a disgruntled duck disturbed by their passage brought Tom out of his self-pitying reverie, but not to the point where he was tempted to speak.

The uncomfortable silence was broken by Ullel himself, who began to name the various ducks and other birds they passed, telling them how this one was good to eat while that one had an elaborate and comical courtship display, while a third would only nest in a particular tree and a fourth produced the best eggs in the whole wide world. This casual friendliness worked to ease the knot of grief and guilt that had settled in Tom's gut and he started to relax, even asking questions when he spotted something new.

A flight of large white birds came in close above their heads, flying in a V-formation, their long necks stretched forward. Tom and Mildra both ducked instinctively, as the ghostly shapes swept over them to land amid great splashes of foam some distance ahead, honking all the while.

"Swans," Ullel said, a soft smile on his lips, "the white queens of the Jeeraiy."

Soon after, the great expanse of water seemed to shrink and contract, as they entered an area which was less open, the land evidently more solid. Trees bordered the waterways and even sprouted from within them. At one point Ullel deftly manoeuvred the boat between the trunks of two such – great towers of wood and bark thrusting out of the water, part of a cluster of perhaps a dozen trees whose bases were completely submerged. They grew uniformly straight, with branches sprouting thickly towards the crown, as if they were arrows shot into the ground by a tribe of giants from amongst the clouds, darts that had ripped down through the sky and water and the mud beneath to lodge deeply in the world's skin.

"Swamp cypress," Ullel supplied. "Very hardy, they have to be – the levels here rise and fall constantly; one day they're growing on land, the next in water."

Tom could have reached out and run his hand along the pale brown bark of the nearest, but it looked coarse and flaking, so he resisted the temptation, concerned that he'd only end up skinning his fingers and looking stupid for doing so. Their brief trespass between the trees was accompanied by raucous scolding from birds somewhere in the canopy; the irritated movement of the unseen avians still causing the foliage to rustle with menace long after the boat had passed through.

Beyond this small picket of trees they found the way cluttered with lilies, their broad leaves glistening as if waxed. The plants grew so densely that individual pads overlapped like the scales of a fish to form one continuous raft. White flowers burst forth at erratic intervals to decorate the verdant expanse. Ullel didn't hesitate. His pole strokes remained as measured and sure as they had been all journey. He angled the boat to cut a course across the lily field, heading towards the bank. Her prow gently pushed the lilies apart, and when Tom looked back it was to see the individual pads already drifting back towards one another. Before long there would be no sign of their passage at all.

A bright red frog, its back marked with regular black spots, watched them dispassionately, refusing to move even when the boat's wake caused the pad it was sitting on to undulate alarmingly. Tom wondered how such a brashly coloured creature survived out here, where it must surely make an easy target for predatory birds. Perhaps that was the point; perhaps its hide was a form of challenge and the creature had hidden defences which the birds knew about and so made sure to avoid.

Tom looked to the front of the boat again and realised that they were not heading for the land after all, but rather towards a narrow channel, the mouth of which had been hidden until now. A willow grew precipitously close to the edge of the bank, leaning outward to weep yellow-green fronds into the water, effectively masking the narrow waterway behind it.

Tom found himself fending off deceptively substantial branches and twigs as the boat sailed beneath them. Mildra simply ducked down, hands covering her head, while, glancing back, he saw Ullel squat and raise a hand to protect his eyes. The fisherman stood up again immediately they were free of the tree's foliage. The nonchalance with which he accomplished the pole, duck, stand, pole again sequence suggested to Tom he'd been this way a few times before.

As they emerged from beneath the concealing willow, the first thing Tom saw was a large wooden shed or barn. Beyond the barn stood a stone-built cottage, reduced almost to the point of insignificance by the wooden building in front of it. It was as if the cottage had been deliberately hidden away behind the larger building, peeking out from its shadow. Tom remembered Dewar's comment as they approached Gayla's village about stone being hard to come by here, and guessed that whoever built the cottage must be either rich or know of a ready means of transporting things into the Jeeraiy.

"Don't take any notice if Leon seems unwelcoming when you meet him," Ullel warned. "He likes to act tough, but underneath his sour words the man has a heart of gold."

If Ullel intended this to settle their nerves, it failed as far as Tom was concerned.

The fisherman brought them to a stop before the shed, which began perhaps half the height of a man above the water and proved to be larger than Tom first realised, while the ground in front of it was smooth and compact, forming a runway down to the channel they were in, any grasses that had once grown there worn away. Close to the shed a trench had been dug, with several lines of dark, near-black mud slabs lain out beside it.

"Peat," Ullel said, seeing the direction of Tom's gaze. "Makes very good fuel once it's been properly dried." He then stepped from the boat and called out, "Leon, visitors!"

There was no immediate response from the house, but a face peered at them from around the corner of the shed. Tom's first impression was that this was a boy, younger than him – no more than seven or eight years old – but with overlarge saucer-like eyes.

Ullel smiled on seeing the boy. "Hey, Squib, is Leon here?"

Evidently reassured by a familiar voice, Squib stepped out from his hiding place. He still looked like a boy, but one who hadn't eaten properly in a while, or perhaps a child's poor drawing of what a boy should look like that had somehow come to life. Tom had never seen anyone so thin. His limbs seemed little more than gangly spindles, which a stiff breeze might snap in two if it caught them at the wrong angle.

"Who are these two?" The boy's suspicious gaze darted to Tom and Mildra. His voice was almost comically high-pitched.

"Friends, Squib, just friends in need of a ride across the Jeeraiy." Ullel's relaxed voice and ready smile were a marked contrast to the hostility evident in the boy's expression. "Is Leon inside?"

"He was, but he's out here now," said a voice far deeper than Squib's. Tom turned to see an elderly man approaching from the direction of the house. Two things struck Tom immediately: the man's pronounced limp – he walked quickly enough but relied on a gnarled redwood cane to do so – and the colour of his hair and whiskers. To call these grey would have been an injustice; they were white, reminding Tom of clouded steam which had somehow been captured and given substance.

"Leon, good to see you!"

"And you, Ullel. How are Gayla and the rest of the village?"

There was an awkward pause, ending when Ullel's began to describe the raid and their current circumstances. Tom watched the grim set of Leon's face as he listened to Ullel speak. "Sorry news, sorry news indeed," the old man said with a shake of his head once the fisherman had concluded. "And you say these two want to be taken across the Jeeraiy?"

"Yes."

"And you're hoping I'll oblige."

"Well…"

Leon scratched his chin, looking at each of his three visitors in turn. "Ullel, I'm not sure I can help this time. You know I think the world of you, of Gayla, of your whole damned village, but times are hard. Running the Mud Skipper costs, and I can't really afford to be taking her out unless there's profit in the trip somewhere. Don't see any here."

"Perhaps you'll find cargo at the far end of your journey," the fisherman suggested.

"Maybe, but maybe and perhaps aren't anywhere near good enough. Sorry, Ullel, really I am, to you and your friends here; I'd love to help, but…"

"Perhaps I could suggest something," Mildra said.

Leon stared at her quizzically. "I'm all ears, young lady."

"I noticed you walk with a stick, so there's a problem with your leg. May I ask exactly what?"

"Too much dampness coupled with too much use over too much time. The knee's worn out, simple as that."

Mildra nodded. "And if I were able to cure that, to restore your knee to the point where you could throw away the walking stick, would that be worth passage across the Jeeraiy?"

"Hah! Lady, if you could do that, I'd give you a guided tour around the whole breckin' continent!"

She smiled. "Across the Jeeraiy would be fine. Now, may I see?"

Leon eased himself down onto the grassy bank, rolled up his trouser and presented the offending leg.

"You're a healer, then, are you?" he said as Mildra knelt beside him.

"When I need to be, yes."

She reached to place her hand on his knee and he flinched, as if perhaps preparing to draw his leg away. She looked at him with arched eyebrow. He gave a sigh and submitted to her touch. "Sorry, long time since any woman's touched my leg."

"Don't think of me as a woman then, just think of me as a healer."

He gave a tight-lipped smile. "That's easy for you to say."

Ignoring him, Mildra bowed her head in concentration, long hair falling to cover her face. Tom couldn't see whether or not she closed her eyes, but Leon certainly did.

The old man's head lolled back, and a few breaths later he admitted, "Actually, that feels real good."

After several moments the Thaistess removed her hands and lifted her face. She looked tired. "Try that."

Gingerly, the old man got to his feet, putting the weight on his suspect leg and hobbling a few steps. "It feels... different," he said, "itchy inside, but..." and he broke into a broad grin. "Yeah!"

Mildra smiled in response. "Good. Your knee was worn away. You had bone rubbing against bone. I've rebuilt the lining of cartilage that would normally prevent that from happening and at the same time smoothed out a couple of bone spurs caused by the rubbing, which would have been painful in themselves. I can't promise the knee will be as good as new, but you should find this a big improvement on what you've been living with, once you get used to it."

"Lady, I barely understand a word of that, but I can tell you that my knee feels better already. You and your friend have got yourselves a ride!"

Ullel seized the opportunity to take his leave.

"We can't thank you enough," Mildra said, "either you or your people. May the goddess watch over you and help you to rebuild."

"Yes," Tom added from beside her, "thanks – for everything." Inadequate, perhaps, but he didn't have the Thaistess's silken tongue, or a goddess to call on.

As the fisherman departed, Mildra turned her attention back to Leon, advising him to take things carefully with the rebuilt joint. She suggested they not head off until the next day to allow it some rest.

"Sounds reasonable," the old man agreed. "That'll also give the opportunity for your missing friend to show up. If he's not here by tomorrow, chances are he never will be."

That comment brought home an uncomfortable truth. As Leon and Squib made preparations for the following day's departure, Tom had a chance to raise the matter with Mildra. "What do we do if Dewar doesn't show up?" he asked quietly.

"We go on."

"Can we, though? First Kohn and now Dewar; they were the strongest of us. What chance do you and I stand without them?"

"The goddess will watch over us and keep us safe."

She'd done a pretty lousy job so far by Tom's reckoning, but he kept quiet, suspecting that her faith might be all that Mildra had left to cling to, that her beliefs were what enabled her to remain so calm. He didn't see much point in undermining that.

Morning came and there was still no sign of Dewar. In his heart of hearts Tom hadn't expected there to be, but he still felt tempted to suggest they wait a little longer, just in case. Dewar was sullen company at the best of times and Tom found his overbearing manner a constant irritation, but, despite that, there was no denying how reassuring it was to have someone of his competence and confidence in charge. The prospect of continuing into the unknown without him was daunting, if not downright terrifying, though Tom chose not to say as much to Mildra, suspecting she already felt the same.

They'd decided on morning as their start time and morning it was going to be; nobody else seemed inclined to delay. While Squib and Leon made preparations for the coming journey, Tom went for a stroll, to collect his thoughts and to settle his nerves, walking away from the house to a position where he had a good view across the Jeeraiy to the mountains beyond. He felt humbled by the vastness of the world, and still wondered at one level what a street-nick from the rundown basement of a mighty city was doing here. Funny, but he didn't mourn Dewar in the same way he had Kohn, regretting the loss of the man's knowledge and skills far more than the absence of the man himself. As Tom stood there, he thought back over the journey so far and the part he'd played to date, feeling a little ashamed of some of his actions and taking little pride in his contribution. He'd been content to sit back and let others do most of the work, relying on Dewar to make decisions and Kohn for his strength. Well, they were both gone. It was down to Mildra and him now, and high time he shouldered his share of the responsibility. He gazed again at the wilderness and at the distant peaks that waited, and felt a new resolve hardening within him. They would do this; they had to, for the sake of the prime master and those waiting back in Thaiburley but, more importantly, for Kohn and Dewar who had sacrificed their lives to give them the opportunity.

Feeling calmer in himself than at any time since they left Thaiburley, he turned and walked back to join Mildra where she stood close to the house.

The Thaistess greeted him with a troubled smile. "We are sure about this, aren't we?"

He nodded. "Certain."

"Good." Her smile widened into one of genuine warmth, as she perhaps saw the new determination in his eyes. "That's good!"

"Where's Leon?" He was anxious to get going while the first flush of his renewed determination remained fresh.

"He and Squib disappeared into the boathouse." Mildra nodded towards the tall, black-boarded shed.

"Ah, so we're finally going to catch a glimpse of this Mud Skipper, are we?"

"Looks like it."

As if on cue, the great doors at the front of the shed swung a little way open. Squib emerged to pull them wide, scurrying from one to the other. This was followed by a great clanking sound, as if a vast chain were being dragged across something, and then a loud coughing. Smoke billowed from a chimney at the top of the boathouse, and the coughing steadied into the pounding huff and growl of an engine. Seconds later, the prow of a boat began to emerge. But it didn't come out of the shed on its own. Two metal joists extended horizontally from the boathouse, appearing from near the roof and slowly lengthening as they stretched towards the water. A series of thick chains hung from the beams, criss-crossing between them. They were attached to a metal cage, a cradle, in which sat what could only be the Mud Skipper. Tom stared in fascination as the two beams and boat emerged in steady unison. From the little he could make out the vessel looked bizarre, though it was difficult to see where cage ended and boat began, so he tried to reserve judgement until he could see the ship properly. Boat and cradle slid slowly down the short slipway amidst a cacophony of clanking and hissing and the groaning of stressed steel. Leon appeared in the doorway to the boathouse, yelling and gesturing at Squib, who raced up to join him. The pair disappeared inside.

Tom glanced at Mildra, who met his gaze with eyebrows raised and a look of pure disbelief. They both grinned, and moved forward for a closer look.

Dark smoke billowed from the boathouse chimney, and the sound of the engine from within intensified, growing simultaneously louder, faster, and higher in pitch, as the caged boat reached the water, where it stopped its outward progress and began to be lowered. Then it stopped, though the sound of the engine didn't relent. For brief seconds the boat hung suspended a fraction above the ground and the channel by which Tom and Mildra had arrived. Then it began to turn, ponderously rotating through ninety degrees with only a little bumping on muddy banks as the boat rocked in its cradle, until the hull paralleled the course of the water.

Squib was back, shouting and giving a thumbs-up in the direction of the shed. With a dramatic hissing sound and renewed screeching as if metal was being ripped apart, clamps released and the cage split, parting in the middle with the two sides lifting high. The burden which the cage had carried from the boathouse dropped the short distance into the waiting water, where it bobbed and settled.

Tom and Mildra had their first unobstructed view of the Mud Skipper.

"Isn't she a beauty?" Leon said, striding down from the boathouse, his cheeks ruddy and sweat on his brow. As he walked he wiped his hands on a large oily cloth, which he tossed casually to Squib as he arrived at the boat.

"She's... certainly impressive," Mildra replied. The response summed up Tom's reaction perfectly. There was no question that the Mud Skipper was striking to look at, but beyond that he had yet to decide quite what to make of her.

The hull was painted white, though none too recently by the look of things, with a blue cabin and bright red funnel. She was far larger than any of the boats operated by the fishermen they'd seen on the Jeeraiy, completely filling the channel which had brought them here. However, it wasn't her size that caught Tom's attention, but rather her paddles. A great towering wheel protruded from her stern, composed of a whole series of paddle blades within twin circular hoops, while smaller versions were mounted on either side.

"What exactly is she?" Tom asked.

"Paddle steamer," Leon said, patting his boat's hull. "A stern-wheeler essentially, leastways she is when she's in the water."

Squib had already clambered aboard, and was now lowering the short gangplank. Leon used this to follow the lad and looked back at his two guests.

"Well, are you coming or not?"

Tom glanced at Mildra, who shrugged. The pair of them went up the gangplank. The boat settled with their added weight, so that the two smaller wheels sank down to rest on the muddy bank to either side – it really was that tight a fit. Squib already had the engine fired up, venting puffs of smoke from the boat's red-painted chimney. Tom and Mildra found seats in the cabin, on Leon's advice: "At least until we're in the open water."

As soon as they started moving, Tom understood why. The great stern wheel began to turn slowly, its broad blades dipping in and out the water. At the same time, the two side wheels began to rotate, their paddles digging into the mud and grass of the bank. The Mud Skipper jolted forward, her motion growing increasingly smooth as they gathered speed. Soon the two side wheels were flying round, gouging into the ground and throwing up a cloud of mud and grass in all directions, which included great clumps at times.

Leon grinned and called in to them from his position at the wheel, behind the cabin, "That's why I named her the Mud Skipper." He continued, proudly, battling against the noise of the engines and the churning blades, "She's equally at home in wet mud or muddy water, and we've plenty of both around here. The stern wheel can be lifted, the side wheels lowered and raised, depending on conditions."

In no time at all the Mud Skipper had exited the curtain of willow branches and scythed a path through the lily pads to reach open water.

"You can come out on deck now," Leon called down.

They found seats near the prow, and Tom was fascinated to see the side wheels lifted and brought in to rest against the cabin walls.

Squib took the wheel and Leon came over to join them.

"Well," he said, "what do you think of her now?"

"Beautiful," Tom conceded, "she's simply beautiful."

Tom and Mildra both agreed that this was definitely the way to experience the Jeeraiy. The Mud Skipper didn't hang around, and they were seeing several day's worth of this sprawling, diverse land all in one go. They passed fishermen in long narrow canoes with stabilisers to either side – something that seemed eminently sensible to Tom as he watched them stand and cast their nets – and villagers who waved and called out greetings. At one point they came close to a party of the same broad-faced animals they'd encountered before stumbling on Gayla's village. The beasts were again submerged, with just their eyes and nostrils visible above the water.

"Best to stay clear of those," Leon advised, pointing. "They can be bad tempered so-and-sos."

For a while their course paralleled that of a wooden causeway standing proud above the water on a forest of stilts. The causeway linked a series of islands together and seemed broad enough for two or three people abreast. Tom even saw a couple of the stocky marsh ponies being led across one section. He could only marvel at the ingenuity and sheer determination that must have gone into making such a raised pathway in this environment.

For the most part on that journey, Tom found himself simply sitting back and relaxing, succumbing to the wonder of this place.

A great shouting broke his tranquil mood. He looked around to see a bunch of gangly-limbed figures rushing towards them, apparently running across the very top of the water.

"Skimmers," Leon muttered, "that's all we need."

They looked humanoid, but at the same time were clearly not human. There was something unsettling about their movements, which were almost insect-like in the way they skated across the surface of the water.

Their limbs and indeed their whole frames were improbably slender, while they wore on their feet the most bizarre boots Tom had ever seen. Great saucer-like fans of translucent webbing supported by a splay of skeletal struts spread out from the base of each leg, enabling the skimmers to glide over the water. They looked to be children, all boys, and all a good deal younger than him. Nor did they limit themselves to shouting. As they came close to the Mud Skipper, they began to pelt the craft with fruit, greeting each hit with a chorus of cheers. They reminded Tom of a group of boisterous street-nicks up to mischief, though these looked far too innocent to be up to anything serious, with their over-large brown eyes and guileless expressions. In fact, there was something vaguely familiar about these spindle-limbed, wide-eyed creatures. Tom glanced from the pack of harassing skimmers to Squib, and back again.

"Yes," Leon said, presumably seeing the direction of his gaze, "Squib is a skimmer, which is why these lowlifes keep giving me such a hard time whenever we're out this way." Squib was at the far side of the boat, jumping up and down, shaking his fists and hurling high-pitched insults back at the chasing posse of youths. If he heard Leon talking about him, he gave no sign. "He was born without the webbing, you see. He couldn't live as a skimmer, couldn't survive. To them he's just a freak. If I hadn't taken him in when I did, he'd have died. So whenever we come this way, we run the risk of this happening – the kids coming out to harass us and taunt him"

Tom stared at the nearest pair of youths, gliding across the surface on their great webbed discs. "You mean those things are their feet?"

"Of course. What did you think they were?"

"I don't know, shoes or something."

"Huh! You really think anyone, human or skimmer, could have come up with footwear as weird as that?"

Leon had a point.

"Squib!" Leon yelled. "Calm down for Thaiss' sake, or you'll end up going overboard."

The youngster's torrent of abuse and aggressive gesticulating had built to an alarming crescendo, with spittle flying from his mouth and body gyrating as if he were on the verge of a fit. At Leon's words he paused and looked round, favouring them with a broad grin. "Aye, aye, skipper."

"Not that I can really blame him," Leon said quietly to Tom and Mildra. "Those skimmer kids are a real pain in the ass."

At that moment, a bright green globe came flying towards them, narrowly missing Tom but splattering on Leon's shoulder. It burst to dribble a trail of viscous pip-rich pulp down Leon's chest.

"Right, that does it!" the old man roared, shaking his fist at the skimmer responsible, who had peeled away and was beating a retreat, laughing triumphantly. "You pesky brecking water fleas! Squib!"

The Mud Skipper's mate was beside him in a flash. "Is it time?"

"Oh, it's time all right." Leon's words were almost growled. He unlatched a panel in the side of the ship's cabin, revealing a coiled-up hose. Squib started to cackle maniacally, hopping from foot to foot in excitement as he accepted the nozzle from his captain.

A piece of rotting fish sailed between them to spatter against the cabin, signalling a fresh chorus of cheers from the circling skimmers. "You'll be laughing on the other side of your faces soon, you maggot-riddled water cabbages. Ready, Squib?"

"Yes yes yes!" The lad had the nozzle over the ship's side, training it at one of his tormentors.

Leon turned his attention to a small wheel in the same recess that had housed the hose, turning it rapidly. A belch of liquid leapt from the nozzle to dribble into the water, followed by another more sustained spurt, which soon developed into a stream. Even then, the hose's discharge still didn't reach as far as the skimmers, despite Squib's best efforts. They continued to circle, jeering all the louder.

"Can't wait for this," Leon confided to Tom and Mildra, grinning maliciously.

"But the hose isn't reaching them," a puzzled Tom felt obliged to point out.

"That's the beauty of it – the hose doesn't need to. Watch."

Even as he spoke, the first of the young skimmers went down, splashing into water that would no longer support him. Two more followed instantly, then another. The jeers had stopped, to be replaced by panicked screams and splutters of dismay. At least, the jeers from the water had ceased. Beside Tom, Squib now launched into a new apoplexy of jumping and fist-clenched air punching, firing off fresh volleys of ridicule and insult interspersed with cackles of unfettered hilarity. Even Leon was laughing and pointing, as the entire pack of youths floundered.

"Oh this was worth waiting for," he said, wiping the corners of his eyes with pudgy fingers, "it really was."

"What did you do?"

"The hose was loaded with a chemical – something I cooked up myself. It lowers the viscosity of water, weakens its skin if you like, so that the skimmers just fall right through. The effect won't last for long, of course – the Jeeraiy will soon disperse the chemical and everything will go back to normal, but for once in their lives those heartless, brainless bullies have been given a taste of what it's like to be Squib; a skimmer who can't walk on water."

The incident put both Leon and Squib in fine spirits for the remainder of the journey, which passed without any great incident. Tom was surprised at how quickly the mountains, which had seemed so distant, loomed above them; wondering how many days it would have taken to get this far without the Mud Skipper. His respect for the peculiar craft rose accordingly.

"This is Pellinum," Leon said cheerily.

The town enjoyed a spectacular setting, no question about that. Some distance behind it, a great curtain of waterfalls plunged down a mountainside, the rumble of their thunder a constant background noise, causing Leon to raise his voice.

"Decent enough folk, but don't let them sell you any of their so-called religious souvenirs; tat, the lot of it. This early in the season you should be able to find yourselves a room cheaply enough, if you've a mind to enjoy a comfortable night before you go on, and I'd advise you to. There won't be much comfort in those mountains you're so determined to explore."

Tom barely heard him. At that moment all his attention was focussed on the waterfalls, which had to be one of the most awe-inspiring sights he'd ever seen.

They moored beside a long wooden jetty, which already had a number of other boats clinging to it like leaves to the branch of a tree, though none were as large as the Mud Skipper. Squib leapt off and secured them to a mooring. Before he'd even finished tying off, a group of children came charging along the wharf, yelling for Leon to sound the boat's whistle. Laughing heartily, the skipper obliged, tugging on a chain to vent three high-pitched toots of steam.

"As you can see," he said, turning back to his passengers, "we're hardly strangers here." The man smiled broadly, clearly loving the attention. "This is as far as we go. Hope you've enjoyed your time aboard the Mud Skipper, and thank you, young lady for sorting out my leg. Never thought I'd hear myself say such a thing, but, Mildra and Tom, may the goddess be with you."

It was Mildra's turn to smile. "And with you, Leon and Squib – not forgetting, of course, the magnificent vessel known as the Mud Skipper."

The marsh man pushed down on the pole with exaggerated care, moving his shallow boat slowly along the edge of a great mat of reeds and grasses. Around his feet lay a number of tubers and two fat fish – his original reason for being out in the boat, before he was lured away from fishing and foraging by the promise of greater reward. He planted the pole again with great deliberation, making sure it was firmly set before pulling on it to haul himself forward. The last thing he needed was to have the thing snag on treacherous roots which would inevitably be lurking just beneath the surface this close in.

A plume of smoke hung above the site of old Gayla's village like some sombre exclamation mark. He didn't need to go any closer to know that the roofs and walls would be smashed and the buildings alight. There were bodies enough bobbing in the water to confirm this as a raid. The water surrounding the nearest one writhed with motion, as a shoal of tiny snippers fed. He could even see the occasional silvered flashes of individual fish as they darted in to tear off a mouthful of flesh with their razor sharp teeth before flitting away again, leaving room for the next, only to return a moment later for a further bite.

He avoided the corpses that were obviously locals – they wouldn't have anything on them worth salvaging – and would normally have been going through belts and pockets of the raiders' dead by now, but he'd spotted one that was potentially even more valuable.

A body lay snagged in this bed of reeds, half in, half out the water. By his clothing it was obvious that this was neither a local nor a raider. A traveller, then; probably a pilgrim on his way to visit the goddess, which meant he would be carrying provisions and the means for buying more, not to mention whatever he might have brought to offer the goddess as tribute. Now there was a prize worth running the risk of a few grass roots.

The goddess was smiling on him today, because no other small boats were here yet – he seemed to be first on the scene, but that wouldn't last. The smoke would be visible for many leagues across the flat openness of the Jeeraiy, and every marsh man with a boat was bound to be hurrying here as fast as they could row or pole. For now though, he had the pick, and he intended to make the most of such rare good fortune, starting with this pilgrim.

The body was lying on its side. By edging the boat right up against it, he was able to half drag, half roll the fellow into the boat, deftly adjusting his own balance and footing to ensure the craft didn't tip over. This wasn't a big man, nor richly dressed, but who knew what might be concealed within his clothing? As the marsh man knelt to investigate, the corpse's eyes sprang open. Startled, he let out an exclamation and jerked back.

Before he could think to do anything further, the suddenly very animated corpse's hands shot out and grabbed his shirt, pulling him downwards once more. At the same time, the man's face lunged up, headbutting him.

Pain exploded across his temples. Caught by surprise, disorientated and hurt, the marsh man lost his balance and fell, vaguely aware that the boat was rocking dangerously beneath him. Somehow he landed in the boat and it hadn't tipped over, but this respite was short lived. Strong hands gripped his shirt, hauling him up, and the next instant he was flung through the air to crash heavily into the water.

Instinctively he tried to suck in a lungful of air but took down a great gulp of foul water instead. He felt himself sinking and struggled to turn around, to get his feet beneath him and kick for the surface. Even as he did so, disaster struck. He felt his foot snag and entangle in the very roots he'd been trying to avoid with his pole. Panicking, he tugged and tugged, but the roots held firm. The water wasn't deep here, and he knew the surface had to be close above his head, yet with his foot trapped it might as well have been a hundred miles away. He was a marsh man. Surely he couldn't die like this?

Knowing it was likely to be his final effort, he pulled for all he was worth, flexing his foot, and felt a surge of relief as his heel came free and the finger-like grip of those clasping roots reluctantly loosened. Suddenly he was shooting upwards, clawing at the water until first his hand and then his head broke the surface.

Sweet air! He spluttered and splashed and gulped in as much as he could, all the while looking round in panic for his boat.

Then he saw it, already some distance away and continuing to move further; the figure of the pilgrim standing straight and working the pole.

"My boat," he gasped, trying to shout. "Come back, you brecking bastard, that's my boat!"

But if the pilgrim heard him he gave no indication, instead continuing to move steadily in the direction of the distant mountains.

SIXTEEN

They came in ones and twos and clusters and groups. The talented. It was less than an hour until globes out. A team of lamp lighters stopped to stare, neglecting their duties as they watched this unprecedented surge of people. Normally most folk were safely indoors by this hour, but today there was a great flurry of activity. And the Tattooed Men were everywhere, knocking on doors, chivvying the reluctant or simply escorting. The lamplighters scratched their heads and conferred in muted murmurs, wondering what the breck was going on, but deciding it was none of their business and probably better they didn't know.

A pair of dun-uniformed razzers, on their way back to the station after completing their final patrol of the day, stopped in their tracks and looked on, bemused. They wondered whether they ought to intervene, or at least enquire, but decided against the idea. There were Tattooed Men involved, after all, and who in their right minds wanted to interfere with them? So instead, in time-honoured tradition, they chose to scamper back to the guard station and report events to their superior. Let someone else decide what to do, if anything.

All the little knots of people were converging on one place: Iron Grove Square, where Kat was already waiting. Two braziers had been lit, their hot coals glowing red through the lattice of black iron that held them, while the smell of roasting nuts wafted on the breeze. Kat was kept busy making sure everyone was given a hot drink or a mug of soup as they arrived. It wasn't really that cold, but the glow of the braziers offered comfort and a sense of homeliness which would be welcome once the globes were fully out, while a drink was the very least they could do.

The apothaker came forward, accepting a mug of warm chocolate and offering Kat a confident smile in return. She had cleaned herself up and taken the trouble to dress smartly for the occasion. "Give her hell!" she said.

"We will," Kat replied, trying to match the other's tone with a confidence of her own.

As the apothaker moved away, Kat took the opportunity to look around her. The square was now dotted with people of all ages, shapes and sizes, standing in groups and chatting, or simply sitting and waiting. For once she felt proud of where she was from, of being a part of a community that produced folk like this; people willing to gather here despite the danger, displaying the sort of gutsy defiance that had seen the denizens of the City Below emerge from the blood and the horrors of the war unbowed and unbroken. They'd seen off the Rust Warriors and the Blade, and by Thaiss they'd do the same with this Soul Thief!

There was no turning back now; this was actually happening. Kat felt certain that the bait would be taken –

how could the Soul Thief resist an opportunity like this? She only hoped the firepower they'd amassed would be enough to stop her. It had to be. For her sake, for her sister's, and for the sake of all these people gathered in Iron Grove Square.

As more of the Tattooed Men started to arrive, their shepherding duties completed, Kat was able to delegate the serving of soup and hot drinks to others. Predictably, Shayna was among the first to offer, leaving Kat free to burn off some of her anxious energy by touring the perimeter and seeing for herself the preparations being made for their special guest.

The square was bracketed on all four sides by what must once have been a grand building. Two storeys of interlinked galleries and passageways boxed in the inner courtyard known as Iron Grove Square. On the north side, the building was punctuated by an imposing arched gateway which granted access to the street. Two large wooden gates, held together by bands of heavy black iron, guarded the entrance. When they first discovered this place, the gates had been as dilapidated as the rest of the building, but the Tattooed Men had restored them. This evening, the gates stood open.

The inner courtyard had been christened Iron Grove Square because of the metal sculpture of a tree which stood at its centre – now rusted, with leaves and branches missing, but still with enough form to hint at its former glory. A description which could easily be used for the whole of the City Below itself.

The Tattooed Men enjoyed a largely nomadic existence, maintaining several safe houses scattered across the under-City but this was by far the grandest and the

most important. The secluded courtyard aside, this neg-
lected fragment of Thaiburley's past boasted one
particular feature which made it ideal as their base of
operations. Partially hidden beneath the rubble that littered the floor of the place, they had discovered a small
stairway giving access to a cellar, and in that cellar they
found a safe. Not just any safe, but the sort of substantial, solidly built strong room which the owners of
banks got all excited about and which most financiers
could only dream of. The door was a wonder in itself,
for this was no blank-faced slab of immovable metal,
but rather boasted a large indented central panel, which
displayed an intricate mechanism of giant cogs and
levers and wheels, of toothed discs and metal bars.
Somehow, Chavver came into possession of the key,
presumably found elsewhere in the house, though
she'd never bothered sharing the details with Kat. The
first time Chavver opened the strong room, all of them
had been there, crowded into the cellar and on the
stairs, craning to catch a view of the interlinking wheels
and components, holding their collective breaths in
hope that the system still worked, which it did, even
after so many years of disuse. Slowly, the cogs turned,
one triggering another, and the solid steel bars and rods
had been drawn back, to leave the massive door free to
be opened.

Kat would never forget the smell that assailed them as
the door was pulled wide. Within, they found a massive
space, steel-lined and shelved but otherwise stripped
bare; empty apart from one thing: the mummified corpse
of a woman, which they had never been able to identify
nor indeed explain.

Despite their best efforts, a hint of that smell still lingered, and Kat had never felt tempted to go down and watch the door being opened again.

She had no idea what sort of wealth the house's original owners possessed, what might require such extreme levels of security, but presumably it must have been substantial; either that or they were extraordinarily suspicious breckers. Of course, the key's discovery was crucial. Without it, the safe would have been no more than an impressive curiosity. With it, this became the perfect place for the Tattooed Men to store their carefully gathered arsenal, confident that the weapons would remain secure.

That arsenal had been carried up from the cellar earlier and was now in the process of being deployed; the weapons checked and loaded, before they were dispersed around the building. Kat enjoyed a sense of grim satisfaction as she walked from room to room watching the Tattooed Men at work.

As she turned a corner, she abruptly found herself confronted by a face so like her own; a little broader, a little rounder, with fuller lips, but unmistakably related. Charveve, who had been coming the other way. The two stared at each other, Kat wishing she was somewhere else but not about to give ground, and her sister looking as if she felt the same. Then Chavver said awkwardly, "I wanted a word."

"What?" Kat must have misunderstood. Surely her sister hadn't just said that.

"A word," Chavver repeated. "About Rayul. After you and that kid left us, he was taken; by one of the Dog Master's creatures."

Kat was stunned. This was the first attempt her sister

had made at any form of communication that didn't involve a blade or a threat in over a year. Kat had never really understood the intensity of Charveve's hatred. Yes, they'd rowed about the leadership of the Tattooed Men and yes those rows had turned nasty and even physical on occasion, but in the end she'd walked away. Kat had seen what their fights were doing to the group, to the people who were the only family either of them had known since their mother's death, and she'd refused to go on. She'd given in because she had to. Chavver was too stubborn to back down, no matter what the cost, so Kat did. She resigned herself to a life of looking out for herself, of being alone, for all their sakes. But that hadn't been enough for her sister. Chavver's enmity had pursued her into the shadows, banning any of the Tattooed Men from even talking to her and threatening dire consequences should she ever cross the group's path again, effectively cutting her off from any hope of support should she need it.

This seemed an extreme reaction even for Charveve, and it had been more difficult to bear than anything Kat had suffered in the Pits. Now, she was beginning to understand, just a little. Jealousy. Of her, and of Rayul. Was that what lay at the bottom of all this: jealousy? The three of them were consigned to the Pits at around the same time and soon became firm friends. Yet Rayul had always been closer to Kat than he was to Chavver. She had become the glue that bound their little team together – the best friend of both. It was Kat that Rayul confided in, Kat that he talked to first. This had been the source of the occasional sulk and angry word even back then, but Kat had never dreamed her sister might harbour deeper resentments. Yet it seemed to fit.

"Thought you should know," Chavver added.

"Thanks, but I already knew."

Chavver looked up sharply. "How?"

Kat could have kicked herself. Why couldn't she have kept her mouth shut? She knew why, of course: because for once she wanted to be one up on her sister. Stupid, stupid, *stupid!* "I'll tell you about it," she said, "but not now. When this is all over."

Chavver held her gaze for long seconds and then gave a curt nod. "All right, but don't think you're running away from this one. Soon as this is ended, we're having that conversation."

Kat bridled and almost responded with a jibe of her own. A year ago she would have done, but there were more important things right now and she'd done a lot of growing up in the intervening months, so she simply smiled and said, "Look forward to it."

Kat returned to the courtyard through one of the four doors – each wing of the building boasted its own – hovering in the doorway and simply watching. There was a great deal of laughter, the mood almost celebratory, and yet she could sense how fragile this was, the tension bubbling just beneath the service. It wasn't exactly forced bravado, but she suspected this atmosphere was only preserved because certain realities were being consciously avoided. She wondered how long the cheerful spirit would linger once globes were fully out.

Somebody, a man, started to sing in a strong baritone. It was a song Kat vaguely recognised but one which she hadn't heard in years, not since her earliest days in the Pits. A second voice joined in, a quavering elderly woman's, rising to complement the man's, and then others followed. Before long the whole square was filled with a chorus of singing. Even those who didn't know the words recognised the tune and were able to hum along, including Kat. She smiled as the song ended amidst a babble of mutual congratulation. Perhaps she hadn't given these people enough credit and the high spirits would survive beyond globes out after all. Another song began almost immediately the echoes of the first had died away. Kat even knew the words to the chorus for this one.

During the singing that followed, a Tattooed Man surreptitiously closed the twin doors to the arched gateway, effectively sealing in those in the courtyard. Others moved around the fringes of the crowd, lighting the bracketed lanterns which were dotted at intervals around the walls. The erratic glow from these lamps highlighted the faces of gargoyles and demons carved into the frames of doorways and gate, lending their faded features a sense of animation which made it seem they were observing those gathered in the courtyard with malevolent anticipation. Kat just hoped this wasn't an omen for what was to come.

Despite the low-key nature of the Tattooed Men's actions, people noticed, and clearly appreciated the significance. Kat heard the singing falter as realisation spread through the crowd. But it resurged almost immediately, as several people – including, Kat felt certain, the original singer – made a concerted effort to sing louder and bring the melody back on course. She had no idea who the baritone was, but determined to seek him out when this was all over and thank him.

Kat strained to spot the faintest sign of life behind any of the windows in the other wings – silhouette of a bald head, slight movement in the shadows, or a stray beam of light reflecting off uncovered metal. The flickering radiance of the lanterns made it impossible to see anything, though she knew the Tattooed Men were there. Waiting, even as she was.

If she couldn't see the ambushers there was a good chance the Soul Thief mightn't either, though surely the monster was rational enough to recognise this as a likely trap.

Kat carried the whip Annie had found for her clipped to her belt, though she wasn't sure why. In truth she didn't have much faith in it. She also had the apothaker's luck potion, which she trusted about as much. After a moment's hesitation, she took out the small phial, removed the stopper and knocked back the contents. A minty sweetness with a hint of cloves, chased down by a kick that might have been alcohol, trickled down her throat. She took a deep breath, drew her two short swords and squatted down to wait, her back against the wall. She wondered precisely where Charveve was now, knowing that her sister planned to be on the building's upper floor when everything kicked off, to get a better view. This was the moment they'd both been waiting for virtually all their lives. Or at least it promised to be, assuming everything went to plan.

Kat occupied herself by trying to guess how the Soul Thief was going to get in here. Would she burst through the twin gates, sending shards of wood and iron everywhere, or would she come straight through the house? Clearly, they'd prefer the former, so had sealed and barricaded both the street entrances into the house proper as firmly as possible, but the Thief had proven many times over that doors in general were no great obstacle to her, so no one was taking anything for granted.

In the event, she did neither.

Kat was looking across the courtyard, not focussing on anything in particular, when a flicker of movement caught her eye. She almost passed over it, but something made her look again, and this time there could be no doubt. A black stain was creeping down the far wall of the courtyard, an irregular patch of night which none of the lamps were able to penetrate.

"The roof!" she yelled out. "Look to the roof, south quarter!"

Whether alerted by her call or not, others had seen it now. There was pointing and exclamations among the crowd, which surged towards Kat as people scrambled to put distance between the south wing and themselves. The stain had gathered substance, swelling to become a soot-dark cloud which slid down the brickwork towards the ground.

A flechette gunner opened up, sending a stream of silvered darts into the billowing mass. The thrum of crossbows sounded and a dozen quarrels sped in the wake of the flechettes. An inchoate shriek issued from the cloud, sounding like wind whistling through a narrow chimney but louder and somehow more aware. The form writhed and twisted, shifting shape in an effort to avoid the stream of missiles, which were chewing up the brickwork behind in a rain of chips and stony shards. Somewhere over there they'd deployed a flamethrower. Kat just hoped those wielding it could bring the weapon to bear and get a clear shot. It was an unwieldy contraption of valves and dials at the best of times, but she was itching to see what the Soul Thief made of a concentrated blast of fire. The flechettes and archers had managed to pin the monster down, preventing it from advancing into the square in pursuit of the fleeing people; and, judging by the increasingly plaintive sounds coming from the creature, they were hurting it, but Kat wasn't convinced they'd done any real damage as yet.

She was working her way through the throng of talented, who had rushed to cling to her side of the square. She had no intention of actually attacking as yet, not wanting to get caught by any of the lethal munitions that had already been brought to bear on the monster, but wanted to be in a position to do so if needed. The longer they could keep the Soul Thief in one place the more chance there was of bringing other weapons into play. A firebomb shattered at the edge of the tattered blackness, splattering the ground and the wall of the house with burning oil, as well as a patch of the creature itself. There was no mistaking the pain in the shriek this time; and the affected patch of darkness *burned!* Where the breck was that frissing flame thrower?

Kat had forced her way to the edge of the throng of people, reminded of their presence and their fear and their bravery when a girl immediately behind her sobbed. She suddenly realised that these people were no longer needed. They'd done all that could be asked of them without complaint and had succeeded, drawing the Soul Thief to where the Tattooed Men waited.

Kat turned around and yelled, "Open the gates. Let these people out!"

"Yes, let us out," someone in the crowd agreed. "Open

the brecking gates!" Others picked up the call and soon the whole lot were demanding release.

Kat glanced back towards the Soul Thief. The flechette gunner had ceased firing, presumably to reload. There now seemed little to hold the monster at bay, at which instant the very ground beneath Kat's feet shook as a huge dart, longer than a man is tall, erupted from one of the courtyard windows to tear across the intervening space in an instant, slamming into the Soul Thief and though the wall behind, bringing a wide section of it down. She just hoped there was nobody still standing in the room beyond. Despite a fresh shriek of anger and pain, the monster just flowed around the shaft of this enormous steel bolt and reformed. Kat knew the giant arrow had been fired from a steam-powered cannon which would take moments to reload. The occasional quarrel from a bow still flashed at the creature but without the incessant attention of the flechette gun this was no longer enough to keep her immobilised, and the black cloud, now looking vaguely human in shape, started to advance across the courtyard towards the trapped people.

"Get this brecking gate opened now!" Kat yelled.

Mercifully, another flechette gun opened up from the opposite side of the courtyard to the first, temporarily halting the creature's progress, and then a second fire bomb shattered on the flagstones in front of it. The flames danced up, partially hidden by the stunted iron tree which stood between Kat and the blaze, its crooked scantily-leafed branches momentarily resembling upturned hands, mimicking an appeal for mercy.

A new weapon opened up, a streak of blue light crackling across the courtyard, seeming to catch a corner of the Thief before spending itself against the far wall. Kat turned her head away and blinked to clear her dazzled vision of the afterimage. When she looked back, the broiling mass of darkness that was the Soul Thief seemed to have grown, swelling until it towered over the residual flames from the firebomb. Flechette darts passed through it now with no visible effect, as if the creature truly were composed of nothing more than smoke.

Then the black cloud detached itself from the ground and started to drift towards Kat and the crowd of talented, floating over the burning oil and the iron tree, drawing ever closer. Until now, everyone had stayed remarkably calm, but people's resolve finally started to wilt and for the first time people around Kat began to panic. Somebody screamed, and the sounds around her grew increasingly desperate. "For Thaiss's sake get that gate open!" the woman closest to Kat shrieked.

As if in response, the two gates finally moved. Kat had no idea whether this was the work of Tattooed Men answering the calls of the crowd or simply the people at the front working out how to release the locks for themselves, nor did she care. At least these folk would have a chance to escape.

Her relief was short-lived, as a fresh wave of screams and shouts erupted – from the front of the crowd, near the gates. Kat couldn't see what was happening. She was too short and so was unable to see over the intervening mass of people, but something was obviously wrong. Desperate for more information she jumped in the air but still couldn't get high enough to make anything out beyond the fact that nobody seemed to be leaving yet, despite the gates being open; and the screams and curses and shouts of desperation were only getting louder.

Kat looked back at the Soul Thief. The bitch was almost upon them. A few more seconds and her foremost dark tendrils would be directly over the crowd. No more blue lightning had leapt forth to oppose her, and Kat wondered if the weapon had only been good for that one shot.

The night abruptly lit up, as a stream of fire erupted from one of the windows to her left, like the breath of some indignant dragon. The flame thrower! Somebody had finally brought it to bear. The heat was intense, even though Kat stood some distance away. The nebulous form of the Soul Thief was enveloped in flame. The black cloud burnt and sparked and crackled, visibly contracting, curling in on itself like an injured spider drawing in its legs. And the thing screamed. A high-pitched shriek of torment which cut through every other sound and caused Kat to wince, as it hurt her ears. She watched with a sense of elation as the still-smouldering bundle of darkness plummeted to the ground.

Yet it fell almost on top of one of the talented, a young woman who screamed and tried to back away but couldn't go far because of the press of bodies around her. A tendril of smoke reached from the diminished Soul Thief, to curl around the foot of the hysterical woman. This seemed to act as a tether and within an instant the creature's entire remaining substance flowed along that tenuous link to engulf the woman in a nebulous grey-black mist. The mist began to darken immediately, gathering substance. Brief seconds after the cloud had surrounded the unfortunate soul, it released her. A desiccated husk dropped to the floor as the now stronger, larger Soul Thief streamed away from this first victim to attack another.

"No!" Kat screamed.

This couldn't be happening. The fire had come so close to killing it, and yet the monster was already restoring itself by feeding on the talented, and with this many of them here, Thaiss alone knew how much feeding it might do. People started to scatter, fleeing the creature and moving away from the gate, enabling Kat to catch a glimpse of the front of the crowd. A solid line of armed men stood across the exit, blocking the gate and penning the talented in.

Who in Thaiss' name were these men? What the breck was going on?

Kat hesitated, torn between the urge to attack the Soul Thief directly and her desire to ensure these people could escape the courtyard. Before she could make up her mind, the decision was made for her. A jet of flame engulfed the Soul Thief once more. It wasn't indiscriminate, but it was all-consuming, as fire tends to be. The Soul Thief and the poor man she was currently feeding on were engulfed, and several people beyond were caught as well. Whoever wielded the weapon had obviously realised that the only way to save the majority was to take the monster down, no matter what the cost. Screams of agony joined those of terror. The cloud of darkness detached itself from its latest victim, a high pitched wail issuing from the creature as it burned, a sound which rose above the human voices. The Soul Thief then fled the withering flame by racing across the intervening ground to smash through the nearest window and into the building itself. A fresh stream of fire pursued it, playing across the smashed window and leaving the surrounding frame and brickwork blackened and charred once the flames relented.

With the Soul Thief having slipped beyond her grasp again, choice was no longer an issue; Kat had only one immediate enemy to deal with. She forced, slid and wormed her way through the panicked crowd of people, not hesitating when she reached the front but instead launching herself straight at the line of armed men. Her erupting from the crowd with twin swords at the ready seemed to wrong-foot them for a second – all the time she needed. Kat caught a glimpse of white open mouths crudely daubed on black shirts. The Fang! Then the thrill of combat roared through her blood, bringing her fully alive and suppressing other thoughts. For the next few moments all she was aware of were blades to block, openings to strike at and adversaries to disable and kill.

The twin swords became an extension of her body, moving as rapidly and unerringly as their wielder, as she struck and parried, blocked and thrust, rolled and twisted and then struck again.

A lull in the fighting allowed her to pause; a degree of sanity returned as she took stock of the situation. Kat was dimly aware of four, perhaps five men having fallen to her blades, and she'd suffered a raking cut to her left shoulder – a blow that narrowly missed taking her ear off – but that had only acted to goad her on at the time. She remembered laughing as the sting of steel kissed her skin, before blithely cutting down the man responsible.

The line of those penning in the talented had broken. The remnants of a melee surrounded her, small knots of struggling figures while many more lay unmoving on the ground. She assumed people must have followed her lead and taken the fight to the Fang. Beyond the gate she could see figures scurrying into the night, so at least some of those who had come to help would make it home.

A figure reared up to her right, face contorted in a snarl, sword already descending. Kat stepped to one side, thrust with her right-hand blade – knee flexing, arm fully extended – then pulled the sword back and let the body fall. She walked across towards the gaping door that gave access to the house proper, hacking down in passing another of the Fang who had two of the talented backed against the wall, fighting for their lives. The pair smiled their thanks and then made good their escape, joining the steady flow of people fleeing Iron Grove Square.

Kat felt she'd done as much as she could here. It was time to find the Soul Thief and finish this.

She stepped into the building, to find the floor of the small gate room littered with bodies. Five or six of the Fang and one Tattooed Man: Adam, one of the oldest and one of the first people to take her under his wing when she was consigned to the Pits. The next room was larger but told much the same story. Heavy fighting had taken place here. She counted seven dead Fang and two of the Tattooed Men. How many of these frissing Fang were there and what the breck was going on here?

She came to a stairwell and heard the unmistakeable sounds of combat from two directions – on the ground floor ahead and from the stairs above. As far as she knew, Chavver was upstairs.

Kat raced up the flight, taking the steps two at a time. Once at the top, she saw the suggestion of fighting – of raised arms and falling swords – cast in silhouette against the wall ahead, like some staged battle scene performed by shadow dancers; though she had little doubt this one was for real.

She charged along the corridor, growing angrier with every step. It had all been going so well until the Fang intervened, trapping the talented and now, apparently, attacking the Tattooed Men. Whatever their part in this, she determined to make them pay, dearly. Judging by the number of bodies she was again stepping over – four more scattered along the corridor – it seemed the process had already begun. They must have brought a small army with them. But why?

As she turned the corner she gained a partial answer. A Tattooed Man sat collapsed against a wall: Rel, badly injured, most likely dying. Two of the Fang lay dead at his feet. A little further along Chavver and M'gruth stood side by side, holding off a group of the Fang and a figure Kat instantly recognised.

"Brent!" Images of the man crossing a city square in conversation with a Fang flashed through her mind and she cursed herself for not pursuing the matter at the time. Too late for regrets now. She leapt forward.

At her snarled exclamation the two nearest Fangs turned to face her. Kat went in low, thrusting upwards simultaneously with both blades, slipping under their guards and running the pair through.

Further yet along the corridor a fire had somehow started, which doubtless explained the elongated shadows she'd seen fighting on the wall as she reached the top of the stairs. Chavver and M'gruth had been pressed back close to the flames. No question this Brent was good; he was keeping Chavver pretty much fully occupied, leaving M'gruth to contend with the Fang. Kat's arrival changed the odds dramatically. The Tattooed Man took advantage of the distraction she'd provided to drop one of his opponents. Kat dispatched another. Three against three; or maybe not, as one of the two surviving Fangs evidently did a little mental reassessing of the odds and didn't much like the sums. He turned tail and ran, heading back towards the stairs for all he was worth. After brief hesitation, the other followed.

Brent disengaged from fighting Chavver, leaping back so that all three of them – Kat, Charveve, and M'gruth – were in front of him. He was breathing hard but still had a smile on his face, as if the odds didn't trouble him all that much.

"You should have told me about this little party, Kat. I thought we agreed to work together."

"I changed my mind."

Chavver and M'gruth were too experienced to be distracted by this little interplay if that was Brent's intention, though doubtless Kat would have some explaining to do once they'd finished off this interfering brecker. The three of them fanned out, making sure Brent had no avenue of escape while maximizing their own space to avoid tripping over each other when they pressed their attack.

"Not that it mattered, of course. Or did you really think something like this could be organised without word spreading?"

"So you thought you'd come along and wreck everything out of injured pride, simply because you weren't included?" Kat didn't believe that for one minute.

They were almost there, almost as far apart as possible.

"No, of course not," Brent replied. "I'm afraid I was a little sparing with the truth when last we spoke. You see,

I wasn't hired to kill the Soul Thief but rather to protect her and to ensure she grows strong."

"What?" Why would anyone want an abomination like that to thrive?"

"My employer's motives remain as opaque to me as they are to you, but once hired I always deliver."

"Not this time you won't," Chavver assured him.

"Really?" That supercilious smile was still there. "Who's going to stop me? You? I thought you might have more pressing concerns."

His eyes shifted to look above Chavver. Kat wasn't about to fall for a trick that obvious, but reckoned with three of them present, one at least could afford to check it out, so she did; and what she saw made her glad she had.

Now at least she knew what had caused the fire. The creature must have fled up here, weakened and smouldering, only to ignite some cloth or piece of wooden furniture in passing. Then it had cowered amongst the shadows in the stucco design of the ceiling, greatly diminished and too weak to escape, while Brent and his Fang cohorts had forced Chavver, M'gruth and the fallen Rel ever closer, until finally the Thief saw her chance.

"Chav, above you!" Kat knew her call was too late. In manoeuvring for the perfect attack, her sister had inadvertently stepped directly beneath the Thief's hiding place. A smudge of blackness fell towards Chavver, covering her face even as she attempted to turn and twist and react. The darkness immediately began to swell and gain substance, taking on an almost human shape.

Kat heard her sister scream, a cry of unadulterated agony.

"No!" Kat ran forward, ignoring the smell of burning overlaid with the stench of something putrid. She hacked at the thing, feeling slight resistance through the handle of her sword, but it verged on the trivial, as if she were chopping through a bag of fluffed-up cotton wool. "M'gruth, the fire!"

The big man was already running towards the blaze. There was no sign of Brent at this point – the brecker had obviously taken the opportunity to flee, but she'd worry about him later.

"Leave her, you bitch!" Kat screamed.

Charveve was thrashing, struggling against the shrouded figure that now seemed to envelope her. The suggestion of a face started to appear amidst the chaos. Kat didn't hesitate, stabbing at the thing's head. As before, the blade passed through with minimal resistance, but this time the creature cried out, as if stung. Kat stabbed again, growing increasingly desperate, the fear of losing her sister something she refused to accept.

"M'gruth!"

Where the breck was he? Then the Soul Thief's face began to take on greater definition, becoming more human, a woman's face, one she knew. "Katerina?"

Kat stopped attacking, her arms suddenly limp. All she could do was stare – at a face she only dimly remembered from her very earliest memories. "Mother? No!" The scream erupted from somewhere deep inside her. "You're not my mother. Don't you dare assume her face."

"Oh, but I am." The voice was like the wind across autumn leaves, dry and ancient. "She lives on in me, as do all I claim. Everything that remains of her is here, a part of me. Would you really kill your own mother, Katerina?"

For answer, Kat attacked with renewed fury, punctuating each stab with a word: "*You... are... not... my... mother!*"

Chavver had stopped moving. The Thief slid off of her, allowing Kat's sister to crumple to the floor; a dried, lifeless husk in black leather armour that now seemed ludicrously overlarge for the withered form within.

"No." Kat suffered a moment of double vision; past and present superimposed, one face overlaying the other. This was exactly how her mother had looked after the monster claimed her. "Goddess, please, no."

M'gruth finally came back, clutching the leg of a chair with fire smouldering at its top. He and Kat shared a desperate look. Too late and they both knew it. Kat felt numb, defeated, robbed of all hope. The Soul Thief flowed across the floor towards a window and all she could do was watch it go. M'gruth flung his burning brand. It sailed through the tattered trail of the killer without discernible effect.

The window's glass burst outward as the Thief paused before it.

Somewhere deep inside Kat the knowledge stirred that the murderer was about to leave. She stumbled forward, realisation that yet again the slayer of her mother and now her sister was going to escape overriding her paralysis and despair. Desperation empowered her and she ran the few short steps to the window, even as the last of that black cloud passed through. And then she remembered Annie's whip.

She yanked the barbed leathery length from her belt and held it properly for the first time, feeling a thrill of energy course up her arm, and dared hope that this seemingly vulgar thing might be more than it appeared to be. Without pause, Kat drew her arm back and cast the tip towards the patch of darker night, leaning out the window to do so, oblivious to the shards of shattered glass that still clung to the frame.

Kat had no idea what to expect. Swords had failed, while flechettes and crossbow quarrels merely slowed the creature down; what good was a whip likely to do? But she was desperate and had nothing else to hand. Her delight when the whip bit and the handle jerked violently was therefore matched by her surprise. There was a shriek of frustration and perhaps even pain from the nebulous cloud, and Kat had to hold tight with both hands to prevent the whip from being jerked out of her grasp. She found herself pulled forward, clothes and skin tearing on the window's glass-fragment teeth. She could have let go then, but refused to; refused to live with the knowledge that her family's killer had escaped again. So instead she clung on for dear life, and was physically dragged through the window.

The wrench on her arms was immense, as they were suddenly asked to take the weight of her entire body. She waited for the whip to pull free, or for the leather to snap, to send her tumbling towards the ground. They weren't high, and she knew how to land. Kat reckoned she could survive a fall from here without too much injury. But it never came.

She found herself carried across the courtyard while the creature above her shrieked its consternation. Perhaps the Soul Thief writhed and twisted, trying to shake off the whip's dogged grip; Kat couldn't say. Her attention was fully occupied with the wall of the opposite wing to the house, which was starting to loom large ahead of her. They'd gained a little height since leaving the window but not enough for her to clear either wall or roof. Fortunately, they weren't travelling quickly. Kat was able to bring her feet up, planting them on the wall and then using them to scrabble up it as she was pulled forward. The same tactic worked with the shallow-pitched roof. She could have let go then and been safe, but the possibility barely crossed her mind. She was in this until the end, however bitter that might prove to be.

They were free of the house now, drifting over smaller, single storey dwellings and still gaining height, little by little. Kat dangled, arms and body extended, like some lead weight hanging from a line. The solid presence of the grand conveyor loomed large. In fact, that seemed to be where the Soul Thief was headed.

She tried not to look down on the rooftops that swayed alarmingly beneath her feet, tried not to think of the muscles in her shoulders and arms which ached in mounting degrees of agony, and tried to focus only on the task of holding on.

No question, the Soul Thief was making for the grand conveyor. The brick-built viaduct with its series of broad supporting arches bestrode this section of the under-City like some multi-limbed colossus.

They were fairly high up now, and Kat wondered whether the Soul Thief was intending to pass over the belt, though to do that she would surely have to go higher still. To her right, Kat could see the chophouse where she'd first encountered Brent; a painful reminder of another score that needed settling. Then they were coming in close, approaching an archway two along from the one housing Coalman's. Kat could see a fissure towards the top of this arch, a dark hollowing in the right-hand wall where some of the bricks had fallen out

or been removed. Of course; no wonder she hadn't uncovered the Soul Thief's bolt-hole despite all that
searching – this was it! She'd never even considered including the grand conveyor, yet it was ideal – within easy
striking distance of the streets. It was also in spitting distance of where Brent had chosen to meet Kat.
Coincidence? She doubted it. The man had been mock-
ing her even then.

They were coming in too high. She was carried above
the archway, and found herself careening towards the
brickwork of the viaduct itself. Glancing quickly up, she
saw that the Soul Thief had stopped, though Kat continued forward, swinging like a pendulum. Presumably a
deliberate attempt to dislodge her.

With her hands fully occupied, she brought her feet
up to absorb the shock of impact. As they connected she
immediately used them to push herself off, as gently as
she could, anxious not to add to the momentum. The result was awkward and only partially successful, her
upper-body continuing towards the viaduct. She twisted
so that her left shoulder took the brunt of the contact.
The Soul Thief was moving again, pulling her away and
then dashing her towards the brickwork once more.

No question now, the creature was definitely using the
viaduct to try to rid itself of this troublesome burden. The
combination of momentum from her kick and the Soul
Thief's movement sent Kat spinning, twirling around on
the whip, which did nothing to improve her concentration. She saw the brickwork racing towards her again.
She tried to bring her feet up, to kick herself off as she
had before, but the spinning made judgement impossible. She slammed into the viaduct sideways, her

shoulder and hip striking with bruising force, followed a split second later by her head. Pain lanced through her thoughts, fracturing her attention.

Kat's right hand slipped, losing its hold on the whip. In desperation she tried to adjust her grip by reaching higher, only for her fingers to close on nothing at all. The horror of that barely had time to register before her left hand's hold failed completely. With no time to react in any way, she was falling. This was no mere drop from a first floor window, she was far higher, fatally so. Her arms were flailing, body tumbling, the brickwork of the conveyor flashing past with sickening speed.

Seemingly from nowhere a dark shape appeared. The Soul Thief, come to claim her life force as it had the rest of her family. Too fast. She barely had time to register its presence before the thing was upon her. Kat felt the juddering force of impact flare through every part of her body. Her last memory was of all-consuming pain.

SEVENTEEN

Above the village there was a definite trail, which came as a relief to Tom, who'd had visions of their having to clamber up the side of a mountain without any form of reference. Thankfully, the going would be a little easier than that, at least initially. Although they were yet too early for the pilgrim season to have started in earnest, this was a well-travelled path, which provided the pair with perfect camouflage. Nobody stopped to question what two such young people were doing abroad in the world alone when they took a room at a moderately-priced inn the previous evening; pilgrims came in all ages and sizes it would seem. In a sense, therefore, the goddess was indeed protecting them, from the curious if nothing else. Tom thought better of sharing this private observation with Mildra.

Before setting out that morning, they did a little shopping. Heeding Leon's advice, they ignored the various forms of bric-a-brac that Pellinum seemed to offer in abundance, but did acquire some warmer clothing, having lost theirs when the horse bolted during the Rust Warrior's attack.

The pair headed into far starker and more rugged countryside, which made it all the more strange to be leaving the Jeeraiy behind. They stopped a few times during that initial climb to gaze back upon the rooftops of Pellinum and watch the sunlight glinting off the waters of the Jeeraiy beyond. It was only then that Tom realised how busy a port this was. There were boats of various types and sizes in the waters around the town, some of which were clearly fishing while others looked to be ferrying either cargo or passengers, but none were as quirky or beautiful as the Mud Skipper, which was nowhere to be seen having left the previous evening.

Their course brought them close to the crown of the waterfalls they'd watched from the deck of the boat. For long moments they stood on a rocky knoll, awed by the power and the majesty of the plunging torrents that fed the watery plains below them; as the mist-like fret from the falls dappled their cheeks and dusted their clothes with glistening droplets, Tom was delighted he was able to gaze down on any of this at all without vertigo overcoming him. Whatever measures the prime master had taken to remove his fear of heights were holding up admirably.

Mildra seemed mesmerised by the falls. Tom had a feeling she would have happily stayed there all day. Eventually, after he'd tugged gently at her arm, they moved on, climbing a little above the course of the Thair, which had carved a canyon into the rock. They walked now beside a broad ribbon of surging white water, bursting with energy and violence, a raging torrent, whose growling voice was their constant companion. This seemed utterly different from the deep dark giant of a river that had carried them in the early

stages of their venture, or from the vast, placid expanse
of the Jeeraiy flood plain that the river would soon become, which made it hard to accept that the same water
comprised all three.

For the first time since the earliest days of their journey, Tom's legs began to ache, particularly the backs of
his thighs, which made him think that the effort of walking uphill must place different demands on the muscles;
wonderful news.

By late morning the terrain had levelled out and the
Thair had calmed a little – the roar of white water replaced by an altogether more soothing murmur. They
came to a lagoon, a spur leading off from the river's
course which may have been a natural feature with later
human embellishments or could have been entirely
man-made, Tom wasn't sure. All he did know was that
decorative paving stones bordered the pool around its
entire perimeter, providing the lagoon with an unnatu-
rally smooth edge, and that directly opposite the inlet
stood a building which simply had to be a Thaissian temple; subtly different in many ways to those he was used
to seeing in the City Below, but similar enough that he
instantly recognised the general type. As did Mildra, who
gave a delighted cry and hurried forward. The path led
them around the lagoon directly past the front of the
temple. Tom's respect and affection for the Thaistess had
grown throughout their journey, but he still felt no inclination to embrace her beliefs, so rather than joining
her inside he sat and waited on the temple steps, studying the water. The surface of the lagoon rippled with
half-glimpsed life, as scaly forms entwined and slid past
one another in some silent ballet. The waters of the pool

seemed to be alive with them, and dark fins frequently cut through to momentarily invade the air before disappearing beneath the surface once more. Tom became absorbed in watching the fish, trying to predict when one would next break the surface, and completely lost track of time.

"Thaasiel," Mildra murmured as she came to stand beside him. She sounded almost in awe. "They're holy fish, the water avatars of the goddess," she explained. "They're the same fish we keep in the temple pools back home, though I've never seen them this big or in such numbers."

Tom stood up and the two of them continued around the lagoon. A girl, swathed in a white shawl, stepped out from the temple and walked daintily down to stand close to where he had been sitting. She commenced to cast a large fistful of something, perhaps nuggets of bread, onto the water. The white pellets soared out, peppering the surface in a broad arc, and wherever they landed the water broiled with scaled forms. The girl was already taking out a second handful from a bowl clasped one-handed to her stomach. After scattering these, she looked across and smiled. Her dark face was narrow and far from pretty, but there was a serene quality about her features and the smile lent them added grace. Mildra raised an arm and waved to her. She took the trouble to pause in the ritual feeding and wave back. No words were spoken, as if such coarse human utterances would spoil the moment.

There was a spring to Mildra's step as they walked away from the lagoon, which lightened Tom's heart far more than the sight of the temple or its fish. She hadn't been quite herself since the raid on the village, lapsing into bouts of sullen silence which he didn't know how to respond to.

As they continued, the landscape around them opened up, the slopes on either side growing gentler and greener, though the path itself was covered in loose shale that had the promise of grazed knees written all over it.

Directly ahead of them rose a particularly verdant slope which seemed oddly marked. At first Tom failed to make sense of what he was seeing, but as they drew closer it became clear. Tier upon tier of low walls decorated the hillside, reminding Tom of his home, the City of a Hundred Rows, except that here the rows were used to separate crops rather than people, partitioning the mountainside into a series of staggered fields.

The green shoots of crops could be seen crowding the gaps between the stark paleness of the dividing walls, and here and there people were also in evidence; small pale motes moving among the green, presumably tending the plants. From this distance they looked a little like cavern ants, scurrying around the walls of chewed up rock and earth from which those busy insects built their nest mounds. Comparing these industrious people to such mindless, instinct-driven creatures seemed hardly fair, but he couldn't fully dismiss the image.

Mildra seemed to delight in everything they encountered, maintaining the smile and carefree demeanour she'd rediscovered at the temple, which prompted Tom to comment, "You look happy."

"I am," she replied. "I am."

With that she laughed and danced ahead of him. He hurried to catch up, breaking into a run, his own spirits lifted merely at seeing her like this. Tom was still coming to terms with the wonder of life; the paradoxical way he could feel so cheerful, giddy even, within a few short days of losing first a newfound friend and then a vital companion. The City Below taught pragmatism but offered little by way of this sort of release. In all manner of ways, the world was proving to be a far bigger place than he had ever imagined.

Much to Tom's frustration they left the cultivated slopes with their neat walls and crops behind without meeting any of the people who were so busy tending them. He had been tempted to dally, to climb up to wherever these people dwelt and learn exactly what was grown with such care in those precarious terraces and how the people farming them lived, but Mildra was keen to press on while the light and good weather held. The clear skies of earlier had disappeared as the day progressed and it was a while since they'd seen the sun, which lay hidden behind heavy clouds. The darker the clouds, the more anxious the Thaistess became, her earlier bright mood evaporating. With the sun's disappearance and the higher altitude, temperatures plummeted, and the pair stopped to unpack some of the thicker clothing they'd bought that morning. By late afternoon Mildra's fears were realised and the first drops of rain started to fall.

Never having seen rain before, Tom thought this was wonderful, holding his face up to feel the heavy drops splatter against his cheeks and forehead. Mildra seemed less impressed.

"You won't be so cheerful when your clothes are sodden through and everything's damp and cold," she assured him.

At her urging they searched for somewhere to shelter, settling on a small cave – little more than a hollow in the rock beneath an overhang, really, but enough to keep them dry. By now the rain had started to fall more heavily and Tom's fascination with the stuff had rapidly faded.

They huddled together for warmth, glad to be under cover as the rain lashed the mountainside in pitiless torrents. Tom was astonished at the ferocity, never having imagined that the sky could hurl down so much water with such vehemence. The path they'd been following now resembled a stream rather than anywhere a person could hope to walk along. The rain stopped as quickly as it had started, but by then darkness had already fallen and they decided to stay where they were until morning, which suited Tom just fine. When they first cuddled, Tom felt awkward, not knowing where to rest his hand. Then, once that hand found a comfortable position somewhere around her stomach, he'd tried hard not to move his fingers, afraid that Mildra might read intent into any slight flexing or involuntary twitch. It took a while for him to relax, but eventually he fell asleep with the warm presence of Mildra's body resting against his side and the smell of her rain-damp hair in his nostrils.

Come morning, everything seemed fresh and new in the wake of the previous day's rain. The clouds had withdrawn and they both felt cheered by the sun's return. It was hard to believe that anything could possibly be wrong in such a bright and beautiful world; apart from the slight crick in Tom's neck where he'd slept awkwardly.

A single great bird soared above them as they set out, splayed wings and strange tail held motionless, giving the impression that its flight required no effort at all. The tail was shaped like the blade of an oar, broad and rounded. An eagle, or so Tom assumed. Despite being high up, the bird was obviously huge, reminding Tom of the Kite Guard who had caught him in Thaiburley's Residences. That made him think of his ill-judged attempt to escape the razzer's clutches which led to his toppling over the wall; the horror of that sickening fall past Row after Row of the city's walls. Not his most distinguished moment, he had to admit.

"Are you all right?" Mildra asked from beside him.

"Yes," He smiled. "I'm fine."

The bird disappeared behind a craggy peak and they walked on, having to press close to the rock face as they walked beneath a waterfall – a cascade that produced a brief curtain of shifting obscurity as the waters tumbled into the Thair. They'd walked for perhaps half the day when a bird far smaller than the eagle caught Mildra's attention; a songbird, all black and yellow stripes with a red flash above each eye. The bird alighted for a second in one of the stunted, thorny trees that bordered the path at this point, trilled a few sweet notes and then took off again, to land in another tree a little higher up.

Mildra impulsively set off in pursuit, leaving the path to clamber over the moss-stained rocks. Despite her urging him to follow, Tom hesitated, strangely reluctant to leave the path. Then, with a shake of his head and a sense that, of the two of them, he was probably supposed to be the reckless one, he went after her. Tom didn't see the bird again though presumably Mildra did, because she kept climbing, and Tom followed.

There was no real path here, and the footing seemed

treacherous enough to demand concentration. Tom was
therefore taken completely unawares as he crested a
rise and came to stand where Mildra had stopped. He
could hardly believe the view that opened up before
him. For long seconds the two of them stood in silence
and simply stared.

They stood at the edge of a high meadow bursting with
colour; a vast open area completely carpeted in flowers.

Nearest them were large and small blooms, pinks and
purples predominant, though there were broad swathes
of red as well, and here and there a splash of yellow, as
if some exuberant artist had been let loose with a palette
of vibrant colours and allowed to toss them freely in
every direction.

"To think we nearly walked right past this without
even knowing it was here," Mildra said quietly.

Tom could only nod. He'd never seen anything so
bright, so vivid, so joyful, and on top of all this visual
wonder there was the intoxicating scent. The air seemed
saturated with sweet perfumes which made him want to
sing and dance and laugh for sheer joy.

Whereas he merely felt such urges, Mildra acted on
them. One moment she was beside him, the next she
was ahead once more, arms outstretched like wings,
skipping among the flowers, her laughter ringing out
over the meadow.

Watching her, Tom felt a grin spread across his face.
He couldn't remember the last time he felt this happy,
this unburdened. He ran after her. Then something
caught his eye which brought him up short. Off-white
and regular, bones poked out from a matt of foliage. He
bent down and tugged away creepers and vines and

small white flowers, to reveal part of the ribcage from what had been a reasonably large animal of some sort.

"Sad," said Mildra who had come back on seeing him stop. "But all things pass, Tom, and if you had the choice and knew your time was near, wouldn't you come here at the end? What more beautiful place could there be to say goodbye to the world."

Nor could he argue. He stood straight again, gazing at the sheer beauty around him, and noticed something new. A multitude of broad-winged insects fluttered between the flowers on quick-beating wings, many of them white, but just as many bore colours enough to challenge the rainbow. The effect was mesmerising.

"Butterflies!" Mildra exclaimed, evidently following his gaze. She laughed and turned to him again. "Aren't they wonderful, Tom?"

And they were, skimming across the meadow, flitting from flower to flower and at times rising in swirling spirals of dancing colour above the pink and purple blooms. One landed on his wrist – red and blue wings, each of which seemed to be daubed with a staring eye. It took off again almost at once, but he delighted in the featherlight tickle of the insect's touch. Others were less welcome, and he swatted at his neck where something had just bitten him.

Mildra was off again, leaping and skipping across the meadow. "Come on, Tom, keep up."

And his feet responded, carrying him after her, while the laughter bubbled forth – an upwelling of joy from somewhere deep inside him. Ahead, Mildra had stopped, to spin on the spot with her arms outstretched and head thrown back, face to the sky. After two such stationary circles she dropped backwards, falling onto a cushion of flowers and grasses. Tom had reached her by then, to fling himself down beside her.

They were both laughing, and the scent of the meadow engulfed him. He stared down at Mildra, and she had never looked more wonderful. Even among all this beauty, hers outshone the rest, and he didn't want to look anywhere else. Without consciously meaning to, he leant forward. She made no effort to turn away, so that her lips were there to meet his. He felt the tip of her tongue dance across his as the kiss progressed, and her hand reached up to stroke the back of his head, his neck. A shiver coursed through his body and for a moment he forgot how to breathe.

A tiny part of Tom's mind remained detached enough to be amazed; he never imagined that his first real kiss would be with a Thaistess. Then even that analytical corner of thought was subsumed by the swell of passion, as her kiss grew more urgent and her hands started to clasp and pull at his clothing. His own hands found the soft mounds of her breasts beneath her shirt, marvelling at how hot and firm yet yielding they were, and he was suddenly desperate to touch and squeeze them unhindered. He tugged at her top, almost tearing it in his haste, dragging the garment upward until the dark peaks of her nipples lay exposed, the shirt compressed to a thick collar of rumpled material caught beneath her arms. He would have abandoned all thought of clothing there but she sat up and was helping him, grasping the hem of the top and drawing it onward over her head, to leave her naked from the waist up.

Before he could take advantage, Mildra was lifting his own shirt up, forcing him to raise his arms and wriggle his shoulders so that the tight garment could slip over them. As his arms and head came free, she fell backward again, to lie on the grass, giggling. He stared at her, mesmerised, yet the same time strangely daunted by the realisation that this nakedness was for his benefit.

She stopped giggling and reached to place a hand on his neck, drawing his face to hers again, his lips to her lips.

Tom was intensely aware of the hotness of her skin against his, the firm feel of her nipple as it pressed against his chest and the tingling thrill of her fingers as they travelled down his back. All the while the scent of the flowers surrounded him, filling his nostrils and entwining his thoughts.

"Tom, Tom." Somebody was calling his name and pulling at his arm.

"What?" He wished whoever it was would leave him alone. He was quite happy sleeping, thank you very much.

"Tom, you have to wake up!"

He blinked his way to wakefulness, feeling cold and shivery and realising that he was naked from the waist up. Night had begun to fall, bringing its customary drop in temperature. Suddenly the memories came flooding back. With a heady mix of shock, embarrassment and arousal, he remembered the cool sensation of Mildra's lips against his, her pulling off his shirt, the overwhelming lust as he felt her naked breasts beneath his fingers, and then... nothing. The next thing he recalled was being woken up now.

"What... what happened?"

"Come on," Mildra urged, as if he hadn't spoken, "we have to go." She was already fully dressed, he noticed, sneaking a quick glance because he couldn't summon up the nerve to look directly.

Tom allowed the Thaistess to help him to his feet, though a petulant part of him wanted to shrug off her insisting hands. In standing up he had to untangle resisting grasses which had somehow conspired to snag his legs and clothing. He fumbled with his top, pulling it on and mumbling an irritated, "I'm cold," as Mildra urged him to leave that and hurry up.

The Thaistess was on her knees, stripping away tendrils of grass that appeared to have grown over their packs; but how could that have happened in such a short time? Then the two of them were running, stumbling towards the far side of the meadow.

Though many of the flowers had closed with the setting sun and their heady scent was all but gone, the place still held an ethereal beauty in the twilight, and Tom felt no real desire to rush away despite the girl's insistence.

"Mildra, what's the hurry?"

"I'll explain in a minute, just trust me for now, will you?"

And he did, so picked up his pace to match hers. They continued like that, with Tom keeping quiet until the ground began to rise and they were among the trees beyond the edge of the meadow, the beautiful carpet of flowers behind them. Only then did the Thaistess stop, dropping her pack to the ground and bending forward a little, hands on her knees as she caught her breath.

"All right, so what was that all about?" Tom wanted to know, panting a bit himself.

"The flowers..." Mildra said between gasps. "Their scent, their pollen... It was drugging us, making us want to..."

Tom stared at her in alarm, remembering their shared

passion, his arousal, but not able to recall where all of that had led to. "And... did we?" he asked timidly.

"No," she shook her head, and he wasn't sure whether to feel relieved or disappointed. "I realised what was going on, managed to exert enough self-control to stop us."

"How did you stop me?"

She looked at him a little awkwardly. "I put you to sleep."

"You what?"

"Sorry, but I had to. The effect of the pollen was so potent I... I couldn't fight it, couldn't rely on my own willpower... So the only thing I could do was remove the temptation."

Tom shook his head, not knowing whether to feel angry, offended, or what. In the end he started to giggle; quietly at first, but then the bizarreness of the whole situation swept over him, and he couldn't stop. Nor evidently could Mildra, because suddenly they were both laughing, and the more he looked at her face contorted with mirth, the more uncontrollable it became.

As the fits of juddering hysterics subsided, with Tom wiping tears from his eyes, Mildra was again picking up her pack. "Come on, we need to move further away from the meadow before sunrise."

Tom bent to collect his own pack and remembered something else. "When you woke me up just now, I had to pull my pack free from the grasses. How did that happen?"

"That was the worst part," she replied, striding away so that he had to scramble to keep up.

"How do you mean?"

"I know this sounds silly, but while we were both still – you asleep and me sitting beside you – the plants started to grow, really fast, extend tendrils over us."

"What?"

"They didn't move quickly enough that you could actually see them grow; in fact at first I thought I was imagining it, but I wasn't. If you watched the same spot for a few minutes, you could see how the shoots had reached out and moved. I had to keep pulling them off of your legs and body. Remember those bones we found on the way into the field? I think the whole place is a trap; beautiful and seductive but deadly all the same. Imagine, with all those plants and greenery, whole herds of deer and other plant eaters probably come wandering in here. The meadow lures them with its beauty and apparent abundance of food and drives them into a mating frenzy with all that pollen and scent, until they collapse from exhaustion. Then the plants snare them and feed."

"And you think that's what would have happened to us?"

"Yes."

He shuddered. "Thaiss!"

"I know."

He tried to imagine what it must have been like for her, sitting there in the field until nightfall, surrounded by danger and knowing she daren't relax and risk falling asleep. "Thank you," he said.

She smiled. "The worst part was working all this out and wondering if the plants could move any faster and knowing what would happen if I fell asleep."

Even in the fading light, he saw the young Thaistess shiver, and wanted to say something to comfort her, but couldn't think what.

"I couldn't wake you for fear that we'd lose control again," she continued, "and all the while I knew that by staying there we risked..."

"… becoming plant food."

"Yes. And there was no one but the goddess to ask if I was doing the right thing. And if the goddess answered, I didn't hear her." She sounded close to tears, and he felt tempted to put his arm around her, but in his mind's eye he felt again her naked breasts, saw her face contorted in passion, and the memory of what had happened between them just a few hours before stopped him. He couldn't stand the prospect of her pulling away.

"Here, this should be far enough," Mildra declared, her voice brimming with fragile bravery.

As they spread their sleeping mats she said quietly, "Tom, don't feel ashamed of what happened. It wasn't your fault, wasn't either of our faults."

He thought about her words as he pulled the coverings up and settled down, his back to hers, and realised that he wasn't ashamed. Slightly embarrassed, perhaps, but other than that he felt excited, exhilarated, and secretly even a little proud. As he closed his eyes he saw again the perfect shape of her breasts, felt her fingers stroking his naked back. In truth, there was a large part of him that regretted the Thaistess had stopped things when she did and wished she hadn't come to her senses until a moment or two later, whatever the dangers of their situation.

That thought did briefly shame him, even when memories of the action itself still failed to.

The hunter had no real problem picking up their trail at Pellinum. An attractive young woman travelling with a teenage boy might not be unusual enough to draw attention, but nor did it go entirely unnoticed; not this early in the year when pilgrims were so few. He strode up the path above the town, not pausing to admire the waterfall – he'd seen plenty such sights before – nor stopping to pay his respects at the temple: he had no time for religious tomfoolery. The pair were no more than a few days ahead and he felt confident of making up the time. After all, they were only a soft and pampered priestess and a wet-behind-the-ears kid, where as he was a professional; a killer born and trained. He'd catch up with them all right.

EIGHTEEN

Sander adjusted the sleeves on his jacket, pulling them down to his satisfaction, then lengthened his stride and hurried towards home. He'd had to work late again, which was threatening to become the norm. Globes were already out by the time he left the office, and was there any chance of claiming overtime? Not a hope, not now that he was considered part of "management". The company seemed to expect him to put in all the hours under the goddess simply out of love for the job. Well if they weren't careful they might soon discover just how much he was willing to take. It was about time they appreciated how vital he was. The place would come to a complete standstill without him.

Take today. The wretched barge from Crosston had been late. Again. Not just slightly this time but by a whole three hours, and of course there was nobody capable of overseeing the unloading but him. All the cargo had to be checked in and fully logged before he could even think of going home. Frissing job!

There was hardly anyone else on the streets at this hour, just the occasional idiot like him. All the sensible folk were already sitting at home with their feet up, hands cradled around a hot drink, no doubt. Having said that, there was a figure ahead, leaning against the wall; a woman by the look of things – probably a whore, though this wasn't one of their usual haunts. If she looked clean, he might even be tempted. He could do with some light relief after the day he'd just had.

Though, as he drew nearer, he was able to see how old she looked, perhaps too old. Shame.

"Sur Sander?"

The words caused his clipped, assured footfalls to falter. *She knew him?* He peered more closely, and suddenly recognised her. The apothaker, the one he'd bought the love potion from.

"Wh... what are you doing here?" he mumbled in dismay.

"Waiting for you," said a man's voice from close to his ear, and he felt the edge of a blade press against his throat while a firm grip closed on his arm.

Sander had never been assaulted before and instantly froze, paralysed by fear. The terror coursed through his body in a cold wave, totally unmanning him. The warm wet sensation of escaping urine steadily soaking his trousers only compounded the misery.

"What do you want?"

"Answers," said a new voice from somewhere behind him; a young woman's by the sound of it.

The blade pressing against his throat vanished, but before he had a chance to feel any relief at this release a hood was dragged roughly over his head and pulled tight via a noose-like cord at the neck, while his hands were hauled roughly behind his back and bound.

"No, please no. This is some mistake, it has to be," he whimpered, wondering how life could possibly be so unfair.

Kat hadn't expected to wake up. As she lost hold of the whip and plummeted towards the streets, she knew this was a fall she couldn't survive, and then, when the dark, vaguely humanoid shape swept towards her out of the night, she was convinced that her fate was to be the same as her mother's and her sister's. So, upon coming to in a soft bed with linen sheets covering her and a pleasant, floral scent in the air, she could perhaps be forgiven for thinking in those first confused seconds that she truly had died and was now in the realm of the goddess.

However, the presence of an acolyte in a grey cassock soon provided a clue that she might be in a slightly less elevated state of existence, a suspicion confirmed when a green robed priestess entered the room soon after.

She wasn't in any Thaissian afterlife at all, merely one of their temples. Oddly, her immediate reaction was an upwelling of huge disappointment. She didn't want to wake up, didn't deserve to still be alive, not when her mother had died so horribly, and then Rayul, and now Charveve. What was the point in living, and why her and not them? She rolled over, turning her back on the priestess and on the world, curled into a foetal ball and lost within her own despair, revelling in self-pity and welcoming the sanctuary of returning unconsciousness.

The second time she woke she felt far more level-headed. The grief and self-loathing were still there, she could feel them, but they were somehow detached and less immediate, as if she were merely sensing an echo of somebody else's emotions rather than her own. It seemed that all those negative, destructive feelings had somehow been clinically severed from the rest of her and then condensed and sealed into a tight knot which had then been tucked into some hidden recess of her being. A second heart, disconnected and dormant for now but ready to spring to life and pump the ice-cold plasma of despair around her body if provoked.

Kat sat up, rubbing her head, trying to come to terms with how odd she felt. Somebody else was in the room; the Thaistess. This time Kat had the presence of mind to take in detail; the elderly, slightly wrinkled face, laughter lines that formed so readily around grey-blue eyes, the small mole that nestled in the crease of a prominent nose, the faintest suggestion of a cleft chin, and the floral, vaguely minted scent that she would always associate with one person.

"Shella?"

"Welcome back, Kat." The woman reached out to squeeze her arm where it rested on top of the bed clothes.

"What... what have you done to me?"

"What was necessary. It seems my lot in life is to nurse you back to health whenever you misuse that body of yours."

Here was the same Thaistess Kat had crawled to when she'd fallen foul of a crooked business deal not long after leaving the Tattooed Men. With no Shayna to turn to, Kat had used the last drop of her failing strength to reach the nearest temple of Thaiss, collapsing at its door. Without the Thaistess's ministrations she would have died that night. Thanks to Shella she had lived, wiser and warier for the experience; or so she'd always hoped.

"How did I get here this time?" Kat asked.

"A Kite Guard brought you to us. He didn't know where else to take you."

"A Kite Guard?" She remembered the dark shape swooping to meet her as she hurtled towards the ground; so, not the Soul Thief after all.

"He was injured himself," the Thaistess continued. "Apparently he caught you as you fell off the grand conveyor...?"

"Not quite, but I can understand why he'd think that."

"Well, at any rate, catching you hampered his ability to fly and caused him to have a rough landing; more in the nature of a crash, from what I can gather. He was lucky, nothing too serious, and I was able to patch him up and send him on his way in no time. You, on the other hand, have taken a little longer to mend."

Kat had no idea what the Thaistess had done to heal her, how the hurt and despair had been excised or at least isolated, but she was willing to accept it as necessary. Kat had been a fighter all her life, but she had woken that first time without hope or the will to go on. Shella had given her the means to master that and to do whatever was necessary in the days ahead.

"Thank you, Shella... again," she said.

Kat left the temple a few hours later; not through any lack of gratitude, but because she was itching to know what had happened in her absence. Besides, she didn't want to outstay her welcome.

Shella would have preferred a little more patience. "You're not strong enough yet."

"I'll be fine, thanks to you." In truth she could probably have done with a little more time to recuperate, but the world wasn't about to pause and wait for her while she did so.

"The Kite Guard wanted to see you once you were awake," the Thaistess tried.

"I'm sure he did, and he may well do, but not right now. I have to know what's been going on."

And therein lay the crux of the matter. She'd been unconscious for a little over two days according to the Thaistess. Who knew what had happened in the meantime?

Kat headed straight to the house at Iron Grove Square, only to discover it deserted. One wing was damaged and blackened by fire, as was a window near the gates, but at first glance there was little other evidence of the titanic struggle that had taken place here just two nights ago. On closer examination she found some flechette darts and a few crossbow quarrels among the rubble, and even the occasional blood stain near the gates, but it all had the air of ancient history, not recent turmoil. There were no bodies, of course. The body boys would had carted those off with their usual efficiency, and that doubtless contributed to the sense of distance. Charveve, her sister, her bitterest rival and the most precious person in her world, had been taken from her; and she hadn't even had the chance to say goodbye.

After Iron Grove Square Kat visited the three safe houses in the vicinity, but without success. There was no indication that the Tattooed Men had visited any of them within the past few days.

It was then that she went to see the apothaker, to make sure she'd survived. The old woman was in fine spirits and even seemed pleased to see her, which Kat wasn't sure she deserved.

The pair swapped stories, the apothaker going first, describing how she'd been in the middle of the crowd when the gates at Iron Grove Square had finally been opened, but she was still able to see the mob of armed men who waited there, forcing their way through the gates and cutting down several of the talented while pushing the rest back. They then broke down the doors to either side of the gateway and stormed into both adjacent wings of the building, while others stayed at the gate to keep the talented penned in.

The apothaker had been among the surge of people who escaped when Kat charged the cordon of men and others followed her lead. She'd come straight home without discovering the outcome of events.

It was then Kat's turn. She described all that she had been through that evening, including her sister's death and her fall from near the top of the grand conveyor. It felt good to tell someone this, almost as if the words that left her mouth and the accompanying images and feelings they conjured helped to ease a burden she hadn't even realised was there. None of which stopped her from quipping as she finished, "So much for your brecking good luck potion; didn't do me any good at all."

"Really?" the apothaker asked. "You're still alive, aren't you?"

Perhaps she had a point; many others weren't, after all.

"The night time killings have stopped at any rate," the old woman reported. "So even if you didn't finish that thing for good, you must have done it some damage."

That was interesting. Had the Thief fled back to the Stain? If so, she was presumably weakened, having claimed only Chavver after coming so close to being killed herself. Had they scared the bitch that much?

"Oh, by the way, someone called here yesterday asking if I'd seen you," the apothaker continued.

Kat felt abruptly tense. *Brent?*

"One of your Tattooed Men," the old woman continued. "M'gruth, I think he called himself. He said that if I did see you, I was to say that he'll be at the Crooked Cockerel for the next few evenings."

Kat knew the Crooked Cockerel; a tavern M'gruth had always been fond of. She found herself smiling for the first time since waking up at the Temple. At least somebody had faith in her still being alive.

That evening, she found M'gruth where and when he said he'd be, and brought him back to the apothaker's. The old woman seemed glad of the company and Kat felt more comfortable talking where they couldn't be overheard. She listened intently as M'gruth filled her in on what had happened after she disappeared over the rooftops. It seemed that the Fang had come to the party mob-handed, but hadn't been overly choosy about who they recruited.

"Must have been around sixty of them," M'gruth told her. "There were some real hard nuts among them but also some wetting-themselves cowards. Because of the way we were spread around the building, mobs of them caught our boys in ones and twos to start with, taking us by surprise. Sheer numbers told and we lost a few."

"How many?"

"Seven; eight including Chavver. Plus two that Shayna worked miracles to save but are still recovering, Rel among them."

That was welcome news. Kat had thought Rel was done for when she'd seen him collapsed against the wall.

"What about the Fang?"

"Broke and ran once we were able to regroup; those that could. We counted thirty two bodies and reckon there were at least a dozen more injured who limped or crawled away."

"The Fang have been throwing their weight around in the streets of late," the apothaker interjected, "but no one's seen hide nor hair of them in the past couple of days."

Kat grunted. "That's something at least. What about the rest of the Tattooed Men?"

"A lot of razzer activity in the aftermath, what with the fire and everything, so we decided to scatter and go to ground for a few days."

Kat nodded. She might well have ordered the same under the circumstances, though it would have been handy to have the men readily available. As they continued to chat, she told the other two about Brent, a discussion which interested the apothaker, who thought the man Kat had seen in conversation with the sinister outsider sounded suspiciously like the client who had visited her immediately before the Soul Thief's attack, a certain Sur Sander...

Kat drew the hood off their prisoner, not bothering to be gentle. The man, Sander, hadn't stopped snivelling since they first jumped him. He'd whimpered as they led him the short distance here, begged for mercy as he was forced to sit in the chair, and had now lapsed into simply crying, as his imagination doubtless painted goodness only knew what pictures of the fate awaiting him. Kat didn't imagine they'd have much trouble getting information out of this one.

There was no question in her mind, Sander was the man she'd seen talking to Brent and a member of the Fang the night she'd been scouring the rooftops in search of the Soul Thief's lair.

M'gruth threw her an apple. She smiled at their captive. Tears and snot ran down his face as he stared back, wide-eyed. She took a bite from the apple, tossed it a little way into the air directly in front of Sander, then whipped up the sword in her other hand to slice through the fruit as it reached the apex of its flight. Sander jumped in his restraints and cried out as the blade flashed close to his face. Two uneven halves of apple fell to the floor.

"Now, Sur Sander, tell us about Brent."

She saw his eyes widen at mention of the name. "Wh... who? I don't know anyone called Brent."

"Liar!" She screamed the word, thrusting her face forward until her nose almost touched his.

He whimpered and shrank away.

"I saw you talking to him a few nights ago." She stood up again. "Now, there are two ways this can go. Either you tell us the truth straight away and we walk out of here without harming you, or you continue to lie, we slice off your fingers one by one, and then you tell us the truth. It's your choice. I don't care either way, but I thought that you might have a preference."

She brought the sword up, pressing the point to his cheek. The man was a mess, unable to take his eyes off of the blade She applied a little more pressure, pricking his skin and drawing a thin line of blood across his cheek. "So, what's it to be, eh, Sur Sander?"

He was crying silently now, his body convulsing within the restraints. "You've no idea what he's like..." he almost whispered between sobs. "He'd have killed me if I'd dared to refuse. I had to do it."

"Had to do what, Sur Sander?" Kat asked, her face still close to his though the sword had been withdrawn, her voice soft, almost soothing. "What was it Brent forced you to do for him?"

"You know, you know!" he cried. "Else you wouldn't have brought me here."

"We do know, yes, of course we know, but we want to hear it from you."

"I... I can't... please."

"Yes you can!" she screamed again.

After a fresh sob, he tried to speak. "I..." The words emerged as if each and every one was an individual torment. "I led her... that thing... to them."

"The Soul Thief, you mean."

"Yes."

"To the talented."

"Yes."

"What you're telling us is that this man, Brent, forced you to lead that abomination to the homes of the healers, the apothakers, the seers and the spirit talkers, to anyone who showed the slightest sign of real talent."

"Yes, yes," Sander whispered, his eyes squeezed tightly shut. "You have to believe me... I didn't have a choice."

"But he paid you, didn't he."

Silence followed her words.

"Didn't he!"

"Yes."

"There's always a choice, Sur Sander. You took this stranger's coin to betray your own kind. You became these people's clients, earned their trust, and then you found an excuse to visit their homes knowing that death shadowed your footsteps, and your pockets grew heavier with each and every one. That was your choice"

New sobs wracked the pathetic man's body. Kat felt nauseous. She wanted to slap him, to spit at him, to draw her swords and run him through, but refrained; not while they needed what he knew.

"What else could I do? " Sander whined. "He's evil, pure evil... I'm sorry, I'm so sorry." This last was spoken in the direction of the apothaker, who had hung back, preferring to stay in the shadows, though she could still be seen.

Kat couldn't bottle it up completely. "You disgust me."

He hung his head, refusing to meet her eyes. Kat paced up and down in front of him, controlling the rage, resisting the urge to leap on this bastard and stab him, again and again. No wonder the Soul Thief had killed so many this time around. She'd had a guide. But who exactly was this Brent, was he really just hired help as he claimed? What was his connection, or his employer's, with the monster that had now killed both Kat's mother and her sister?

She stopped in front of Sander's chair again. "And where can we find your friend Brent right now?

"I don't know."

"That's a shame. We were doing so well, and then you have to go and lie to me again." She looked up, to where a muscular figure stood behind the chair. "M'gruth, free his hands would you? And bring the right one forward where we can all see it. We'll start by taking off the little finger I think."

M'gruth grabbed the prisoner's arm, about to comply.

"No, no wait, please. Mill Lane, he's staying on Mill Lane."

"That's better. See how easy it is? Now, whereabouts in Mill Lane?"

"A tavern... a small place called the White Ox."

Kat looked to M'gruth, who shook his head. He didn't know that one either. "And that's in Mill Street, you say?"

"Mill Lane, not Mill Street, north end, on the conveyor side. But don't tell him you found out from me, please."

He sounded genuine. She felt sure this was the truth in as far as he knew it. "Oh, we won't, don't worry. I doubt there'll be much conversation of any sort when we catch up with Sur Brent."

Kat nodded towards the grim-faced M'gruth. The two of them headed towards the door. She didn't spare Sander another glance.

"Wait, where are you going?" he called out. "You said you'd set me free if I told you the truth."

"No, I didn't," Kat replied without stopping. "What I said was that we'd leave without harming you, and we are."

"But I'm not leaving," the apothaker said, stepping forward. "At least not until you and I have had a cosy little chat about my Kara, about what you brought into my home and how you helped to murder her."

"No, please, you can't leave me here   not with her," Sander called after them. "I told you everything you wanted to know... please!" Kat didn't blame him for pleading on that score. The apothaker might seem elderly and frail, but Kat had seen the look in the woman's eyes when they'd discussed the plan, and didn't doubt she'd make Sander pay for his betrayals.

Even after the door was shut behind them, Kat could still hear his desperate, whining voice, though the sound didn't bring the satisfaction she'd hoped for, not when set against all the loss she'd suffered of late. Still, there was every chance that the anticipated meeting with Brent would prove of greater help on that front.

Once outside the building Kat stopped, turning to M'gruth. "Wait here, would you? See that the old woman gets home safely." Night time in the under-City was not a place anyone her age should be abroad without protection.

M'gruth wasn't happy with the idea. "You can't take him alone, Kat. You've seen him fight. He stood toe to toe with Chavver and held his own."

"True," Kat admitted. "I've seen him fight. Tell me honestly, M'gruth, in a no-holds-barred scrap between me and Chav, who do you think would have won?"

He shook his head, as if about to duck the issue, then he looked her in the eye and sighed. "Truthfully... I don't know. You're both formidable. Chavver was a little stronger, you a bit quicker..." He shrugged.

"Exactly. I'm quicker, and Brent's never seen me fight. He's going to gauge me by what he knows of my sister."

M'gruth didn't seem convinced. "And you think that's going to be enough?"

"It will be, don't worry." She smiled, placing a comradely hand on the larger man's shoulder. "This is something I have to do, M'gruth. Alone."

"I know," he said after a pause.

"Just look after things this end for me. I'll see you before morning."

With that, she turned and walked away. Thirty paces later she heard a series of muffled sounds. Surely they weren't screams? No, couldn't be. They'd have to be really loud for her to have heard them from this far away. They certainly sounded like screams though.

Kat knew Mill Lane – a stubby passage which ran between Mill Street and the Whittleson Road, close to where the grand conveyor terminated at the Whittleson factory, but she'd never registered the presence of a tavern there. The buildings were two storey and the walls appeared to be grimy and dark, which added a claustrophobic sense to an alley which already seemed too narrow. There it was – a small sign sticking out from above a door otherwise indistinguishable from any of the others. Through the flaking paint she could just make out the crudely painted image of an ox. This looked exactly the sort of place in which a person could hide away without being noticed. The tavern was not yet open, so, stopping under the sign, she dropped one hand to her belt close to a sword hilt and then rapped twice on the door with the other.

Kat was fully attuned to the rhythms and nuances of the City Below; she knew how the world worked and so summed up the man who answered the door in a flash, reckoning that bravery would not prove his strongpoint. He opened the door a fraction and poked his head out.

"Is it a room you'll be after, little 'un?"

Long lank greasy hair framing an angular leather-skinned face which was dominated by a pair of small, darting eyes, all preceded by what had to be the worst breath Kat had ever encountered.

"No," she replied, pushing the door further open, forcing the man back and doubtless surprising him with her strength. "Information."

He was retreating rapidly towards a small bar and presumably either a sword or staff that lay hidden behind it. "I... I don't know nothing," he assured her. "Now stay back! I'm warning you, I've got friends among the razzers."

Kat doubted that, doubted he had much in the way of friends anywhere. She laughed. "Fine, you call your friends and I'll call mine: the Tattooed Men."

He stopped in his tracks and stared at her, clearly re-assessing who stood before him. He ran his tongue over his upper lip and then said, "What do you want?"

"There's a man staying here, name of Brent; an out-sider, from the East." She wasn't sure why she'd added the last, except that the words of the odd man from the chophouse came back to her. "Tall, thin, wears an un-usual brown coat."

"Hah!" The man laughed, showing a missing front tooth. "Was staying here, you mean."

"He's left, then?" Her heart sank. That had always been the danger – that Brent had fled the city straight after Iron Grove Square.

"Oh, he's left all right, though not by choice. The razzers came and took him yesterday afternoon."

The razzers? "Some of your friends, were they?" He looked sheepish. "Did they say why?"

"What, explain themselves to the likes of me? Proba-bly the same reason they ever do anything, because somebody paid them to."

True enough, but who else would be interested in Brent?

"So what's so special about this Brent anyway?" the man asked slyly.

"Trust me, you really don't want to know."

Kat walked away from the Crooked Cockerel with a mounting sense of frustration and anger. In a way this reminded her of the Pits, where she had been completely at the mercy of others. Once again she felt manipulated and used. There were things going on around her which she didn't understand, and whenever she tried to discover what they might be she found only more questions at every turn. It was time to regroup the Tattooed Men. Once she had them properly organised she intended to seek out a certain Kite Guard and find out what he knew, if anything. One way or another she was determined to get some answers.

NINETEEN

Tom couldn't decide whether he should consider this a particularly large village or a small town. The houses seemed to be crammed into the canyon, straddling the river, with a wooden bridge connecting the crowd of buildings on the far side to the nine or ten that he and Mildra were approaching on this side. It was late in the day, and the prospect of spending a night with a roof over their heads added an extra spring to Tom's step.

The bright colours of the houses' walls and low-pitched roofs – red bricks and tiles in places, blue painted ones in others – struck Tom as strangely appropriate, as if they represented an attempt to bring brightness to this otherwise sombre setting, nestled as these buildings were between buttresses of stark, grey rock. Likewise the triangular pennants in red, yellow and blue which fluttered listlessly from jauntily angled flagpoles somewhere towards the settlement's centre. There was a permanent sign planted in the ground on twin metal stakes immediately in front of the first house they came to. Tom ignored it; he couldn't read and had never seen any point in the written word so long as people had voices to speak with. Besides, he was more interested in the building itself. Now that he could see it close up, he was amazed at just how precariously the house perched on the mountain's side. Not just this one; all the buildings seemed to be situated in dizzyingly hazardous positions, and they were clustered closely together, as if to draw comfort from one another in the face of the mountain's might, or perhaps the river's, whose waters frothed and raged through the heart of the community.

They had an opportunity to experience that might from a new perspective, as they crossed above the torrent via the bridge. Despite the handrails and the bridge's apparently solid construction, Tom was never at his best when it came to heights and felt anything but secure. He had to continually suppress such thoughts as: *What if one of the boards is rotten and breaks beneath my feet?* and, *should the bridge really bounce this much at every step?* He walked stoically forward, focussing on a particularly bright roof on the far side and refusing to look down. He wasn't about to test the blocks the prime master had placed on his vertigo to that extent. In surprisingly short time they were across, stepping onto solid ground once more beneath twin cords of gold and silver foil streamers, which struck Tom as yet another fruitless attempt to lift the community's collective spirit.

As ever, the local people accepted the arrival of two strangers in this remote and inaccessible town without any apparent surprise, and if Tom had thought Pellinum boasted a lot of garish tat, this place surpassed it. Children kept running up to them with charms and crudely painted hand-carved statuettes of the goddess Thaiss.

The town had a strange atmosphere, an air of expectancy, as if the whole community was holding its breath, waiting for something or someone. The pilgrims, Tom suddenly thought. He and Mildra had been told in Pellinum that they were early, and surely that was why this place existed: to cater for pilgrims who hadn't arrived yet. No wonder the place seemed to be missing something; it was. He went to tell Mildra this flash of insight but stopped himself.

The Thaistess had gone out of her way all day to be friendly and happy, as if to emphasise that what happened in the flower meadow hadn't changed anything as far as she was concerned, but now she seemed distracted, troubled. Tom initially thought she was offended by the kids' trinkets, which commercialised and even trivialised the beliefs she'd built her life around, but it turned out to be more than that.

"Did you see that sign as we entered the town?" Mildra asked as they took shelter from the street hawkers in a café. He confirmed that he had. "And did you see what it said?"

"No, I didn't." The last thing he wanted to do was admit to her that he couldn't read.

"Well, the top line read 'Pilgrimage End' and below that was written 'Welcome to the source of the Thair'." She looked at him, clearly expecting a reaction.

"You mean we've arrived?" he asked, having frankly anticipated more. "*This* is where your goddess is supposed to live?"

"No," she said, "and that's the problem." Mildra turned to the waiter who was delivering them drinks – two plump earthenware mugs of *doolhd*, a recommended local speciality which consisted of warmed goats' milk infused with mint and mountain herbs. "Excuse me, but could you tell us how far we are from the source of the river Thair?"

"Why, you're no distance at all, young pilgrim." The man's face split into a broad grin, revealing a gold tooth which Tom found annoyingly distracting. "Because the source of the sacred river is right here, in this very town!" Again the gold tooth glinted from beneath the man's moustachioed nostrils – any upper lip he might have possessed was completely obscured by the whiskers. "At the northern end of town you will find the great Temple of Thaiss, where you may meditate undisturbed for as long as you wish in a gallery over-looking the holy waters, before leaving your offerings, safe in the knowledge that they will be received by the goddess herself." Drinks safely deposited on the table, he clasped his hands together in front of his chest at these final words.

"But that can't be right," Mildra protested. "The river continues on beyond this town, so how can this be the source?"

The man was shaking his head. "I understand your confusion, dear pilgrim. You see, beyond this point the Thair becomes nothing more than fractured uncertainty – a bewildering tangle of many streams and falls, like the roots of a tree, spreading out in all directions, fetching water from the peaks, all of which combines to form the blessed torrent that flows through our humble commu-nity. Trust me, Pilgrimage End; this is the first point where the Thair can be clearly identified and the flow of water is worthy of being called a river."

"None of which makes this the source, surely."

The man's smile was beginning to look a little strained. "The Thair has a thousand sources in the melt waters of the mountains, all feeding this, the true source, where the goddess Thaiss dwells in her temple. Rejoice, young pilgrim, for you have reached the end of your journey." With that, he moved away to serve another customer.

Mildra looked far from satisfied.

"Perhaps we should pay a visit to this temple," Tom suggested.

"The sooner the better," the Thaistess agreed.

They each sipped tentatively at their lukewarm beverages. Tom smacked his lips after the first taste of the aromatic emulsion, trying to decide what to make of it. He concluded that while the taste wasn't entirely unpleasant – tangy but mellow – he didn't much care for the fatty feel it left in his mouth. All in all, Tom reckoned he could happily go the rest of his life without sampling *doolhd* again. Judging by the look on Mildra's face, the Thaistess liked the drink even less than he did.

She grimaced and said, "How does right now sound?"

"Fine by me."

Pilgrimage End struck Tom as rather a pompous title for such an oddly structured town. True, there were *some* level surfaces, where streets and paths had been created, but the terrain undulated dramatically, with buildings on one side of a given street liable to have doors higher than those on the other. Small flights of steps were used everywhere to try and bridge the differences, yet there remained a sense that this was a rag-tag collection of buildings which happened to have been built in the same place rather than a proper town. At least it wasn't all that big, and, despite the unconventional geography, they had little trouble in finding the temple.

This was very different from any temple of Thaiss Tom had seen in the City Below, or the one they'd encountered lower down at the lagoon. Situated at the north most edge of the town, it was evidently the largest building in Pilgrimage End and, Tom suspected, the gaudiest. The facia in particular struck Tom as horrible. Gold and red pillars fronted imposing arched wooden doors that were themselves painted gold; currently thrown open so that they looked like great golden wings framing the doorway. The temple stood on three levels, each smaller than the one above it, like some elaborate celebratory cake.

A flight of stairs led up to the imposing doorway, which, in effect, opened into the building's second storey. To either side of the doors, the wall was divided into a series of panels, each intricately decorated and gilded. As Tom came nearer, he could see that some of the detailing here was astonishing. At the top of each panel a line of powerful looking animals were depicted, carved in miniature and facing outwards on a series of plinths, all designed to appear as if they were holding up the top of the frame that surrounded each panel. There were lumbering beasts that resembled oxen but with large flapping ears and noses ridiculously extended and curling to disappear under their bodies, great snarling cats with heads thrown upward and tails lying flat along their backs, claw-footed spill dragons with jaws spread wide, all where a simple small support would have sufficed, or just a plain unadorned wall. Even the tiny plinths supporting the beasts were embellished with meticulous scrolls and motifs. Tom had never seen such elaborate decoration.

The building was topped with a bright golden-yellow roof, its edges artfully scalloped so that each point coincided with one of several ornamental half pillars, also golden, built into the wall of the upper storey. The latter at least Tom could forgive, since the roof was in keeping with much of the rest of the town, but gold pillars?

Inside, the temple floor was paved in polished tiles. Despite the two doors being flung open, the end of the broad pillared chamber which they found themselves in seemed dark due to a lack of windows, especially beyond the fringes of the doorway's illumination. The far end, in contrast, was ablaze with light. As they walked nearer, Tom could see why. In addition to the broad expanse of glass windows that formed the temple's furthest wall, the floor also contained a number of glass panels, through which could be seen the rushing torrent of the Thair. Tom took an involuntary step back, as he realised that the temple had deliberately been designed to jut out over the river.

They weren't the only visitors. There were some half dozen genuine pilgrims present, a couple simply standing, gazing at the torrent below, while most were on their knees, clutching beads or simply clasping their own hands before them, all bar one with heads bowed and eyes closed. A priest in white robes approached them. He looked to be fairly young but was shaven headed, which made it hard for Tom to be certain.

"Can I help you?"

Mildra smiled and bobbed her head respectfully. "Dear brother, I am the Thaistess Mildra, who has travelled the long journey from the city of Thaiburley to bring greetings and to renew my order's faith with our mother, the goddess."

Had she declared herself to be Thaiss incarnate Tom doubted the priest could have looked more astounded. He immediately went in search of "the Blessed Mother", whom Tom assumed to be the head of the holy-sorts around here, inviting Mildra to follow. Trusting the Thaistess and having less desire to get involved in a round of religious greetings and pleasantries than he would leap into the freezing Thair naked, Tom chose to stay where he was.

Curiosity overcame his caution, and Tom edged forward to peer down through one of the floor windows, making sure not to disturb any of the pilgrims in the process. The sight of the frothing white torrent directly below was certainly impressive, but, he suspected, no more so than the view available from the bridge dissecting the town. Of course, he couldn't confirm this, since he'd made a point of not looking down when they'd gone across. As he edged along the window's side a little further, he was able to see that a series of broad steps had been carved into the rock, leading down to the Thair, presumably from the ground floor of the temple beneath. More pilgrims were there, and a pair of white robed, shaven-headed priests. Some ceremony seemed to be in progress, with the priests lifting water from the Thair in an ornate golden bowl and tipping it over kneeling pilgrims.

Looking back at this happening behind and beneath him provided Tom with an odd and interesting perspective, but he was more focused on the implications of what he saw. It struck him that the river itself was being treated as divine here; people acted as if the Thair was a god in its own right, not merely a channel for the influence of the goddess as the Thaissians in Thaiburley believed.

He was itching to hear Mildra's take on this observation, but realised he'd probably have to be patient for a good while yet before doing so. How long was an audience with "the Blessed Mother" supposed to take, in any case? Not as long as he'd feared, apparently. Having watched the ceremony below reach its conclusion, and the priests and acolytes climb up the steps and out of his view, Tom crept away from the windows and examined the intricate carvings of the temple's inner walls. As detailed and expertly realised as those on the outside, though not as garishly painted. He was just resigning himself to a long wait, when Mildra reappeared, accompanied by the same priest. They smiled at each other with apparent equanimity and even warmth in parting, but Tom knew Mildra well enough to sense how shallow an expression hers was.

For once he curbed his impatience, at least until they were out of the temple and back in the streets again.

"So?" he said at last, when the Thaistess still hadn't volunteered anything.

Mildra stopped in her tracks, glared at him while taking several deep breaths, and looked fit to scream. "This place is really trying my patience."

She said it with sufficient vehemence to draw a startled look from the storekeeper whose shop they'd stopped beside. The man was busy stacking empty wooden crates along the side wall, but hurried back to the front as if to avoid what he presumably took to be an argument.

"Thought you were a bit quick with her blessedness."

"Huh! She'd have had me there all day if she could. She wanted me to take part in ceremonies and hymnal incantations, which, from what I could gather, are so pompous and elaborate it's a wonder they ever have time to actually think about the goddess herself." More deep breaths. "I don't understand this place, this town, so close to the holy source and yet the people here all seem to be out for what they can get, with cheap trinkets and souvenirs, talk of offerings to the goddess... What goddess? She isn't in their precious temple, that's for sure. I think the 'offerings' are claimed by the priesthood, not the goddess at all."

"The priests then, they're false as well?"

"No, no." She shook her head, as if frustrated by her inability to express herself. "They strike me as devout, dedicated and holy people, but the faith they follow, the way they express it, seems so... misguided, so gaudy and materialistic. Whatever happened to the simplicity of worship?"

Tom felt increasingly out of his depth. Never having worshipped or even believed in any deity, he wasn't sure how to respond to this.

"Oh, I don't know," Mildra said. "It's just that coming here, so close to the source of everything I've always believed in, I expected this to be incredible, an uplifting, inspirational experience... And it isn't. Not in the least."

Tom couldn't bear to see Mildra like this, on the verge of questioning beliefs so central to who she was. "Maybe things will be different when we find the true source," he said. "Remember, this isn't it. We're going on from here."

"Yes, you're right." Her shoulders sagged a little. She looked at him, and smiled. "Thank you. The sooner we leave this place, the better."

As if to emphasise her point, a cocky voice said, "Well

what have we got here? Couple of pilgrims come to pay tribute, by the look of it. Which is good news all round."

Tom looked up, to see three youths standing a few paces away, close to the shop front. The largest brandished a stout stick, while one of the pair flanking him stood toying with a knife, as if to do so was the most natural thing in the world. Tom cursed under his breath. He'd become so absorbed in the conversation with Mildra he'd let his guard down.

"Yeah," the third kid said, sniggering, "'cos we're here to collect."

"We don't want any trouble," Tom said.

"Course you don't."

"We've just been to the temple," Mildra said. "We don't have anything to give you."

"See, Jed," the sniggerer said, "they're on the way back. We should have got them on the way going, like I said."

The big lad, presumably Jed, shrugged. "Doesn't matter. They still gotta get home, so they'll have coin, food, stuff to barter with, enough for the journey at least."

"Oh yeah, so they will." And with that, the trio started towards them, the stick-wielding Jed to the fore.

"Stand back!" Tom drew his sword, not at all reassured when the sniggerer laughed out loud and the others grinned, with no sign that the weapon worried them in the slightest. Jed's stick whirled around at dizzying speed, to sweep down and crack Tom on the hand with bruising force. He cried out at the sudden pain and promptly dropped his sword.

The stick twirled in the lout's hand again, coming around in an arc which Tom just knew would end on his head. He reached sideways to grab hold of the wooden crates, ignoring the agony in his right hand which throbbed where the stick had hit it. He half dragged and half threw the top two crates at the three local boys. Seeing his intent, Mildra did the same with the next stack.

"Run," Tom yelled, acting on his own advice. Mildra turned to run beside him as the crates tumbled over in their wake.

Angry shouts pursued them as they charged down narrow streets and raced up steps, ducking beneath a line of washing strung across an alleyway, hurdling a stool placed in front of a doorway, nearly bowling over a pair of startled elderly women who were suddenly in front of them as they tore round a corner. Tom felt like laughing; he could almost imagine he was back in the streets of the under-City again, running rings around incompetent razzers.

Except that Mildra had never been used to running anywhere and despite the vague sense of familiarity these were not Thaiburley's streets, not the streets he knew.

"Tom," the Thaistess said, stumbling to a halt, "I can't go on." She held her sides and bent forward, doubling over and gasping for breath. "Sorry. You keep running... maybe they'll ignore me."

Maybe, but he wasn't about to take that chance.

A clatter of running footsteps behind them heralded the arrival of two of the youths; while at the same moment a shout came from ahead, where the stick-bearing Jed had appeared, effectively cutting them off. Naturally they'd know these streets better than Tom; their turf, not his.

Tom grabbed hold of his exhausted companion's hand and urged her forward. "Come on, Mildra, just a few more steps, you can do it." He dragged her in his wake as he ran towards Jed.

Tom had taken on plenty of bigger kids in his time and would far rather face one opponent than two or three, irrespective of size. He didn't look back, didn't want to know where the other two were. His attention was focused on this one, the leader, the kid with the stick, Jed, who was charging towards them even as they stumbled towards him, so that the gap closed in no time.

Tom eased Mildra down into a sitting position, in the process palming a couple of small stones from the ground. Then he stood, drew his knife and waited as the lummox came forward. His hand still throbbed but he didn't care. He felt a whole lot more comfortable now than he ever had when holding the sword.

No, not his turf, not the streets he knew, but for once on this trip it was his kind of fight.

Jed closed in, grinning, confident. Tom waited until he was almost in range of that staff before hurling the first stone. Too close for Jed to avoid, the missile struck him on the left temple, causing him to flinch, turn his head and pull his chin to his chest, while his free hand and shoulder rose instinctively to provide protection. Tom closed in, stepping within the arc of that stick, flicking out with his knife and cutting the bigger lad's raised fore-arm to add to the pain and confusion before punching him hard in the gonads, the second stone still clenched in his fist. The stick clattered to the floor and, with a strangled howl of pain, Jed followed, sinking to his knees, both hands covering his abused groin.

Tom was immediately behind him, grabbing Jed's hair and pulling his head back, knife pressed to the bigger youth's exposed throat.

As he'd hoped, the other two kids were ignoring Mildra, their attention focused on the unfolding drama. Both were flushed with either anger or fear and neither seemed inclined to snigger anymore.

"Now, as we said, we don't want any trouble." He tried to put as much menace in his voice as possible. "If that means I have to kill Jed here or even all three of you to ensure that we don't get any, I'll do it. Understood?"

The pair nodded. Mildra climbed to her feet but made no move to intervene.

"Drop your weapons."

After the briefest hesitation both tossed their knives to the ground, close to Jed's fallen stick. Mildra did move then, collecting the two knives and the stick before coming to stand at Tom's shoulder.

"Right. I'm going to let Jed here go and then count to five. By the time I reach five, I don't want to be looking at any of you. If I am, I'll assume you want to continue the fight, except this time we'll be the ones with the weapons."

He whipped his own blade away from Jed's throat and pushed the larger boy in the back, so that he landed on all fours.

"One..."

The other two came forward, helping Jed to his feet.

"Two..."

The trio scurried away, Jed stumbling in the wake of the others, managing a lurching bandy-legged gait and needing their help to keep up.

By the time he reached five, Tom's shoulders were shaking and he couldn't control the laughter, nor could Mildra beside him.

"Well done," the Thaistess said, and kissed him on the cheek.

The laughter drained out of him and visions of her naked breasts and her impassioned face flashed through his thoughts. She looked suddenly embarrassed, as if the kiss had been instinctive, something she now regretted and wouldn't have done had she thought things through.

"Are you... feeling all right now?" he asked in an effort to breach the awkward silence.

"Yes, thanks. Sorry about your sword."

He shrugged. "No real loss. I was never any good with it in any case."

She grinned. "True."

That easily, they put the awkwardness behind them and walked back to the café they'd visited earlier, if not arm in arm, then at least still side by side.

With evening drawing in the place was busier, and seemed to be slipping smoothly into a new identity; that of bar rather than café. A few of the patrons looked to be locals, but they were in the minority. Most were clearly visitors, pilgrims such as they'd encountered at the temple; nor were all human. Three Kayjele clustered around a table on chairs clearly designed to accommodate beings of their size. Tom stared. These were the first of their race he'd seen apart from Kohn, and he was fascinated to note both the similarities and the differences to his fallen friend.

Mildra seemed delighted to see the trio of giants here, and rummaged in her pack to pull something out; Kohn's heart stone, which she held up to show Tom, smiling triumphantly.

"Do you really think–" But before he could say any

more, she was up out of her seat and darting the short distance across the floor to the Kayjeles' table.

Tom watched with interest as the three giants – their faces as different as any similar group of humans might be – stopped what they were doing and stared at the Thaistess. All were male, Tom noted. Presumably they were talking in the fashion of Kayjele. What must that be like? Could Mildra hear all three of their mental voices at once, and did they sound different? Or did she have to talk to them one at a time? There was nothing in their facial expressions or movements to give anything away.

After a few moments Tom saw Mildra hand the heart stone to one of the trio and she then came back to join him. "There," she said, obviously pleased with herself. "They promised to make sure the pendant gets back to Kohn's family."

"But can they be trusted?"

"What do you mean?"

"Well, I was just thinking, imagine a man, any man, just a traveller, in a strange place – the land of another race or tribe – and one of this race comes up and hands him a precious jewel, saying that it belonged to a friend of his who was human but has died, and asking the man to make sure this jewel reaches his family. I just wonder how many men would even bother trying."

"Oh." She looked crestfallen. "I hadn't even thought of that."

No, of course she hadn't – not until he went and opened his big mouth. He could have kicked himself. "Mind you, that's to judge the Kayjele by human standards," he said quickly, making it up as he went along. "I'm sure they're nothing like us and our friends over there will deliver the pendent as promised. They're pilgrims, after all."

"Yes," she gave an uncertain smile, "I'm sure you're right." But she wasn't, not any more, he could see that in her eyes. And that was his fault. Tom swore silently. Surely by now he should have learnt to keep his thoughts to himself, or at least to be a little more selective when voicing them.

"What was it like?" he said, both to change the subject and because he genuinely wanted to know. "Talking with three of them at once, I mean."

"Actually, that was a bit strange, especially to begin with..."

Before Mildra could go any further, the gold-toothed waiter from earlier that afternoon appeared to ask for their drinks order. The pair exchanged a knowing grin and both scrupulously avoided ordering the doolhd.

"Did you visit our wondrous temple?" the obsequious man asked, glinting gold at every word.

"Yes, it's very beautiful," Mildra temporised.

"Ah, I'm so happy your pilgrimage has reached such a fulfilling conclusion." He again clasped his hands, as if to bless their joyous journey.

"Actually," Tom replied, "we're not so sure it has reached a conclusion. We'd still like to explore the river higher up, above the town."

"But why?" The man looked horrified. "There's nothing up there but snow and rocks and cold and slipperiness. It's dangerous, and you're both so young!"

Eventually, once convinced of their seriousness and determination, Gold Tooth admitted that the town had a few hunters who ventured that way and knew the trails as well as anyone. By happy coincidence, one such was his brother, whom he'd be delighted to introduce them to.

Within the hour they were talking to a man who looked much like Gold Tooth – swarthy skinned, with a flat, broad nose and heavy eyebrows – but lacking the golden dental enhancement and also the bushy moustache. In place of the latter, Ky, the hunter, sported salt and pepper stubble around his chin, as if to emphasise that here was a rugged man who courted the wilderness and lacked the time for such niceties as regular shaving. There was something behind the man's eyes that made Tom uneasy. A cunning calculation that caused him to doubt the wisdom of entertaining the hunter at all.

"I can take you further up, for sure," he told them. "It's not an easy climb though. No real path up there any more, just game trails at best."

"You say 'any more'…?" Mildra cut in.

"There is an old temple, half a day from here. Abandoned now because of the severe conditions, but there used to be a trail leading to it. We'll follow that to begin with, as far as we can at least."

And so it was settled; they would leave first thing the following morning.

TWENTY

The tingling in the prime master's arm was growing progressively worse. There were techniques at his disposal that could dull the feeling if not tackle the actual cause. He used them without hesitation. Not because he was afraid, although he very much was, nor because he was attempting to deny the truth or avoid the inevitable, but because the sensation could be a distraction. If, as he presumed, there was only a very limited time left to him, then he intended to maximise that time. There were things he needed to do, arrangements to be made and events to set in motion while he still could.

The prime master didn't tell anyone about the tingling. What would be the point? He was in constant touch with Jeanette and knew that she was still a long way from finding a cure, so what could anyone else do? Nothing, except look worried while they pitied him, make a fuss and tell him to take things easy, and generally get in the way and slow him down; all things he could do without. So he determined to keep quiet until the last possible moment.

In the meantime he had something new to worry about, as if such were needed.

A ridiculous number of documents crossed his desk each day – far more than any one person could be expected to consider in detail, though he tried to look at as many as possible, if only briefly. Most were reports of things done and action taken, things which protocol insisted he be notified of though they didn't really merit his attention, but not all. Among all this mass of triviality and routine, one caught his attention. Perhaps it was pure luck or the machinations of some predestined fate that brought this particular sheet of paper to his attention, though the prime master liked to think that after all these years he had a knack for such things. One name caught his eye, that of a man he had seen a lot of in the past few days: the Kite Guard, Tylus.

During the recent unrest in the under-City, one of the sun globes had come down, visiting death and devastation on the people and buildings below. To the best of the prime master's knowledge, this was an event unprecedented in Thaiburley's history, though it was difficult to be certain since the damage inflicted on the core during the war. In a commendable display of initiative, the local Watch officer had evidently prevailed upon Tylus to investigate the incident. The Kite Guard had discovered a small partially crushed mechanism which he couldn't explain and had sent it for analysis.

Doubtless Tylus himself had since forgotten all about this, but as a result of his keen eye for detail, a document had eventually been produced, to find its ways – one of so many – onto the prime master's desk. The significance of the report was enough to momentarily eclipse even his concerns about bone flu. The prime master read it again, to make certain he'd not misinterpreted the conclusions. But no, there they were, recorded in a box with such apparent innocence.

How could somebody have written this without immediately flagging it for more senior attention? Without shouting the findings from the rooftops for Thaiss's sake!

This seemingly mundane piece of paper contained news that threatened the security of all Thaiburley. For, according to this, the war, which everyone thought had ended generations ago, was still continuing. The report threw a whole new light on the recent unrest in the City Below, on the schemes of the Dog Master and the subversion of the street-nicks. The prime master had sensed at the time that there was a hidden hand behind those events, and now, at last, he felt sure he'd unmasked the true villain.

According to this report, the mechanism Tylus had sent for analysis was part of an Insint – an Instability and Intelligence Unit – one of the enemy's most successful weapons during the war. It would seem that somewhere – presumably in the Stain or it would surely have been discovered long before now – one of these lethal organic-mechanical hybrids still operated, patiently plotting the city's downfall.

If the prime master had time to do just one thing before his body calcified and his heart was stilled forever by a fist of encroaching bone, then let it be this. He refused to die before Thaiburley was safe from this insidious machine stubbornly fighting a war that the rest of the world had been trying to forget for generations. And he believed he'd hit upon a means of doing exactly that.

• • • •

Ky was waiting for them the next morning as promised. Tom trusted this brother of Gold Tooth's about as far as he could see with both his eyes closed, but he and Mildra had discussed matters the previous night, after they had been left alone, and both accepted that the huntsman wasn't just their best chance of finding the Thair's true source, he was probably their only chance.

At least he seemed to be taking the expedition seriously, insisting they were kitted out with appropriate clothes and providing both of them with stout staffs. The clothing included gloves, which Tom had never worn in his life and instantly hated. They made his hands feel trapped and far too hot. The knuckles on his right hand had stiffened up in the night and were badly bruised from where Jed's stick had caught them during the previous day's fight, so he transferred the staff to his left. On reflection, he should probably have asked Mildra to do something about the bruising before now, but he was reluctant to keep running to her with every minor gripe.

"You'll need those for when we get further up, into the snow," Ky explained, indicating the staffs.

Tom couldn't argue about it being cold. Breath formed plumes of vapour as they spoke, and every inhalation brought a chill to his mouth and throat. They walked through the town, drawing the odd curious glance from the locals, and then past the temple at the northern tip of habitation. The golden doors were firmly shut and the place looked altogether less impressive in the absence of priests and worshippers.

"In another month or so you won't be able to walk through here like this," Ky told them. "The place will be packed with people even at this hour, all patiently queuing,

waiting for their chance to pray to the goddess and leave
their tributes at the temple."

This was said with a hint of disdain which Tom
found curious in a man who made his home here, even
though a large part of Tom felt much the same way, but
Mildra stepped in, saying, "Yes, I often feel humbled by
the dedication of the faithful," which struck Tom as the
perfect rejoinder.

Ky led them between two imposing boulders, following
a narrow track which barely merited the name. Without
him their progress would have been far slower, assuming
they could even have found the way forward. He moved
with calm assurance, leading them ever higher, until they
were able to look back at the brightly coloured roofs of
Pilgrimage End – a scattering of children's sweets cast
upon the landscape, red, yellow and blue.

As they walked it started to snow; not heavily, just
large flakes drifting on the breeze, but this was yet another first for Tom, and he watched fascinated as a fat
fleck of whiteness landed on his gloved hand, melting
slowly because of the insulation locking in his body's
heat. He'd seen snow on the peaks of the mountains for
the past few days, but this was the first time he'd seen it
close up and felt the icy kiss of flakes striking his cheeks.

Their way was constantly intersected by streams and
trickles feeding into the river, and twice they saw spectacular waterfalls on the opposite side hurling torrents
down into the Thair, but they'd yet to see a fracturing of
the main river's course as Gold Tooth had predicted.

Their first real hurdle came not long after the roofs of
Pilgrimage End had disappeared from sight. A wider
stream, which over the years had carved out its own

small canyon. At the bottom of the treacherous looking crack water frothed, tumbling over and around rocks and boulders in a broiling surge of white spume, all the while hissing like a room full of over-excited serpents. Ky didn't pause, nonchalantly leaping across without even bothering to warn his two companions to be careful, as if challenging them to cope as readily as he had.

It wasn't that wide, the dramatic setting being the only thing that made this seem even remotely daunting. Tom knew he could make the jump comfortably but wasn't so sure about Mildra. However, she gave him a confident smile, gathered herself, then ran a few short steps and sailed across the narrow gap with arms outstretched like a dancer. Tom was reminded of the rooftop dash he and Kat had made, and how her elegance had made him feel awkward and clumsy. He decided to stop worrying quite so much about the Thaistess and concentrate on getting across safely himself.

As morning wore on the snow stopped falling, but they now travelled across a patchwork landscape of brown and white, and the ground underfoot became increasingly treacherous. Still the Thair sang its warbling song beside them.

They came to a point where the river divided, and each branch was itself fed by a number of tumbling, melt-swollen streams. Perhaps Gold Tooth hadn't been entirely wrong after all. Ky continued along the right-hand fork without hesitation.

"Is that right?" Tom asked Mildra quietly.

"I... I'm not sure," Mildra replied. "I think that's right, but the goddess's presence is so strong around here that I seem to sense her everywhere."

Soon after, the three of them rounded a rocky bluff. Ky stood to one side and simply grinned, apparently waiting to see their reaction.

Tom came to stand beside the hunter; only then did he understand why. The view was spectacular. The rocks here were of a deep, dark brown, starkly prominent against the blanket of pure white snow which might once have covered them completely but now did so imperfectly, as bold rock thrust through the whiteness, tearing gaping wounds in the virginal mantle. Dramatic enough in its own right, this scene was relegated to a supporting role – that of mere backdrop – by what stood in the immediate foreground.

An abandoned temple; stonework weathered and brown, seemingly ancient. The stones the buildings had been hewn from were a perfect match for the rocky slopes around them, as if the temple were an extension of the very mountain, sharing the slow strength and majestic wisdom of ages. Columns had been built of great flat stones piled one on top of another, each an individual shelf – those at the bottom marginally broader than those above so that they formed squat, tapering towers without ever actually reaching a point. From one such solemn buttress the image of a great beast snarled at them – a stylised lion, Tom decided, though it wasn't easy to be certain. The whole place seemed old in a way that Thaiburley never managed to.

None of the buildings were overgrown – there were no tangles of vine or shoots reaching into nooks and crannies to strangle the stonework and pull apart the structures – though here and there water dripped from the corner of a roof, as if the rock was wringing itself fully dry.

"The High Temple of Thaiss," Ky said. "Abandoned now, of course."

"Why?" Mildra wanted to know. Tom agreed; there was some rubble, yes, a few fallen pillars, but on the whole the place seemed in remarkably good condition.

"Because for much of the year this temple is buried under snow and ice. Only for the few months of summer's thaw does it emerge." Which perhaps explained the absence of invading plants. "Generations ago the priests would come and go with the thaw and the snows, but not anymore; easier to remain at the temple in Pilgrimage End than to constantly migrate with the seasons."

A large black crow alighted on the lion's head to stare at Tom inquisitively. It opened its maw as if preparing to screech either welcome or warning, though no sound emerged. Then the bird launched itself into the air, to be joined by a mate. The pair spread splayed black wings and soared away out of sight.

Following the bird's flight, Tom's gaze came to rest on Mildra. Only then did he stop to wonder at her reaction to this place. In the passage of days they'd spent together he had all but forgotten that she was a Thaistess, a fact brought starkly back into focus at Pilgrimage End. Certainly it wasn't a Thaistess he was thinking of when he recalled in such vivid detail their encounter in the flower meadow. Whatever did or didn't lie between them, now or in the future, faith was one facet of this girl who had come to mean so much to him which he would never be able to share.

He wondered what was going through her head now as they stood on the threshold of this lost place of ancient worship. It was a far cry from the commercial temple they'd visited the previous day; this place had a presence, a sense of inherent importance that even Tom could sense. It made him want to creep around on tiptoe out of sheer respect.

As he watched, Mildra stepped forward between the first two pillars. Her eyes seemed focused only on the temple, as if she'd forgotten about her companions entirely; but then she surprised him by looking to him and smiling. "This," she said, "is a lot more like it."

Ky came up beside him and put a friendly hand on his shoulder. "Really something, isn't it?"

"Definitely," Mildra agreed, without looking round.

Tom felt a slight scratch to the underside of his chin when Ky's arm withdrew, as if he'd been caught by a sharp edge on a ring or some such.

Mildra was staring up towards the temple's roof, which looked to be intact despite the neglect. "I can't believe they'd abandon this place."

"I know," Ky agreed as he sauntered up to stand beside the Thaistess.

And then he hit her. A vicious swipe of the fist that came out of nowhere. Caught completely off guard, Mildra sprawled to the ground.

Tom went to react; he tried to shout out, to rush to Mildra's aid, to move… to do anything, but he couldn't. To his horror, he was frozen to the spot, paralysed. He was still breathing, but other than that only his eyeballs would respond; he couldn't even blink.

Mildra seemed to fumble with something, her knife; but Ky wrenched it from her hand. "Now, now," he told her. "Behave and this will all go a lot easier on you. And don't expect any help from the boy. He won't be able to lift a finger." The man laughed, presumably at his own attempt at humour. "A nerve poison, distilled from a local plant found around the temple, as it happens. By the time you and I've finished having our fun, he'll be dead. Don't worry, though, he'll live long enough to see most of it."

Mildra tried to struggle, a desperate lashing out of legs and fists, but Ky struck her again, slapping her in the face. The Thaistess sagged back, either stunned or unconscious.

"Pretty girl like you is wasted on a kid like him in any case. It's not right. What you need is a real man." As he spoke, the hunter was tugging at his belt, pulling his trousers down.

Tom could only look on. He tried desperately to move a hand, even a finger, but failed. Nor could he feel anything anymore, as if the nerve endings had fled from his skin. In his head, he screamed, but no one heard it except himself.

Ky had obviously been planning this all along. Tom and Mildra were pilgrims, who was going to miss them? And in the unlikely event someone did, how could anyone be blamed? After all, they'd insisted against all advice on striking out into the icy wilderness beyond the town. Whatever happened to them after that was obviously their own fault.

Gold Tooth. Was he in on this, feeding his brother likely victims to drag off into the back of beyond to rape, rob, and quietly murder? Tom could picture the pair of them huddled together late that night, smirking as they split their gains. They were no better than the thugs who had attacked him and Mildra with sticks and knives as they returned from the temple, merely more sophisticated.

Tom watched in horror as Ky, trousers now pushed back around his ankles, drew a knife and reached towards Mildra, who was moving feebly.

Tom remembered how he'd broken Magnus's command to halt and kept running when fleeing from the wall. If he could defy the power of a senior arkademic, surely he could fight this. He focused on the little finger of his left hand, willing it to move, if only a fraction, but nothing happened.

Everyone kept insisting he was special, powerful; he'd saved the whole city for Thaiss's sake, and yet here he was, helpless to save someone he cared about, not to mention himself. What good his much vaunted abilities now? They worked only against mechanisms... Or did they? Mildra had told him he could be a healer with the proper training, and his original talent, that of hiding in plain sight, had been used on people from the very start...

He needed to concentrate but couldn't close his eyes, so instead he stared intently at Ky, drawing on that part of himself he'd tapped into when striking down the Rust Warrior, that coil of something deep inside which he'd always accepted as a part of his *self* without ever questioning its import. Tom stared at the hunter, refusing to be distracted by what the man was doing – now kneeling between Mildra's knees as he forced her legs apart – and instead willed his senses to reach beyond the man's clothing and skin, into the body itself. At the same time he sought to project thoughts of savagery, of rending and tearing and destruction, without any sense that this was necessarily the right thing to do, just the hope born of desperation that it might be.

Ky stopped in mid-motion, as if afflicted with the same drug he had administered to Tom. His eyes widened and he suddenly threw back his head and screamed, like some primordial beast baring its soul to the stars. He rolled or, more accurately, threw himself to one side, Mildra hastily drawing her feet out of the way. The hunter was on his back, thrashing legs and arms, body convulsing in violent spasms.

Tom stared in morbid fascination: did he do that, just by willing it?

Even as he wrestled with feelings of thrilled excitement mingled with disbelief, a hooded figure arose from the rubble behind Mildra. Swathed in thick clothing which looked to be a patchwork of rags, the figure seemed a part of the wilderness itself. Tom had no idea where this apparition had come from; all he registered was that this man towered over Mildra with a drawn knife in hand. He didn't hesitate, but lashed out with the same power that had just felled Ky. The newcomer froze, convulsed, and collapsed, the knife tumbling from his hand.

Mildra was screaming. Not simply in terror, there were words. She was trying to tell him something. "Tom, stop it! You have to stop whatever you're doing. That's Dewar, Tom, it's Dewar!"

Finally the words' meaning penetrated. He stopped instantly, horrified. *Dewar?* It couldn't be. The figure he'd seen, the figure he'd struck out at, had been menacing Mildra with a knife. He was sure of it. *Why would Dewar do that?*

Mildra had scrambled over to the newcomer, who was convulsing as if in the throes of a fit, his limbs thrashing the ground. Nearby, Ky lay supine and still, eyes open and staring at the heavens. The Thaistess pushed back Dewar's hood and placed her hands either side of his head. Tom could see it was Dewar now; unshaven, with several days' growth peppering upper lip and chin, but obviously Dewar. Why hadn't he been able to see that before?

Part of Tom wanted to take offence that Mildra had gone to Dewar first. After all, he was the one who had been poisoned and was slowly dying here. But the larger and less selfish part of him recognised that Dewar's need was the more immediate, and that the man wouldn't be in this state at all if not for him, so perhaps he didn't deserve the Thaistess's help at all.

Dewar stopped moving. Tom wasn't sure whether that was a good sign or a bad one. Mildra withdrew her hands, rocked back on her haunches and took a deep breath. Her shoulders sagged as if from weariness. Then she gathered herself, stood, and came towards Tom. *Her face!* Only now did he get a proper look at the split lip and angry welt where Ky had hit her. He wanted to reach out, to hold her and comfort her, and wondered whether any of that showed in his eyes as she met his gaze, smiled a little crookedly, and said, "Thank you, for saving me."

Her hands reached out to either side of his face, as they had with Dewar, and he thought he could feel them, faintly, though that might have been pure imagination. Slowly, feeling did begin to return and with it, control. He could blink, could feel the warmth from Mildra's touch, then he could move his mouth and take his first deep lungful of cold mountain air in what seemed an age. Mildra didn't stop to acknowledge this success. Her eyes were closed, brow furrowed in concentration. With agonising slowness the sense of warmth spread throughout his body and, with it, the ability to move began to return.

His hands were among the last to regain feeling, his feet the very final part. As he felt his toes obey the command to wriggle, he was prepared to accept that he might live after all. Not that he doubted Mildra's abilities, but he'd never seen her have to work this hard before. Mildra's hands slid away from his face, and, with a snort of expelled air, she wilted.

Tom caught her under the arms, and her eyes half-opened. "Sorry," she mumbled. "So tired."

Her feet scrambled against the slippery ground, and between them, she and Tom managed to lower her into a sitting position, back against a wall.

"Dewar?" he asked.

She shook her head. "Don't know."

Tom grabbed some food from his pack – a moist, sugary cake favoured by travellers because it was said to boost energy levels. The Thaistess thanked him and ate mechanically. Several mouthfuls disappeared before she said, "Enough." Her eyes flickered shut almost immediately and she fell into exhausted sleep.

In contrast, Tom felt buzzing with nervous energy and didn't want to sit down, afraid that the paralysis might return. He'd seen corpses aplenty in the City Below, many of them a good deal closer than he'd cared to, but none as unsettling as Ky's. Though lying on its back, the body seemed twisted, compressed, while the limbs were arranged at odd angles, like a marionette whose strings had been severed in midstride. But it was the face Tom found hardest to look at, contorted as it was into a frozen scream, with eyes wide open, mouth snarling, drying spittle on the chin. What made it especially difficult was the knowledge that he was responsible, that he had done this.

He was also responsible for what had been done to Dewar, but at least their former companion was still alive and, following Mildra's ministrations, sleeping peacefully as far as Tom could tell. He covered Dewar with a blanket, rolled Ky's body over so that the eyes didn't seem to follow his every move, and made Mildra as comfortable as he could; then he hunkered down to wait, knowing that he wouldn't be going anywhere until the Thaistess and hopefully Dewar woke up again.

TWENTY-ONE

Time disappeared rapidly as Kat and M'gruth made the rounds, leaving a note under a stone at a prearranged spot, whispering in a barmaid's ear here, a shopkeeper's there, standing on the right corner at the right hour to speak to a man who knew somebody – the full gamut of measures necessary to spread the word and ensure that all those who needed to be reached had been. It took two days, but they were here now, those who remained of the Pits' survivors, the Tattooed Men – some thirty-odd souls in total, including the still-recovering Rel. Kat swallowed on a suddenly dry throat, oddly nervous about addressing these people whom she knew so well. She leapt up onto a low table, planting her feet firmly as she turned to face them. Conversation stilled; somebody shifted in their chair – the grating of wood on stone floor strident in the gathering silence – then all was quiet.

"We've been slow," Kat began, "or maybe distracted." And if so, she'd played more than a small part in that herself. "The streets are changing. When we came out of the Pits we found ourselves in a place that had already been carved up into territories and sections by the street-nick gangs and others. Perhaps we should have been stronger then, but everything was new to us and, after all we'd been through, we didn't want to take on the world. So we fitted into the cracks, the shifting borders where gang turfs meet, the no-go areas dividing this territory from that. And so the Tattooed Men have lived ever since, roaming the streets, going where we will; the nomads of the under-City. But we don't need to, not anymore. We can stake our own claim. If the Fang have done anything useful, it's to prove that even half-wits like them can establish a territory in this new world. Well, we've broken the Fang, and now we'll take what was theirs, and the shopkeepers and traders will welcome us with open arms. Who wouldn't after being forced to pay protection money to scum like the Fang?"

She had them; not entirely perhaps, but enough. Nods and smiles outnumbered the furrowed brows and uncertain glances.

"No more being constantly on the move, no more packing and unpacking; we can stay put and organise life so that it becomes what we want it to be." More smiles now and even a few calls of "yeah".

"Then, of course, there's the Soul Thief. If the Fang hadn't stuck their noses in when they did we'd have finished her off at Iron Grove Square, but thanks to them she got away, and we all know what that cost us." There were nods and murmurs at that. "Near as we can figure out, the bitch raids the streets every couple of years, kills a bunch of folk, feeds, builds up her energies or whatever, and then disappears into the Stain again until the next time.

"The thing is, if she has gone back to the Stain now – and we still haven't heard of any more attacks so that seems more than likely – then she's going to be hungry. We took her for almost everything she had the other night, and it seems as if the only thing she's had to feed on since is Chavver." Kat almost lost it then; she could hear her own voice quivering at those last words. She paused and cleared her throat before continuing. "So the bitch will be coming back, sooner than usual, much sooner, and when she does, she'll be coming into *our* turf, where we'll be nice and settled in and waiting for her. This time, there won't be any Fang to crash the party and we'll finish what we started at Iron Grove Square."

"Yes!" Applause from all quarters and even a few cheers; there was no doubting their support. Kat let out a ragged breath, surprised at how nervous she'd been. It was more than a year since she'd stood in front of the Tattooed Men and spoken like this, and even then Chavver had been beside her; this was the first time Kat had ever addressed them alone. Much of the pain might have been suppressed, but Charveve's absence was a blank space inside her and in the world around her, and she still hadn't figured out how she was supposed to live the rest of her life without her sister being there.

"Sorry to interrupt," said a mild voice from behind her. Kat spun around, to see somebody stepping from the shadows, a man she recognised. "But do you really want to wait until the Soul Thief returns, when you could go hunting for her now?"

"You!" It was the man who'd spoken to her outside Coalman's Chophouse, warning her about Brent. People were moving, weapons being drawn. Whoever this might be he was brave, or more likely stupid, to sneak into a meeting of the Tattooed Men, particularly so soon after all that had happened at Iron Grove Square. Kat jumped down from the table, which was too unstable if things turned nasty; her hand hovered by a sword hilt.

"Who the breck are you?" she demanded. "And don't hang around with the answer if you know what's good for you."

"Ah yes, introductions. Quite right." The man smiled. If he was intimidated by the situation he hid the fact brilliantly. "You are Kat, friend of Ty-gen and of Tom, sometimes Death Queen of the Tattooed Men, and I... am the prime master of Thaiburley."

"No brecking way!" Kat gawped.

There was movement behind the elderly man. More figures emerged from the shadows. Kite Guards, half a dozen of them, and first among them the officer she'd met in the streets, the one she presumed had saved her life at the grand conveyor.

"He's perfectly serious," that Kite Guard said. "This really is the prime master."

There was a surge of movement behind her; the soft sigh of steel gliding over steel from all around. M'gruth was suddenly at her side, clasping his drawn sword, and others with him.

The old man's smile hadn't wavered. "Please, we're not here to cause trouble, merely to put a proposal to you."

"We're listening," Kat assured him.

"Thank you. Perhaps if your friends would lower their weapons, just a little, we could all relax."

Kat glanced at M'gruth and nodded. Swords were dipped, though not sheathed; the Tattooed Men had no reason to love Thaiburley's masters, not when the city had sanctioned the Pits for so many years before eventually seeing fit to close them down.

"To be blunt, I need your help," the prime master said. "Thaiburley needs your help, and at the same time, I'm in a position to help you." That winning smile shone forth again. "So I'm proposing a trade, if you will, an agreement where we work together to help one another." Kat remained silent, waiting to hear him out. "I know you were caught up in the recent disturbances in the under-City, and that you played your part in securing a favourable outcome. What might come as a surprise to you is that the Dog Master wasn't working alone when he subverted the street-nicks. He had help from an even more dangerous enemy, a leftover from the war devoted to bringing down all of Thaiburley, without any consideration for how many lives might be lost in the process. And this villain, this enemy of the whole city, is hiding in the Stain. It's vital for the security of us all that he's dealt with before he can strike again."

"The Stain?" Kat laughed. "You're not seriously suggesting we go in there?"

"Oh, but I am. Not alone, of course. As I said, we work together, so this will be a joint undertaking: the Tattooed Men and a company of Kite Guards under the command of Captain Tylus here. Your mission will be twofold: to hunt down this ancient enemy and at the same time to take care of the Soul Thief once and for all."

Kat shook her head. "Sorry, not meaning any disrespect, but you must be mad if you think we'd go into the Stain, with or without your pretty fly-boys. Blundering around in there would be suicide."

"Agreed, but who said anything about blundering? What if I told you that Captain Tylus could lead you straight to the Soul Thief? Once the small matter of our wartime relic is dealt with, of course."

Kat looked sharply at the Kite Guard, the one she'd met before. "And how exactly would he manage that?"

"Somebody must have caught the Soul Thief with a weapon – a rope, a net, a whip – it doesn't really matter what, but this weapon would have had small jewel thorns imbedded in it."

Kat nodded confirmation.

"I don't know how you came by such a thing, since that's a specialised item fashioned by the arkademics, but it's our good fortune that you did. Some of those thorns have detached, as they're designed to, and have been absorbed into the creature's very substance. There's nothing it can do to get rid of them, they're now a part of the monster, and they're emitting a signal, one which will lead us straight to the Soul Thief no matter where it chooses to hide." Really? Kat made silent apology to Annie for ever doubting her. "We also have a small piece of our hidden enemy, recovered by Captain Tylus from the scene of the sun globe crash..."

"You mean this 'enemy' of yours was responsible for that?" Another score to settle, since the globe had fallen almost directly on top of her and Tom.

"Indeed." Was it her imagination, or was there a hint of satisfaction to the prime master's smile? She had the feeling he'd dropped the matter of the sun globe into the conversation to judge her reaction, perhaps suspecting she'd been there but wanting confirmation. Clever, very clever; she was going to have to be careful when dealing with this one.

"There'll be no blundering around," the prime master assured her. "We can pinpoint both targets, so this will be an incisive strike into hostile territory, taking out first one then the other, before pulling out again. Clean and simple."

Kat licked her upper lip. This was tempting, and he made it sound so simple. There was no Chavver to consult, no Rayul. She glanced quickly at M'gruth, who was as seasoned, experienced and level-headed a warrior as anyone could wish for. He gave a slight shake of his head, without ever looking away from the prime master. His negative backed up what her own gut was saying.

"Sorry, prime master, but even if we know where the target is, the Stain is still a living hell. We've taken some pretty heavy losses of late, and I don't think we want to be lining ourselves up for any more right now."

"I see. I'd heard the Tattooed Men are the most formidable warriors to be found in the City Below. Was I misinformed?"

"No, you were told right, but we're not stupid. No one knows all the nightmares that are hiding in the Stain, and we don't fancy being the first to find out. We're the best all right, but I'd want a lot more muscle behind me than even we could provide before I'd attempt to take on the Stain."

The prime master smiled broadly on hearing that. "Ah, I see. More muscle. Lucky for all of us then that I brought some along with me."

More shapes stepped forward from the shadows; half a dozen towering ebony figures. Every weapon the Tattooed Men carried rose in unison, as did a collective growl. Kat stared, overwhelmed by a confusion of awe and horror. "The Blade!"

"Yes. I'll put six of the Blade under your direct command until the mission is completed. Will that give you the extra firepower you were looking for?"

There was a general murmuring and shuffling of feet and harness around her. The Tattooed Men were responding as one, fight or flight instincts to the fore. Kat couldn't blame them. The Blade were a curse word anywhere in the City Below; the atrocities they'd been a party to while stationed here during the war had become the stuff of legend – bitter memories that ran deep. The prospect of being allied to them in any way was almost unthinkable. Yet if they genuinely represented a chance to put an end to the Soul Thief, could she afford to react as all her instincts were urging her to do and refuse them?

Every eye was focused on her and she knew this to be a crucial moment. First she and Chavver had commanded the Tattooed Men between them and then her sister had done so alone. Now Kat stood here for the first time as their sole leader and immediately faced a decision daunting enough to test anyone. What she said now would define her future, determining whether or not she deserved to lead the Tattooed Men. If she asked the prime master for a moment to consult the older, wiser members of the group as she so wished to do, it would mark her as weak, unfit to command alone, while the wrong decision, however boldly taken, could lose her the confidence and support of her followers.

The different options didn't so much parade through her thoughts as flit and collide and rebound in a chaos of possibilities. Eventually she settled on one. It was a compromise of sorts, one which she hoped might satisfy everybody. More importantly, it satisfied her.

She smiled at the prime master, hoping she projected a level of confidence she only wished she felt. "All right then. As you may have heard just now, we've made a few plans of our own, plans to secure a more stable future, and I'm not willing to put those on hold to go traipsing off into the Stain. At the same time, I agree that this venture of yours might benefit all of us. So here's what I'm willing to do. I'll lead a dozen of the Tattooed Men into the Stain with your Kite Guards and your Blade, and we'll take out the Soul Thief and hunt down this enemy of yours. The rest of the Tattooed Men will stay here and set about establishing a territory in the streets, ready for when we come back again."

She sensed approval from the people around her, and hoped that wasn't just wishful thinking on her part. She'd made the choice which felt right to her, and reckoned that was as much as anyone could ask of her.

The prime master chuckled. "Ty-gen told me you were sharp. He wasn't exaggerating, was he? Very well, a dozen Tattooed Men matched by a similar number of Kite Guards and the Blade. Somehow, I suspect the denizens of the Stain are in for a shock."

"One more thing," Kat said quickly.

"Go on." The prime master replied in a voice that suggested she was in danger of trying his patience.

"The razzers have arrested a man, someone you know, an outsider name of Brent. We've a score to settle and I want him handed over to us."

For a taut second their two gazes locked. "Brent was taken into custody on my explicit order," the prime master said slowly. "We suspect him of being mixed up in all manner of things. It isn't the city's policy to use criminals as bargaining chips."

Damn, had Kat pushed things too far?

"However," and that warm smile returned. "Once we've finished interviewing him and are satisfied that he's told us all he can, we may well decide to exile him from Thaiburley rather than enforcing a custodial sentence. Should that prove to be the case, I could always make sure you were alerted as to the time and place of his release. Such details aren't considered secrets, after all."

Kat smiled and nodded. "Fair enough; then I think we might just have ourselves a deal."

They couldn't wake Dewar.

Mildra examined him and thought that he was all right physically, but he remained in a deep sleep. She didn't want to leave him but was convinced they were near to their goal and was desperate to continue. The man was too heavy to carry. In the end they pulled him into a more sheltered position and decided to leave him, reasoning that this was the only sensible thing to do. They wrapped him warmly and left a parcel of provisions beside his sleeping form, vowing to return once they'd found the river's source and take him back to Pilgrimage End somehow, whether he was awake or not.

They set out in subdued mood, recent events weighing heavy on both their minds, as Mildra demonstrated when she asked, "Do you think Ky was anything to do with Seth Bryant, or just an opportunist?"

"Opportunist, I reckon, and I don't suppose we're the first he's done this too."

"At least we know we'll be the last," Mildra said, which put him right back to thinking about what he'd done to Ky and Dewar, which both fascinated and frightened him. Simply leaving their erstwhile leader behind seemed wrong, especially as this wasn't the first time, but he couldn't think of an alternative.

Above the temple the river, now shrunk to a width no greater than two men lying head to toe, ran through a desolate landscape of grey brown rocks and ice. The air seemed incredibly clear and pure, and bitterly cold, while the sky was an impossibly bright blue. They came across a cluster of rusted tins and canisters and what might have been the remains of a sled; proof positive that people had been here before, though not recently by the look of it.

The river appeared to be leading them directly towards a sheer rock face, or perhaps ice face; it was now difficult to be certain where pale rock ended and muddied ice began. Sure enough, a little further and the frothing white waters disappeared under a low rock/ice ledge, or rather emerged from beneath it.

"An ice cave," Mildra murmured, before turning to him, her face aglow. "This is it, Tom, the source of the Thair, home of the goddess."

Tom did his best to respond with a smile, though in truth he found it hard to match her enthusiasm. He felt too tired, too cold, and too numbed.

At the cave's mouth a chunk of melting, permeated ice sat in the water, its sharp edge jutting skyward. It looked defiant and menacing – a warning of intent to any trespassers.

A narrow ledge ran into the ice cave on their side of the river, just above water level and all-but invisible until

they were almost upon it. Without hesitation Mildra entered the cave, though she had to duck down to do so,
as did Tom behind her. They were so close to the water
that it was impossible for feet and legs not to get splashed
time and again by the gushing, bubbling neo-river, so
that socks and trouser legs were quickly soaked through
and cold, while the very wall they were forced to press
against radiated a level of chill that leached warmth from
the body. Despite their thick clothing, Tom's face, hands
and feet soon felt so frozen that he was convinced they'd
never fully thaw again. Under any other circumstances
he might have given up and insisted they turn back, but
after all the two of them been through to get here, that
would have been ridiculous. So he pressed on, increasingly concerned that neither of them were likely to leave
this ice cave alive, that their strength would run out before this tunnel did.

Just when it reached the point where he didn't think
he could take the cold or his back aching, or his legs
hurting from the cold and the demands of this new bent-
over form of walking, the wall beside him vanished, and
the claustrophobic presence of rock and ice so close
above his head lifted. He and Mildra were both able to
stand straight again; tentatively at first, as if not quite
able to believe they were able to do so, but they did.

"Some sort of chamber," Mildra said, almost whispering.

Tom knew how she felt; it was if they had stumbled
into some mystical grotto where no mere humans were
meant to tread. But another matter concerned him more.
"How come we can see?" he wondered aloud. "Where's
the light coming from?"

"No idea."

It seemed to emanate from all around them. A soft, pale, bluish and appropriately icy light. They could see, and they could stand straight again, but it was still bitterly cold.

The chamber was a small one. The frothing water vanished beneath another wall, this one appearing to be far less ambiguous; it was clearly a sheet of ice rather than rock. Mildra was already examining it and beckoned him over.

"Look at this."

Embedded in the wall, at around shoulder height to Tom, was the outline of a human hand. The indentation was obvious when you stood close to it, but from six or seven steps away it was invisible, with nothing to differentiate it from the rest of the ice.

"What do you think it is?" he asked.

"A door," Mildra replied instantly. "I think a hand pressed into this will open some sort of door, one which we can't even see as yet."

The two looked at each other. "You try," Tom said. "Since this is your goddess we're supposed to be visiting."

"True," and she smiled. "But I think this is something you have to do. After all, you're the one the prime master sent here. I just came along for the ride."

Tom raised his eyebrows, wishing he could argue the point, but instead he reached forward to press his right hand firmly into the depression. He was grateful for the glove. Without it, his hand would probably be frozen in place.

Nothing happened.

"I think it's supposed to be done with a naked hand, Tom," Mildra said quietly.

Unfortunately, Tom had a feeling she was right. Taking a deep breath, he pulled off the glove, spread his fingers and, before he could think about what he was doing, pressed firmly against the indentation, which was larger all round that his actual hand. There was no give, in fact no obvious response at all. To his considerable surprise, there was no sense of cold either. Perhaps, despite appearances, this wasn't ice after all.

"Keep your hand there," Mildra urged. Tom did so, but after another uneventful second he was about to stand back and suggest the Thaistess have a go, when there came a low rumbling; not loud, but seeming to emerge from somewhere deep in the ground.

The wall in front of them, which they'd taken to be a sheet of ice, started to rise. Water ran from its edges and dripped down from above, where the wall appeared to be sliding up into a wide slot in the ceiling. Beyond was darkness. Light from the open doorway fell onto the stone floor of what could only be a vast cavern but threw little illumination onto whatever waited further inside. The faintest of outlines were all that Tom could make out. The floor was solid, the waters of the nascent Thair emerging from somewhere beneath it. That was as much as Tom registered before the lights flickered to life, and the room's contents were revealed.

Two large caskets stood close to the back wall, dominating the room. Grey, moulded, perhaps metallic, although he couldn't be certain, they were supported by a complicated system of braces, almost upright but tilting slightly backwards. Each looked large enough to house a Kayjele and they were unmistakably humanoid in shape. There were other things behind, arranged against the wall, equipment and wonders enough for any curious mind, but Tom barely noticed them; the two caskets claimed his attention completely. Mildra, though, gasped on seeing them, her gaze sweeping along the various objects.

"Some of these things…" she murmured. "I recognise them. We have equipment similar to this in the temples."

Tom led the way into the room, Mildra at his shoulder, each absorbed by their own fascination. As a result, it was Tom who noticed the change first, who saw that the casket to his left was showing signs of – what? – life? Signs of something, at any rate.

"Look, the casket," he murmured, pointing.

The front no longer looked plain and grey, no longer resembled metal or anything else Tom could name. Instead its substance seemed to slide and shift, as if it were liquid rather than solid; a viscous gel that moved sluggishly but with apparent purpose. And it glittered, shimmering with internal light.

Beside him, Mildra's breath seemed to catch, giving rise to a quiet, "Oh."

Whatever transformation they were watching gathered pace – the gel no longer moving slowly but instead seeming to race around within the confines of the casket's front, rippling with colour and light that spread across it in waves.

Mildra sank slowly to her knees, hands clutched before her breast.

Tom didn't.

He thought about doing so, if only for Mildra's sake, but instead determined to meet the goddess or whatever they might be about to face as a man, standing on his own two feet.

The bursts of light increased until they became dazzling, causing Tom to shield his eyes. For one horrifying moment he was reminded of the Rust Warrior, but as the light faded and he was able to look again, any such fears disappeared.

The front of the casket had vanished. The interior was padded in what looked to be soft off-white cushioned material. Cosseted within this nest was a figure that was unmistakably a woman. Outlandishly dressed in a pale blue one-piece suit which left only her head exposed, she was tall, slender, and had a face that looked to be set-tling comfortably into middle age, with high cheek bones and well-sculpted features – a face that could be de-scribed as handsome, though hinting that it might once have been a good deal more than that. The unkempt hair hung long and straight, falling to her shoulders, and it was grey, though not lank or lacking in lustre. This was the grey of burnished steel.

Then she opened her eyes.

Dark, incredibly dark, like Tom's.

"Holy Mother Thaiss, we welcome you," Mildra said.

The goddess ignored her and stared straight at Tom. "You're late," she snapped.

Tom stared, uncertain of how to respond. He wanted to look at Mildra for guidance but didn't dare. "I'm sorry," he said carefully, "when were you expecting us?"

"At least a hundred years ago," the goddess replied. She stretched her neck, flexed her arms. "Is Thaiburley still standing?" Barely pausing, she then answered her own question. "Of course it is, or you wouldn't be here. I'm amazed it's survived this long." She rubbed her eyes, and then skewered Tom with that intense gaze again. "The city is still standing, isn't it?"

"Yes," he assured her. "Yes."

She seemed to relax a little. "Good, then there's still hope."

The prime master scrutinised his hand, turning it over so that the vein in his wrist stood proud, then opening and closing the fingers, moving from the aggression of clenched claw to the spread of earnest entreaty and back again. No visible signs yet, but he knew it wouldn't be long. He could feel the joints stiffen, the skin solidify, and knew that scaly hardness lay just beneath the surface.

In the past few days he had utilised every discipline to stifle emotions, measures that were known to be infallible. So why did he sit here still feeling such fear, such frustration, such despair?

The weight of years suddenly sat heavy on his shoulders. The prime master sighed, bowed his head, and allowed himself the luxury of a single tear. It trickled from the corner of his left eye to drop from his cheek, a pinpoint of moisture sitting proud on the desk before him.

Was this really how his life was destined to end?

EPILOGUE

Ol' Jake looked around the familiar taproom of the Four Spoke Inn. These were strange times and no mistake; Seth and Wil vanishing like that – here one night, gone the next morning. It had been the talk of Crosston for days. Things hadn't been the same since. At times like these a man needed the reassurance of familiar surroundings, and the Four Spoke Inn could at least be counted on for that.

He took a sip from his tankard, savouring the maltiness of the brew.

Jake was of an age where he didn't much care for change. A steady routine, things in their place and faces where he expected to see them; that would do him just fine thank you very much. Nor was he one for asking too many questions, not like some folk around here.

The regulars were thin on the ground tonight. Not even Matty had put in an appearance as yet, which meant Jake was short of good company. He could always go and join Col Blackman, but in truth he'd rather squat over a nest of agitated ladder snakes than share a drink with that twisted soul. He wouldn't trust him as far as he could throw him, and at Jake's age that was no distance at all.

A high pitched squeal drew his attention away from Blackman and he looked round in time to see the young barmaid Bethany slap the face of a garishly dressed merchant. That minx would come a cropper one day, but not this one it would seem; the merchant was clearly furious and looked fit to take things further, but his two friends were laughing and slapping him on the back. Jake hid a smile behind another swallow of beer as he watched the red-faced pompous ass fight down his initial anger and attempt to muster a laugh of his own, more worried about losing face in front of his fellow fops than he was about seeking petty vengeance on an uncooperative tavern girl

Bethany flounced back to the bar with the empties, her long, straight, strawberry blonde hair bouncing in time to the jiggle of her pertly modest bosom. Every eye in the house was on her – an occurrence she always enjoyed.

The girl wrinkled her pretty little nose and batted her eyelids at the landlord as she set the empty glasses down.

"Everything all right, Bethany?"

"Of course," she responded, with a gratuitous flick of her dark-gold locks.

Jake and the landlord exchanged knowing glances, which fell just short of grins.

Jake had come to accept that life presented far more questions than it ever did answers. No point in fretting over that, it was simply the nature of things. Definitive explanations were rare, particularly where men such as Seth Bryant were concerned. Not that Jake minded in the least. He was simply glad to have Seth back behind the bar at the Four Spoke Inn.

"Same again, Jake?"

"Oh, go on then, Seth. One more never hurt anybody."

Something Jake had learned long ago: the more things change, the more they stay the same, and, as far as he was concerned, all was again right in the world now that Seth was back where he belonged.

ABOUT THE AUTHOR

Ian Whates lives in a comfortable home down a quiet cul-de-sac in an idyllic Cambridgeshire village, which he shares with his partner Helen and their pets – Honey the golden cocker spaniel; Calvin the tailless black cat; and Inky the goldfish (sadly, Binky died a few years ago).

Ian's first published stories appeared in the late 1980s, but it was not until the early 2000s that he began to pursue writing with any seriousness. In 2006, Ian launched independent publisher NewCon Press. That same year he also resumed selling short stories, including two to the science journal *Nature*.

He is currently hard at work on the final book in this trilogy, *The City of Light & Shadows*.

www.ianwhates.com

EXCLUSIVE PREVIEW
City of Light & Shadows

The third book of the City of a Hundred Rows trilogy, City of
Light & Shadows, *is coming soon. Here is the first chapter.*

Stu hated this place with a passion; it gave him the creeps.
Typically, he'd drawn the short straw, so the responsibility of
carrying out the day's final inspection fell to him. *Inspection?
Of what, for Thaiss's sake? Weren't nothing here except a
load of stiffs.* Literally. And it wasn't as if they were ever going
to cause trouble for anyone anytime soon.

Bone flu victims, row after row of them lined up along the
floor side by side and then piled up on top of each other
when there weren't no more room on the floor; each one as
dead as the next.

There was something eerie about seeing a human body en-
cased in a sheath of bone, like some hard-case method of
embalming, let alone the couple of hundred that occupied
the vast hall Stu was charged with patrolling. Especially when
you considered that they'd all been alive just a few days before. And the bodies kept coming: more and more brought
in every day.

The one saving grace was that you couldn't see their faces, which meant you could kid yourself these weren't people at all but just great big dolls or statues or something, newly made and waiting to have their faces painted on. That's what Stu did, that was how he coped.

This late inspection though, when there was no one else around – just him and the stiffs – he didn't like this, not one bit. It was easy to let your imagination run wild, to believe that these ominous figures with their knobbly off-white coatings weren't dead at all but were only sleeping, waiting to catch some poor soul on their own. Just like he was now.

If it were up to him the stiffs would have been burned straight away, the lot of them, or buried, or whatever it took to get rid of the breckers. Course, nobody ever asked for his opinion, and the doctors, they wanted all the victims stored so they could study them and try to work out a cure. All well and good he supposed, but did they really need *this* many?

This inspection was going to be a quick one, and to hell with regulations. It was dark. The wan illumination that much of Thaiburley benefited from during daylight hours – thanks to an ingenious system of mirrors, crystals and glass tubes leading from the walls – had disappeared with the sunset, and this area didn't merit electricity, it wasn't posh enough. Nor were there any oil lamps lit here in the hall. What use did the dead have for light? So all Stu could call on was his big black battery powered torch. He hefted it in his right hand, reassured by its solid weight; a useful weapon if need be.

He strode quickly down the central aisle, swinging the torch from side to side, its beam playing across the dull white surfaces of the bone-encased bodies. Halfway. That was as far as he intended to go. The torch could reach the rest of the way from there. He'd play the light along the back wall, take a quick look to make sure everything was all right, and then get the hell out of here, job done.

Two more steps and he reckoned that was about far enough. So he stopped... which was when he heard the cracking sound. A sharp, loud snap, and it had come from his left and a little ahead. He whipped the torch around, cursing as the beam flickered, but it steadied again almost immediately. Nothing. Just the same gnarly effigies of human form; there was no sign of movement and he couldn't see anything obviously out of place. He stood there, conscious of his heart pounding and of his own heavy breathing, too loud in all this stillness. So what was he supposed to do now? Any further investigation meant stepping out among these things, and he was hanged if he was going to do that. Ignore it, that seemed the best option.

No sooner had he reached a decision than the sound came again. He jumped, nerves frayed. It had been closer this time, almost at his feet. Stu shone the torch at the nearest bony cadaver. Had it moved, just as the light reached it? His feet shuffled a few steps backward. Was that a crack? He craned forward despite himself, leaning down for a closer look. Yes, definitely a crack, running down the side of where the face would be, from the top to the chin.

Then came the loudest sound yet, like an explosion, as the figure split completely, ripping apart. The small crack expanded all the way to the body's groin and the two halves gaped wide. Light streamed from the resulting gap, causing Stu to stumble backwards, shielding his eyes. Squinting and looking through the cracks between his fingers, he watched as something stirred and a figure began to emerge from the calcified body.

Stu hadn't got a brecking clue what this was, but he knew they didn't pay him enough to hang around and find out. He turned and bolted for the door, dropping his torch in the process. But he was too slow; far, far too slow.

Assembly Member Carla Birhoff entered the grand hall and paused, casting her gaze around the room one final time before the first guests arrived. Her aim was not to focus on anything in particular – every detail had been scrutinised and approved according to her exacting standards during previous inspections and she now felt confident that each individual element was as perfect as it could be. No, it was how those components fitted together that concerned her at this stage, the assemblage which she had so meticulously planned. Her gaze, therefore, swept across the room, taking in the whole that was the sum of its many parts.

First impressions were paramount. The entire décor had been chosen with this one view in mind and geared towards maximum impact. She would greet her guests here on the mezzanine level, causing them to pause at the top of the small flight of steps that led down into the room proper. Then, as they turned to descend those steps, the whole vista opened up before them. She was determined that it should wow every single one of them.

And it would, it *would*.

White tablecloths – one traditional detail she had insisted on, though the potential starkness was alleviated by fine wide-mesh golden-brown gauze which flowed from the middle of each table to cover roughly two thirds of its area. At the very centre sat an arrangement of bright red berries nestled among autumn leaves and pine cones, while flecks of gold leaf had been sprinkled over the web-like gauze, causing it to sparkle. The fanned napkins before each place setting matched the golden brown of the arrangement, and the stylish chairs were wooden framed, boasting deep burgundy upholstery. Small gifts in gold boxes awaited each lady when she arrived at her seat: tiny khybul sculptures – predominantly birds and fish. Simple pieces certainly, mere tokens, but all those in attendance would know the value of khybul and appreciate the cumulative price of so many pieces, no matter their size.

The evening's seasonal theme was picked up again in a display that dominated the long wall directly opposite the stairs. A cascade of gold, brown and russet veils tumbled from ceiling to floor, transformed by artfully directed air currents and clever lighting into the wild rush of an autumnal waterfall. The illusion was completed by brown drapes gathered and pinned to the wall in imitation of rocks around which the veils flowed.

Another treat awaited guests at the bottom of the stairs. In order to find their appropriate seats, they would need to consult the table plan which stood to their right. Proudly displayed on a glass plinth beside the plan was Carla's latest acquisition: by far the largest, most intricate, and breathtakingly beautiful khybul sculpture she had ever seen. Here, depicted in sparkling crystal, was an exquisite representation of Thaiburly itself. The straight walls of the city seemed to erupt from a base of rugged rocks, shooting upwards to culminate in a dazzling array of delicate spires, chimneys and crenulations. The design cleverly encapsulated the spirit of Thaiburley's wondrous roof, while the walls of the piece were marked with the suggestion of tiny windows and even, here and there towards the top, a balcony or two. And if the ninety-odd floors of the City of a Hundred Rows were not all here, who would quibble? None could dispute that this was an inspired work and that the unknown artist had captured the spirit of Thaiburley in all its grandeur.

The piece had been far from cheap but Carla didn't begrudge a single penny. As soon as she clapped eyes on the sculpture she simply had to have it. Others might own khybul figures but none had anything in their collection to rival this.

Determined that no one would miss its magnificence, she had arranged for lights to be embedded in the glass stand, which then shone up through the sculpture and caused the whole piece to glow, while the tips of the spires sparkled with fairy light.

On the wall above and behind the crystal city hung a large painting, almost lost against the sculpture's magnificence. It was by the artist Arielle, once feted as the greatest painter of her generation. Completed more than two decades earlier, the picture depicted a ball, a lavish function much like the one about to commence. All present were evidently having a wonderful time. Faces glowed, smiles beamed, pale golden and deep burgundy wines flowed, the women were elegant and beautiful, the men dashing. Vibrant colours leapt from the canvas and it was hard to imagine that anyone involved had a care in the world. As you studied the painting, your eyes were inexorably drawn to the figure at the very centre of the composition: a woman, so young, so beautiful, so unmistakably Carla.

She had always loved this painting, for its vibrancy and the pure joy of life it expressed, as well as the memories it stirred and the emotions it evoked, yet she hadn't looked at it for some fifteen years; not since the scandal. Arielle had once been Carla's closest friend and then her bitterest rival. Look at them now. The once celebrated artist had disappeared, her reputation sullied and her work forgotten, never to be seen in polite company again, while Carla had gone from strength to strength, becoming a respected member of the Assembly – the administrative body of Thaiburley's government – and the darling of the Heights' social circuit.

Carla looked at the painting again. In truth, she would

have been hard pressed to explain the whim that had caused
her to take it from storage for this, her big night, except that
it seemed fitting somehow that the painting should be present as she reaffirmed her position as society's queen; not as
a centrepiece, no, but in the shadow of something even more
beautiful, acting as a faded reminder of rivals vanquished and
glories past.

Her gaze finally reached the stage to her far right, where
the multi-stringed duoharp was already in position, the great
chordophone resembling a stylised heart. Its twin opposing
soundboards met at the base, where they converged on the
central pillar of polished wood and gleaming metal embellishments before sweeping upwards and outward like wings.
Identical curved necks connected the rounded shoulders of
the soundboards to the pillar's crown.

The instrument was to be played by the Gallagher Sisters,
said to be among the finest musicians in all Thaiburley. The
dark haired girl – older and prettier than her sibling – was already in place, studiously tuning her half of the harp, but the
seat opposite her was empty. Carla felt a flash of irritation
that both girls weren't ready and she was about to call out
when the blonde sour-faced one hurried over to take her
seat, licking her fingers and chewing on something, as if having snatched a bite to eat before the performance.

Carla pursed her lips. She was tempted to take the girl to
task but in the end decided to put it down to artistic tem-
perament. Instead she returned her attention to completing
her survey of the room, which ended with a glance down at
her own dress. Commissioned from Chanice, one of the
Heights' hottest designers, the gown featured a beautifully
arranged skirt of layered silks graduating from autumnal rus-
sets at the bottom to shimmering scarlet at the top, matching
the bodice. The dress was so artfully cut that the skirt

avoided being billowy while still drawing in tightly at the waist to emphasise her slender figure. Carla had studied herself from every angle before coming here, and was confident that she looked fantastic. Scarlet could be an unforgiving shade, one she probably wouldn't dare risk in another five or ten years, but she felt bold tonight and knew she still retained enough of her youthful glamour to get away with such audacious display. While she could, she would.

Finally satisfied, Carla allowed herself a small smile. Everything seemed in readiness; soon the great and the good of Heights' society would be here to pay her tribute. She would accept their compliments with an appropriate degree of grace and modesty, of course, while privately secure in the knowledge that she had earned each and every plaudit.

An hour later found Carla in her element, meeting and greeting, sharing a few words with this couple, a sentence or two with another and a joke with the next, before flitting away to greet a late arrival. The Gallagher Sisters were playing divinely, though as more people arrived and the volume of conversation grew louder it was becoming increasingly difficult to hear them unless you were standing right next to the stage. Not that it mattered. The fact that Carla had secured their services when others had failed to do so for their own functions was reward enough.

She handed a barely touched flute of finest Elyssen champagne to a waiter – she had been holding the glass for far too long and the wine had lost much of its chill and fizz – and took a fresh one, savouring a sip of cool dry effervescence before the customary smile slipped back into place. She laughed politely at the end of someone's anecdote, a tale she'd only half been listening to. The smile was one which had been perfected over many years: the expression of a hostess who knows her evening is a success and is confident that it will only get better. In the corner of her eye she saw white jacketed waiters circulating with what should be the final trays of warm canapés. It would soon be time to usher the guests to take their seats for the meal. Glowing comment had already been made about her khybul sculpture, most pleasingly from young Xyel, a pretty little thing who saw herself as something of an emerging rival to Carla. Poor deluded girl. Her Summer Soirée had been pleasant enough but she still had a lot to learn. Carla reserved a special smile for her.

A ripple of polite applause ran through the section of the room closest to the stage as the Gallagher Sisters finished their latest piece – surely the penultimate one of their set – and Carla noted waiters returning to the kitchen with empty salvers. She looked across and caught the mâitre d's eye. He nodded, to show that he was on top of the timings. If things continued to run this smoothly, she might even be able to relax a fraction and enjoy herself during the meal.

It was a little thing really in the context of everything else that was going on: the scream that heralded such a dramatic change of fortune for Carla and all those present. Most wouldn't even have heard it. The only reason Carla did was because she happened to be at the top of the small flight of steps, at the spot where she'd greeted the guests, and so was close to the door. The scream came from outside; high pitched and unmistakably a woman's. Conversation on the mezzanine level died and for a second there was a bizarre contrast between the silence to Cara's left and the continuing hubbub from the rest of the room to her right.

When no further indication of disturbance came, those closest to Carla resumed talking, with a shrug of their shoulders or a knowing rise of the eyebrows, and muttered comments such as, "Kids!"

Jean, the mâitre d', had moved across to speak to the door-man, but nobody seemed concerned and Carla was about to dismiss the incident as a minor glitch soon forgotten, when the doors burst inward and Hell strode through the opening.

The first figure was merely a giant, towering above Jean and the doorman. The latter tried to block the intruder's way, but the burly man was picked up and tossed into the room in one motion, crashing into a knot of startled guests. The mâitre d' was simply brushed aside.

More than one scream rent the air now.

Further figures were pressing through the doorway behind the first. One or two had human features but most seemed composed of nothing more than silver light, dazzling to look upon. All were of similar stature to the first. Carla gaped, un-able to rationalise what she was seeing. She couldn't move, didn't know how to react. She was supposed to be the perfect party host, ready for any eventuality, but not for *this*.

Several things then happened at once, snapping her out of her paralysis. The tall windows which dominated the wall op-posite the stage shattered, seemingly all at once, sending shards of glass raining down on those nearby, and more of the silver light giants strode through the broken windows. This registered only at the periphery of Carla's awareness, whose attention was focused elsewhere. She stared in horror at the shimmering figure who reached out towards Jean, while the mâitre d' was still recovering from his brush with the first giant. As a glowing finger touched him, a cocoon of light enveloped Jean's body and he froze, all except for his face, which took on an expression of wide-eyed horror that swiftly transformed into one of excruciating agony; eyes screwed shut, mouth thrown open as if screaming, though Carla couldn't hear him. It was a moment she would never forget, as if every tortured line of Jean's face burned itself into her retinas and hence into her memory. A second later the expression was gone, vanishing as his face exploded. No, that was wrong, the process was less dramatic. Jean's face, his whole body, seemed to simply drift apart. One moment there was a shape within the glow that was recognisably Jean, the next nothing human stood there at all. In the brief instant before the glow which had surrounded the mâitre d' faded, Carla watched a cloud of russet flakes drop towards the floor like ruddy brown rose petals.

The glowing silver giant was no longer silver or glowing. It now looked like Jean.

Only then did Carla grasp the full horror of what was happening here; only then did she realise their doom.

She stumbled away in a daze, with no clear idea of where she was going, just the certainty that she had to get away from these creatures. Somebody bumped into her, causing her to stagger, and she was abruptly aware that pandemonium had broken out and that *everyone* was trying to get away. The thin veneer of politeness, of etiquette, had been abandoned, to be replaced by the drive to survive. Men, women, young or old, it didn't matter; all were screaming, fighting, pushing and elbowing in their desperation to reach the stairs and escape. Never mind that more of the creatures waited below, a whole cordon of them, herding folk towards the stage, instinct still drove people to flee the most immediate threat, and a bottleneck started to form at the top of the mezzanine stairs.

For those at the back there was no hope of escape. The silver giants moved implacably forward, killing with a touch. The ones that had already adopted a semblance of human form simply killed. The crowd discovered new levels of desperation. Carla watched an elderly woman, resplendent in diaphanous gown and diamond jewellery, knocked from her feet and trampled by her fellows, with no chance of recovering.

A small part of Carla's mind remained detached, refusing to accept any of this as real. A symptom of shock perhaps, but that small corner of sanity brought her hope. She realised that the stairs which all around her were straining towards offered only temporary respite, that even those who reached them would still be trapped. Then her gaze fell upon the door, off to one side, evidently overlooked by everyone. The kitchens, deliberately designed to lead off the mezzanine to ensure that a supply of freshly chilled champagne was always on hand during greetings and that diners could fully appreciate each new dish as it was paraded down the stairs prior to serving. She started to forge her way in that direction, moving across the flow of panicked people. She prised a woman's chest away from a man's back and inserted first an arm and then her whole self between. Moving against the human tide proved to be an unexpected advantage. While others were faced with a wall of backs and had nowhere to go, she could slip through – with a little persuasion. Somebody dug her in the ribs with an elbow, someone else struck her shoulder with bruising force. She ignored the minor flares of pain and kept going, focussing only on that door.

Doubtless she *knew* these people, many of them would be her friends, yet terror and desperation had converted their faces into those of strangers. She pushed, kneed and fought with the best of them, forcing a passage, closing her vision and her mind to everything else and refusing to think about how close the death-dealing giants were coming.

She was nearly there, with just a few more people to fight through, when it happened. In her eagerness to find sanctuary she overstretched across intervening legs and feet. Somebody trod on her gown, her beautiful gown, tearing it, and she was jostled as she tried to bring her trailing leg through. Carla stumbled and tripped, falling heavily onto a man's knee and then the floor. Desperately she tried to pull herself along, no longer keeping track of the number of bumps and bruises. Somebody stepped down on her calf and she cried out, barely hearing her own voice above all the screaming and the shouting, which suddenly seemed to intensify.

A woman to her left, oblivious to her presence, looked about to repeat the act of stepping on her but this time in stiletto heels, when the woman froze and her body began to glow. Carla scrambled away, pulling her legs in, desperate not to touch that nimbus. Within seconds the woman imploded, disappearing in a cascade of rusty flakes, some of which fell onto Carla's exposed arm and legs.

She lost it then. All rational thought deserted her as she opened her mouth and shrieked and writhed and kicked, not even aware that she had broken through the crowd of people until the door to the kitchen loomed before her nose. She pulled it open and half-rolled half-crawled inside, to collapse, her body wracked with sobs.

Heat washed over her. The lights were still on but the kitchen was deserted, the cooks and waiting staff having presumably fled. The rich aromas of cooking, which normally Carla would have breathed in deeply and relished, now only made her feel nauseous. She reached up to grip the edge of a table, pulling herself to her feet, and stumbled across the empty room towards the service door which she knew to be there. Two thirds of the way across, her stomach heaved and she was forced to double over, throwing up onto the floor. It seemed an age before the retching subsided and she could move forward. Not even pausing to find water and wash the sour taste of vomit from her mouth, she finally reached the door, thrusting it open and staggering into the corridor beyond.

She stopped to draw in fresher, cooler air, amazed at how muted the noise from the ballroom had become. From out here the shouting, the screaming, the sounds of people being slaughtered, it could almost be mistaken for over-enthusiastic revelry. Almost.

There was no one in sight. Part of Carla was glad, conscious even now what a mess she must look and relieved that there was no one here to see it, but guilt immediately swept such concerns away as the implications sank in. Surely others must have escaped? She couldn't be the only one; but, if so, they were already long gone. Not that she could blame them.

Carla took a deep breath and braced herself. It was time to forget that she was Carla Birhoff, celebrated socialite, and re-member that she was Assembly Member Birhoff. Her city needed her.

She wriggled her feet and kicked off the impractical shoes that still somehow clung to them, gathered up the skirt of her ruined gown, and started to run; a somewhat shuffling gait perhaps, but it was the best she could manage – more than a decade had passed since she last attempted to move this quickly. As she ran, she bent over to spit out the taste of sick from her mouth, all decorum forgotten. Such considerations seemed no more than petty affectations in the light of what she had just been through.

Carla determined to find the city watch, to alert the Kite Guard, to rouse the Assembly, to mobilise the Blade. The peo-ple of Thaiburley needed to be warned, they had to be told the unthinkable truth. The Rust Warriors had returned.

Example of the 20' x 30' print proportions (actual print is in color)

Own the Art of Greg Bridges

The stunning cover art of this book is now available as a Limited Edition Art Print as well as free wallpaper* for your iphone™

See what this cover art looks like without typography and download it free for your iphone™. You can also own the cover art of this book, to hang on your wall in a magnificent color reproduction.

"When you view this work larger you will discover, over time, new things you didn't see before. It is the nature of Greg's work. He meticulously works on every detail, so you can enjoy the work for years to come. There are mysterious objects and hidden images that will surprise and tantalize you through the years. What makes Greg's work unique is his exceptional ability to let us look into his worlds and feel like we are there."

Premium quality reproductions capture the intense essence of Bridges' works magnificently. Printed on heavy duty archival paper or canvas, there is an edition for all budgets from unsigned open prints to large signed and numbered archival editions for the serious art collector.

• To view, or order a print now, please download the print info and ordering details at www.gregbridges.com/prints/printinfo.zip

• To download your free Gregory Bridges iphone™ wallpaper art of this cover go to www.gregbridges.com/iphone/cityofhope.zip

• View more of Gregory's world-acclaimed work at www.gregorybridges.com

GREGORY BRIDGES

* For iphone wall paper, make a new folder in your iphoto library - name it Greg Bridges Art , and drag the downloaded image into it. In itunes, with your iphone connected, in the pictures section, tick the folder Greg Bridges Art and sync it. In your iphone go to settings/wallpaper/Greg Bridges Art and select the image
* iphone is a trademark of Apple Inc.